# THE OLD MAN and Lesser Mortals

# THE OLD MAN
# and
# lesser mortals
## Larry L. King

THE VIKING PRESS    NEW YORK

The author bows deeply to all publications
permitting the reprinting of articles appearing,
though often in slightly different form,
in their pages; they will find
their respective names at the conclusion
of each article where applicable.

*This book is dedicated to the memory of my late father*
CLYDE CLAYTON KING
*and my late wife*
ROSEMARIE COUMARIS KING
*—two people I loved*

# Contents

# Introduction

WRITERS AND PROSTITUTES grow accustomed to being asked why they do the things they do. There is no easy answer. Of the two trades, writing appears the more mysterious simply because there seem fewer sane reasons to take it up. I can't imagine writing being fun in the way, say, that orgies or even office parties are. Certainly it is great fun to see one's name blinking from book jackets or magazine covers . . . but that's not *writing*—that's preening before the mirror, indulging one's distaste for the crowd's natural anonymity, rejoicing once the crops are laid by.

Why the notion persists that writing is woman's work is one of those mysteries preserving life's spices. It is the verdict of one who has picked cotton and pissanted heavy objects for small profit that no work is harder than writing. It may be accomplished indoors, away from extreme temperatures or foul-talking gang bosses, but its disadvantages include such tediums as organization of raw materials, interpretations of characters and events, the ability to semicoherently progress from one point to the next, and enough thinking to cleverly restate the philosophies of others should the writer be blessed with none of his own. More terribly, however, the act demands an iron ass and unnatural disciplines: sitting before the typewriter in crippling solitude while knowing that somewhere others are laughing or smoking dope or making love with no thoughts of guilt or reprisals. I hope they choke.

Worse, much journalistic writing forces one to visit the cold outside world there to accost strangers with impertinent or improbable questions they tolerate for reasons I never shall understand. That, for me, is the most difficult part. Despite a whisky tendency to aggressively claim attention, I tend to shrink inside and stammer when faced with interviewing people. I am not worth a farthing at asking whether people sleep in the nude, why they learned to tap dance, or whether they expect to vote the Vegetarian ticket. The smallest question suddenly weighs eighteen stone and tuppence as it drags reluctantly past the lips; my head registers empty of all save wind and dishwater; I feel duh-duh dumb, a clumsy interloper. For those reasons I work slowly, preferring to observe for two weeks rather than interview for two hours. My goal becomes, simply, to wear the other fellow down: to hang around until he forgets my purpose and carelessly begins to consider me a part of the scenery worth rapping to. If one is blessed, one's subject then reveals himself by his actions, commentary, or snarls with only an occasional guiding question necessary.

Time consuming and not recommended for the wire-service reporter dealing in quick facts and hot deadlines, this bashful technique is not wholly ineffective when applied to magazine journalism with its more leisurely demands. There is the opportunity to roll one's material around in one's head, to squeeze, weigh, divergently view and generally torment it. The technique is not always surefire. In the case of some subjects reluctant to reveal themselves (among them Nelson Rockefeller, Johnny Unitas, Peggy Lee, Jack Anderson, Jane Fonda) I wrote inferior pieces or, more wisely, abandoned the projects altogether. The reader should be almost pathetically grateful in being spared such muted or mutilated offerings here. The articles here collected, with one or two exceptions, were crafted after an earlier grouping, . . . *And Other Dirty Stories,* which was published in 1968. Where it seems appropriate I have written a short afterword or introductory note, as in the earlier work.

Dross reposes, I know, among the gold. At their best, I'd like to think, these pieces reflect the America where I have come to middle age: the America I have observed, been obsessed with, chronicled. At their worst, hopefully, they will at least reflect one working writer's condition in his time and his place—even if only his peculiar preoccupations or prejudices or the things he did for money.

Two of these pieces—"The Old Man" and "A Country Lawyer and How He Grew"—were particularly difficult because of close personal involvement with the subjects: my late father and an old, dear friend named Warren Burnett. My work was made no easier by the knowledge that each of them, eloquent employers of the English language in their respective ways, shaped and coached me by their verbal examples in the dim past. There was a danger, then, of not seeing the forest for the trees: of being overly protective or conveniently selective in one's recollections. Face it: I pulled a punch or two. In each case friends or relatives have judged that I missed the mark—though all had different reasons as to the particulars. "The Old Man," for reasons more personal than the fact it has become the most critically commended and the most anthologized, remains a career favorite.

Precisely because it required the sort of dogged interviewing and sweaty spadework I dearly despise, "The Road to Power in Congress" lightly kisses my vanity. I think it not a bad study of an American institution in its internal threshings. Throwing modesty to the winds, let the same be said of "Blowing My Mind at Harvard." If permitted one more advertisement, I recommend "Whatever Happened to Brother Dave?" It's funnier to read than it was to do: I found the experience full of the terrors, mistrusts, and suspicions of our age. In many of these articles—in most of them, I guess—I intrude with personal experiences or recollections or otherwise get in the way. So be it: I am of the school of personal journalism and can't seem to learn new tricks.

Enough. When my teen-aged son Bradley, was ten, he advised that he never troubled to read introductions. I admonished that the introduction told something of what a book was about, what the author intended, his purposes and secretions. "If the book's any good," my son said, "it will tell you all that itself."

He could be right.

# THE OLD MAN and Lesser Mortals

# THE OLD MAN

**W**hile we digested our suppers on The Old Man's front porch, his grandchildren chased fireflies in the summer dusk and, in turn, were playfully chased by neighborhood dogs. As always, The Old Man had carefully locked the collar of his workday khakis. He recalled favored horses and mules from his farming days, remembering their names and personalities though they had been thirty or forty years dead. I gave him a brief thumbnail sketch of William Faulkner—Mississippian, great writer, appreciator of the soil and good bourbon—before quoting what Faulkner had written of the mule: "He will draw a wagon or a plow but he will not run a race. He will not try to jump anything he does not indubitably know beforehand he can jump; he will not enter any place unless he knows of his own knowledge what is on the other side; he will work for you patiently for ten years for the chance to kick you once." The Old Man cackled in delight. "That feller sure knowed his mules," he said.

Sons rarely get to know their fathers very well, less well, certainly, than fathers get to know their sons. More of an intimidating nature remains for the father to conceal, he being cast in the role of example-setter. Sons know their own guilty intimidations. Eventually, however, they graduate their fears of the lash or the

3

frown, learn that their transgressions have been handed down for generations. Fathers are more likely to consider their own sins to have been original.

The son may ultimately boast to the father of his own darker conquests or more wicked dirkings: perhaps out of some need to declare his personal independence, or out of some perverted wish to settle a childish score, or simply because the young—not yet forged in the furnace of blood—understand less about that delicate balance of natural love each generation reserves for the other. Remembering yesterday's thrashings, or angry because the fathers did not provide the desired social or economic advantages, sons sometimes reveal themselves in cruel ways.

Wild tigers claw the poor father for failures real or imagined: opportunities fumbled, aborted marriages, punishments misplaced. There is this, too: a man who has discovered a likeness in his own image willing to believe (far beyond what the evidence requires) that he combines the natural qualities of Santa Claus, Superman, and the senior saints, will not easily surrender to more mature judgments. Long after the junior partner has ceased to believe that he may have been adopted or that beating off will grow hair on the hand while the brain slowly congeals into gangrenous matter, the father may pose and pretend, hiding bits and pieces of yesterday behind his back. Almost any father with the precious stuff to care can adequately conceal the pea. It is natural in sons to lust—yes, to *hunger* for—an Old Man special enough to have endowed his progeny's genes with genius and steel. Or, failing the ideal, to have a father who will at least remain sturdy, loyal, and *there* when life's vigilantes come riding with the hangman.

You see the fix the poor bastard is in, don't you? He must at once apologize and inspire, conceal and judge, strut and intervene, correct and pretend. No matter how far he ranges outside his normal capabilities, he will remain unappreciated through much of the paternal voyage—often neglected, frequently misread, sometimes profaned by his own creation. For all this, the father may evolve into a better man: may find himself closer to being what he claims, a strong role having ways of overpowering the actor. And if he is doubly blessed, he may know a day when his sons (by then, most likely, fathers themselves) will come to love him more than they can bring themselves to say. Then, sometimes, sons get to know their fathers a bit: perhaps a little more than nature intended, and surely more than yesterday would have believed.

There was that blindly adoring period of childhood when my father was the strongest and wisest of men. He would scare off the bears my young imagination feared as they prowled the night outside our Texas farmhouse, provide sunshine and peanut butter, make the world go away. I brought him my broken toys and my skinned knees. He did imitations of all the barnyard animals; when we boxed he saw to it that I won by knockouts. After his predawn winter milkings, shivering and stomping his numb feet while rushing to throw more wood on the fire, he warned that tomorrow morning, by gosh, he planned to laze abed and eat peach cobbler while his youngest son performed the icy chores.

He took me along when he hunted rabbits and squirrels, and on alternate Saturdays when he bounced in a horse-drawn wagon over dirt roads to accomplish his limited commercial possibilities in Putnam or Cisco. He thrilled me with tales of his own small-boy peregrinations: an odyssey to Missouri, consuming two years, in covered wagons pulled by oxen; fordings of swift rivers; and pauses in Indian camps where my grandfather, Morris Miles King, smoked strong pipes with his hosts and ate with his fingers from iron kettles containing what he later called dog stew. The Old Man taught me to whistle, pray, ride a horse, enjoy country music, and, by his example, to smoke. He taught that credit buying was unmanly, unwise, and probably unforgivable in heaven; that one honored one's women, one's flag, and one's pride; that, on evidence supplied by the biblical source of "winds blowing from the four corners of the earth," the world was most assuredly flat. He taught me the Old Time Religion, to bait a fishhook and gut a butchered hog, to sing "The Nigger Preacher and the Bear."

I had no way of knowing what courage was in the man (he with no education, no hope of quick riches, no visible improvements or excitements beckoning to new horizons) that permitted him to remain so cheerful, shielding, and kind. No matter how

5

difficult those depression times, there was always something under the Christmas tree. When I was four, he walked five miles to town in a blizzard, then returned as it worsened, carrying a red rocking chair and smaller gifts in a gunnysack. Though he had violated his creed by buying on credit, he made it possible for Santa Claus to appear on time.

I would learn that he refused to accept the largess of one of FDR's recovery agencies because he feared I might be shamed or marked by wearing to school its telltale olive-drab "relief shirts." He did accept employment with the Works Progress Administration, shoveling and hauling wagonloads of dirt and gravel for a road-building project. When I brought home the latest joke from the rural school—WPA stands for We Piddle Around—he delivered a stern, voice-quavering lecture: "Son, the WPA is an honest way some poor men has of makin' their families a livin'. You'd go to bed hungry tonight without the WPA. Next time some smart aleck makes a joke about it, you ought to knock a goddamned whistlin' fart out of him."

Children learn that others have fathers with more money, more opportunity, more sophistication. Their own ambitions or resentments rise, inspiring them to reject the simpler wants of an earlier time. The son is shamed by the father's speech, dress, car, occupation, and table manners. The desire to flee the family nest (or to soar higher in it; to undertake some few experimental solos) arrives long before the young have their proper wings or before their parents can conceive of it.

The Old Man was an old-fashioned father, one who relied on corporal punishments, biblical exhortations, and a ready temper. He was not a man who dreamed much or who understood that others might require dreams as their opium. Though he held idleness to be as useless and as sinful as adventure, he had the misfortune to sire a hedonist son who dreamed of improbable conquests accomplished by some magic superior to grinding work. By the time I entered the troublesome teen-age years, we were on the way to a long, dark journey. A mutual thirst to prevail existed—some crazy stubborn infectious contagious will to avoid the slightest surrender.

The Old Man strapped, rope whipped, and caned me for smoking, drinking, lying, avoiding church, skipping school, and laying out at night. Having once been very close, we now lashed out at each other in the manner of rejected lovers on the occasion of each new disappointment. I thought The Old Man blind to the wonders and potentials of the real world; could not fathom how current events or cultural habits so vital to my contemporaries could be considered so frivolous—or worse. In turn, The Old Man expected me to obediently accept his own values: show more concern over the ultimate disposition of my eternal soul, eschew easy paths when walking tougher ones might somehow purify, be not so inquisitive or damnfool dreamy. That I could not (or would not) comply puzzled, frustrated, and angered him. In desperation he moved from a "wet" town to a "dry" one, in the foolish illusion that this tactic might keep his baby boy out of saloons.

On a Saturday in my fifteenth year, when I refused an order to dig a cesspool in our backyard because of larger plans downtown, I fought back: it was savage and ugly—though, as those things go, one hell of a good fight. But only losers emerged. After that we spoke in terse mumbles or angry shouts, not to communicate with civility for three years. The Old Man paraded to a series of punishing and uninspiring jobs—night watchman, dock loader for a creamery, construction worker, chicken butcher in a steamy, stinking poultry house, while I trekked to my own part-time jobs or to school. When school was out I usually repaired to one distant oil field or another, remaining until classes began anew. Before my eighteenth birthday I escaped by joining the army.

On the morning of my induction, The Old Man paused at the kitchen table, where I sat trying to choke down breakfast. He wore the faded old crossed-gallus denim overalls I held in superior contempt and carried a lunch bucket in preparation of whatever dismal job then rode him. "Lawrence," he said, "is there anything I can do for you?" I shook my head. "You need any money?" "No." The old Man shuffled uncertainly, causing the floor to creak. "Well," he said, "I wish you good luck." I nodded in the direction of my bacon and eggs. A moment later the front door slammed, followed by the grinding of gears The Old

7

Man always accomplished in confronting even the simplest machinery.

Alone in a Fort Dix crowd of olive drab, I lay popeyed on my bunk at night, chain smoking, as Midland High School's initial 1946 football game approached. The impossible dream was that some magic carpet might transport me back to those anticipatory tingles I had known when bands blared, cheerleaders cartwheeled sweet tantalizing glimpses of their panties, and we purple-clads whooped and clattered toward the red-shirted Odessa Bronchos or the Angry Orange of San Angelo. Waste and desolation lived in the heart's private country on the night that opening game was accomplished on the happiest playing field of my forfeited youth. The next morning, a Saturday, I was called to the orderly room to accept a telegram—a form of communication that had always meant death or other disasters. I tore it open with the darkest fantasies to read MIDLAND 26 EL PASO YSLETA 0 LOVE DAD. Those valuable communiqués arrived on ten consecutive Saturday mornings.

With a ten-day furlough to spend, I appeared unannounced and before a cold dawn on the porch of that familiar frame house in Midland. The Old Man rose quickly, dispensing greetings in his woolly long-handles. "You just a first-class private?" he teased. "Lord God, I would a-thought a King would be a general by now. Reckon I'll have to write ole Harry Truman a postcard to git that straightened out." Most of the time, however (when I was not out impressing the girls with my PFC stripe) a cautious reserve prevailed. We talked haltingly, carefully, probing as uncertainly as two neophyte premed students might explore their first skin boil.

On the third or fourth day The Old Man woke me on the sleeping porch, lunch bucket in hand. "Lawrence," he said, "your mother found a bottle of whisky in your suitcase. Now, you know this is a teetotal home. We never had a bottle of whisky in a home of ours, and we been married since 19-and-11. You're perfectly welcome to stay here, but your whisky's not." I stiffly mumbled something about going to a motel. "You know·better than that," The Old Man scolded. "We don't want you goin' off to no blamed motel." Then, in a weary exasperation not fully appreciated until dealing with transgressions among my own offspring: "Good God, son, what makes you want to raise ole billy hell all the time?" We regarded each other in a helpless silence. "Do what you think is right," he said, sighing. "I've done told you how me and your mother feel." He went off to work; I got up and removed the offending liquids.

The final morning brought a wet freeze blowing down from Amarillo by way of the North Pole. The Old Man's car wouldn't start; our family had never officially recognized taxis. "I'll walk you to the bus station," he said, bundling in a heavy sheepskin jumper and turning his back, I suspect, so as not to witness my mother's struggle against tears. We shivered down dark streets, past homes of my former schoolmates, by vacant lots where I played softball or slept off secret sprees, past stores I remembered for their bargains in Moon Pies and then Lucky Strikes and finally Trojans. Nostalgia and old guilts blew in with the wind. I wanted to say something healing to The Old Man, to utter some gracious good-bye (the nearest thing to retroactive apologies a savage young pride would permit), but I simply knew no beginnings.

We sat an eternity in the unreal lights of the bus station among crying babies, hung-over cowboys, and drowsing old Mexican men, in mute inspection of those dead shows provided by bare walls and ceilings. The Old Man made a silent offering of a cigarette. He was a vigorous fifty-nine then, still clear eyed, dark haired, and muscular, but as his hand extended that cigarette pack and I saw it clearly—weather cured, scarred, one finger crooked and stiff jointed from an industrial accident—I suddenly and inexplicably knew that one day The Old Man would wither, fail, die. In that moment, I think, I first sensed—if I did not understand—something of mortality; of tribes, blood, and inherited rituals.

At the door to the bus The Old Man suddenly hugged me, roughly, briefly: not certain, perhaps, such an intimacy would be tolerated by this semistranger who bore his name. His voice broke as he said, "Write us, son. We love you." I clasped his hand and brushed past, too full for words. For I knew, then, that I loved him, too, and had, even in the worst of times, and would never stop.

We took a trip last summer, one The Old Man had secretly coveted for a lifetime, though, in the end, he almost had to be prodded into the car. "I hate like the devil to leave Cora," he said of his wife of almost six decades. "She's got to where her head swims when she walks up and down the steps. She taken a bad spill just a few weeks ago. I try to stay close enough to catch her if she falls."

The Old Man did not look as if he could catch much of a falling load as he approached eighty-three. Two hundred pounds of muscle and sinew created by hard work and clean living had melted to a hundred-sixty-odd; his senior clothing flapped about him. He had not worn his bargain dentures for years, except when my mother insisted on enforcing the code of some rare social function, because, he complained, they played the devil with his gums, or gagged him, or both. The eagle's gleam was gone from eyes turned watery and rheumy; he couldn't hear so well any more; he spoke in a wispy voice full of false starts and tuneless whistles requiring full attention.

He was thirteen years retired from his last salaried job, and he had established himself as a yard-tender and general handyman. He mowed lawns, trimmed hedges, tilled flower beds, grubbed stumps, painted houses, performed light carpentry or emergency plumbing. In his eightieth year my mother decreed that he might no longer climb trees for pruning purposes. Though he lived with that verdict, his eyes disapproved it just as they had when his sons dictated that he might no longer work during the hottest part of the desert summer days. The Old Man surrendered his vigor hard, each new concession (not driving a car or giving up cigarettes) throwing him into a restless depression. He continued to rise each morning at five, prowling the house impatiently on rainy days, muttering and growling of all the grass that needed mowing or of how far behind Midland was falling in unpainted fences. At such times he might complain because the Social Security Administration refused him permission to earn more than twelve hundred dollars annually while continuing to merit its assistance: he sneaked in more work by the simple expediency of lowering his prices. Except on the Sabbath (when, by his ethic, the normal joy of work translated to sin), he preferred the indoors only when eating or sleeping. He had long repaired to a sleeping porch of his own creation, where it was always twenty degrees cooler in winter and correspondingly hotter in the summertime; one of the curses of modernity, he held, was "refrigerated air."

On my mother's reassurances that she would spend a few days with her twin sister, we coaxed The Old Man into my car. Years earlier I had asked him whether he wanted to see some particular place or thing and whether I might take him there. To my surprise (for The Old Man had never hinted of secret passions) he said yes, he had wanted since childhood to visit the state capitol in Austin and the Alamo in San Antonio: he had read of them in books his mother had obtained when his father's death had cut off his schooling. I had long procrastinated. Living in the distant Sodoms and Gomorrahs of the East, I wandered in worlds alien to my father in search of ambitions that surely mystified him. There were flying trips home: an hour's domino playing here, an evening of conversation there. Then the desert would become too still, dark, and forbidding: I would shake his worn old hand, mutter promises and excuses, grab a suitcase; run. Last summer my wife effectively nagged me to deliver on my old pledge. And so, one boiling morning in July, we departed my father's house. He sat beside me on the front seat, shrunken and somehow remote, yet transmitting some youthful eagerness. The older he had grown, the less The Old Man had ever troubled to talk, contenting himself with sly grins or solemn stares so well timed you sometimes suspected he heard better than advertised. Deliver him a grandchild to tease and he would open up: "Bradley Clayton King, I hear turrible things on you. Somebody said you got garments on your back, and you have ancestors. And word come to me lately that you was seen hesitatin' on the doorstep." With others, however, he was slow to state his case.

Now, however, we had hardly gone a mile before The Old Man began a monologue lasting almost a week. As we roared

11

across the desert waste, his fuzzy old voice battled with the cool cat's purr of the air conditioner; he gestured, pointed, laughed, praised the land, took on new strength.

He had a love for growing things, a Russian peasant's legendary infatuation for the motherland; for digging in the good earth, smelling it, conquering it. "Only job I ever had that could hold a candle to farmin'," he once said, "was blacksmithin'. Then the car come along, and I was blowed up." Probably his greatest disappointment was his failure as a farmer—an end dictated by depressed prices in his most productive years and hurried by land worn down through a lack of any effective application of the basic agrarian sciences. He was a walking-plow farmer, a mule-and-dray-horse farmer, a chewing-gum-and-bailing-wire farmer. If God brought rain at the wrong moment, crops rotted in the mud; should He not bring it when required, they baked and died. You sowed, tilled, weeded, sweated: if heaven felt more like reward than punishment, you would not be forced to enter the Farmer's State Bank with your soiled felt hat in your hand.

World War II forced The Old Man off the family acres: he simply could not reject the seventy-odd cents per hour an oil company promised for faithful drudgery in its pipeline crew. And he felt, too, deep and simple patriotic stirrings: perhaps, if he carried enough heavy pipe quickly enough, the fall of Hitler and Tojo might be hastened. He alternately flared with temper fits and was quietly reflective on the fall day in 1942 when we quit the homestead he had come to in a covered wagon in 1894; later, receiving word of the accidental burning of that unpainted farmhouse, he walked around with tears in his eyes. He was past seventy before giving up his dream of one day returning to that embittered soil, of finally mastering it, of extracting its unkept promises.

As we left behind the oil derricks and desert sand hills last summer, approaching barns and belts of greenery, The Old Man praised wild flowers, dairy herds, shoots of cotton, fields of grain. "That's mighty good timberland," he said. "Good grass. Cattle could bunch up in them little groves in the winter and turn their backsides to the wind." He damned his enemies: "Now, Johnson grass will ruin a place. But mesquite trees is the most sapping thing that God lets grow. Mesquites spreads faster than gossip. A cow can drop her plop on a flat rock, and if she's been eatin' mesquite beans they'll take a-holt and grow like mornin' glories."

One realized, as The Old Man grew more and more enthusiastic over roadside growths and dribbling little creeks, just how fenced in he had been for thirty years; knew, freshly, the depth of his resentments as gas pumps, hamburger outlets, and supermarkets came to prosper within two blocks of his door. The Old Man had personally hammered and nailed his house together in 1944, positioning it on the town's northmost extremity as if hoping it might sneak off one night to seek more bucolic roots. Midland had been a town of maybe twelve thousand then; now it flirted with seventy thousand and the chamber of commerce mindlessly tub-thumped for more. The Old Man hated it: it had hemmed him in.

We detoured to Eastland County so he might take another glimpse of the past. He slowly moved among the tombstones in a rural cemetery where his parents rested among parched grasses and the bones of their dear friends: people who had been around for the Civil War; God-fearing, land-grubbing folk who had never dreamed that one day men would fly like birds in the sky or swim like fishes beneath the sea. Though he had on his best suit, he bent down to weed the family plot. I kneeled to help; my young son joined us. We worked in silence and a cloaking heat, sharing unspoken tribal satisfactions.

We drove past stations he recognized as important milestones: "Right over yonder—the old house is gone now, been gone forty years—but right there where you see that clump of them blamed mesquites, well, that was where your brother Weldon was borned. Nineteen-and-fifteen, I reckon it was. We had two of the purtiest weepin' willers you ever seen. I had me a dandy cotton crop that year."

We climbed an unpaved hill, the car mastering it easily, where the horses or mules of my youth had strained in harness, rolling their eyes under The Old Man's lash. "This durn hill," he said. "I come down it on a big-wheel bicycle I'd borrowed when I was about fifteen. First one I'd seen, and I was taken with it. Didn't know no more about ridin' it than I did about 'rithmetic. Come whizzin' down so fast my feet couldn't match them pedals: didn't have sense enough to coast. Wellsir, I run plumb over in the bar ditch and flipped over. It taken hair, hide and all." He laughed, and the laugh turned into a rasping cough, and the cough grew so violent that veins hammered at the edge of his sparse hair and the old face turned crimson. Through it all he joyously slapped his leg.

We stopped for lunch in a flawed little village where my father had once owned a blacksmith shop. The café was crammed by wage hands and farmers taking their chicken-fried steaks or bowls of vegetable soup seriously, men who minutely inspected strangers and muted their conversations accordingly. Weary of the car and the road, The Old Man chose to stand among the crowded tables while awaiting his order. He was grandly indifferent to the sneaked upward glances of the diners, whose busy elbows threatened to spear him from all sides, and to the waitress who, frowning, danced around him in dispensing hamburgers or plates of hot corn bread. "Tell granddad to sit down," my teenage daughter, Kerri, whispered. "He's all right," I said. "Well, my *gosh!* At least tell him to take off his *hat!*"

The Old Man startled a graybeard in khakis by gripping his arm just in time to check the elevation of a spoonful of mashed potatoes. "What's your name?" he inquired. The old nester's eyes nervously consulted his companions before he surrendered it. "Don't reckon I know you," my father said. "You must not of been around here long." "Twenty-some years," the affronted newcomer mumbled. "I had me a blacksmith shop right over yonder," The Old Man said. He pointed through a soft-drink sign and its supporting wall. "It was in the 1920s. My name's Clyde King. You recollect me?" When the old nester failed the quiz, my father abandoned him to his mashed potatoes. "What's *your* name?" he inquired of a victim mired in his blackberry pie. My twelve-year-old son giggled; his sister covered her humiliated face.

He walked along a diminutive counter of ketchup bottles, fruit pies, and digestive aids, reading only those faces grizzled enough to remember. An aging rancher, deep in his iced tea, nodded: "Yeah, I remember you." The Old Man pumped his hand, beaming. "I was just a kid of a boy," the rancher said. "I was better acquainted with your brother Rex. And the one that run the barbershop. Claude, wasn't it? Where they at now?" The Old Man sobered himself. "Well, I buried 'em within three weeks of one another last month. Claude was seventy-eight and Rex was seventy-four. I'm the only one of the King boys still kickin'. Oldest of the bunch, too. If I live to the eighteenth day of next February, the Lord willin', I'll be eighty-three year old." "Well, you look in right good shape," the rancher said.

When The Old Man sat down at our booth my daughter asked, too sweetly, "Granddad, you want me to take your hat?" He gave her an amused glance, a look suggesting he had passed this way before. "Naw," he said. "This a-way, I know where it's at if this café catches a-fire and I need it in a hurry." Then he removed the trespass to his outer knee and slowly crumbled crackers into the chili bowl before bending to feed his toothless face.

His bed was empty when I awoke in an Austin motel shortly after sunrise. He could be seen in contemplation of the swimming pool, turning his direct gaze on all who struggled toward their early jobs. Conversing with a black bellhop when I claimed him, he was full of new information: "That nigger tells me he averages a dollar a head for carryin' suitcases. I may buy me some fancy britches and give him some competition. . . . Folks sure must be sleepyheaded around here. I bet I walked a mile and didn't see two dozen people. . . . Went over yonder to that governor's mansion and rattled the gate and yelled, but didn't nobody come to let me in." "Did you *really?*" I asked, moderately appalled. "Thunder, yes! I'm a voter. Democrat, at that." Then the sly country grin flashed in a way that keeps me wondering in the night, now, whether he really had.

We entered a coffee shop. "Lord God," The Old Man said, recoiling from the menu. "This place is high as a cat's back. You mean they git a dollar eighty-five for two eggs and a little dab a bacon?" I smiled—how much did he think our motel room had

15

cost? "Well, the way things is now, I expect it run ten or twelve dollars." No, the price had been thirty dollars. His old eyes bulged: "For *one night?* Lord God, son, let's git us a blanket and go to the wagonyard!"

"This here's a heap bigger place than I thought it would be," he said in a hushed voice as he inspected the polished chambers of the Texas House of Representatives. He read the faces of past governors hanging in the rotunda, pointing out his favorites (selecting three good men and two rank demagogues). He stood shyly, not having to be reminded to remove his hat, when introduced to a few stray legislators and when led into Governor Preston Smith's office. Probably he was relieved to find the governor was absent, for The Old Man had never prospered in the company of "big shots": a big shot may be defined as one who wears neckties in the middle of the week or claims a title; I was never certain what fine distinctions The Old Man made in his mind between a United States senator and a notary public.

He marveled at the expanse of grass on the capitol grounds, inspected its flower beds, inquired of an attendant how many gallons of water the grounds required each day, and became stonily disapproving when the hired hand did not know. In the archives of the General Land Office he painstakingly sought out the legal history of that farm his father had settled in the long ago. He was enchanted by the earliest maps of Texas counties he had known as a boy.

That night he sat on his motel bed recalling the specifics of forgotten cattle trades, remembering the only time he got drunk (at age sixteen) and how the quart of whisky so poisoned him that he had promised God and his weeping mother that, if permitted to live, he would die before touching another drop. He recited his disappointment in being denied a preacher's credentials by the Methodist hierarchy on the grounds of insufficient education. "They wanted note preachers," he said contemptuously. "Wasn't satisfied with preachers who spoke sermons from the heart and preached the Bible pure. And that's what's gone wrong with churches."

A farmhand and apprentice blacksmith, he had not been smitten blind by his first encounter with my mother at a country so-

16

cial. "I spied another girl I wanted to spark," he grinned. "Next day I seen that girl and several others go into a general store by the blacksmith shop. I moseyed over like I was out of chewin' tobacco. Lord God, in the daylight that girl was ugly as a mud fence! I couldn't imagine wakin' up to that of a-mornin'." He laughed. "Then I taken a second look at Cora—she was seventeen—and she had the purtiest complexion and eyes and . . . well, just *ever*thing." Scheming to see her again, he pep talked his faint heart to encourage the boldness to request a date.

"Didn't seem like I'd ever do it," he confessed. "I'd go up to her at socials or church and make a bow and say, 'Miss Cora.' And she would bob me a little curtsy and say, 'Mister Clyde.' Then I'd stand there like a durned lummox, fiddlin' with my hat, and my face would heat up, and I couldn't think of a consarned thing to say." He laughed in memory of the callow swain that was. "It was customary in them days for young women to choose young men to lead singin' at church. I know within reason, now, that it was to help tongue-tied young hicks like myself, but I was pea green then and didn't know it. One night Cora picked me. Lord God, it excited me so that I plumb forgot the words to all the hymns I knowed." One could see him there in that lantern-lighted plank church, stiff in his high collar and cheap suit, earnest juices popping out on his forge-tanned forehead, sweet chaos alive in his heart. His voice would have quavered as he asked everyone to please turn to number one-forty-three, while matchmaking old women in calico encouraged him with their wise witch's eyes and young ladies with bright ribbons in their hair giggled behind fluttering fans advertising Sunday-school literature or pious morticians.

"Somehow I stumbled through it. Never heard a word the preacher said that night—I was tryin' to drum up nerve to approach Miss Cora, you see. Quick as the preacher said amen to his last prayer I run over fat women and little kids to git there before I got cold feet: 'Miss Cora, may I have the pleasure of your company home?' When she said, 'Yes, if you wish,' my heart pounded like I was gonna faint!

"Her daddy—ole man Jim Clark, *Lord God,* he was a tough case—he didn't allow his girls to ride in no buggies. If you wanted to spark a Clark girl, you had to be willin' to walk. Well-sir, I left my team at the church. Walkin' Cora home I asked if I could pay a call on her. I never dated no other woman from then on. There was another young feller had his eye on Cora. Once I had paid her three or four courtin' calls, I looked him up to say I didn't want him tryin' to spark her no more. Because, I said, I had it in mind to marry her. 'What'll you *do* about it?'—he got his back up, you see. I said, 'Whatever I got to do. And if you don't believe me, by God, just you try me!' He never give me no trouble."

The Old Man revealed his incredulous joy when, perhaps a year later, his halting proposal had been accepted. "Do you remember what you said?" my intrigued daughter asked. "Durn right! *Ought* to. I practiced on it for some weeks." He laughed a wheezing burst. "We had just walked up on her daddy's porch one evening and I said"—and here The Old Man attempted again the deeper tones of youth, seeking the courtly country formality he had brought into play on that vital night, reciting as one might when called upon in elocution class in some old one-room schoolhouse—" 'Miss Cora, I have not got much of this world's goods, and of education I haven't none. But I fancy myself a man of decent habits, and if you will do me the honor of becoming my wife, I will do the best I can by you for always.' " He bowed his head, hiding his tears. "Granddad," my daughter asked, "did you kiss her?" "Lord God, *no!*" The Old Man was sincerely shocked, maybe even a bit outraged: "Kissin' wasn't took lightly in them days."

Between Austin and San Antonio we drove through San Marcos; a prominent sign proclaimed that Lyndon B. Johnson had once earned a degree at the local teachers college. "That's a mighty fine school," The Old Man said. I remained silent. "Yessir," he said, "a *mighty* fine school." Only the purring air conditioner responded. The Old Man shifted elaborately on the seat. "Why, now, I expect that school's as good a school as the New-nited States has." By now he realized that a contest was joined: whatever joke he wished to make must be accomplished in the absence of my feeding straight-line. "I doubt if that Harvard out-

18

fit up yonder could hold a candle to this school," he said. "I expect this school would put that Harvard bunch in the shade." My
son, less experienced in such games, provided the foil: "Granddad, why is it such a good school?" "*Got* to be," The Old Man
said. "It learned ole Lyndon to have sense enough to know he
couldn't get elected again." He enjoyed his chortle no less for the
delay.

"Didn't you like President Johnson?" my son asked.

"Naw. LBJ told too many lies. I wouldn't a-shoed horses on
'credit for him."

"Who was your favoriate president?"

"Harry Truman. Harry wasn't afraid to take the bull by the
horns. Wasn't no mealymouth goody-goody in him like in most
politicians. Ole Ike, now, they blowed him up like Mister Big
and all he ever showed me was that silly grin."

"Did you ever vote for a Republican?" my son asked.

"Yeah, in 19-and-28. Voted for Herbert Hoover. And he no
more than put his britches on the chair till we had a depression.
I promised God right then if He wouldn't send no more depressions, I wouldn't vote for no more Republicans."

"Do you think God really cares who's president?" I asked.

"I reckon not," The Old Man said. "Look at what we got in
there now."

What did The Old Man think of this age of protest and revolt?

"It plagues me some," he admitted. "I got mad at them young
boys that didn't want to fight in Vietnam. Then after the politicians botched it so bad nobody couldn't win it, and told lies to
boot, I decided *I* wouldn't want to risk dyin' in a war that didn't
make sense."

It was suggested that no wars made sense.

"Maybe so," The Old Man said. "Bible says, 'Thou shalt not
kill.' Still yet, the Bible's full of wars. Bible says there'll be wars
and rumors of wars. I don't think war is what all the ruckus is
about, though. I think young people is just generally confused."

"Why?"

"They don't have nothing to cling to," he said. They had been
raised in whisky homes; their preachers, teachers, politicians, and
daddies had grown so money-mad and big-Ikey nothing else

19

counted. Too much had been handed today's kids on silver plat-
ters: they got cars too soon and matching big notions. They went
off chasing false gods. Well, didn't guess he much blamed 'em:
they didn't have nothing waiting at home except baby-sitters,
television, and mothers that cussed in mixed company or wore
whisky on the breath.

"I seen all this coming during the Second World's War," The
Old Man said. "People got to moving around so much with good
cars. Families split up and lost their roots. The main thing,
though, was the women. Women had always stayed home and
raised the kids: that was their job. It's just nature. And the man
of the family had to be out scratchin' a living. But during the
Second World's War, women started workin' as a regular thing
and smokin' and drinkin' in public. Triflin' started, and triflin' led
to divorces. I knowed then there was gonna be trouble because
*somebody's* got to raise the kids. You can't expect kids to turn
out right if you shuffle 'em off to the side."

There was little a divorced man could say.

"I'm thankful I raised my family when I did," he said. "World's
too full of meanness and trouble these days. Every other person
you meet is a smart aleck, and the other one's a crook. Them last
few years I was workin' for wages, there wasn't one young feller
in fifty willin' to work. All they had in mind was puttin' somethin'
over on somebody. Down at the creamery docks, the young
hands would slip off to play cards or talk smut or sit on their
asses any time the boss man wasn't standin' over 'em. They
laughed at me for givin' a honest day's work. I told 'em I'd *hired
out* to work, by God. I wouldn't a-give a nickel for any of 'em.
Didn't put no value on their personal word. I'd lift them heavy
milk crates—lift a dozen to their one—and when the drivers come
in and their trucks had to be swamped out and cleaned, I'd look
around and be the only hand workin'." He shook his head. "They
didn't care about nothin'. Seemed like life was . . . well, some
kind of a joke to 'em.

"Now," he said, "I think the niggers is raisin' too much sand.
Maybe I'd be raisin' ole billy myself if I'd been kinda left out of it
like them. I dunno—it's hard to wear the other feller's shoes. But

I just wasn't raised up to believe they're supposed to mix with us. It don't seem natural."

"Dad!" I said. "*Dad . . . Dad . . .*"

"Oh, I know," he said. Impatience was in his voice. This was an old battle fought between us many times without producing a victor—even though we had selectively employed the Bible against each other.

"You still mowing Willie's lawn?" I asked.

"Every Thursday," The Old Man said. "Durn your hide," he chuckled. Then: "Naw, Willie's moved off to Houston or someplace." Willie was a male nurse and had been the first black man to move into my father's neighborhood eight years ago. Not long after that community despoiling I visited home: great were the dire predictions having to do with Willie's staying in his place. Six months later we were sitting on the front porch. The black man walked into the yard. "Hey there, Old-Timer," he said.

I stiffened: surely The Old Man would burn a cross, bomb a school, break into "The Nigger Preacher and the Bear."

Instead he said mildly, "How you, Doctor?"

"Can you do my lawn a couple days early next week? I'm having some people over for dinner Tuesday night."

"Reckon so," The Old Man said. "Whatcha gonna have to eat?"

The black man smiled and said he thought he might burn some steaks on the grill.

"You can *tip* me one of them beefsteaks," The Old Man said, looking mischievous. "I'm a plumb fool about beefsteak."

They laughed; the black man complimented my father on his flower beds before giving him instructions on exactly how he wanted his shrubbery trimmed. The Old Man walked with him across the street to inspect the particulars. When he returned to ease back into his chair, I said—affecting the flattest possible cracker twang—"Boy Hidy, if that chocolate-coated sumbitch don't stay in his *place* . . ." The Old Man's grin was a bit sheepish. "I wouldn't mind 'em if they was all like ole Willie," he said. "He works hard, he keeps hisself clean, to my knowledge he don't drink, and I don't believe he'd steal if he was hungry." Then came one of those oblique twists of mind of which he was capable: "I don't take his checks though. I make 'im pay cash."

Now, some years later, we were approaching San Antonio. "I always figgered this for just another little ole Meskin town except for havin' the Alamo," he said. Soon he was marveling at the city's wonders, at the modern office buildings, old Spanish-style homes, green parks and easy-riding rivers. The Old Man happily waved to passing paddle boats as we idled under a tree at a riverfront café, laughing through the tears at himself when— mistaking a bowl of powerful peppers for stewed okra—he spooned in a country mouthful requiring a hard run on all available ice water.

He approached the Alamo with a reverence both enthusiastic and touching. "Right here," he proclaimed—pointing to a certain worn stone slab—"is where Travis drawed a line with his sword and told all the boys willin' to die for the right to step across. All of 'em stepped across except Jim Bowie, who was sick on a cot, and he had his buddies *carry* him across." Just why he had selected that particular stone not even historians may attest: the much-restored Alamo must make do with the smaller original artifacts and the wilder romanticisms. Indeed, where much of the blood was spilled a prestige department store now stands.

He moved among display cases containing precious bits and pieces of a more vigorous time: wooden pegs serving purposes later to be preempted by metal hinges, square-headed nails, early Colt firearms, crude chisels and hand-operated bellows, arrowheads, saddlebags, oxen yokes, tintype photos, the earliest barbed wire, a country doctor's bag with crude equipment such as an old uncle had carried in the long ago. He assembled his descendants to explain the uses of each relic, carefully associating himself— and his blood's blood—with that older time and place. He came to a new authority; his voice improved. Soon a group of tourists followed him about, the bolder ones asking questions. The Old Man performed as if he had been there during the siege. Choosing a spot on the outer walls, he said with conviction that right over yonder was where the invaders had fatally broken through. ("Daddy," my daughter whispered, "will you *please* get him to stop saying 'Meskin'?")

Taking a last look, he said, "Ma bought me a book on the

Alamo. I must of read it a hundred times. I read how them damn Meskins done Travis and his brave boys, how ole General Santa Anna had butchered all them Texas heroes, and I promised myself if I ever seen one of them greaser sons-a-bitches, why, I'd kill him with my bare hands." He laughed at that old irrationality. "But did you notice today, half the people in that Alamo was *Meskins?* And they seemed to think just as much of it as we do."

Now it was late afternoon. His sap suddenly ran low; he seemed more fragile, a tired old head with a journey to make; he dangerously stumbled on a curbstone. Crossing a busy intersection, I took his arm. Though that arm had once pounded anvils into submission, it felt incredibly frail. My children, fueled by youth's inexhaustible gases, skipped and cavorted fully a block ahead. Negotiating the street, The Old Man half laughed and half snorted: "I recollect helpin' you across lots of streets when you was little. Never had no notion that one day you'd be doin' the same for me." Well, I said. Well. Then: "I've helped that boy up there"—motioning toward my distant and mobile son—"across some few streets. Until now, it never once occurred that he may someday return the favor." "Well," The Old Man said, "he will if you're lucky."

Three o'clock in an Austin motel. The Old Man snores in competition with jet aircraft. On an adjoining bed his grandson's measured breathing raises and lowers a pale banner of sheets. Earlier, the boy had exorcised his subconscious demons through sheet-tugging threshings and disjointed, indistinct private cries. The Old Man snores on, at peace. *Night battles never plagued me*, he once said in explaining his ability to sleep anyplace, anytime. *I never was one to worry much. What people worry about is things they can't do nothin' about. Worryin' always seemed like a waste to me.*

The bridging gap between the two slumbering generations, himself an experienced insomniac, sits in the dark judging whether he would most appreciate a cold six-pack or the world's earliest sunrise. Out of deference to The Old Man, he has known only limited contacts with those bracing stimulants and artificial aids for which his soft, polluted body now begs. The only opium

23

available to him is that hallucinogenic agent the layman calls "memory"—a drug of the most awful and powerful properties, one that may ravish the psyche even while nurturing the soul. Stiff penalties should be affixed to its possession, for its dangerous components include disappointing inventories, blocked punts, lumpy batters, and iron buckets of burden. It is habit forming, near-to-maddening in large doses, and may even grow hair on the palms.

I remembered that we had compromised our differences in about my twentieth year. My own early assumption of family responsibilities proved healing: in the natural confusions of matrimony, one soon came to appreciate The Old Man's demanding, luckless role. Nothing is so leavening to the human species as to gaze upon the new and untried flesh of another human being and realize, in a combination of humility, amazement, and fear, that you are responsible for its creation and well-being. This discovery is almost immediately followed by a sharply heightened appreciation of more senior fathers.

We discovered that we could talk again. Could even sit at ease in long and mutually cherished silence. Could civilly exchange conflicting opinions, compete in dominoes rather than in more deadly games, romp on the lawn with our descendants, and share each new family pride or disappointment. For some four years in the early 1950s we lived in close proximity. The Old Man came to accept my preference for whisky as I came to accept his distaste for what it represented; he learned to live with my skeptic's atheism as I came to live with his belief that God was as tangible an entry as the Methodist bishop.

The Old Man was sixty-six and I was twenty-five when I went away for good. There were periodic trips back home, each of them somehow more hurried, fleeting, and blurred. Around 1960 it dawned on me that The Old Man and his sons had, in effect, switched roles. On a day I cannot name, he suddenly and wordlessly passed the family crown. Now the sons were solicited for advice or leadership and would learn to live uneasily in the presence of a quiet and somehow deeply wrenching paternal deference. (*Weldon, you reckon it would be all right if I got a better car?* Well, now, dad, I believe I'd go slow on that. Maybe you

24

don't see and hear well enough to drive in traffic very much. *Lawrence, what would you say to me and your mother goin' back to the farm?* Now, dad, why in the world? People have been starving off those old farms for fifty years. What would you do out there in the sticks, miles from a doctor, if you or mother got sick?)

The heart of the young blacksmith continued to beat in that shrinking frame, however. He could not drive a car any more; he nodded off in the middle of the sermon at Asbury Methodist; meddlers had barred him from climbing trees. He remained very much his own man, however, in vital areas. Living by his sweat, The Old Man saved an astonishing amount of his paltry pensions and earnings, fiercely guarded his independence, took pride in his age, seldom rode when he could walk, tended the soil, ate well, and slept regularly.

On that motel bed slept a man who, at age twelve, had fallen heir to the breadwinner's role for a shotgun-widowed mother and eight younger siblings. He had accepted that burden, had discharged it without running off to sea: had drawn on some simple rugged country grace and faith permitting him no visible resentments then or later. He had sweated two family broods through famines and floods, Great Depressions and World Wars, industrial and sociological revolutions. Though a child of another century, really, he walked through the chaos and tediums of his time determinedly—as Faulkner wrote of women passing through grief and trouble—"able to go through them and come out on the other side."

The faintest dawn showed through the windows when The Old Man sat up in bed, yawning: "Lord God, is it dinnertime? Must be, you bein' awake!" He examined my face: "Didn't you get no sleep?" Some. "How much?" Three or four hours, I lied. "You ain't gonna live to see fifty," The Old Man predicted. "What you ought to do is buy you a cotton farm and work it all day. I bet you'd sleep at night, then."

He almost hopped into his trousers from a standing position, amazingly agile in that fresh hour he most cherished. Noting my inspection he asked, "Reckon you can do that at eighty-two?" Hell, I said, I can't do it at forty-one. The Old Man celebrated

25

this superiority with a pleased grin. The previous night he had insisted on playing dominoes past midnight in the home of a favorite nephew, Lanvil Gilbert, talking it up like a linebacker: *Say you made five? Why, that makes me so mad I'll play my double-five—and gimme fifteen while you got your marker handy. . . . I forgot to tell you boys I run a domino school on the side. Got a beginner's class you might be able to git in.* Back at the motel he had again explored the distant past until his grandchildren yawned him to bed. *Old Man,* I thought, *what is the secret? What keeps you interested, laughing, loving each breath?* I remembered his enthusiastic voice on the telephone when I told him I had given my son his middle name: "I'm puttin' a five-dollar bill in the mail to buy him his first pair of long pants. Put it up and keep it. I want that exact five-dollar bill to pay for my namesake's first long pants." Grand satisfactions had visited his face earlier on our Austin trip when my son brought him a gigantic three-dollar pocket watch. The boy had shoved it at him— "Here, granddad, this is for you, I bought it out of my allowance"—and then had moved quickly away from the dangers of sentimental thanks and unmanly hugs.

As we started down to breakfast, The Old Man said, "Why don't we take Bradley Clayton with us?" Sure, if he wants to go. The Old Man gently shook the boy. "Namesake," he said. "Wake up, namesake, you sleepyhead." The boy rolled over with reluctance, blinking, trying to focus. "Git up from there," The Old Man said in feigned anger. "Time I was your age, I had milked six cows and plowed two fields by this time-a-day."

"*What?*" the boy said, incredulous.

"I'll make you think what!" The Old Man said, then repeated his improbable claim.

The boy, pulling his wits together, offered The Old Man a sample of the bloodline's baiting humor: "Was *that* what made you rich?"

The Old Man whooped and tousled the boy's hair, then mock-whipped him toward the bathroom.

We talked late on my final night. The Old Man sat in his jerry-built house, on a couch across from a painting of Jesus risking retina damage by looking directly into the celestial lights. Pictures of his grandchildren were on the walls and on the television top, along with a needlework replica of the Dead Kennedys appearing to hover over the U.S. Capitol, and a Woolworth print depicting a highly sanitized village blacksmith. One of his sons, thinking to please The Old Man, had given him the latter: while he appreciated the thought, he had been amused by the artist's concept. "Lord-a-mercy," he had chuckled, "the feller that painted that thing never *seen* a horse shod or a blacksmith shop either one." The painting revealed a neat, sweatless man effortlessly bending a horseshoe as he worked in an imposing brick edifice surrounded by greenery, while little girls in spotless dresses romped happily among gleaming anvils possibly compounded of sterling silver. The Old Man enjoyed comparing it with the realities of a photo made in the 1920s, showing him grease stained and grimy in a collapsing wooden structure filled with indescribable debris.

His hands—always vital to his lip movements—swooped and darted, described arcs, pointed, performed slow or vigorous dances according to the moment's chin music. Just before bed I asked in a private moment whether he had any major regrets. "Two," he said. "I wish I could of done better financially by your mother. I never meant for her to have such a hard life. And I wish I could of went to school."

On the morning of my departure he was spry and fun filled. Generally such leave-takings were accomplished in tensions and gloom; for a decade the unspoken thought had hovered that this might be the final good-bye. Last July, however, that melancholy tune was but faintly heard: The Old Man was so vigorously alive that I began to think of him as a sure centenarian. I left him standing on the front porch, wearing his workman's clothes, shaking a friendly fist against what he would do if I didn't write my mother more often.

Six weeks later he gathered a generous mess of turnip greens from his backyard vegetable garden, presenting them to his wife with the request that she concoct her special corn bread. A few hours after his meal he became dizzy and nauseated. "I just et too many of them turnip greens," he explained to his wife. Persuaded to the hospital for examination and medications, he insisted on returning home on the grounds he had never spent a night in a hospital bed and was too old to begin. The next morning, in great pain, he consented to again be loaded into my brother's car.

The Old Man mischievously listed his age as sixteen with a crisp hospital functionary filling out the inevitable forms. He ordered nurses out when a doctor appeared, extracting a promise from my brother that "no womenfolk" would be permitted to intimately attend him. When the examining physician pressed his lower abdomen, The Old Man jerked and groaned. "Is that extremely sore, Mr. King?" Well, yes, it was a right-smart sore. "How long has it been that way?" About ten days, he reckoned. "Why didn't you tell me?" my exasperated brother inquired. The old eyes danced through the pain: "Wouldn't a done no good, you not bein' no doctor."

He consented to stay in the hospital, though he did complain that his lawn mower and supporting tools had been carelessly abandoned: would my brother see that they were locked in the backyard toolshed? Then he shook my brother's hand: "Weldon, thank you for everything." He shortly lapsed into the final chills and fevers, and before I could reach home he was gone. I saw him in his final sleep and now cannot forget those magnificently weathered old hands. They told the story of a countryman's life in an eloquent language of wrinkles, veins, old scars and new. The Old Man's hands always bore some fresh scratch or cut as adornment, the result of his latest tangle with a scrap of wire, a rusted pipe, a stubborn root; in death they did not disappoint even in that small and valuable particular. No, it is not given to sons to know everything of their fathers—mercifully, perhaps— but I have those hands in my memory to supply evidence of the obligations he met, the sweat he gave, the honest deeds performed. I like to think that you could look at those hands and read the better part of The Old Man's heart.

Clyde Clayton King lived eighty-two years, seven months, and twenty-five days. His widow, four of five children, seven of eight grandchildren, six great-grandchildren, and two great-great-grandchildren survive. His time extended from when 'kissin' wasn't took lightly" to exhibitions of group sex; from five years before men on horseback rushed to homestead the Cherokee Strip to a year beyond man's first walk on the moon; from a time when eleven of twelve American families existed on average annual incomes of $380 to today's profitable tax-dodging conglomerates; from the first presidency of Grover Cleveland to the midterm confusions of Richard Nixon. Though he had plowed oxen in yoke, he never flew in an airplane. He died owing no man and knowing the satisfaction of having built his own house.

I joined my brother and my son in gathering and locking away The Old Man's tools in that backyard shed he had concocted of scrap lumbers, chipped bricks, assorted tins, and reject roofing materials. Then, each alone with his thoughts, we moved in a concert of leaky garden hose and weathered sprinklers, lingering to water his lawn.

*Harper's*
APRIL 1971

## afterword

When Willie Morris was my editor at *Harper's*, titillated by my whisky stories about The Old Man, he urged me several times to write about him. Each attempt failed. Only six weeks before The Old Man died, I tried again. A month later, on a damp day over drinks in a Lexington Avenue bar when I felt unusually used up, I morosely confessed failure: "Goddammit, I'm intimidated by it. I guess I just don't understand him well enough." Willie generously said he agreed with my first declaration, though he doubted the latter.

Flying home for The Old Man's funeral, I began to sort him out in my mind. Though not aware of doing so, I probably was beginning the writing process even then. I remember openly and carelessly puffing several sticks of pot between Washington and Dallas, and seeing mystical, tantalizing, undefinable clues to what it was all about in the puffy drifting cumulus formations outside the sealed window. When Willie Morris telephoned his condolences about two hours after we had buried The Old Man, I blurted, "Willie, I can write it now."

The task required about thirty days or, more accurately, nights. Emotional ones; I cried a lot. Though the article came in at about twelve thousand words, I wrote nearer to forty thousand in the original draft. Always it was a process of defining, of evaluating, of winnowing and cutting down. To my amazement, I discovered much about The Old Man—and about myself, and larger subjects—that I had not previously suspected. I came to believe that perhaps what life is all about, with its uncertain currents and puzzling tugging tides, is the extensions of the generations trying to work it all out. I once read somewhere that writing is, ideally, an act of discovery; certainly it was for me in that case.

"The Old Man" brought other satisfactions. One was hearing my mother say, almost two years after publication, "Rereading that piece about your daddy gives me back a little of him for a while." Another occurred one night shortly after I learned the article had several times been reprinted abroad. Swooshing down a dark Texas highway, the headlights showing only vast empty reaches and the car radio thrumming indigenous country music, I thought: *By God, they're reading about old Clyde King tonight in Warsaw and Moscow!* It was a great feeling, like giving to someone you love, only slightly dampened by the thought that I would have given anything to hear the wry, self-deprecating thing The Old Man might have said about such an absurdity. A third windfall came when I heard my son precisely quoting something The Old Man had said in the article: " 'A cow can drop her plop on a flat rock, and if she's been eatin' mesquite beans they'll take a-holt and grow like mornin' glories.' " He quoted his grandfather with a pleased smile, and with a chant sensing not only the rhythm but the poetry of the utterance. In that moment I could have wished or imagined no greater reward.

# BLOWING MY MIND
# AT HARVARD

On a windy February morning almost twenty-one years ago I woke up before first light, tossed a duffel bag and a scruffy suitcase into a friend's pickup truck, and went off to college.

I was twenty-one, just discharged from the army, eager to accept the best cerebral gases on deposit at Texas Tech. I brought as qualifications a scroll attesting the U.S. Army's satisfaction with my score on its high school equivalency test, and valuable civilian experience as a cotton picker, oil-field roustabout, summer postman, and counterman at a drive-in restaurant. I had less than fifty dollars, and not a book or a dress shirt.

I might just as easily have been heading for any of a half dozen small southwestern schools, each having expressed interest in my football potential to the exclusion of my scholarly possibilities. I chose Texas Tech because my mother's cooking was only three hours' decent hitchhiking away; agents of the athletic department had efficiently recognized a youngster who might respond to shameless flattery and promissory lies. I had no course of study in mind. In general terms I aspired to make All-American, write a best-selling novel, and be forever revered in the hearts of shapely coeds. I lasted one and one-third semesters.

On a slightly muggy morning in September of 1969 I got up before first light in Washington, fought with my wife over the cargo limitations of a late-model convertible, and twenty-six impossible loadings later drove off again to college.

This time I was forty-one and a grandfather. I was better supplied than formerly—both in books and dress shirts. A monstrous color TV on the back seat, surrounded by electrical appliances, precluded hitchhikers. My experience now included five years as a newspaper reporter, a decade in the viper pits of political Washington, five years of backbiting at Manhattan literary cocktail parties, two marriages, three children, and a satisfying old dalliance or two, many of life's routine bruises, and not a few moderately deep cuts. I had been drunk in the company of Louie Armstrong, Lyndon B. Johnson, Bubba Smith, and Norman Mailer. I had shared a predawn walk in Washington with Harry Truman, and in a moment of midnight Manhattan madness had explicitly, if unsuccessfully, solicited the affections of Lauren Bacall. I no longer believed life to be everlasting or its fruits without number, had learned that the answer is not always clearly printed in the back of the book.

Now the old Texas Tech dropout was going to Harvard. I had applied for a Nieman Fellowship because I was "old, ignorant, and critically in need of rest"—the language notifying my agent and editors that the reliable old word machine had slipped its cogs. I wanted, in the words of Adlai Stevenson, "to sit on the sidelines for a while, with a glass of wine in my hand, and watch the people dance."

The Lucius W. Nieman Foundation, established in 1937 by the widow of the late publisher of the *Milwaukee Journal* for the purpose of "elevating the standards of journalism"—an ambition, then and now, pregnant with potential—annually brings to Harvard a dozen American journalists and three or four from abroad. With rare exceptions, all of Harvard's facilities are available. Except for loosely pledging not to write for commercial purposes while in attendance, and a requirement to perform all assigned work in one course of his choice for one semester, the Nieman Fellow is free to do what he wishes. One former Nieman ran in the twenty-six-mile Boston Marathon, finishing 586th. Another put together the best-selling sex spoof, *Naked Came the Stranger*. Another committed suicide. Ed Lehey, a legendary member of the original Nieman class, who made at Harvard life-long friendships with Felix Frankfurter and Archibald MacLeish, probably spoke for many successors when he said he wished he could do it again sober.

I was entertaining my fifteen-year-old daughter and twelve-year-old son at a North Carolina beach resort when word came of my selection—an event inspiring much merriment among the offspring, who had trouble seeing daddy in school. Nor was one cheered when an old friend wrote another, ostentatiously spreading around carbon copies, "In the matter of *King v. Harvard,* I will take King and give fifty-two pints." "You at Harvard?" a telegram said. Rumors spread that I would major in astrology and Christian Science. One eventually found himself baited into accepting a bet that he dared not offer for the Harvard football varsity.

When the grandfatherly Nieman Fellow examined the histories of the 1969–1970 Fellows, he found little comfort. He was the class elder by anywhere from three to fifteen years ° and his curriculum vitae was nakedly exposed by Harvard's version of our biographical sketches. "Mr. Montalbano," a typical blurb ran, "holds degrees from Rutgers and Columbia universities, and was an IAPA Scholar at the Universidad Nacional de Buenos Aires in 1964." "Mr. Smith was graduated from Williams College and attended Oxford University." "Mr. Van Aal has degrees from the Lycée Janson de Sailly, Paris, and the Université de Paris." "Mr. King attended Texas Technological College." "For about thirty minutes," an anonymous admirer scrawled on a *New York Times* clipping.

For years the would-be scholar had hidden his academic deficiencies behind the darkest mendacities, claiming when pressed to be a graduate of this university or that, bestowing high honors or exotic degrees on himself. Not a set of his old applications for employment exists free of their scholastic deceptions, including a former success on file with the U.S. Congress. With experience one became less inclined to fortify his shoddy academic walls with liar's mortar. There came a time when it seemed advanta-

° His morale would slightly improve upon the appointment of Lou Banks, editor of *Fortune,* fifty-two, as the first Nieman Senior Research Fellow.

geous to stress one's lack of formal intellection. Yet for all his boasting of official ignorance one never knew when Ben Franklin's voice might whisper in the private darkness, *An investment in knowledge always pays the best interest,* or Horace Mann might thunder, *Schoolhouses are the republican line of fortifications,* or Halliburton might suggest, *A college education shows a man how little other people know.*

No matter that for years one had been a voracious reader, half digesting great lumps of Faulkner, Kafka, Dickens, Ruskin, Twain, James, Tocqueville, Bierce, Kipling, Burke, Sandburg, Mencken, Mailer, the biblical prophets—even taking cautious samples of Euripides, Joyce, Freud, Shakespeare, Gogol, Kierkegaard, Plato, Marx, Céline, Yeats—devouring in wild, undisciplined fury tomes on primitive mythology, spelunking, Machiavellian politics, race relations, public accounting, ancient wars, girls' basketball, sometimes consuming the *Congressional Record,* Sir James George Frazer, Mickey Spillane, Krafft-Ebing, Sears Roebuck, Brendan Behan, and *The Texas Cattleman.* No matter that libraries contained books with his own name on their spines, or that he had disputed Norman Podhoretz's literary word to his face. No matter at all: for he had no scroll with his name affixed, unless he counted his old GI high school equivalency certificate.

It is hard to describe what Harvard represented in the mind's private country to one whose sensibilities were shaped in the provinces, whose reluctant civilization judged educational institutions by their football successes, whose family tree boasted not a single marginal scholar. To say in the words of former president Charles William Eliot that his institution was "the oldest, the richest, and the freest" of America's academic clusters was simply not enough. "I don't think you understand what it means back in Kansas City to come East to college," I later would hear a young Harvard professor accuse a history honors class, and the fifteen select seniors—predominately eastern, affluent extensions of Jewish intellectualism—verified the professor's suspicion by their blank expressions.

My father's favorite talmud had taught that nothing was more useless or contemptible than "educated fools"—those long on book sense but bereft of the common sense he judged vital to the world's daily tasks. It was axiomatic that the man who fastidiously used the language could never satisfactorily milk a cow. My country forebears talked colorfully and well in their country idioms of adventures among snake-handling religious cults or experiences along the creek banks, and they provided helpful instructions in the arts of coon hunting, blacksmithing, and crop tending. It was not easy, however, to catch them discoursing on ideas.

Our politicians of the McCarthy era made it clear that the nation's most dangerous men were Harvard educated. Snobs were known to prevail there, as rich as they were arrogant. We feared, despised, and envied Harvard's sons for their radical notions, old money, eastern breeding, and elegantly effete and snobbish ways. "Bright, scholarly men like McNamara, Bundy, and Fortas had a lot of influence on his thinking," Sam Houston Johnson would complain in *My Brother Lyndon*, "because he regarded them as part of an intellectual elite. There was a hint of awe in his attitude toward them. He knew he was basically as smart as they were—smarter in some respects—but their way of talking and their whole educational background—Harvard, Yale, and all of that—somehow got to him more than it should." When I visited the undergraduate house off Harvard Yard to which I had been loosely assigned, the Master so offended me by imitations of my Texas accent and remarks about my preferring hard cider to gentlemanly rations of sherry that I never again by choice went near the hatchet-faced, beret-wearing, supercilious Ivy League smartass.

One arrived in Cambridge burned not only by academic and regional paranoias, but obsessed over how to preserve his privacy. The grandfatherly Nieman Fellow had a distaste for group activities surpassing all reason. He had never been a team man (preferring in his youth to lose a football game by three touchdowns when he had personally enjoyed an exceptional night, rather than win one in which he had performed to only perfunctory applause). He had hated the innumerable luncheons, airport rallies, fund-raising dinners, and committee meetings so necessary to the political calling—all those goddamned people, each on earth to intrude, push, shove, crowd, hoo-haw: *Gimme, gimme, my*

35

*name's Jimmy.* There remained old friends he enjoyed, and periodically he recharged his social juices through three or four nights of determined reveling. As he grew older, however, even these diversions became less vital. The longer he worked as a writer, free of all obligations except his compulsive appointments with the typewriter, the more he came to cherish seclusion among his books, his deadlines, and his private detachments. On arriving in Cambridge he bought a ton of books with which he planned to read himself into intellectual grace, installed a plug-in telephone, and vowed to contact the outside world only in moments of personal convenience.

It began pleasantly enough in the September sunshine. Deans and professors honored our introductory luncheon in the genteelly shabby old Harvard Faculty Club. This was intended as a mixer: Nieman Fellows and faculty getting to know you. In truth it resembled two distinct celebrations. Nieman Fellows circled each other warily from afar, sizing up the fraternal competition. Faculty men formed their more sedate circles; one heard them speaking as cold war congressmen spoke of the Russians: "No one knows what to expect of them after last spring." "There's a rumble that they're holding a strategy session tonight." "It's difficult to know if they truly seek to communicate or merely to agitate." The enemy was the Harvard students. One began to suspect an interesting year.

A rebellion occurred immediately after our luncheon, when antisherry forces seized control and marched the captive Niemans in a body to King's Men's Bar on Harvard Square. Here Scotch, bourbon, and beer carried the day as we sixteen strangers wore our most convivial faces, accepting as fresh material even the hoariest city-room yarns, routinely turning the other fellow's grinners into knee-slappers, each of us careful to make fluttery passes at modesty when it became necessary to air our respective capes of personal accomplishment. Not a man spoke of what every heart surely had in it: *If I've got to spend a year with these people, it's important to discover the fools, charlatans, and infidels.* Those who hoped to meditate in solitude feared close connections with anyone who might bang on the door at midnight or plot excessive "Nieman family" picnics. Those with only modest appreciation for small children were naturally on guard against those who owned several. It was a subtle process of winnowing and judging, and those who didn't know it didn't belong in the league.

Only The Drunk revealed himself on that first day. More time and oceans of sherry would be required before one could name from among his associates the Corporate Straight Arrow, the Lover, the Supercilious Fat Man, the Harmless Wry Pun-Maker, the Country Cynic, and the Cool Cat. The Drunk soon became a living advertisement for Prohibition, indulging in weepy midday jags, becoming more garrulous the closer he approached his semi-comas, never hesitating at seminars to repeat a complex question he had asked fifteen minutes earlier but had simply forgotten in the fog.

The Lover, originally revealed after telephoning select Nieman Fellows' wives to solicit private appointments when their husbands were in class, became the best public peep show in town as he steered the various objects of his abundant affection into what he thought to be cozy corners, there to flutter his bedroom eyes and whisper his endearments, oblivious to large and appreciative audiences. To witness the Corporate Straight Arrow unable to concentrate on the dramatic productions at Loeb Theater because of his compulsion to greet anyone whose face was marginally familiar, or anyone known to be well connected in the faculty community, was a quick lesson in corporate climbing. To observe the Country Cynic shaking his head and delightedly saying "sumbitch" as such mortal exhibitions verified his natural suspicions was to feel that mankind might yet be uplifted.

Those early days were not bad for the spirit. This was before the Nieman wives had the opportunity to think of certain of their counterparts as bitches or bores, before snow, before one grew weary of the same old faces. One's ego received vital refurbishings as he played almost every down in a fourteen-to-twelve Nieman football loss to lithe young *Crimson* hearties, a foolishness that left him bruised and bedridden only for three days.° One

° His plan to offer for the Harvard football varsity was aborted when a humorless functionary of the athletic department failed to discern by tele-

discovered an impossible number of exciting courses in the Harvard catalog. He decided to risk public exposure, choosing economics, history, the drama, sociology, American literature, foreign affairs—the law, astronomy, and the Divinity School tempted him. The would-be scholar began to cultivate a knowing air two weeks before classes began. He skulked around The Coop, eyeing Harvard chairs and crimson sweat shirts, wondering when the White House might solicit his advice on problems requiring light touches of culture.

One temporarily spurned an old habit of writing by night and sleeping by day, rising to stroll about Harvard Yard or Harvard Square with the early sun and the morning dew, frisky squirrels and yawning storekeepers as his incidental companions. He made an honest effort to acquire the feel of history by reading chipped gravestones (looking incongruously like cardboard cutouts from Hollywood's notion of Boot Hill memorials) in the old burial ground near Christ Church, where lay the Revolutionary soldiers and Harvard's earliest bloods. Or he quietly contemplated stone memorials such as the one off Cambridge Common that stated, rather matter of factly, that here, under a certain large old elm, one night in April of 1775, villagers gathered to march in defense of Concord against the British. Other markers reminded him that Cambridge had been founded in 1630, that Harvard began only six years later, that here, in Wadsworth House, General Washington of the Continental army had briefly made his headquarters before moving over to Vassall House on Brattle Street.

Yet it was unreal: it did not come alive despite one's dogged efforts to call up thudding hoofbeats of Revere's mount, the righteous rattle of colonial muskets, the canings of Harvard's first sons by its first president. Too many traffic lights intruded on the dream, too many subway rumblings, too many signs advertising pizza or cocktail lounges with Inez-at-the-keyboard; too many stray beards slipped up behind the history seeker to demand spare coins. He discovered that he dwelt more efficiently in imaginary tents of the past when in his native desert Texas, where

---

phone the intriguing possibilities. Things went well after the grandfatherly Nieman said he had once played at Texas Tech, until he responded to the matter of when by confessing to 1949.

the sight of rocky foothills, salt domes, and flat brown miles marching unbroken to distant horizons suggested the ice-age glaciers inching down from Canada, inactivated old seas, the earliest Spanish expeditions; suggested prideful Comanches who for four hundred years made their murderous ponyback raids into Mexico while dispatching all reciprocating invaders; buffalo herds belly-deep in grasses; the old Butterfield Stage and Judge Roy Bean and prehistoric Midland Man who wandered that desolate land twenty thousand years ago. He knew that Harvard had graduated students two hundred years before settlers stopped killing Indians around Dallas; yet he walked where Washington had stood, and Henry David Thoreau and the earliest of Saltonstalls, by Queen Anne and Tory and old Georgian houses, unaccountably convinced that it had all started here no earlier than 1936.

For by midmorning Harvard Square would be packed by hairy wrecks and braless butterballs hawking their wares—Fem Libs, Black Panthers, SDSers, Weathermen, nihilists, hedonists, devil worshipers, and unspecified crazies all proclaiming The Only True Salvation; chanters of Hare Krishna/Hare Krishna/Krishna Krishna/Hare Hare, wearing their peach-colored togas, with shaved heads and rattling tambourines. Agents of bug-eyed spiritualists, peace marches, and coffeehouses thrust their documents into his hand, while teenyboppers from South Boston and juvenile runaways from Indiana made their ersatz Harvard poses. Bellbottoms and miniskirts. Pot smokers and panhandlers. Green-eyeshadow gals and anticosmetic feminists. Hairy heads suggesting cockleburs and ticks. Jivers and schemers and round-the-clock dreamers. Merchants posting notices proclaiming Absolutely No Bare Feet Inside. Through it all wandered occasional gray old faculty heads wearing the tweeds and ties of another day, sometimes muttering to themselves.

Exactly the type of thing, of course—along with student protests and "fuck" appearing frequently in the columns of the *Crimson*—to inspire the old grads of '09 or '53 to write letters threatening to dry up alumni generosity or to point their heirs toward Yale. "The Bright Lexicon of Youth," wrote Bernard A. Merriman, '09, in a letter to the Harvard *Bulletin:* "Guys, chicks, twerps, latrine, grass, abortion, pregnant, shrink, seduced, hysterics, and nervous breakdowns all needed to describe the life of happy sharing. Harvard College appears ready to diffuse this barnyard culture throughout its Houses. I do not feel obligated to assist." What triggered B. A. Merriman '09 was an article heralding the arrival of coeducational dorms, making it all the easier for the Radcliffe lamb to lie down with the Harvard lion. Such things happen—may have happened as early as '09 (though surely without community cooperation, which probably only made it all the sweeter). May it comfort old grads: some of Harvard's sons first to bivouac officially in Radcliffe quarters complained of young ladies taking breakfast in bathrobes and curlers, while Cliffies complained of Harvard men who regurgitated their stag liquors and were slow to open doors, carry books, or request dates.

Harvard is not what it used to be. Nothing is: Harvard or the single wing or McGeorge Bundy's image or the taste of baked sweet potatoes. College kids, especially, are not what they used to be. Presidents who lovingly speak of peace while aggressively waging war no longer fool them. Old fossils who vote to send them to die for corrupt Asian governments in the name of obscure freedoms, while closing their eyes to acts of genocide against the Black Panthers, are quickly recognized as frauds. Screwing is better than killing, to say nothing of being ever so much more moral, and the young know this where their fathers did not. Pot being no worse than alcohol, they know the insanity in an alcoholic judge's sending a pothead to jail on the word of a drinking prosecutor slowly murdering his own liver—while Washington subsidizes tobacco growers and cancer research from the same pocket. They know that Eisenhower lied about our U-2 spying missions, that LBJ lied about the Gulf of Tonkin and much to follow, that had the Pentagon told truths all these years about its "kill ratios"—seven to one; ten to one; more—then the Vietcong would be more severely damaged than we now find it. They know the wide gap existing between the claims of institutional advertising and institutional performance, as is provided in malignant forms when they attempt to place Manhattan telephone calls or when a black man can't secure a loan outside the lairs of loan sharks or when doorknobs fall off or basements leak in new fifty-thousand-dollar split levels and when the rich architects of faulty automobiles assign private detectives to dig up dirt on Ralph Nader. They know that careless ecological crimes are committed by our industrial kings against the land they are supposed to inherit (provided they don't die in Asia, on the campus of their personal Kent State, or attending a Democratic National Convention) and that Dr. Billy Graham, the Nixon administration's official moralist, has not provided leadership on a major social crisis in twenty years, if ever: let them eat platitudes. They know that John Wayne, Bob Hope, Mendel Rivers, and other patriots who most publicly proclaim the need for more efficient killing tools and young men to enthusiastically employ them, have never served a military day in their comfortable fat lives. They know that J. Edgar Hoover is a despot, a tyrant, a vainglorious bureaucrat who runs his G-man corps with all the daily democracy attending a banana republic—and that not a man in Congress, or the White House, has guts enough to say so.

Much, of course, is unknown to Harvard's young. They know nothing of the tricks of parenthood, of the debilitating pressures of chickenshit bosses, of being locked by age, habit, financial obligations, mean circumstances, or mature cowardice into loveless marriages, dead-end careers, and advancing physical infirmities. They understand little of the depression's old chills or of the numbing fears of McCarthyism, and they sense practically nothing of what boiling insecurities those events inspired in their elders. They have no viable solutions to many of the problems they rail against; while they will resent its being said, they simply lack the seasoning, judgment, or experience to run the world as efficiently as they presume they would should its care be suddenly thrust upon them. One met young fools at Harvard as well as old.

On their down days, Harvard's sons and Radcliffe's daughters cry many damnations: the most heralded of their professors (whose campus presence may have originally motivated them to Cambridge) are mostly aloof strangers, difficult to communicate with even in their posted office hours, generally content to sur-

41

render their charges to obscure teaching fellows while removing themselves to write books, perform distant lectures, or accomplish research. Students often feel they are no more than passing numbers in the institution's scheme, unknown by name or distinguishing characteristics to those who lecture them in lots of two hundred or more, strangers even to their classmates, with little voice in student government (of which Harvard effectively has almost none). They are as impatient with Harvard's varied study commissions as they are with Washington's, seeing fewer reforms than new commissions. Despite Harvard's reputation for excellence, a surprising number of students complain of not being sufficiently challenged; it is impossible, they claim, to fail a course as long as one is not suspended for disciplinary reasons or unless one too vigorously contradicts a professor's favored dogma. "I don't think a Harvard education means what it once did," Frank Rich, an editor of the *Crimson,* said to me. "Many of us at the *Crimson* spend our time and our energies here. I don't know anybody who does all the required reading or who worries much about attending classes. On the other hand, I don't know anybody who's failing."

Sam (we shall disguise him), a bright young midwestern junior originally shipped to Harvard because his wealthy parents thought it necessary to be saved from radical elements (and who has learned to smoke dope and who is not entirely without sympathy for the Weathermen), is depressed over joining his innocent parents in Washington for their annual Easter pilgrimage to national shrines. "We visit all the stone monuments," he says, "then we call on the old relics in Congress my father contributes to. Everyone sits around reaffirming mutual prejudices. What they hate most is militant blacks and college students. I remember when they mostly hated Northern Democrats and Fifth Amendment Communists." Gloria telephoned her wealthy parents' seaboard home in tears to ask if someone could please make sense of the campus killings at Kent State. "Don't call here in hysterics again," her mother said. "For a minute I thought you were pregnant or had been busted for pot." Another Cliffie, Elaine, is hung up by the double life she leads at age twenty, a schizophrenic contrast between home and school. "I've practically lived with this boy for a year, but when I'm home for the holidays I'm not permitted phone calls after ten." Some safe old gaffer draws a low draft number from a fish bowl in Washington; a love affair goes bust; Ted Kennedy jeopardizes the immediate future by driving not quite all the way across the wrong bridge; cops invade Harvard Yard to crack heads with billy clubs; there is a sudden drought of LSD—and desperate calls go home; quarrels erupt between friends; suicide is contemplated; five or six or seven out of ten seek the services of a shrink. "I don't know anybody happy here," one hears from a significant number of students.

One should remember, of course, that self-dramatization comes easily to the young. It is particularly chic these days to claim more cancerous disaffections than the next fellow, although God knows (and Nathan Pusey should), there are enough to go around. Fred once told me that he almost never went to class, seldom did the required reading, and did not trouble himself with exams to the extent that his friend Stan did. Stan told the same story—except that he reversed their respective roles.

Of the five or six classes I audited, attendance figures were much more stable and consistently higher than the students led me to believe. Even a large majority of those students who complain loudest admit that they probably would choose Harvard if they had to do it over.

I agree that faculty lions generally permit minimal student contacts, considering their students little better than necessary nuisances or worse. At several Cambridge dinner parties one heard faculty types discuss—to the exclusion of mentioning their students for good or ill—institutional politics, their glory days in Washington when Camelot reigned, their books or research or career frustrations. John Kenneth Galbraith, Warburg Professor of Economics and Harvard's most determined triple-threat man of letters, spoke with refreshing candor to E. J. Kahn, Jr., author of *Harvard: Through Change and Through Storm:* "I've never been able to put my mind on anybody else's problems. The fact that some students may be exploring the structure of poverty in the United States or the means of financing the Boston Symphony doesn't attract me. I've never been able to give the same standing to someone else's problems that I give my own." Perhaps President Pusey himself establishes the institutional example; in his *Ambassador's Journal*, Galbraith describes visiting Pusey to inform him of plans to resign on receiving his appointment as ambassador to India: "He received the news with great equanimity and said he hoped it might be early in the academic term so there would be a minimum of academic disturbance. The interview, *the only one I ever had with him* [italics supplied] took about five minutes." The president of Harvard is a busy man, of course, and one cannot expect him to conduct constant interviews or to hunker down in the Yard rapping with radicals. Particularly not Nathan Pusey, who can go cold and flinty when offended, and who—since calling in police during the spring uprising of '69—has become something of a public scold against the rebellious young. He does not grant newspaper or television interviews except on the rarest occasion, and I discovered only two or three students who had had a personal word with him.

One observed unhealthy suspicions not only between faculty and students, but among faculty members themselves. Events of the famous spring bust of 1969, when tradition was violated by outside cops invading Harvard Yard, radicalized many undergraduates and polarized the faculty. Since that time, well-publicized conservative and liberal caucuses have been held among divergent faculty groups at the slightest provocation. It was not uncommon to hear faculty members or their wives speak of old friendships broken or old trusts betrayed. "We used to meet at the Faculty Club and talk of our husbands' academic projects," one faculty wife said to me, "but now we whisper of campus politics—or we don't talk at all. I rather suspect it must be the same among partisans in Congress at times." A certain Harvard sophistication cloaks these fresh wounds, though one senses the deepest seethings beneath the outward civility. President Pusey has opted for early retirement, if that's any clue.

No longer believe that Harvard students are all rich preppies tracing their Harvard histories back almost as far as the Saltonstalls (of whom nineteen had been graduated by the start of the twentieth century). A substantial percentage of sons of Harvard sons remain (up to a quarter was normal until World War II, though the figure is appreciably fewer now) but old Crimson blood doesn't count for as much as it once did. There is more concern than formerly with social, economic, cultural, and ethnic mixes; perhaps 60 to 65 per cent of the students now come from public schools, and there has been a recent effort to welcome students who won't jump off the Cambridge water tower should they finish in the bottom quarter. Harvard is a place of rawer democracies than formerly, more permissive than its students now realize. The traditional eating clubs do not matter much any more, or snooty connections, or tweedy jackets affecting leather elbows, or button-down shirts and tasteful narrow ties. One night a kindly old house master, veteran of many a proper gentlemanly meal where his boys appeared with scrubbed faces and "sirs" on their lips, regretted over sherry that coats and ties at dinner had ceased to be obligatory—remarking, in some amazement, that a persistent minority attempt to claim dining-hall rights in their T-shirts.

Neither believe, however, that barbarians reign triumphant: Harvard currently accepts only 1 in 5.2 applicants, almost three-fourths of these taking honors. A high percentage spend summer vacations in interesting and useful ways: working with Ralph Nader, doing labor in Israel, writing for newspapers, cutting sugar cane in Cuba, interning in Congress, or hitchhiking through Europe. As a group they are intelligent, articulate, more concerned and serious than their elders suspect. For all the agony smiting the class of '09, the students are only moderately radical. Of forty-eight hundred Harvard undergraduates and twelve hundred Cliffies, only three hundred participated in the original seizure of University Hall. Of three thousand persons present in Harvard Square for the celebrated post-Cambodian trashings last spring, only a small minority participated. Even the hairiest radicals are not wholly devoid of reason: following the Kent State killings, when two hundred of them marched on the campus ROTC building with thoughts of burning it, an equal number circled the building to protect it; after a lengthy debate, rather than fisticuffs, the militants were successfully persuaded against torching. When fifteen or so Weathermen in-

45

vaded the Center for International Affairs to attack faculty members and secretaries in a senseless hit-and-run raid, they were denounced by varied SDS factions and, indeed, by almost every organization on campus. From Cambodia's invasion forward, however, one observed a generalizing spread of radicalism.

An old head there sees numerous sociological differences between this collegiate generation and his own. Fewer barracks boastings prevail about the astonishing amount of nooky one gets, probably because more youngsters are busy in its efficient harvestings. Where we considered a weekend lost in the absence of getting all vomity drunk, today's youngsters are more likely to content themselves with acid-laced orange juice, marijuana, or mild beer busts. ("They don't drink," a young Harvard professor said. "When I was an undergraduate here seven years ago, we organized our social life around booze. These kids don't really care for it.") Where we stood in fear before professors or other symbols of authority, today's students are quite cavalier, fearless, and not easily intimidated. Where we made a big thing of family pedigrees or finances, social station, personal histories, and introduced ourselves down to our middle initials and hometowns, today's kids say only, "I'm Scott" or "I'm Frank" or "I'm Ann." The idea, they explain, is to accept other humans at face value; they don't give a damn what has gone before. This ignoring of the personal past may somehow serve the ideal of a pure democracy, though as a writer obsessed with every man's story and as one who thinks understanding of the past is vital to lessons of the present, it blows my mind.

The old Nieman's resentful juices boiled when he heard undergraduates sneer at their parents' fears of premature pregnancies, or criticize their fathers for their economic preoccupations, or jeer at the family chaos resulting from a mother's vacation discovery of pot caches, or otherwise speak with contempt of their elders. When a student whose writing seemed mature and perceptive complained in honest outrage of his long-divorced father having cut off his sustaining child-support payments now that the student had turned twenty-one, I found myself cheering the old boy (*Yeah! Go, Dad!*) and then delivering a stiff little lecture telling the young barbarians how many of my own youthful contemporaries were expected, at the age of fifteen or sixteen, to largely make their own ways in the world or at least to pay weekly board into the family coffers. When the Nieman Fellows, publishing a special issue of the *Crimson*, attacked that publication for (1) having no blacks on its staff, (2) paying less than union wages to its back-shop help, and (3) barring press coverage of their annual banquet, I thought the editors' whines and protest unbecoming.

One would be drinking beer with *Crimson* staffers, considering himself their calendar equals, and then a bright young Cliffie would remark, "Oh, it happened a long time ago—Kennedy had just been elected president, and I was in about the fourth grade." The old Nieman would recall that his first conversation with John F. Kennedy occurred sixteen years ago, when Kennedy was a junior and very skinny U.S. senator who appeared ill at ease and who stammered his speeches in a high, reedy voice. In one class I mentioned the execution of the Rosenbergs, an event that seemed to me to have taken place about a week ago Wednesday, and a voice in the back asked, "Who in hell were the Rosenbergs?" "God," one Cliffie said to another as I walked past them, "Sally's hooked on this old guy who teaches school in Providence. He's *got* to be thirty-two or thirty-three." Dr. Richard (Kip) Pells, a gifted young professor of history, remarked in the first class I attended, "I was born in the time of Pearl Harbor"—somehow making it sound as if the Zeros had zoomed in only about two hours after Christ fled the tomb.

One evening at a party a young lady remarked on a magazine article revealing my early prejudices against black people. She said that writing it must have required unusual courage. No, I said, because those youthful indiscretions had not been performed by the man who wrote the article: the boy who had held those attitudes died, in effect, about twenty-five years ago; I remembered him well enough, but he simply wasn't with us any more. A senior I had come to know, a mature young man of serious purpose, followed me to the kitchen bar: "Did you mean that? I mean, I can't imagine ever getting so outside myself I would become another person. How can you become that alienated from yourself?"

My young friend was bright and sincere. He had not lived long enough to understand that just as the body changes in cellular structure, just as hair falls out and teeth decay, there are storms of change in the mind, the heart, the soul, the psyche—so varied, so alternately exhilarating and debilitating, so capable of lighting a dark corner of the brain or permanently bruising some tender psychic spot that it throbs in the sleepless nights of other decades, that *not* to become someone other than we once were would constitute the true mutation of nature.

He should not (I said) be embarrassed or intimidated by his former selves. He should make them welcome—study them like slides under a microscope, the better to understand the place he had come to, the paths by which he had arrived. I tried to say that in future years—when my young friend had made inevitable journeys back into his past—old ghosts would reach out to demand accountings, to defend, to accuse.

Probably I said it badly, halting and fumbling there in that Cambridge kitchen in my Scotch haze, for the young man turned away, nodding no more than politely. Later, back in the party's circle, the host jocularly asked what I had learned at Harvard to date. I was feeling a little foolish and used up. I said, "Every snake must shed its own skin." There was a clumsy silence, the kids sneaking glances, wondering whether I had uttered a profundity or was just another old codger out drunk in the snowy night. Then a young woman said, "Groovy," and someone said, "Yeah, groovy," and then somebody else got up to advance the rock music's decibel level just in case it wasn't coming in loud and clear down in Boston at the Old North Church tower.

In his winter of discontent the would-be scholar was startled to observe how closely his behavior matched his experience at Texas Tech. As in the earlier time, his mind in the presence of most lecturing voices dreamed and wandered like a hobo. He stared sightlessly out of windows. He methodically baited his sweet wife as he had once tempted the mild farm boy who had been so unfortunate as to draw him for a roomie at Texas Tech. And, as before, he lived with an old Baptist guilt that nagged him like a fishwife for his bungled opportunities.

For all his small samplings, the grandfatherly Nieman had never been overwhelmingly enamored of academicians. He judged them a bloodless breed, saw much in them of accountants, astronauts, career civil servants; men of large pompEsities and little hammers; men who kept one foot on third base and would have shriveled if flashed instructions to steal home. He suspected that R. Milhous Nixon might have prospered at some prairie school where high marks were awarded for memorizing dates of history and the faculty enjoyed pep rallies. He saw them as narrow specialists, untroubled by runaway imaginations, too little concerned with robust fun or the good vinegars of democratic confrontations. Harsh judgments, these. Judgments from one who had listened too closely when his old father had preached so long ago of educated fools.

He had looked to Harvard to repair these misconceptions. Instead he had discovered academicians who honored his father's definitions. There was the semicelebrated Harvard law professor (a former aide to two Kennedys and a McNamara protégé) who, finishing second in the Nieman seminar debate, suddenly shouted *didn't we know who he was?* and then branded another Harvard professor—whose sin had been to criticize The Institution in disagreement with the semicelebrated law professor—as unfit to be a member of the Harvard faculty. There was the biologist who came touting a new product fatal to useless insects, and when somebody joshingly asked whether the scholarly tout owned any stock in the miracle-working formula, why, it developed after some stuttering, that he certainly did. There was an evening at the Signet Society when a number of academicians-statesmen, representing Washington service under four presidents, produced three hours of what Harry Truman called "gobbledygook" on a subject entitled "Difficulties of Interdepartmental Communication in Foreign Policy," which meant, dogged listening revealed, how best to shuffle papers from one State Department office to another so that the buck remains in a state of free passage. (Dr. John Knowles—denied appointment in the Nixon administration as head of the Public Health Service thanks to opposition from the American Medical Association's most reactionary nooks—and a fellow visitor whispered that I define several of the more precious complexities. When I confessed that I could not, we began to canvass the faculty members, taking copious notes. "I'm not certain," the first said. "I'm not exactly clear on that," a second responded. A third, thoughtfully tugging his briar pipe, cleared his throat several times before admitting he was mildly puzzled by the terminology. "Jesus," Knowles whispered, "maybe the AMA did me a favor.")

I rejoiced, it must be said, when my Harvard year ended. What I heard from Huntley-Brinkley or read in the *Boston Globe* might have been bulletins from another planet, for all the connections I felt. Nor could I identify with many events occurring in full view: when Harvard's young men remained all night by their radios, listening for their draft numbers to be announced, *that* wasn't real to one who had completed his military obligation by the time they were born. One who had made his domestic court appearances could hardly thrill as he listened, in Dr. Theodore Morrison's creative-writing class, to a series of original short stories revealing the triangular tragedies afflicting campus infatuations. One who had observed the organizational climbings of powerful senators was not entertained in observing the same techniques at the faculty level. One who knew the uncertain motives in his own modest writings was unlikely to feel rapture in hearing professors authoritatively explain exactly why Céline or Barth or Donleavy had done it this way, and then—as if reciting unimpeachable catechisms—blithely reveal the hidden meanings and deeper secretions of the authors. One who knew the natural agonies of delivering unheralded books cringed while students easily proclaimed *Catcher in the Rye* irrelevant and juvenile, or damned Bellow, Steinbeck, or Arthur Miller for their "minor themes"; he came near to striking a sophomore who confidently said of *Death of a Salesman*, "Actually, it's just a story about this old guy who was hung up on job security."

One who had for several years enjoyed the luxury of not much caring what folks thought about him, in small matters, anyway, could only enjoy the irrational angers he generated when he thoughtlessly appeared to accept his certificate of completion from President Pusey (and to pose for the official class photographs) in knockabout corduroys and a bright orange sweater. When passing undergraduates, spotting the Nieman Fellows stiffly posing on the steps of Widener Library, demanded our identifications he called out in response, "The New Canaan Chamber of Commerce Committee to Eradicate Potato Bugs," "The Green Bay Packers of 1937," and "Friends of Louise Day Hicks." No, he could not escape the campus quickly enough.

But perhaps, in ways he has not had time to comprehend, the Harvard experience may even have improved the grandfatherly Nieman. He obtained some insights into a world previously unknown to him and sampled the minds of a new generation. He read a number of books that might have eluded him had he been busy fighting deadlines, and he sat and thought a bit. For all his churlishness, he joined a few new friendships of value. He has warm memories of observing Barlow Herget, the twenty-six-year-old editor of a small daily in Paragould, Arkansas, challenging the word of former presidential advisers and locked in thumb wrestling with Norman Mailer. It was good to watch Lou Banks shed fifteen years. There were fine evenings spent happily comparing the latest absurdities with Wally Terry, a colleague from *Time,* and with special young friends from the *Crimson.* The grandfatherly Nieman came to appreciate the fact that while Harvard might not be perfect, she permits the individual to go his way without excessive restrictions or institutional demands.

I cannot imagine that in some future date I will forget the loneliness of Cambridge evenings where the soul was as dark and icy as the February outdoors, coming to speak only of good and glorious times as do Veterans of Foreign Wars convening down at the lodge once their chests have slipped, their hair has thinned, and their shrapnel scars have whitened. It may be, however—come a future November or two—that for the first time

I will show some small sneaky personal interest in whether Harvard (if one can believe it) beats Yale.

*Harper's*
OCTOBER 1970

## afterword

Three years have passed. Like many an aging geezer, I now remember it better, perhaps, than it was. Somehow the cold dark ices of February don't seem so important any more. In retrospect, troublesome personal events appear funny. Such as the night that William Styron, speaking to the Nieman Fellows at my request and after sharing with me two fifths of Scotch and numerous clouds of Mexican Boo Smoke, had what the unknowing thought a spectacular heart attack. Doctors at a Cambridge hospital, more experienced, wisely prescribed immediate bed rest; by morning, save for a remembered hallucination or two, the man of letters was never healthier. Rumors ran through the Harvard community, however, that I had poisoned Styron's drinks with LSD, or worse. People in high places considered me a bounder and a cad.

Then there was the late evening lecture delivered, in the home of John Kenneth Galbraith, on the many deficiencies of Harvard and how the institution might be improved. Only later would I learn that the young law school professor to whom I had directed the tirade was named Derek Bok; within a year he became president and, to date, has called on me for minimal additional assistance. One assumes, therefore, that one solved all his problems in the single sitting.

My wife, Rosemarie, would know her last truly ambulatory year at Harvard. Soon cancer would reduce that proud vital spirit to crutches, then wheelchairs, and, ultimately, the deathbed. It is good to have memories of her cheerfully hosting parties for Mailer and Styron; being a vivacious dinner companion at the Faculty Club; monitoring classes in drama, music, literature and economics; walking in the sunshine near the Charles River, or—stoned on high-quality grass—digging the freak show that was

Harvard Square. Though she knew her own dark nights of the soul there, she also experienced some of her last great times.

I understand why the campus was in such upheaval that year —given Cambodia, Kent State, and the other madnesses of the period—but I wish it had been more tranquil. Nieman Fellows as well as undergraduates found it difficult to concentrate on academic pursuits when the Outside World trembled, shook, and sometimes seemed about to attain its final explosion.

If I did not come away from Harvard speaking Latin or assigning a constant value to $x$, I did learn something personally comforting if institutionally disturbing: that one no longer felt it necessary to skulk through life because he had not been favored by an Ivy League education. Lyndon Johnson would have been ever so much more an effective president, I think, had he not been burdened by the provincial notion that Ivy Leaguers were born knowing half of it and learned the other half at Groton. There are other fond memories: all that idle time to read, rap, drink, and think without the pressures of deadlines. Like Ed Lehey, I'd like to do it again sober.

# WHATEVER HAPPENED TO BROTHER DAVE?

t is warm and muggy for North Carolina in late May, a very southern night, with flying bugs and scents of grass in the air. Young men cruising with their car windows down sound mating calls on their nightly inspections of root beer stands or What-a-Burger palaces, while on many city porches old men cherish their post-supper memories of farms they will never till again. We must escape Charlotte's shopping-center vapors and downtown exhaust clouds to savor it, though once in shaded residential sections or on semirural lanes, the grass fragrance is green, clean, and nostalgic, inspiring thoughts of forgotten alfalfa growths, of discovering Faulkner, of parking near the football field on summer nights a world ago to wrestle the price of the evening's movie and popcorn out of the sweetly moist flesh of Becky Sue or Alma Mae or Betty Lou.

Though oven temperatures prevail as the visitor drives ten miles out of Charlotte to the ordered and pastoral campus of little Davidson College, that school's football team is grimly grunting and maiming its sweaty way through the merciless tortures of spring practice. Along the rural roadways are young Huck Finns taking their country pleasures, "antique shops" with their $3.98 chenille bedspreads and old vases probably certified all the way

54

back to 1947, Confederate flags or decals superimposed on license plates. Old country stores thrive near new red-brick ramblers with camp trailers or motorboats near at hand, and, further on, are declining shacks where poor whites or poorer blacks take the sun on rude wooden porches in the presence of ragged kids and peeling old Buicks parked in the front yards. Near midnight, en route to Charlotte's Pecan Grove Club to catch the second show, the car radio offers gut-jangling country tunes and advertisements for Chick Starter (which is not a new aphrodisiac for hippie girls, but a product to feed infant chickens) while warm-weather fliers dash themselves into eternity and gooey gobs against the windshield. They can whoop of the New South with its rapid industrialization and economic or cultural leaps all they want, but some things cannot be paved over by asphalt or changed by factory smokestacks—things rooted deeply in the southern soil, the southern soul, the southern psyche.

Welcome home. Welcome to Klan Country, as a giant billboard says.

A couple of Good Ole Boys in butch haircuts and white short-sleeved sport shirts temporarily disadvantaged by neckties are drinking from a brown bag out on the unpaved parking lot at the Pecan Grove Club, sneaking a few manly snorts in rebellion against the mixed potions their wives force on them inside, and one is volunteering probably louder than he knows that the goddamn Tar Heel football team won't never amount to a shit till they hire a big-time coach like ole Bear Bryant. The sight of a dude in a beard and an eastern-cut suit obviously too flannelly for southern latitudes is enough to bring them pause. When their eyes begin to calculate exactly where the heavy artillery should be unloaded, the visitor consults with his Confederate ancestors and offers in his best drawl, "Evenin', fellers, how y'all?" Then he slouches on by like he was moseying down to the 7–11 to buy hisself some Moon Pies and Ara-Cee Colas. This inspirational act passes him by without fisticuffs, though when the ole boys see how his hair hangs over his collar in back one says *Shee-ee-it, Hon!* and the explosive laughter sends the visitor's heart flying out in empathy toward the ghost of Thomas Wolfe.

The Pecan Grove Club is dark enough to conceal from the curious those gentlemen who might be in the company of ladies to whom they hold no clear titles. The coatless, tieless, and paunchy combination maître d'hôtel and floor bouncer, who points the path to tables by flashlight, is clearly miffed that a naked Scotch bottle should be openly flaunted rather than decently masqueraded in the obligatory brown bag. His eyes accuse the visitor of inferior breeding, inspiring one to marvel again at that limitless capacity the South has for self-deception, for honoring show over substance, for choosing illusion when reality might better serve. This is a bottle club, meaning that for six dollars per head cover you sneak your own booze in as if freshly stolen and obliged to be smuggled past a convention of Methodist bishops. In exchange for such cooperative deceptions, which in no way violate or improve the law but do faithfully serve tradition, the house provides gratis setups. Beer is free on demand, delivered as regularly as one of several yawning waitresses may be provoked into action; nothing moves them quicker than the clear beacon of a green bill exposed to the uncertain light. Dinner is extra, an expenditure all except a dozen of the fifty-odd customers have avoided because they must later settle the claims of baby-sitters. Between musical numbers the bandleader endorses generosity by reminding customers that waitresses work strictly for tips. Out in the bar area a tough-faced little brunette complains of those SOBs at table four who expect tons of ice, Cokes, beer, and ass-pinching privileges in exchange for each four-bit gift.

Except for probably a few airline hostesses or young secretaries in miniskirts and their mildly sideburned escorts, this could be 1960 again. Women wear domed and lacquered beehive hairdos; bristling crew cuts prevail among the males. Dancing is dogged, more of duty in the couple's motions than of soul or fun. They shuffle and two-step to such vintage ballads as "Misty," "I Wish You Love," and "Poke Salad Annie," while The Frantics, who prefer to blow their music à go-go, are so obviously bored you get the impression they are all chewing gum. When The Frantics can no longer tolerate imitation Lawrence Welk or, occasionally, Johnny Cash, they up the tempo and the decibel level enough that the dance platform could not be more efficiently cleared by a black with a switchblade. And that is the signal for

Brother Dave, out in the wings, to light a fresh cigarette and to prepare to spring onstage.

The Pecan Grove Club seats 550 in enthusiastic circumstances. On evenings such as this, however, owner David Rabie doubts whether Soldier Field has more unoccupied seats in a midnight snowstorm. Rabie is a swarthy, intense man who published poetry at age sixteen and who in the 1950s was a United Nations correspondent for an Israeli publication. Somewhere in there he came to Charlotte to peddle oriental rugs, and somehow about eight years ago he found himself owning the Pecan Grove Club. Tonight he is full of passionate bulletins that anyone eager for the same foolish experience can buy him out for a song and a loose promise. He stands outside shortly before the second show, slapping at flying creatures and fingering a dead cigar, under a sign proclaiming the feature attraction: a comedian billed as Brother Dave Gardner. "I'm losing my ass," the reformed poet confides. "I'm paying this guy a thousand bucks a night. And look at the house."

Then why had he booked Brother Dave?

"I had him here about three years ago and made good money. He was doing more straight comedy then—not so much of this political nonsense. A year later he was deeper into the political thing and I just broke even. This time he's knocking everything —religion, the colored, even the dead Kennedys. It's a disaster. People are calling up to complain." The disaffected club owner turns his mind back from Tuesday to Friday and the special disaster of opening night: "You never saw such a house! I spent eighteen hundred dollars for promotion and then had to refund three thousand at the door when he didn't show. Kidnapped by Indians! Can you imagine that? He says he was kidnapped by the Cherokees!"

"Detained" is the word Miss Millie Gardner used when the visitor arrived at a Charlotte motel on Monday afternoon and telephoned the comic's three-room suite to inquire how the show had been going. Miss Millie, a weathered blonde who acts as her husband's booking agent, did not supply a standard response. "Well, we didn't make opening night on account of the Cherokees."

Beg your pardon?

"We were detained by some Indians. I've called in the FBI."

Ah . . . yes ma'am?

"They have the full report. And I've reported it to Congressman Jonas's office."

Yes. Well. How does one go about getting, ah, detained by Indians in the America of 1970?

"We'll talk about it after the show," Miss Millie said. "I'm not sure I trust the telephone."

The first time he appeared on the "Jack Paar Show," back in 1957, Brother Dave Gardner was a minor comic who for ten years had played tired strip joints and dingy bottle clubs throughout the Bible and boll-weevil belt, working close to the horns of bullish hecklers and walleyed drunks. He had sometimes entertained Rotarians in the assault on their weekly veal cutlets, or discouraged traveling salesmen who gathered in third-rate hotels rather desperately to court fun between the exhortations of their sales managers to get out and more aggressively hawk the aluminum siding, fire insurance, or farm machinery that rode the saddles atop their small pinched lives. He had played drums on something called the "Winkie Martindale Show" in Memphis, where he first began to crack jokes, and he had a straight singing record, "White Silver Sands," that, in the long run, excited him more than it did others. He was best known in the deeper boondocks. If they wore brown shoes, white socks, clip-on bow ties, or butch haircuts, then Brother Dave likely had made them laugh at one way station or another, where laughter was no small gift. He was of and from them, the son of a Tennessee carpenter who liked to think of himself as being "in the construction industry"; he knew what it was to drop school in the tenth grade, to not make it with the quality chicks because your clothes were not the best and because you were scrawny and had never been outstanding at book reports or athletics. He knew what it was to work at dull jobs where they paid you in small coin every Friday and would not have lamented your death except as your funeral hindered commerce.

He rated no seat on the celebrity couch where Paar's favored guests grouped to smile, to crack limp jokes about Ike's golf or the hole in Adlai's shoe or the pelvis of Elvis, all the while preening and plugging their latest movies, records, new noses, or fuzzy theories. Horatio Alger was still to be believed in the America of 1957, and so when they offered Brother Dave a four-minute stand-up shot (wedged between a network station break and spiels by Hugh Downs for dog food) he nearly knocked 'em down getting into position.

Brother Dave rattled off a monologue presenting Brutus in the execution of Caesar, product of a wildly inventive brain that some later would suspect of having influenced Mort Sahl, Jonathan Winters, Bill Cosby, Lenny Bruce, Dick Gregory, Flip Wilson. The studio audience, Paar, and the folks out there in television land broke up as in corn-pone accents Caesar put the final question: *Et tu, Brute?* And Brutus, who had known trouble keeping his toga out of his bicycle spokes and who had earlier heard yon Cassius described as a "picky eater and about half smart," answered, "Naw man, I ain't even et *one*." Paar received a thousand letters and telegrams begging more. NBC-TV welcomed the unknown comic to a three-year association to include sixty-odd appearances on the Paar show alone, and RCA provided a lucrative recording contract. His first album, *Rejoice, Dear Hearts!*, sold almost as frantically as hula hoops. *Kick Thine Own Self* and seven other album successes followed, each a combination of hip, headlines, and down-home wit. He appeared in a Broadway play, banked up to thirty thousand dollars per week for campus one-nighters, and made connections with Las Vegas gambling emporiums where a hot comic smart enough to avoid house tables could depend on a weekly take-home of twenty-five thousand dollars plus free lodgings. Miss Millie, a slender blonde who married him in 1947 within six weeks of his first booking in the small St. Louis club where she bossed the hatcheck concession, knew opportunity's knock; in her role as traveling manager she efficiently guided him away from the perils of roulette wheels and chorus girls, which was not always easy, because little in Brother Dave's natural instincts rides him toward the more pious precincts when he is rolling free.

His Brutus-dirks-Caesar routine became a comedy classic, as

did the bit reporting on David's slaying of "the overgrown Philadelphian," Goliath, with a smooth stone "wrapped up in a bluesuede tennis-shoe tongue." Probably his best-known tale involved the high-speed deaths of two Alabama motorcyclists, Miss Baby and Mister Chuck. In that routine he appeared to put down lawmen, Dixie customs, blacks, cyclists, truckers, and casual bystanders while showing no special malice toward any. He was Andy Griffin running downhill with the brakes off, slightly zonked, and maybe plotting a practical joke to severely embarrass nice old Aunt Bea—or maybe more than embarrass her: his routines had a way of stressing humor in death. There was about him some combination of fun and menace, one sensed, slices of the high school dropout who perhaps had read Shakespeare on his own but who still might efficiently (and not always fairly) clean your pockets at the pool hall, or deliberately direct Yankee tourists to the wrongest possible road should they be foolish enough to inquire the most direct route to Birmingham.

He increasingly became a social comic, putting the knock on JFK, on Castro, on the latest absurdity as reflected in newspaper headlines or by the careless utterances of our kings or pharaohs. If he speared Hoffa in one breath then surely in the next he would gig McClellan; if he made Democrats feel comfortable at the expense of Republicans they soon would discover ecstasy to be a two-way street. On the Paar show, after making professional liberals nervous through his near-perfect imitations of the ill-advantaged but irrepressible Roosevelt, Jabo, and Willie ("home boys," he called them), he would say in his thick winter-molasses accent that he believed in one race, the human race, and then the libs could expel their nervous do-gooder air while Paar beamed and the studio audience applauded. Yes, dear hearts, he enjoyed a merry ride, accumulating a thirty-two-room Mediterranean villa on a Hollywood hill, a luxury yacht, multiple Cadillacs, a second fine home on Biloxi's expensive sands. It was a glorious cruise, save for a little choppy water such as when he accidentally left Miss Millie behind in a West Texas motel room and didn't recall it until several days later in Louisiana, and also excepting that one major misunderstanding in 1962 when Atlanta police charged him with being in the company of an excessive number of amphetamine tablets and assorted other "uppers"—a condition inspiring Jack Paar to fresh public tears and Brother Dave Gardner to the successful investment of five thousand dollars in attorney's fees. And then, shortly after John F. Kennedy's assassination, he disappeared from the national scene.

Last winter among the snows of Cambridge, I listened again to Brother Dave's old records with a black friend, Wally Terry. We debated whether the comedian's lines sometimes bordered on racial bigotry, or whether he simply was a funny man with a rare gift for the exploitation of sensitive ethnic material, a pacesetter who so pinpointed the various insanities of our social confusions that he may have been a decade ahead of the times. Given Brother Dave's weird and conflicting pronouncements, far-out sound effects, and amazing gift for reproducing all regional accents, our repeated listenings only muddled the issue. "Whatever *happened* to Brother Dave?" Wally asked. In that instant I determined to find out.

Celebrity Services inquiries on the East and West coasts failed to locate him. He was not currently registered with any agent known to the major booking agencies. NBC and RCA disclaimed pertinent knowledge. His California home stood vacant and boarded; he had apparently left no forwarding address. Telephone operators ruined several rumors in failing to make connections in Nashville, Memphis, Biloxi, New Orleans. Then a writer friend in Charlotte, John Carr, telephoned to say that Brother Dave would be playing his city in late May.

Brother Dave appeared to "When the Saints Go Marching In," amending the original lyrics to include information that among the marching saints he expects to count Congressman L. Mendel Rivers, Spiro Agnew, Martha Mitchell, and Georgia's Lester Maddox. He was smaller than one had remembered, perhaps five and one-half feet tall, with stubby arms and a welterweight's torso. A sallow, lined face and a pompadoured crown of wiry silver hair made him look older than his forty-four years. "I'd smoke in my sleep if I had somebody to hold 'em, and I'd smoke chains if I could light 'em," he said of his nicotine habit, and taking a couple of quick drags he went to work.

"All who love America shout *Glory!* . . . Oh, dear hearts, don't you wish the other side could hear us? Wouldn't it shake up their fuzzy old heads? All this and Spiro too! *Glory!*" (*Cheers.*) "Martha Mitchell, ain't she good?" (*Cheers.*) "Beloved, the old liberal commie long-haired traitor hippies"—interrupted by applause before reaching the punch line, he joined the laughter—"Yeah, them crazy cats say Brother Dave am against minority groups. No such thing, dear hearts. I'm *for* the minorities—the armed forces and the po-leece. I wouldn't even mind paying taxes if it all went to them. Somebody say, 'You mean Brother Dave's for the heat?' You damn right, beloved. That ole pig, as the hippies call him, he's out there protecting society. And if you ain't a part of society, dear hearts, then what right you got to go around throwing rocks at it?

"And the military, I love 'em so much I send my shoes to Fort Bragg to get 'em shined. Somebody say, 'Yeah, but ain't it ugly for a soldier to kill?' Naw, man, that's his *gig.* You know, dear hearts, ain't nothing wrong with patriotism. By God, I *groove* on it. You can fly as high on patriotism as you can on acid. I'd love to join a patriotic outfit—I'd join the Klan, only I ain't got enough morals." (*Cheers, applause.*) "Let's all shout *Glory!* for the Israeli army." (*Uncertain applause: why cheer the Christ-killing Jews?*) "Yeah, man, that Israeli army fought them rag heads for six days and on the seventh day they rested. Dear hearts, the Israelis are fighting for state's rights just like we are." (*Boisterous cheers, now that the ideology is clear.*) "Them Jews is patient cats. It took 'em two thousand years to get their Wailing Wall back. Dear hearts, how long you think it'd take a Southern Baptist to get his *church* back?" Southern Baptists were apparently well represented, for the responsive roar sent Brother Dave into a further exploration of religious territory. This caused no break in his regular routine, simply because there is no set routine; he jumps from subject to subject, going where the laugh lines guide him, much in the manner of a presidential candidate whose basic speech is capable of alterations fitting all local conditions.

"I put one over on the Supreme Court today, beloved. Yeah, man, I sneaked off and prayed all morning! Prayer's *good,* beloved. Prayer is askin' for it and meditating is waitin' for it.

Somebody say, 'Brother Dave, how come you talk so much about God in nightclubs and honky-tonks?' Dear hearts, on account of it's against the law to mention Him in school! Yeah, man, spirituality is where it's at. Course, you turn the other cheek today and some damn hippie'll take a brick and knock your jaw off.

"Dr. Billy Graham—he's all right, I dig Billy. Yeah, except he disappointed me when he got on TV and tooken up for the hippies and yippies. Said they was good cats. Billy's a Christian, you know—he thinks you *supposed* to love everybody, and I'm one of them eye-for-an-eye cats. I'm for Billy, though: he's got so many guts he prays in public. He even prays at the White House when Crafty Richard posts him some of them palace guards with their cute little Hitler hats. But Billy got on TV and said"—and here Brother Dave gave an accurate imitation of Dr. Graham in the practice of dime-store Churchill—" 'I was coming out of the el-a-va-*tor* in New Ya-wuk recently, and one of those hippie fellows came along, and he *spoke* to me.' And I said, 'Hell, Billy don't you know that cheap trash will speak to anybody who'll speak to 'em?' Somebody say, 'You know good and well Dr. Graham couldn't hear him say that! Brother Dave's flipped out and is talkin' to hisself.' Yeah, beloved, ain't nothing wrong with that! Talk to yourself, dear hearts. By God, you'll enjoy the rare pleasure of listening to somebody with some damn sense."

The beehives and butch cuts were bobbing in merriment now, David Rabie's being perhaps the only grim face in the room, but then he was counting empty tables. Now Brother Dave combined spirituality and sex: "People say motels is sinful. Say, 'Motels am the devil's own doing.' Naw, dear hearts, you drive by them motels at two or three in the morning and you can hear folks digging on spirituality. Services never cease! Yeah, you can hear 'em in there saying, 'Oh, *God! Lord Jesus!* Ain't it *good.*' . . . You know, the Catholics got a terrible advantage over us Baptists and Methodists and Campbellites and whatnot: they can take a friend to the Holiday Inn and bounce her off the walls for thirty-six hours and then go confess it to a priest. *We* do it and then can't tell *nobody.* . . . I ain't got nothing against sex education in the schools, dear hearts, except it makes us parents feel like we didn't do it right. . . . Can you imagine the vanity of that civil wrongs song, 'We Shall Overcome'? Now, beloved, how can any mortal do *that?*"

The good ole boys had loosened their ties, their laughter contained more of steel on stone, drinks flowed a bit quicker from the brown bags. The bouncer, who had earlier ignored a lone heckler, moved over to encourage his silence after a flower from the bush of Southern Womanhood called out of the darkness, "Shut up, you Yankee smartass!" Her command clued Brother Dave to his next line: "Some people say I hate Yankees. Naw, beloved, I love 'em when they come down here bringing money to invest and fleeing them damned crumbling cities and welfare lines and the demands and street barbecues of our 'New Citizens.'" (*Cheers as he pursed his lips into exaggerated thickness, then hopped around scratching himself under the arms and hoo-hoo-hooing like Cheetah in some Tarzanian rage.*) "Yankees are moving south in droves! The South's integrated now, see, and they're segregated up North and they're getting spooked about it." (*Cheers and laughter: take that, you two-faced Yankee swine.*) "The only Yankees I don't like are them that stay up yonder and grow long hair and raise liberal young'uns who dodge the draft and smoke aspirins and shoot up peanut butter."

From here he made a natural leap into dope jokes—and here he lost the crowd. Charlotte's beer addicts and whisky heads sat unmoved when Brother Dave took a deep whiff of his cigarette lighter and then pantomimed euphoria. When Little Orphan Annie was nominated as the "first acidhead—you ever dig them eyes?" they made no response. "I discovered you can get high on smog, beloved. Yeah, and as soon as Washington found out you can get your head together on smog, man, they outlawed it! . . . You know, dear hearts, if them SDS cats and Weathermen and hippies and yippies and all them other crazies would smoke more and burn less, this ole world would smell sweeter and swing higher." He told a story of two hip cats in a restaurant, one saying to the other, "Let's blow this joint," and getting the response, "Naw, man, let's pass it on to the waitress." Only laughter from the band signified a familiarity with certain cultural sophistications among showfolk and hippies.

64

The act was now going sour before folks convinced that marijuana is pure ole dope and dope inspires you to cut up grand-
maw with bread knives. Brother Dave retreated to politics: "I
pulled for Barry Goldwater and he only carried five states. I
pulled for George Wallace and *he* only carried five states. I believe if God was to run He'd only carry five states—and they'd all
be in the South." (*Cheers: this they understood.*) "Beloved, I love
the South!" (*Cheers.*) "And I love America!" (*Cheers.*) "All who
love 'em shout *Glory!* . . . Ah, that's wonderful, beloved. Don't
you wish they could hear us up in Washington?" (*Cheers.*) "And
you know, by God, *lately I think they do!*" (*Cheers, applause,
Rebel yells.*) "Man, I don't know how to act since we finally got
us a president!" (*Bull's-eye.*) "You know, the ole Yankee newspapers put the ugly mouth on those good people down in Lamar,
South Carolina. Yeah, man, said they'd beat up on some New
Citizens' little schoolchildren. Naw, beloved, that ain't true! They
didn't hurt them lovely children—all they did was take some
chains and whip up on some old school buses." (*Loudest cheers
of the night, brown bags banging on tables.*) "Course, it made the
professional liberals slobber at the mouth—but we all know what
a professional liberal is: somebody that's educated beyond their
capacity. Like Bill Bullblight—err, Fulbright. Crafty Richard say
to Senator Fulbright, 'Bill, I think we ought to go in there, by
God, and bomb Hanoi and blow them damn slopeheads plumb
off the damn map,' and Fulbright say, 'Oh, us doesn't dare do
that, Richard, 'cause then us won't have nobody to negotiate
with.' . . . Do y'all remember, dear hearts, when they awarded
that Nobel Peace Prize to the late Dr. Junior on account of his
efficiency in teaching our New Citizens to riot? Man, what's that
Nobel cat doing giving a *peace* prize, after he done went and in-
vented dynamite? . . . Some say that segregation is evil and integration is correct. Now, if that be the case, why do we have ladies' rooms? But we gonna get our country back one day soon."
(*Cheers.*) "Yeah, beloved, them Green Berets and the po-leece
and the National Guard and them other good guys has had just
about enough and by God, dear hearts, they can beat you into
bad health." (*Rising cheers.*)
Then he hit them with the line that caused a sudden shocked

65

silence, a line that even many of the Good Ole Boys deepest into the mysteries of their brown bags were not braced for, and it stunned them, caused gasps, a quick dark murder of laughter. Maybe the wild grin on his face, the sheer exuberance of his delivery, were as petrifying as the line itself: *"God, wasn't that a clean hit on Dr. Junior?"*

The hard core cheered, and somebody up front shouted *Glory!* At least ten people got up and made for the exit, however. A heavy middle-aged blonde in green eyeshadow and an overflowing green pants suit descended on the visitor, who sat morosely smoking at the rear of the hall: "Are you with that idiot?" No, not really. "Well, he's gone too damned far. I love the South and I love my country, and that idiot is putting 'em down. Where's the manager?" David Rabie came with a pained look to take three minutes of perfected abuse, periodically spreading his hands in unconditional surrender. "His damn jokes are forty years old," the blonde raged. "You call this shit entertainment? Jokes about murder? I'm gonna call the *Charlotte Observer* and tell 'em what you got out here. Why did you hire that idiot?" David Rabie explained how it was to be a businessman, saying that entertainers of all creeds had played the Pecan Grove Club. He rattled off names—Brenda Lee, Maxine Brown, Roy Hamilton, LaVerne Baker, Count Basie, The Four Freshmen, Lee Dorsey—noting that "several of them are colored." When the storm blew out he turned to the visitor: "For God's sake, talk to him! Ask him to leave that offensive material out. People want to hear the old routines that made him famous, not this crap. Look at the house—count it!" The visitor did; there now remained twenty-one revelers. By the time Brother Dave ended his turn with a trap-drum recital, there were thirteen survivors.

The faithful lingered under pecan and oak trees while two black men ran to fetch their cars. A citizen in a butch haircut and a $29.95 suit straight off the rack led forward a blind man with his seeing-eye dog: "Brother Dave, this ole boy is blind and everything, but he don't beg or peddle pencils or nothin'. He's got this little newsstand down at the YMCA, and, by God, he *works.*"

"Bless your heart, beloved."

"He don't set on his ass and howl for help just because he's blind," the citizen clarified.

"God bless you," Brother Dave cooed, shaking the blind man's hand. "You know, they got a rule up in Washington that if you break a sweat they'll take you off welfare."

The blind man beamed; his sponsor whooped.

"Course, a cat that sweats don't want it nohow. Don't y'all give up, you hear? We gonna get our country back someday."

He ducked into a gold Cadillac driven by his sixteen-year-old son Junior, and within ten minutes was back in the motel room where Miss Millie waited with a barking French poodle named Mister. Mister may wear a rhinestone collar and sport sissy little ribbons atop his iron-gray head, but let a stranger approach Miss Millie even to light her cigarette and Mister has conniptions in the voice of a surly Doberman pinscher.

Miss Millie, who took her meals off trays in the room, and whom the visitor never discovered outside a gauzy green dressing gown during his six-day observation, was reading one of her seven books by H. L. Hunt. "How was the show?" Miss Millie asked.

"Nothing wrong with the show," Brother Dave said. "The goddamn house is the problem. You could of fired a .410 and not hit anybody at the second show."

"Damn those Cherokees," Miss Millie said.

Yes, *how about* those Cherokees? What had happened? It was the fifth or sixth time the visitor had put that question, receiving only vague and disjointed reports.

"We're driving along Highway 19, coming down from Tennessee," Brother Dave said. "Hell, I didn't know we was on a damned Indian reservation. Me and Miss Millie was in the lead Caddy and our son was trailing in the other one. The Cherokee patrol stopped him, man. Wouldn't let the cat go."

Why?

"They wouldn't say. But you can figure it out." When the puzzled visitor remained mute, Brother Dave added, "They're part of this third-world thing."

Beg pardon?

"Aw, man, don't you know what's happening? Who attacked a meeting of the Klan here in North Carolina two or three years ago, when the Klan cats wasn't doing nothing but burning crosses and singing hymns?"

The Cherokees?

"Damn right, beloved. They're part of this thing!"

"Dave," Miss Millie said, "the FBI asked us not to talk about this."

"Aw, he's all right," Brother Dave said with a nod in the visitor's direction. "Don't you hear that accent? He's from Texas, just like ole H. L. Hunt. Beloved, do you know Mr. Hunt?"

Only by reputation.

"Then you don't know him at all!" This from Miss Millie, suddenly and with surprising heat, her voice crackling and smoldering like a summer storm. "The left-wing press has smeared him all his life. They even tried to link him with JFK's assassination, and we all know that was ordered by Moscow."

"I got interested in Mr. Hunt's patriotic work about six years ago," Brother Dave said. "So I checked him out and he checked me out, and we got our heads together. We've become real good friends. Miss Millie and me have been his guest in that big ole house he lives in—the one patterned after George Washington's. That's the nicest, kindest, gentlest, smartest ole boy in the world. He ought to have the Congressional Medal of Honor. If America is saved, beloved, he's the one who's saved it nearly single-handed. Here, let me show you what Ruth gave us. That's Mrs. Hunt." He produced what appeared to be a catalog advertising furniture, which Mrs. Hunt had mysteriously autographed along with sentiments speaking well of friendship and patriotism. Which seems like a minimal gift from the wife of the world's richest man or thereabouts.

Does H. L. Hunt in any way subsidize Brother Dave's work?

"Naw, man. I ain't asked him for nothing. In the first place, I don't need to: I've got bread and investments so I don't have to work, except I want to get my message across. All Mr. Hunt's got that I want is his wisdom. He's my teacher."

"You should read *Alpaca*," Miss Millie said. "It's the best novel I've ever read. There's this model constitution in there that H. L.

Hunt wrote." (The "model constitution" recommends that each citizen be given a number of votes in direct ratio to his net financial worth and would preclude anyone drawing a government salary, pension, or welfare check from voting; citizens would be permitted to sell their votes to others with greater interests in good government.)

Back to the Cherokee caper: what reason had they given for detaining Junior?

"They just said he was on Indian land. When we swung around to see what the score was, they told us it was none of our damn business and to clear out. We begged, pleaded, flashed our identification—all they said was, 'Get moving.' Then they threatened us with guns."

"Dave!"

"All right, Miss Millie. They held us up about an hour or more. But it took four or five hours to get our son out of that damn mess, and that caused us to miss opening night."

And how had they ultimately freed junior?

"Dave, now, we just can't talk about this," Miss Millie instructed in schoolmarm tones.

"Them cats *had* to know who I was, dear hearts. It wasn't no accident. By God, you wait until that Bureau of Indian Affairs gets through with 'em!"

"Dave!"

The comedian invited the visitor into an adjoining room, where he offered a recording by comic David Frye. "This cat cracks me up. Only thing is, he propagandizes for the leftists. But you got to hear this one track, man." David Frye imitated Richard Nixon taking a few experimental marijuana pokes and then trying to talk hip, the humor grounded in "Nixon's" continuing to sound (even when stoned beyond the capabilities of Mount Rushmore) like the eight year old who received a black leather briefcase for Christmas and who, furthermore, was delighted with the gift. "Can't you imagine ole Crafty Richard turned on?" Brother Dave cackled.

Junior entered from the main room. "Dad, quick! J. Robert Jones is out here."

"Oh, my God!" Brother Dave pinched out a little something he and the visitor had been smoking, frantically fanning the air. "Look, beloved, would you mind waiting in here with the boy? I've got some personal business with this cat."

Junior is lanky and wiry, six feet two, with a mop of long blond hair which his mother despises and which his father disapproves of but defends on the grounds that his son would be disadvantaged in the romance department should he look exceedingly square in a hip age. In military schools for six years before withdrawing a few months ago, he is convinced that neither Harvard nor Yale teaches as much as he'll learn on the road with dad. After he had exhibited various karate chops, Junior demonstrated with flourishes the most effective methods for quickly extracting a switchblade. He was performing his third or fourth guitar solo, between lectures explaining the basic uses of girls, when Brother Dave reappeared from the main quarters: "Come on in, beloved, and meet a friend."

A small, dark-haired man wearing a sly country grin sat in an easy chair, not bothering to rise for handshakes. "This is J. Robert Jones," Brother Dave said. The visitor's mental equipment whirred and clicked: *J. Robert Jones . . . North Carolinian . . . Grand Dragon and Holy Terror of the United Klans of America . . . convicted of contempt of Congress . . . recently released from federal prison.*

Mister, the bejeweled toy watchdog, was growling and snapping another irritating concert at the visitor's heels. "Come on dog," the visitor said. "You should be adjusted to me by now."

"Maybe he don't like hippies." Though the Holy Terror smiled, his eyes seemed to calculate how much bearded beef might dress out by the pound.

"Well, I'd hoped my accent might help."

"Yeah, Bob," Brother Dave said. "He's from Texas."

"Everybody got to be from *some*where," the Holy Terror said. "Ole Lyndon's from Texas, but he never amounted to much."

"Look, beloved," Brother Dave said, laughing nervously. "Would you mind seeing me tomorrow?"

Junior escorted the visitor to his room, only a small lawn and a swimming pool away from the Gardner quarters. "You know who that was you just met?"

"No," the visitor lied.

Junior produced the Grand Dragon and Holy Terror's calling card, which was as neatly and professionally done as that of any Wall Street broker. He produced another, this one from a Klan branch located in Natchez, and bearing the red-letter legend: You are WHITE because your grandfather believed in SEGREGA-TION. These documents reduced Junior to helpless laughter: "Man, don't that blow your mind?"

"Have you dug those cars?" The visitor looked in the indicated direction to observe two cars parked near the Gardner quarters. He noted the silhouettes of several men. "You know who they are?" Junior asked.

The visitor guessed they might be associates of the Holy Terror.

"Yeah, man! I bet they got enough guns to waste half of North Carolina."

This was not comforting as a bedtime thought. The visitor peered through the muggy night, lamenting that he had never learned to identify automobiles beyond their color, being unable to distinguish a Ford from a Lincoln unless he discovers clues written in manufacturer's chrome.

"They'll be there when the sun comes up, man," Junior chortled. "The Klan watches after Dad everywhere he goes. And they can see *your* room as well as my old man's." Much cheered by the thought, and stabbing the air with a switchblade, he turned back to the family quarters, where sleep is always taken in shifts as added protection against midnight conspiracies.

Three or four days and nights had carelessly mingled since the visitor had been introduced to the Holy Terror. The same jokes at the club, the same laughter, had burned the mind like acid. The house had been building nightly, in size and frenzy. The first night following the apperance of the Holy Terror, Rabie counted more than three hundred; Junior had slyly intimated that the gate's quantum jump had not been merely coincidental with that visit.

Since Brother Dave performs his guard watch by night and sleeps by day, many nocturnal sessions had revealed a plethora of conspiracies. He strolled about in an old dressing gown, incessantly smoking, periodically peeking through the parted drapes to determine, one assumed, whether any amphibious assaults might be headed our way from the pool.

"Beloved," he said during one such seance, "do you know why Congress inserted 'under God' in the Pledge of Allegiance at near about the same time the Supreme Court ruled there couldn't be no prayer in the schools?"

By now the visitor did not know whether it was a plot of the Federal Reserve Board, International Jewry, charity rackets, Julian Bond, or the television networks, all of which had received their due licks. So he just said no.

"Man, to *confuse* us. To *divide* us. That's the way this thing works, see." And he would be off down the steepest ideological slopes, waving his arms and wildly scattering cigarette ashes, delivering private monologues of which the following is a typical composite: "I've always been conservative and believe in segregation for them that wants it, dear heart, and nothing not being forced on nobody. But for years, man, I trusted my government —even believed what I read in the newspapers. Then I got to thinking, 'Dammit, something's bad *wrong!*' We had the biggest bomb in the world and couldn't win no wars. And we lost China and three-fourths of Europe and Cuber and all them damn Mau Mau nations, man, and then some good Americans uncovered Alger Hiss and Harry Dexter White and them other spying Communist cats and I started seeing a pattern in it. Man, the problem *had to come from within!* And the more I looked into the thing, I decided that was only part of it: *within* was doing the mischief, but *without* was calling the signals, you dig? Like, you think the people elected Roosevelt, don't you? Naw, man, that's what the big money combines conditioned you to think. Hell, man, the *Rothschilds* put FDR in. The House of Morgan. And they started us toward one-world government. And now, beloved, we can't even control our kids. We can't even be white without having to make excuses for it, and I'm sick and tired of making excuses for being white. Old Nixon, hell he's better than what we've had, but don't you know that cat ain't his own man? *Nelson Rockefeller* put him in office. Yeah, man, set him up in a big rich New York law firm and moved him in that same fancy building ole Rocky lives in, and then went out and spent six million dollars pretending like he was running against him!"

Here Brother Dave collapsed into helpless laughter at how clever the Rockefellers, Rothschilds, Stalins, and possibly the Denver Mint had been in their conspiratorial deceptions, a thing he frequently does when revealing the larger menaces, as if to say, *Hoo, boy, didn't they put one over on humanity that time?*

"I mean, man, you can even see it in *little* things." (*Laughs.*) "Like why do our post office buildings just say 'U.S.,' dear heart, without adding 'of America'?" (*Laughs.*) "How come, beloved, the Supreme Court and the hairy kids and the damned spades all started acting up *at once?*" (*Laughs.*) "And how come JFK and Dr. Junior rode in open convertibles or stood out on balconies where folks could get clean shots at 'em?" (*Laughs.*) "Man, don't you know them cats was following orders to be *sacrificed?*" (*Laughs.*)

Then he would sober himself as quickly as he had laughed, marching about and saying a military coup d'etat might soon be the only method left for preserving America's precious freedoms, defending the Ohio National Guard in its conduct at Kent State, enthusiastically endorsing New York hardhats in their Wall Street attacks on beards, declaring himself to be the only strict constructionist in show business and assigning even John Wayne and Bob Hope to the liberal camp. He offered a grim warning represented as being in the visitor's best interests: "Look, man, I know they wear that damn long hair and face fuzz up there in New York. But you gotta realize, beloved, the revolution is *on.* It's *here.* People are going by appearances now, dear heart, 'cause everybody's choosed up sides. I worry about my own son getting hit by a sniper because of that damn long hair. It's dangerous to walk around looking hairy, man. You could get zapped."

To Klansmen visiting the camp had been added Green Berets and their wives down from Fort Bragg, and a local lady with skinny legs and a zealot's gleam who spoke frequently of the occult, of haunted houses, of reincarnation, of séances, of a devout belief in the prophesies of Jeane Dixon and in the profits of racial

73

segregation. There had been a young sailor with a Confederate flag stitched inside the lining of his jumper so that when he unbuttoned his sleeve and rolled it back the flag winked and blinked in all its lost glory, and the sailor in outraged young innocence had proclaimed after one midnight show that those Communists *in the Pentagon*, now, must soon be stopped. There had been private screenings of a film produced at a small college in Searcy, Arkansas (represented as having been shipped in by H. L. Hunt for Brother Dave's continuing education), which told of a conspiracy linking the Black Panthers, Ho Chi Minh, student rebels, and large segments of Congress.

One night at the Pecan Grove Club the visitor noted with shock the arrival of a party of black people. Within three minutes of Brother Dave's opening blasts he was not surprised to hear loud and disgruntled comments from their direction. Whites at neighboring tables glared and shushed. Just as the dispute approached cussing terrain David Rabie appeared, agitated about one silly millimeter short of pure panic, to say how delighted he would be to refund money. The visitor sighed in concert with the club owner when the blacks accepted. (Rabie later said, "I told them at the door, 'I don't think this is your type of show,' but they didn't get the message.")

There had been one wild adrenaline moment when two Good Old Boys in discouragingly robust health had paused at the visitor's table to sneer as Brother Dave accomplished cadenzas of abuse against long-haired traitors abroad in the land: "*Here's* one of them bastards." The visitor negotiated the best possible grip on his Scotch bottle, felt himself tense to deliver a desperate overhand smash should that necessity descend, felt some reckless ancient joy of combat surging up that he had long presumed civilized out of him, and then, fortunately for his skin and for his long years of refurbishing, a waitress came running with the bulletin, *No, no, he's with Brother Dave, y'all leave him alone, now, you hear?* The ole boys laughed sheepishly and stuck out their rough workmen's hands, telling the visitor they hadn't meant nothing by it, that they was real sorry, and one had begged a private introduction after the show in behalf of his father-in-law visiting from Pine Bluff.

74

There had been moments, too, with Klansmen in close proximity to the visitor's bed, with intrigue heavy on the night air, when paranoia had proved contagious. The visitor debated whether to telephone friends in the East to give some clue to his associates, in the event he should be discovered in some southern creek bed wrapped in more chains than he might conveniently swim in. After rejecting the notion as melodramatic, he had surrendered to it in a midmorning relapse. Later he had informed Brother Dave of his precautions, adding (to the tune of much merriment from among Green Berets and assorted other camp followers) that should anyone offer him a guided tour of the city it would take all hands plus the goddamn dog to load him in the car.

As the weekend of the Charlotte 600 Stock Car Races approached, Good Ole Boys and their ladies flocked in from all over Dixie. Less fun and more pure damn mischief entered Brother Dave's act: "Albert Gore is a whore." James Baldwin made the show as a "low-life, bug-eyed, queer nigger." Senator Fulbright slipped from being Bullblight to a "sissy-britches traitor." The louder the cheers the more he spewed venom, and the more venom the louder the cheers.

The cheers told the visitor something it sickened him to hear, reaffirmed something dark and crazy and ancient he had hoped, and had half believed, might be drying up in southern blood. *They didn't hurt them lovely children—all they did was take some chains and whip up on some old school buses.* Yes, the mood was as openly belligerent as before Selma Bridge, before Bull Connor's police dogs and fire hoses, before the murder of Martin Luther King. It had become unfashionable, after all that highly publicized violence had pushed Congress into a mildly militant civil rights mood, to flaunt one's prejudices. Meddling Justice Department agents, scolding from newspapers and presidents and chamber of commerce finks motivated by the almighty dollar, had caused one to defend the Southern Way of Life only in fairly gentlemanly terms. But a new mood had come to Washington, a thing called Southern Strategy had arrived there, along with a president who received hardhats in his office on the heels

75

of their public assaults and a vice-president whose words could be as inflammatory as any George Wallace ever uttered. Even the best people could now telephone newspaper editors to demand the crucifixion of a United States senator without losing face. *Martha Mitchell, ain't she good?* Busing of students slowed down; the Justice Department for the first time in sixteen years *opposed* integration of certain southern school districts; and when four Kent State students lay dead, our president said through a spokesman that, well, play with fire and you'll get burned. *God, wasn't that a clean hit on Dr. Junior?* Not only gas jockeys, traveling salesmen, and Klansmen were among the cheering faithful; it was no trouble to discover lawyers, schoolteachers, merchants, and physicians in the overflowing house.

So there are few surprises left in the visitor as we rejoin him yawning on the edge of his bed before dawn. The telephone rings. "Come on over, beloved. I got a little surprise for you."

*Surprise!* There is a black man in the room, a muscular cat with a T-shirt showing his chest to good advantage, the sleeves ripped out the better to exhibit his biceps. This dude has some hustle in him, a little jive, for earlier he has sidled up to the visitor to announce that if a man want something to love or smoke that he cannot immediately get from room service, why, then, he know where it might be got. The black man is sitting near a large color photo stuck in the edge of a mirror, and in the photo— *Surprise!*—am de Grandest Dragon and Holiest Terror ob de Newnited Klans of America, and his wife, the happy couple in colorful silk robes with tassels and decals and braids until Kingfish himself could not have conceived more ostentatious costumes for the boys down at the Mystic Knights of the Sea Lodge.

Brother Dave guides the visitor to a chair, leans over, and delivers his biggest surprise in a near whisper: "Hey, man, I been putting you on. I don't really know H. L. Hunt! What's that cat ever done for anybody? You ever hear of that rich ole thing giving a dime to charity? Naw! You know a little something else, dear heart? Brother Dave am not what you think he am. Beloved, he am a secret *liberal*. Beloved, he am believe most faithfully in the Democratic party. He am a counterspy."

Yeah, the visitor says, he am personally believe strongly in tooth fairies.

"Naw, man, I'm telling you like it is! This whole thing is an act. It's a big put-on." Brother Dave leans against a table and laughs until one thinks he might choke, enjoying what is apparently the biggest political joke since the Reichstag fire.

Junior enters from stage left, as opposed to stage right where Miss Millie is presumably in blissful slumber. He jerks his thumb toward the room he has vacated.

"You think about it, beloved," Brother Dave instructs. "I'll be back in a little bit."

During Brother Dave's absence, Junior flashes his Klan cards for the edification of the black man: "Don't that blow your mind?" "Naw, man," the black cat says. "I done lived down here too long." The visitor dozes on the couch, only dimly aware that Junior is teaching the black man karate, that Mister is admitted to the room after scratching on a door, that the television switches from a test pattern to the early news and market reports. He is slumbering soundly when Brother Dave wakes him by wafting hot coffee under his nose. They are alone.

"You thought about what I told you, beloved?"

"It won't wash," the visitor said. "That story contradicts your entire history. I suspect you've checked me out with H. L. Hunt. If I believed in security as much as you do, I would have checked me out the minute I walked in the door."

"Why didn't you tell us you had read *Alpaca?*" Brother Dave asks in injured tones. "Not only that, beloved, but had knocked it in some damn book review."

"Dear heart, nobody asked me." There is an exchange of humorless smiles.

What had the Dallas report revealed about the visitor?

"Well, he's got all you cats computerized. I told him your name and within three minutes he gave me your middle initial— it's *L*, dear heart—and he said that you're an enemy of the people."

An enemy of the people? *Glory!*

"You didn't fool Miss Millie for a damn minute," he said.

"Or Mister." Again the humorless smiles.

"I wish you could meet H. L. Hunt, beloved. I think he might straighten you out. I mean, I don't want to talk *down* to you, man. But the trouble is that people like you are being exploited through your political ignorance."

Who is my exploiter?

"Beloved, you know that as well as I do. Oh well, as long as two cats can smoke aspirins together, man, I feel like there's always hope. Let's don't talk no more politics, 'cause we might have a fistfight or Miss Millie might sic the dog on you." (*Laughs.*)

Why had he so abruptly disappeared from the national scene? Had a boycott been enforced against his political views?

"Naw, man. I could be on national TV if I wanted to push it. But after that funny plane crash in 1966, I decided against it."

Funny plane crash?

"Yeah, I'd charted one of them executive jobs out of Biloxi for my whole family. About ten minutes before we was to take off, they said something was wrong with it and shifted us to another one. Dear heart, it didn't fly twelve miles till it fell. *Blap!* Killed the pilot, buggered up the copilot, and broke hell out of all the rest of us—Miss Millie, she still hasn't recovered. I got the message. Somebody up there don't like me. Maybe I know too much."

Such as?

The big stage grin: "I am know multitudes and reveals but small particles. I am know long division and secrets of Hinduism. . . . Beloved, let me fix you another of them nasty ole Scotches and maybe we'll soon have one less fuzzy liberal with a functioning liver. And from here on, dear heart, let us speak nothing but trash and joy."

There was inconsequential chatter, Brother Dave startling his guest by saying how he digs black comedian Dick Gregory ("Dick didn't know what he was getting into when he went on that freedom ride in Mississippi, man, 'cause he's from Chicago") and Garry Moore—a Jew—who had been extremely nice to him when he first broke into television and Paul Newman ("who's politically ignorant but has the guts to act for his beliefs'").

As the visitor prepared to leave, Brother Dave produced a document for his inspection. From a mobile-home outfit in Alabama, and sent to transmit certain brochures, it appeared to be a routine business letter with its half-formal, half-friendly pitch; one had seen its cousins mailed out by the thousands from congressmen to their voters, from magazines soliciting subscriptions, from countless outfits with wares to hawk. As he puzzled over its significance, Brother Dave's finger pinpointed the closing sentence: *We highly value your interest in Such-and-So Homes.*

"That means a lot to me, beloved," he said. "That shows you what they think of me in the South. They love me down here."

There was a mob scene in the Gardner quarters on the visitor's last night before he would catch a plane to the decadent East, Brother Dave in a euphoric state because an overflow house had cheered his wildest salvos. Junior ran in and out with a series of young belles, Green Berets in high spirits popped beer cans, photographers took Brother Dave's picture, and Mister almost collapsed with so many strangers to intimidate. One was reminded of getaway day when the visiting ball club has concluded a successful road tour, has swept its last series, and now looks forward to a long stand at home.

Not all was happiness or joy, alas. David Rabie and the comedian quarreled over their failure to reach a satisfactory financial adjustment owing to Brother Dave's missed opening night, this leading to more dithyrambs against the Cherokees. Then a beribboned Green Beret sergeant, skinheaded and badly wounded in Vietnam and really quite a sincere ole boy, cursed the New Army's coddling of recruits so that discipline had gone to hell and you couldn't hardly find recruits with enthusiasm for killing any more. And, finally, it had been confided that Miss Millie had taken to her bed with a headache rather than be in the visitor's presence once her suspicions of his character had been verified.

Standing by the swimming pool in the warm North Carolina air, Brother Dave touched the visitor's arm. "Look, man, if you ever get your head about half straightened out and decide you want to know where it's really at, politically, get in touch. I'll be your teacher. There's not much time left, beloved, to save America."

He turned away, himself only a few hours from the road and a dozen one-nighters in Georgia, providing Miss Millie did not carry through her threat to cancel them because of race wars in Augusta. At the door he pursed his lips thickly, gave the clenched fist of the black power salute, and shouted, "Power to the people." Laughing, dear hearts. Laughing.

*Harper's*
SEPTEMBER 1970

## afterword

That one was spooky. Full of chill distant winds. One felt an actor in some Theater of the Absurd, part of an improbable cast out of a novel by Flannery O'Connor with her trembling zealots, foolish prophets, and grotesque doomed innocent children of unavoidable dread. The nation's deeper cleavings and suspicions, born of the tumultuous 1960s, became sharply personal. Coming directly from a year in Harvard Yard into the low-rent scene of seedy clubs, plastic motels, and irrational angers not only intensified the cultural shock but served to heighten the sense of deep national divisions.

Originally, of course, I had come (as had Brother Dave) from hard-scratch working-class people in the rural South. And while I no longer believed with Brother Dave and his disciples, I understood something of how and why they felt as they did. It was like stepping back in time. Going home again, to be greeted by angry old ghosts. Brother Dave and I had, each in his own way, broken outside the routine vocations and expectations of our original places; we had sampled the wicked cities of the mystic East, new wines, exotic herbs and spices not native to our bogs. So much of the same clay we were, and yet we stood shouting our conflicting absolutes across acres of an ideological no-man's-land. All we seemed to share were our certain fears. It became apparent during that strange zonked paranoid week that its hairy experiences might be more general, more kin to our national hates, suspicions, divisions, and knee-jerk madnesses than not. Perhaps Brother Dave said it all, in warning against the dangers of my beard and hair: *People are going by appearances, now, dear heart, 'cause everybody's choosed up sides.* Thus the gathering of data for the Brother Dave piece and its writing was simply no fun despite my satisfaction with its craftsmanship.

Well, before we become so ponderous and philosophical that old bar room friends commence to hoot and snicker, let's talk about how a journalist works. Originally I had a series of questions to pop, questions to quickly ferret out how Brother Dave felt in his innards about race and war and taxes. Miss Millie's unconventional response to my mild inquiry about how opening night had gone (*Well, we didn't make opening night on account of the Cherokees*) alerted me to the possibility of simply following my nose. I instinctively decided to observe and record rather than push Brother Dave with impeding questions: he would be permitted to reveal himself at his own pace. This meant six days and nights of near round-the-clock observations (I'll never know how he survives on catnaps) and seeing his show a dozen times. With the possible exception of the late Louie Armstrong, Brother Dave obliged by revealing himself more fully than any other of my pen's subjects. In fact, often feeling a strange, warped kinship for him, I acted as a voluntary censor by leaving out a couple of incidents that surely would have put him deep in Miss Millie's doghouse.

Just why people should permit journalists to rummage the private luggage of their lives is difficult to understand. In Brother Dave's case he frankly coveted the national publicity. Despite Miss Millie's early suspicions of my purpose, he said, safely out of her hearing, "Write anything you want, dear heart. Just so I get that national exposure." Showfolk, politicians and other flimflam men feel dependent upon public exposure, of course, and so they welcome us to come in and disappoint them with our observations, judgments, and interpretations. They simply never learn that a writer's business causes him to plumb seemingly insignificant acts or events or utterances, to see—or *think* he sees—more than meets the eye. More accurately, they never seem to remember, until it is too late, that men rarely see themselves as others see them. Most journalists will tell you that it is routine for their subjects to cry foul, gnash their teeth, or speak of betrayals once they've inspected our handiwork. Peggy Lee's postpublication reaction to what I thought a sympathetic piece in *Cosmopolitan* (passed through her public-relations man, causing me to understand not to expect any more of her random breathy sweet midnight telephone calls) was, "Tell him he's a great writer . . . and a poor reporter." Nelson Rockefeller, on reading in *Harper's* a piece I now consider "soft" and kind in the extreme, wailed to a staffer, "But the fella seemed so *friendly,* so decent!" Lyndon B. Johnson is said to have branded my Capitol Hill recollections of him a "dirty story," though some of his intimates judged my word portrait funny and accurate. Other dissatisfied customers have questioned my ancestry, told it that I had taken up with stray blondes or that I wore a beard to conceal a weak chin. So when Brother Dave (whose agent had written *Harper's* in quick protest of my interpretations) several times tried to telephone me, I did not respond. No profit in it for either side, ours being a natural adversary circumstance where never the twain shall square dance.

So why are we professional busybodies permitted our alleged poison-pen practices? Well, let me relate a few of my own experiences—at the other end of the pen. On book-promotion tours or speaking tours, others have come to interview me. I allowed it because (1) I was hustling a product and (2) I considered myself so lovable and flawless that no man or woman might find evil, duplicity, or ambiguity in my sterling character. Such a perfect specimen obviously could not suffer harm at the hands of the clumsiest or the vilest of pens, right? Well . . . not exactly.

No, for the bright young student writer from the campus paper at SMU remembers me in the Dallas airport as lumbering, barrel chested, thick waisted, half drunk, loudly profane, a pitchman of wares. I distinctly recall being svelte, lithe, friendly, informal, and modestly willing to admit to small touches of genius—though openly and democratically thirsting for one more Scotch. A Los Angeles *Women's Wear Daily* correspondent lamented I hadn't been "full of that wit and verve" she somehow expected, telling everybody how I was fatigued and dispirited and grumpy and stared moodily into many glasses of strong vapors. My own recollection is of mightily wanting to cuddle that young cushy correspondent—Oh, Foul Male Chauvinist Pig!—and, consequently, of smiling crookedly like Clark Gable while being so generally dashing that mere "wit and verve" wouldn't have come close to touching my best assets. And a lady in Houston, after I'd talked for two hours about Great Literature and Art and Philosophy and other Serious Matters, remembered the one or two times when I put my elbow in the butter dish or spilled an occasional drink or said ain't got no. The headline on that little prize was: "A Hick from West Texas." I mailed her a filthy postcard transmitting many New York obscenities.

Some six months before this writing, a nice young lady at Columbia University flattered me by tales of how I write so great she was composing a lengthy academic paper about me. Of course, I immediately consented to be interviewed. I thought the job would take two hours, a really terrific estimate for one who spends up to thirty days on his own small journalistic woolgatherings. The first time she came my Boswell stayed a week. She has been back innumerable times. I cannot cough or scratch without it going down on her cursed tape recorder. She has interviewed my oldest friends, my relatives, and my ancient enemies and has come back to ask why I have so many fistfights or drink so much or tell so many lies. She reminds me that as a child I preached passionate hellfire sermons over dead mice and dead baby chickens in a cemetery of my own creation, that I may have stepped on several necks on the way up life's ladder with hardly a pause to extend apologies, that my oldest friend judges me "capable of murder," and that in my youth I suffered the shame of dropping out of Famous Writers School. And, always, she wants to know why. *Why?* Not knowing, I am disadvantaged and cannot say. If the lady completes her masterwork within my lifetime, I shall never again consent to be interviewed. This course I recommend to all good Americans. Once I am rich and famous, once I don't need them—them with their diggings and pryings and interpretations and shatterings of long-cherished illusions—I shall tell all who seek interviews to go butt a stump, suck a lemon, store their pens someplace warm and moist.

Well, anyway, most of them. Depends, I guess, on their circulation figures.

# IT'S ONLY A GAME

'm a damned hypocrite when it comes to football.

Yes, I take judicial notice of its well-recorded evils: routine pains and brutalities, greedy or ambitious owners and coaches who advance or profit from those sweats and terrors extracted from the regimented young. Neither am I certain it is healthy for soft or frustrated Americans to assemble themselves to cheer a game that, like war, claims its certain victims and casualties. Some of my most intelligent friends turn into raving maniacs in football stadiums or at TV side, cursing for their mistakes or inefficiency the men who could make mincemeat of them and passing far harsher judgment on athletes than they do on their politicians, lawyers, or physicians. And each time I have observed football at its locker-room level (whether among schoolboys, collegians, or burly professionals) the game's dark side shows itself. Knowing it will happen, I never fail to be shocked, surprised, and resentful; conversely, I rarely turn down a football-story opportunity. Perhaps my obsession for the game traces to my boyhood in Texas. There a poor boy, seeking a spot in the social hierarchy, lusting for acceptance among his peers, knew his greatest opportunities. Even if stardom was out of the question, there were honors and recognitions for becoming a starter, a letterman, or even a member of the traveling squad. Those were the days of the ancient single wind and the old seven-diamond defense, when the game was ever so much more primitive. Today's athletes are bigger, quicker, stronger, smarter; I am sure they are vastly superior, from schoolboy units up through the pros, to my contemporaries. We suffered the same sweats, fears, and humiliations, however; I find it impossible not to identify with both the horrors and the glories of today's game.

# The Beasts of Baltimore

IT IS TUESDAY, and the pressures have not yet started to build in the six-foot seven-inch frame of Charles Aaron (Bubba) Smith, as they may a bit closer to Sunday's kick-off. "May" is the operable word, for Bubba sometimes has trouble psyching himself—"getting up"—to accomplish his job effectively.

Bubba Smith is the defensive left end for the Baltimore Colts, defending champions of professional football. His job requires that he survive the assaults of at least two blockers, sometimes three, to achieve his goal of sacking quarterbacks or riding swift and treacherous ball carriers aground before they damage his team's territorial rights. To accomplish this requires a certain insensitivity to pain and fatigue, or maybe mud or rain or snow, to say nothing of the grunts, groans, verbal brutalities, and the thousand desperate little cheatings indigenous to survival in the pit. When Bubba Smith—268 pounds of mobile muscle buckled and padded and bent on mischief—goes snorting and chugging across that scrimmage line, he may be gouged, kicked, pinched, held, cuffed, helmet-whipped, kneed, elbowed, and—yes (though neither the commissioner's office nor those goody-goody play-

86

by-play TV experts will tell it)—cursed for everything from a plain vanilla bastard to a dumb spade to a particular kind of pervert. Pro football is a mean game ideally played by mean men. If it builds character, so does street mugging.

Sometimes Bubba Smith is very, very good at his job; other days he is simply good; on a few occasions he has permitted himself to flirt with mediocrity. No matter how well Bubba performs on a given Sunday, several dozen someones—writers, coaches, fans, or even a teammate or two—will say he might have done better: he could be as great as he wants to be; he has no more than scratched his mighty potential; he has a tendency to dog it; goddammit, ole Bubba just ain't *mean* enough.

Bubba is very tired of hearing all that. A hyperactive publicity man at Michigan State, where Bubba was All-America in 1966, taught the cheering sections to chant "Kill, Bubba, kill." In this age of runaway imagery, poor Bubba was stuck with a reputation for meanness he neither made nor fit. A story got into print that as a college all-star, Bubba, on the game's first play, sacked quarterback Bart Starr of the Green Bay Packers and growled, "Old man, Big Bubba's gonna ride your ass all night." Good story, except that nothing remotely like it happened. "Everybody expected me to eat nails," Bubba says. Instead, he was injured early in that initial pro season, lost forty pounds, sat on the bench behind tough and experienced ole Billy Ray Smith, and became so confused that he several times forgot to take the field with the kicking team as required. It took the persuasions of his father, a successful football coach in Texas, to prevent his quitting the game. He was, if one may quote the current president of the United States on another matter, a "pitiful giant" in that first go, and only his father's appeal to pride—of which Bubba Smith has tons and tons—saw him through. Though Bubba has known numerous fine Sundays since that impossible beginning five seasons ago, he remains keenly aware that his critics persevere. And so, from about Thursday on, he attempts to psych himself for Sunday's rough business: to will himself mean.

Now, however, it is only Tuesday afternoon. Bubba remains loose and affable. He is stretched out full length in his bachelor pad in a Baltimore high-rise, on a purple-robed bed large enough to accommodate Bubba and/or others. Over the bed is a ceiling mirror, cut to exact bed proportions, where Bubba and/or others may watch themselves sleep. A furry white rug snuggles the floor; there are African art objects, velvet drapes, football trophies, and a huge combination TV-radio-stereo console plastered with blue-and-white Baltimore Colt stickers.

Bubba is drinking a Big Orange while watching a band of television Indians whose savage whoops are drowned out by rock 'n' roll music crashing through the apartment and probably rattling the china at the Lord Baltimore Hotel next door. There are no books in this room and few in any other, though each room has its own telephone and at least one electronic amplifier helping deafness along.

A telephone rests on Bubba's upper torso; each time it rings he snatches the receiver as if fearing it might wake the baby. The instrument remains silent for no longer than three consecutive minutes. It ultimately dawns that Bubba does not know a high percentage of the callers: he is talking to all these *strangers*. "Well, yeah," he admits, "I'm in the book." Yep. There he is, listed along with the Smiths who do not see their pictures plastered on the *Baltimore Sun's* delivery trucks or who do not, in most cases, drive rust-red Cadillac convertibles with custom equipment, or get themselves named to pro bowl squads: Smith Bubba . . . 727-6893.

Bubba is a bit embarrassed, because earlier he had declaimed against crowds, intrusions, and other snares of celebritydom; his teammates know him as a loner they rarely see off the football field. He explains: "Well, you know, it's interesting to speak to all types of people. Find out what's in their heads." Don't the kooks, nuts, and barroom habituals drive him crazy? "Aw, it's not so bad. Most people are nice; they call up and say 'good game' and like that." A big grin. "And hey, my man, I meet a lot of chicks that way." Bubba, who neither smokes nor drinks, describes his appreciation for sweet women as "my only dissipation."

Telephone roulette is particularly hazardous this day. Victory breeds unusual traffic; the Colts have opened a new season with a satisfying 22–0 conquest of the New York Jets. Bubba has enjoyed a rowdy afternoon, and once again is a folk hero. A ninth grader calls to report that he, too, is a working defensive end; Bubba's contribution to the fraternal shoptalk is limited to a half dozen "yeahs," select "uh-huhs," and one "I got to go, son, you stay after 'em." When a nineteen-year-old girl requests the pleasure of Bubba's company, he says, "Send me your picture. Huh? Aw, just send it to Bubba Smith, care of the Baltimore Colts. And hey, look here"—going a bit bedroom husky in the throat— "maybe you better mail your birth certificate along." Joe Fan calls from a bar to ask if this is *the* Bubba Smith, no kidding, honest to Christ? He then permits his several companions a beery word with the Big Man. Bubba responds in monosyllables, obviously not caring a flip what's in their heads. A young schoolmarm complains that Bubba has not honored an ancient promise to address her junior high school class. "Well, all this week I'm being interviewed by this uh . . . intellectual magazine, and uh . . . well, lotta things have been happening to me." He renews his pledge, sort of: "Look here, now, I'll make it one day soon when I get myself together." Bubba sighs and regrets that occasionally a particular old involvement follows a man around, barking.

Now he discourses on the virtues of being mean: "Tody, he's so damned mean it's unreal." Little Brother Tody Smith, a mere sapling of 250 pounds, is a rookie lineman with the Dallas Cowboys. "I wish I had that mean streak, but I don't. I have to compensate in other ways. With speed and quickness. A lot of people associate size with meanness. But here I am, nearly seven foot tall and weighing 295 on the official program, and I'm a pussycat compared to Tody or Mike Curtis. Just nothing very mean lives in my soul. You've got to *arouse* me. I don't care who's on the field. Mike Curtis has *got* to be the naturally meanest man on it. He may be the meanest man in the world.

"Me, I try to avoid touching anybody. The quicker I get rid of 'em, the quicker I reach that quarterback. And I'm paid to sack quarterbacks. I don't care, I could make three hundred tackles up and down that line—but unless I get to that quarterback, I'm just a mediocre defender. I guess Gino Marchetti was about the best defensive end that ever lived, and he once told me, 'Bubba, don't play no games. Your job is to dump that quarterback. It's the same thing as a touchdown to a halfback.'

"No, I don't know what makes one guy meaner than another. Tody, he's twenty-one to my twenty-six, and growing up we used to beat him up a lot, me and my big brother Willie Ray. I guess maybe it turned him mean. Mike Curtis, I talk to Mike a lot, but I've yet to figure him out. I've read that when he was young he used to kill kittens and ride his bike into trees and brick walls. For *fun*, man." Bubba laughs and shakes his head, as if doubting the joy of such recreations. "Mike's so intense he oughta teach hypnotism. He goes so hard that he can recover from a mistake without you knowing he's made one. He'll flatten our backs in practice—not to hurt 'em, exactly, that's just Mike's way. The coaches had to set him down a time or two for the good of team health, and one time Johnny Unitas hauled off and hit him in the face with the football. I don't know what causes Mike to be like he is, but it's nice to have that crazy dude on *our* side."

Bubba has earlier surrendered his persistent telephone to an answering service and is now checking every eight to ten minutes for vital messages. Unable to live with the thought of lost opportunities, he orders the phone switched back to operative. Thirty seconds later a young woman is apologizing for being tardy: her car has cratered; she's been detained by repairs. Fem Libs will not appreciate Bubba's method. He scowls and looks mean. "Don't spend no time *telling* me about it," he growls into the phone. "Get on over here. I've been sitting and holding my hands all day." He slams down the receiver and grins. The grin turns into chuckles and then into a chesty rumble, like distant rolls of thunder. "Hey man, to tell the truth I had forgotten anybody was coming over today. Let's talk about being mean another time. That chick makes me tender."

They call him "The Animal," "The Brute," "Iron Mike"; his coach once joked that when the Baltimore Colts go on the road they ship Mike Curtis ahead in a cage. All that talk is public-relations flackery, of course, not to be taken seriously except by those who move their lips or drool while reading—or perhaps writing—the gee-whiz pap of sports pages. Mike Curtis views his image ambivalently: he *is* tough and is rather proud of his leather; on the other hand he is embarrassed, sometimes, by the "animalistic references." A bridegroom of a year's duration, he would not like his future children to think that their father may have been some freaky brute.

Curtis looks nowhere near as hard as his reputation; nor is he as physically imposing as official progarms advertise: six feet two inches; 232 pounds. With his straw-colored hair, blue eyes, and shy country grin, you wonder—Bubba Smith's testimony to the contrary—whether he belongs among the world's meanest three or four hundred. In faded blue jeans, Duke University T-shirt, a weathered denim jacket, and heavy-duty shoes suitable to the cow lots, he appears to be the original open-faced Farm-Boy Innocent presumed to have disappeared along with sleeve garters, penny candy, and unpolluted streams. In the hairy locker-room world of derisive barracks humor and summer-camp grab-ass, he nods politely to strangers, speaks of little more than the job at hand, and exhibits a bland countenance.

Most people aren't as simple as they look, and neither is James Michael Curtis. Though a genuine ole farm boy from Rockville, Maryland, he has been around the sharpies and bullies of the National Football League these seven years now, exposed to the fast diversions of the wicked cities, so hayseeds no longer sprout wild in his hair. There is a touch of the put-on artist in him, a dash of actor, generous measures of the cynic, sloshes of the romanticist, slices of quince, a hard streak that might be coveted by a hanging judge. Difficult to say what other compounds Mike Curtis harbors, or what chemical in his private moments may dominate, for he is not inclined to quick trusts. He is a man who often finds the world's natural imperfections agitated by the clumsy ministrations of incompetents and buffoons. Perhaps that is the price he pays for having majored in history, or maybe the world has so shaped him—though, if so, the how of it remains a mystery. About all he says of his formative years is, "We were not real poor, but the threat of it was there"; his conversation often arrives at the importance of financial security, of salting a little something away. Men in group associations tend to choose the outstanding personal idiosyncrasy of each of their peers for purposes of humor. When the Colts are not joking about Mike's animalistic qualities they compare his parsimony to that of Ebenezer Scrooge, Jack Benny, or George Halas. Curtis has earned this reputation by cadging locker-room coins for soft drinks, and by developing one of the slowest moves toward a billfold or a check in the National Football League.

Mike Curtis was the only name player in the NFL to report for summer drills when the players' association called a strike a couple of seasons ago, and he bluntly states—as has many a loyal, independent Company Man bending submissively over a lathe or a shovel—that he is basically antilabor. Animals, including those naked apes making up the human race—if we are to trust Desmond Morris—fight for purposes of establishing dominance in a social hierarchy or for control of a given territory. In other words, (1) for the right to belong and (2) to attain those securities guaranteed by acquisition. Should we pursue the theory across the horizon, of course, we might conclude that John D. Rockefeller would have made the ideal middle linebacker, except, maybe, for being a bit loose with his dimes—so let it lay. But don't bury it. For Mike Curtis really didn't care all that much about the game of football at Richard Montgomery High School, "until I discovered that being a football name made me a part of things, gave me a place, opened up opportunities."

At Duke University Curtis starred as fullback on offense and linebacker when the ball changed hands. In 1965 he was drafted number one by the Colts, just as Bubba Smith would be two seasons later. Curtis originally languished as third-string fullback and spot-relief linebacker. Injuries to two Colts linebackers provided a starting opportunity, and no one has thought of displacing him since.

Curtis had a great year in 1968. By the time the Colts reached Miami to prep for their Super Bowl swoon against the New York Jets, the animal image was almost out of hand. Writers and flacks gathered around to demand explanations of his extraordinary meanness. Well, Mike said, as a kid he ran into brick walls, enjoyed B-B gun fights at close quarters, and murdered baby chickens. "That's what they wanted to hear," he now says. "I laughed when I made up those stories, but those writers swallowed it whole and played it straight."

Mike Curtis holds journalists in minimal high regard, believing with fellow Marylander Spiro Agnew that the unbiased reporter is not yet one of the world's real statistics. He also holds with the vice-president on matters of law and order, sharing a fine antipathy for longhairs, peacemongers, those who would accept the dole or encourage a general permissiveness. Strangely, though he is not one of the several Colts who have discovered Mexican boo-smoke, Curtis thinks marijuana laws are overly harsh and favors liberalized abortion laws: these matters, he believes, involve dearly personal freedoms not properly the concern of the state.

Curtis sees himself as a Viking, a gladiator, a white knight rushing to the rescue. "Sir Lancelot" he has called himself—though he had the grace to laugh. "There's an element of danger in football. You can test yourself, find what you've got in the way of bones and courage, and do it without risking your life as you would in war. I've always wondered how I'd react in a combat situation. Football's as close as I can come to testing myself.

"I really like to hurt—well, not really *hurt* so much as *hit*—people. I honestly get a thrill throughout my body in making real solid contact. I like to dominate. I want to be the best. Call it the pursuit of excellence.

"People try to make this game a helluva lot more complicated than it is. Television and sportswriters have done that, and some coaches. Hell, football is a very simple game. It helps to have an instinct for it, but basically you've got to blow in there, got to like that contact. I get awful frustrated if anybody beats me.

"I hit hard in practice, because what is the purpose of practice? To get ready, right? When I smash into our offensive linemen, that helps both of us get ready. When I see one of our backs come cruising through, all loose and relaxed, I stick it to him. He won't be cruising that way in a game situation. If he tries it, they'll knock him loose from that football. No, I don't think my teammates resent it. I don't take any cheap shots in practice, and the guys know my purpose. We've had a few flareups when I was overly zealous, but it's soon forgotten. Football players know that this is a contact sport."

Of late it sometimes has been said or written that Mike Curtis is the best middle linebacker in football, though that contention inspires raspberries among the partisans of the Chicago Bears' Dick Butkus and the Kansas City Chiefs' Willie Lanier. Does Curtis think he's the best?

"I don't think anybody can beat me," he says, unblinking. "Butkus and Lanier may be physically stronger than I am—hell, I'm probably only fourteenth or fifteenth in physical strength on the Colts. But I'm quicker. I can play the pass better than they can, and I think I can hit with 'em. Of course, I'll be the best only when what you might call 'the New York writers' agree that I'm the best. They've got the power. They're the persuaders. When Sam Huff was playing linebacker for the Giants, the writers gave him the title—even though many people in the game weren't sure he deserved it. Butkus has it now. That's the reality of it. I can't help but believe my time is coming."

By Friday noon Bubba Smith has managed to sour his personality. Driving through downtown Baltimore—much of which looks like post–World War II Berlin, half hollow and sleazy and rotting in dull reds or grays—Bubba is reading the morning sports page with one eye on the hazards of traffic. His name is not in the Colts story of the day, which inspires him to fling the paper disdainfully into the back seat. He is edgy, too, because on Fridays the Colts weigh in, and he will not be permitted the joys of breakfast until he has satisfied the scales. He casts covetous glances at three sandwiches wrapped in silver foil reposing on the front seat; immediately after weigh-in, Bubba will wolf them down.

"Man," Bubba says, "I haven't slept in two nights. Getting all these flashbacks." Flashbacks? "Yeah, you know. It's like a movie running in my head. I get all these visions of what the game could be like, how it could come out. I never played against this dude before so I don't know what to expect." The dude in question is the Cleveland Browns' Bob McKay, a 260-pound offensive tackle two years out of the University of Texas. Bubba complains that McKay "owned" the Houston defensive end operating against him the previous week. Bubba has worked especially hard for the Cleveland game, doing extra wind sprints on his own and trying to keep his weight down. Bubba is quicker at 270 or so than he was at the 295 he once carried; the additional weight puts a strain on his amazingly thin lower legs and ankles.

Mike Curtis, disturbed that he isn't mentally "up," is delighted to hear of Bubba's concern. "That's great," he says. "Bubba's big problem is motivation. Most of the time he doesn't pay a damn bit of attention to the films. You can ask him who the offensive tackle against him is, and he won't even know. He just blows in and does his thing, and lets the other guy do the worrying."

"It used to be that way," Bubba later will admit. "But since John Sandusky started coaching me, I'm hip to what's happening. Sandusky has put me in touch. In the past, when I'd be having trouble with some dude and ask some coach what to do about it, he'd say, 'Goddammit, Bubba, don't worry about it. Just play football.' What kind of answer is that? I haven't really had any coaching since my father coached me in high school. Duffy Daugherty didn't teach me beans at Michigan State. John Sandusky tells you how to beat the problem. I go into the games better prepared."

Friday's is the last tough practice before Sunday's game. Saturday will be a breeze, light work on the kicking game and no contact. By way of celebration, a number of Colts crowd into a tavern near the practice field: Curtis, the incomparable Johnny Unitas, center Bill Curry, defensive backs Rick Volk and Jerry Logan, linebacker Ted (The Mad Stork) Hendricks, tight end Tom Mitchell, guard Dan Sullivan, tackle Fred Miller. The favorite beverage is beer, and the talk is of money, women, and each other's various personal quirks. It is rough, not for the squeamish. Rookies cluster at a distant table. Only one of their number—Don Nottingham, a fireplug running back who came unheralded from Kent State University, the very last collegian to be drafted—is included at the table of old pros. This means that young Mr. Nottingham has a bright future, indeed, for there is a social hierarchy among pro athletes that might be the envy of official Washington.

Though fourteen of the forty men on the Baltimore squad are black, only whites have gathered to drink. "That disturbs me," Curtis says. "I'd really like to see the colored guys come out with us. It would unite the team more. They seldom do. You know, they segregate themselves at the training table. I sat down to eat with 'em a couple of times, trying to set an example, but I found I just didn't have much to say to them. I think it's a cultural gap more than a racial one. They like different music, sharp clothes, a looser style. But we're better off than a lot of teams. I really don't think there's any racism on this team. We're all together."

Bubba Smith might not always agree. About three years ago a fellow Colt, now retired—a tough, literal red-neck and hardened veteran given naturally to gouging, cussing, and bullying—took umbrage when Bubba strolled through a hotel lobby in the company of a fine blond lady. He sought Bubba out. "You're gonna get a bad rep. We don't go for that where I come from." Bubba rumbled, "Then you better go on back there, man, 'cause things are changing and I don't have much appetite for crap!"

About the time the beer-drinking white Colts adjourn to their homes or other appointments, Bubba Smith seeks out the comforts of the Baltimore Playboy Club. He spends an astonishing amount of time there for one who drinks nothing stronger than Big Orange, because he likes the "living decor." From bartender to Bunnies, it is "Hi, Bubba!" or Bubba-this-and-Bubba-that, so much so that he momentarily forgets the importance of psyching himself mean and begins to improve his mood.

"My family's very exceptional," Bubba says. "My father is the absolute king. Couple of seasons ago he called me and Tody home to Beaumont after football season. The high school team my father coaches had been about 8–2, Tody's Southern Cal team was something like 6–4, and the Colts hadn't done worth a damn, didn't even get in the playoffs. My old man sat us down at the kitchen table and said, 'We all had bad years, and we're not gonna have another one.' Well, he worked our tails off all summer: run, run, run. Tody had a good year, my old man went undefeated, and we beat the Dallas Cowboys in the Super Bowl." Bubba is waxing eloquent about his mother ("She's a teacher, a Ph.D., and knows more football than most coaches") when the spell is broken.

A long-limbed young Bunny, quite a morsel, pauses near the

table with a hearty helping of roast beef. "Excuse me, is one of
you named Bubba?"

"Yeah," Bubba growls.

"Which one?"

Bubba cannot believe it. "You putting me on?"

"No, sir. I was told to bring this roast beef to somebody
named Bubba. Are *you* Bubba?"

"I ain't Ray Charles," Bubba says, claiming the plate and digging in.

A moment later the Bunny returns. "I'm sorry, I really didn't
know who you were. They just told me to bring it to Bubba. I'm
new here, and I don't know many of the customers."

In deep communion with the roast beef, Bubba mumbles, "OK,
that's all right."

Sweetly, the Bunny says, "I hear you're quite a baseball
player."

"*Baseball?*" Bubba breathes. He stabs viciously at his dinner.
Suddenly, one worries for the health, on Sunday, of one Bob
McKay.

Late evening on a Baltimore expressway. Bubba Smith drives
easily in a dreamy, euphoric state. Mellow. Oncoming cars, like
strings of bright yellow tinsel, create a psychedelic light show.
Bubba, exclaiming over the effect, says how it complements the
pounding rock music. The air conditioner circulates sweet, pun-
gent smoke you can't get by burning mere tobacco.

A companion says, "Do you have an occasional existential
thought about the future meaning of all the perpetual, licensed,
disciplined brutality of pro football?"

About four miles whiz by, and the question is repeated—the
terms discussed a bit. Bubba shakes his head. "I don't think like
that. Football's a job. Violence, brutality—part of the gig. I don't
have any fear of getting hurt or of hurting anybody. Just before a
game, I fear not doing well. But that's all."

Well, the visiting theorist says, wars usually are fought—no
matter the oblique banners or idealistic slogans flying over them
—for purposes of holding or acquiring territory, and . . .

"I don't groove on war," Bubba volunteers.

Right. But football, too, is basically a fight to control territory —to gain or defend ground—and there are other comparisons. Even the terms derive from war: blitz, shock troops, aerial attack, sweep the flanks, in the trenches. So is each game not a small war, replete with its losses, retreats, casualties, walking wounded?

Stubbornly, Bubba says: "It's a *job*, man. I used to think it was a game. But the test came when I asked myself, 'Would you play the game without money?' And the answer is no. So it's a job, see, and I don't worry my head trying to make anything else of it."

To Mike Curtis, football is strictly a game. "Given enough security, I'd play for nothing. Oh, sometimes I look at myself playing hurt, bandaged, or in a cast, and I say, 'This is a *game*?' To me it really is, though. I feel a little funny about going through life playing a game, and sometimes I reflect on how much longer I can. I just don't relish getting a job. When I'm financially secure, I'd like to run a fishing boat. It's important to enjoy what you do.

"Fear injury? No, but I keep my eyes open for cheap-shot artists. Brutality? Ah, that's overrated. Sports-page talk. Box office. Football players don't think about it much." Curtis is right. Sunday mornings, most players watch cartoons before the afternoon mayhem. More card games than books occupy the team airplane flights. One hears virtually no talk of politics; absolutely none of literature or philosophy. These are men who have been exposed to books in college—maybe even to a few stray ideas—but they seem to have left them behind with great relief, as a furniture mover might unburden himself of a piano: quickly, and with a sigh.

"Discipline is an asset," Curtis is saying. "Society could use more of it. The only thing I don't like is the pressure. Really, I guess, it's pressure I put on myself. I missed an open-field tackle in preseason against Oakland, and it ruined my whole weekend. I saw it in the films, and my stomach knotted up. I felt inferior. If anyone had said anything, I'd have felt worse—or wanted to have hit them. Maybe, for me, the pressure is a secret part of the fun. Just part of the game."

Sunday was a slow, chill weep of rain. Overcast skies painted midmorning in the shadowy hues of twilight. East Baltimore Street derelicts abandoned their alleys and doorways to troop like a ragged, gray, defeated army into quick-stop eateries, scarred funky bars, a warm bus station. A day with no good in it. Great funeral weather.

Baltimore's Colts woke in a motel on the city's outskirts, having been gathered from their homes like suspected felons at 9:00 p.m. on Saturday; after the 11:00 p.m. bed check they were locked away. Fathers, studs, or heroes they may be, but professional football players—even worn-armed old men like Johnny Unitas, rapidly sneaking up on forty—are not considered reliable enough to get through the pregame night on their own. Since football men almost uniformly agree that the game is dependent on emotion, the players are carefully gathered to encourage esprit de corps. They are expected to wear Game Faces, which is to say they are to assume the grim expressions of painful surgery, constipation, or unrequited love. Coaches have been known to trade or bench gladiators who chanced to smile or otherwise appeared to enjoy the human experience a bit too close to the kickoff. Ideally, locker rooms are grim stations full of tensions, muted talk, and muscle-bunching gum-chewings.

There are artificial aids more stimulating than gum—though, again, the commissioner's office dislikes hearing talk of it. Players are permitted to get themselves ready as they will. Some few may depend on prayer or positive thinking. Others, however, may require deadening shots, the speedy surges of barbiturates or amphetamines, or small doses of whisky. There is a great deal of looking the other way, a grand official winking, for unit honors and personal pride and big money are the stakes. It is, let it be said again, a mean business.

Playing at home, where they have consecutively performed to fifty-odd capacity houses, the Colts are the six-point darlings of bookies. In the locker room, Coach Don McCafferty—not much for brimstone oratory—says to his warriors that they are in for a "hell of a ball game" and reminds them that Cleveland on three consecutive occasions has taken victory home from Baltimore.

When the public introductions are accomplished, Bubba Smith receives the rowdiest greeting of all—until, a moment later, the cheer for Mike Curtis eclipses all prior records. Bedlam. No other word for fifty-six-thousand-plus screaming partisans. Down in the bench area the sound is physical, a great noisy surf washing the nerve ends. The fired-up Colts respond, belting and jostling each other, crying encouragement and curses. Tight end Tom Mitchell repeats a private litany: *stick the bastards stick the bastards stick the bastards* . . . Mike Curtis, face to face with yet another personal testing, stares past all backslaps and salutations. Bubba's eyes are two dark and shining stones; he takes deep breaths.

Right away it has the makings of a doggy day. Twice in the first quarter, Cleveland chews from its own twenty to within the Baltimore thirty, nothing spectacular, just grunt gains on guts running and play-action passes. Mike Curtis, raging up and down, exhorts the Baltimore line; the sideline Colts curse, whoop, mutter. From the bench you can hear every thud, grunt, or cry, and that keeps the bench very much in the old ball game, cheering or goddamning with fortune's changing tides. Coming to the sideline after a Cleveland drive has been stopped, Bubba huffs. "I haven't got to the quarterback one time. Not *one* mothering time." Someone remarks that Bubba has almost blocked a kick. "*Should* have," he grumbles. "I didn't know I was that close, and I let up to keep from roughing the kicker."

It happens to Mike Curtis with 2:57 left in the first quarter. LeRoy Kelly, taking a pitchout, sweeps wide left from the Colt forty; he is hit by Curtis after about ten yards. It is not a clean hit: Curtis slides off and Kelly stumbles several steps before collapsing. Mike Curtis rises shakily, holding his right arm. He stares at his hand as if it has somehow betrayed him. By the time he reaches the bench, the base of his thumb is beginning to puff. "Bent it back," he gasps. "I think his shoe got it." Mike is very pale, muddy, sweating. The team physician gives the thumb an experimental tweak, and Mike Curtis—"Iron Mike"—yelps like a small puppy and closes his eyes.

"It may be fractured," the doctor says.

"I want to play," Curtis says, sounding wispy and faint.

"Everybody wants to play," the doctor says, unwrapping muddy and grass-stained tape from the linebacker's hands. He pushes Curtis back down on the bench when Mike rises to see what the crowd is whooping about.

The partisans are whooping because Rick Volk has intercepted a pass on the Colt four—then groans when the Colts are called for offside, and Cleveland is given new opportunities. "Penalty on Bubba Smith," the public-address system booms, and out on the scrimmage line the culprit paws the ground. "*Goddammit Bubba!*" people are screaming from the bench.

Aroused, Bubba smashes through on the next play to deflect Bill Nelsen's attempted pass. On fourth down he breaks through to rush Don Cockroft's field-goal attempt so that it sails wide, and the Colts temporarily escape damage. Mike Curtis, however, is being led off to the dressing room by the team physician and is humpbacked in pain.

Mike does not come back. The Colts lose a very sweaty, physical tough one, 14–13. The defense has played magnificently, scoring the Colts' only touchdown, but the offense—with old Earl Morrall and *his* senior, Johnny Unitas, throwing five interceptions between them—also turns the ball over on fumbles three times.

Sitting naked on a footstool fronting his locker, Bubba plasters Band-Aids on little mountains of lumps and assorted small cuts. Earl Morrall, heading for the shower, slaps his shoulder: "Good game, big Bubba." Bubba grunts: "Not good enough." To the other defensive end, Roy Hilton, Bubba says privately, "The offense gave it away. Eight damn turnovers." Hilton nods, then sighs. No one is very talkative. Bubba explains why he traded blows with Cleveland center Fred Hoaglin at midfield in the fourth quarter, and then shook a warning finger in Hoaglin's face: "Aw, the whistle had blown a play dead, and I let up. That damned dude kept blocking on me."

He is showered and dressed within twenty minutes; though he signs autographs for fans clustered at the exit, he does it hurriedly and without comment. The fans, sensing his mood, do not push him.

The car radio booms rock 'n' roll music with the turn of the ignition key. Breaking into traffic with the aid of a policeman who recognizes him, Bubba holds his head in one huge hand: "God, I'm speeding. Can't come down." A few hundred yards into the bumper-to-bumper traffic, fretful and impatient, he slaps the steering wheel. "*Damn*, but I hate to lose. Nobody *knows*, man. They say I'm not motivated. Shit, if anybody wanted to win today more than I did, they must be off hiding their face and crying." Told that official statistics credit him with four tackles, two assists, one sack, and one deflected pass, Bubba snorts. "I know I got more than that. Well, no matter. Losers weepers."

Safely in his pad, Bubba stretches out on the big bed to watch on television Oakland's mopping up of a five-touchdown win over the San Diego Chargers.

The telephone rings repeatedly. Though it is close at hand, Bubba ignores it: Mr. Smith regrets that he isn't at home today. The phone echoes through the darkening apartment, falls briefly silent, then repeats its shrill, neglected cries. In a nearby hospital they are wheeling Mike Curtis into surgery. Soon steel will probe into a hand made not of iron, after all, but only of flesh and blood; Mike Curtis will be temporarily lost to the game he craves. Sunday night in Baltimore, and still the rain comes down. No joy in Mudville.

*The Atlantic Monthly*
JANUARY 1972

# Getting 'em Ready for Darrell

THE DAY WAS MISERABLY COLD and wet for mid-October, the wind cutting down from the north with a keen blade. A ghostly mist blew in about midnight. By daylight the

Texas desert air knew a coastal chill, clammy and bone-numbing. Soon Midland's flat paved streets flowed like shallow rivers.

Seventh and eighth graders of the city's three junior high schools on awakening may have groaned into the weather's wet face, but they pulled on their football jerseys in compliance with a tradition requiring them to set themselves apart as gladiators each Thursday, which is Game Day. They would wear the jerseys in their classrooms.

Three hundred strong, ranging in age from twelve to fourteen years, they comprised the dozen junior high football teams—four to a school, two to a grade—that play blood-and-thunder eight-game schedules with provisions for the more successful to play through to a city championship. Each team practices from two to two and one-half hours per day, except on game days; no homework is assigned to football players the night before a game.

A blond twelve year old named Bradley, who weighed all of 107 pounds and limped on a swollen left knee, was having a more modest thought than of the city championship. "Maybe we can score on a wet field," he said. "We haven't done so good on a dry one." His team, the San Jacinto Seventh Grade Blues, had not known the dignity or solace of a touchdown in four previous outings. Their frustrated coach, a chunky, red-faced young man only recently out of college, had promised to run two laps around the football field for each touchdown his Blues scored against the unbeaten Trinity Orange. This prospect made Bradley grin. "You gonna play on that bad knee?" Bradley's visiting father asked. "I played on it last week," he shrugged.

There were perhaps a dozen shivering spectators behind each bench—mostly parents—when the Blues kicked off to Trinity at 3:30 p.m. Bradley, who had started all four previous games, was chagrined to find himself benched. "Maybe the coach is protecting your knee," his father suggested.

But Bradley believed he had been benched because he had missed two practice sessions that week, due to the death of his grandfather.

Trinity marched through the Blues for four consecutive first downs, most of the damage done by a ponderous fullback who, though slow, had enough strength and size to run over the smaller defensive kids. Even so, his performance did not satisfy his coach. "Come on, Don," he shouted from the Orange sideline. "Duck that shoulder and *go!* You're just falling forward out there!"

Meanwhile, the Blues' coach exhorted his collapsing defense: "Get mean out there! Come on, pop 'em! Bobby Joe, dammit, I'm gonna come out there and *kick* you if you let that ole fat boy run over you again!" Bobby Joe, who may have weighed all of a hundred pounds, sneaked a timid glance at the sideline. "You look like a *girl*, Bobby Joe," a man in boots and a western hat shouted through his cupped hands. "I'm his father," he said to a glaring visitor, as if that mitigated the circumstance.

Trinity fumbled five yards away from a certain touchdown, losing the ball. The Blues jumped and yelled in celebration, while over on the Trinity side the Orange coach tore his rain-wet hair and shouted toward the sullen heavens. "Start runnin', coach," a skinny Blue said, picking up his helmet. "We're gonna score." "Way to *talk*, Donny!" an assistant coach said, slapping the youngster's rump as he ran on the field.

But scoreless San Jacinto could not move the ball. Backs, attempting double and multiple handoffs, ran into each other and fell. Orange linemen poured through to overwhelm the quarterback before he could pass. "We gonna have us some blocking practice at half time if you guys don't knock somebody down," the Blue coach screamed. As if in defiance, the Blue line next permitted several Orange linemen to roar through and block a punt near their own goal line. "Blocking practice at the half!" the Blue coach screamed, his face contorted. "I mean it, now. You dadgummed guys didn't touch a man!" The Orange in four plays plunged for a touchdown, then ran in the two-point conversion for an 8–0 lead.

"I told you guys to get in a goal-line defense Mike!" the Blue coach raved. "Dammit, *always* get in a goal-line defense inside the ten."

"I thought we was *in* a goal line defense," Mike alibied, his teeth chattering in the cold. He turned to a teammate: "Gene, wasn't we in a goal-line defense?" Gene was bent over, his head between his legs, arms hugging his ribs. "Somebody kicked me in the belly," he answered. The Blue coach missed this drama. He was up at the fifty-yard line, shooing off a concerned mother attempting to wrap the substitutes in blankets she had brought from a station wagon. "They won't be cold if they'll *hit* somebody," the coach shouted.

"Same ole thing," Bradley muttered from the bench as his team prepared to receive the kickoff. He had been inserted into the game long enough to know the indignity of having the touchdown scored over his left tackle position. "I had 'em," he said, "but then I slipped in the mud." Nobody said anything, for Bradley had clearly been driven out of the play like a dump truck.

Midway in the second quarter Bradley redeemed himself, fighting off two blockers to dump a ball carrier who had gotten outside the defensive end. He ended up at the bottom of a considerable pile and rose dragging his right foot, hopping back into position while grimacing at the sidelines as if in hope of relief. The coach did not see him, however, for he was busy chastising the offending end: "Paul, dammit, don't give him the outside! Protect your territory!" "Bobby Joe," his father yelled, "*crack* somebody out there. You just standin' around." Bradley played the remainder of the half, limping more on the injured ankle than on the swollen knee. Rain was coming down in windblown and near-freezing torrents when the young teams ran to their respective buses for half-time inspirations.

Four or five fathers shivered near the fifty-yard line, asses turned to the wind, smoking and talking of the 41–9 crusher applied to Oklahoma by the University of Texas. "They sure looked good," one of them said. "I think ole Darrell Royal's got his best team."

A mother in red slacks, her coat collar turned up and her nose red, approached the men. "I think it's just terrible to play those little fellers in weather like this," she said. The men chuckled indulgently. "Well," one of them said, "we got to git 'em ready for Darrell." The men laughed.

A balding, portly man in a mackinaw puffed up. "How's Jerry doing?" he inquired. "Well," one of the men hedged, "none of our boys lookin' *too* good. Especially on offense." "I went to see my other boy play the first half," the newcomer said. "His bunch was ahead 19–0. They looked great. 'Course, they're eighth graders."

When the teams returned to the field the newcomer grabbed his son, a thick-legged little back. "Jerry," he said, "son, you got to get tough. Leland's lookin' tough. His team's ahead 19–0."

"We got to *hurt* some people," a stubby little towhead with the complexion of a small girl said. "We got to *kill* us some people." The men laughed.

Bradley, soaking wet like all his teammates, was dispirited. What had the coach said to the Blues at half time? "He said we're better than they are and that we can beat 'em." The disapproving mother had returned with her blankets. Having wrapped up the bench warmers, she approached Bradley, who shrugged warmth off with a grunt: "I'm starting." An assistant coach, moving in to confiscate the coddling blankets, thought better of it when the mother stood her ground. "Damnfool *men*," she muttered, glaring.

The Blues drove sixty yards in the third period, their best-sustained drive of the season, inspiring their coach to whoop and holler like a delegate to the Democratic National Convention. "Way to *go*, Jerry!" the portly father shouted on play after play as he ran up and down. "Get outta them blankets!" the assistant coach yelled at the bench warmers as soon as the corrupting mother had fled to her station wagon. "If you don't think about being cold you won't *be* cold." Ten yards short of a touchdown three Blue backs collided behind the line in attempting a tricky double reverse, fumbling the ball and losing it in the process. The coach threw his red baseball cap in the mud and stomped it some.

"Coach," the visiting father said, "don't you think your offense is pretty complicated for a bunch of kids? I mean, why not have simple plays they can execute?"

The harassed coach cast a suspicious glance at the visitor. "We teach 'em the same basic system they'll need in high school," he snapped, turning away.

Trinity's Orange picked up a couple of first downs and then fumbled the ball back. The Blues, trembling in a new opportunity, came to the line of scrimmage a man short of the required eleven. The coach grabbed Bradley and thrust him into the game at right guard. Four plays later, failing to pick up a first down, the Blue offense trooped off the field. Water ran down their young faces. Two little girls in short cheerleaders' skirts gave them soggy rah-rahs from beneath a tent of blankets, their voices thin and self-conscious.

"Coach," Bradley said, "I don't know the plays for guard."

"You *don't?* Well, why not? Didn't you study the playbook?"

"Yeah, but you never *played* me at guard before. I'm a tackle."

"Oh," the coach said. "Well . . . Bobby *Joe,* dern you, *hit* somebody!"

"Way to *go,* Jerry!" the portly father shouted, breathing heavily as he kept pace with the action, jogging up and down the sideline. He turned to a bystander, puffing and beaming: "Jerry's not the ballplayer Leland is. 'Course, Leland's an eighth grader."

The visiting father touched the wet arm of his downcast son. "Bradley," he said, "you're standing up on defense before you charge. That gives the blocking linemen a better angle on you. Go in low. If your first charge is forward instead of up, you'll have so much power the laws of physics will guarantee your penetration."

"*Wow!*" one of the teenybopper cheerleaders said. "The laws of physics! Outta sight!" Her legs were blue in the cold.

"Way to *go,* Jerry!"

On his next defensive opportunity, Bradley charged in low and powerfully, his penetration carrying him so deep into the Orange backfield that he overran the ball carrier—who immediately shot through the vacated territory for a twenty-yard gain. Bradley stood back at the fifty-yard line, hands on hips, shaking his head in disgust and staring coldly at the visiting father, who suddenly studied his shoes.

San Jacinto's scoreless Blues got off a final fourth-quarter drive, aided by two unnecessary roughness penalties against the Orange. "Coach," one of the bench warmers sang out, "they're playing dirty."

"Let 'em play dirty," Jerry's father responded. "We'll take that fifteen yards every *time*, baby."

But balls were dropped and young feet slid in the mud, and in the end the Blue drive ended ignominiously. San Jacinto's Blues were fighting off another Orange advance when the game ended. They lost again, 0–8; their coach was safe from running laps.

"We gonna work in the blocking pits next week," he promised his young charges as they ran through the rain to their bus.

Bradley, showered and dressed in street clothes, limped slowly to his visiting father's car. His right shoe was unlaced because of the swollen ankle; by nightfall it would show dark blue around the shinbone with bright red welts running along the heel base.

"I'm sorry I didn't do better," Bradley said. "I got confused. You yelled one thing at me and the coach yelled another. *You* said charge hard and *he* said just stay there and plug up the hole."

"Well," the visiting father said lamely, "I'm sorry I yelled anything at you." There had been too much yelling. "Can't you get heat treatment for that ankle? Or at least some supporting tape?"

"Naw," Bradley said. "They don't give us those things until high school."

They drove along in the rain, the windows steaming over. They passed Robert E. Lee High School, where a squad of perhaps sixty young men drilled in the rain, padless, tuning up for their Friday-night game against Abilene. Thousands would drive the two hundred miles east, some of them drunk or drinking. Probably at least one would hit another car or a telephone pole.

"I may not play in high school," Bradley blurted. "I may not even play next year. The eighth-grade coach came scouting around last week, and he asked me some questions and I told him I might not even *play* next year." His blond hair was wet;

his creamy young face was red. He looked angry and haggard and somehow old.

"Way to *go*, Bradley," his visiting father said.

*Texas Observer*
NOVEMBER 1970

## afterword

A love-hate relationship with football may rest deep in the family genes. My son came to me shortly after "Getting 'em Ready for Darrell" had appeared in the *Texas Observer* to indicate—with a bit of bashful toe digging—that he might try football for one more year. Why? "Well," he said with an abashed grin, "I kinda liked the publicity." He was on the verge of quitting a second time when the article was reprinted in *Chris Schenkel's Football Sportscene*—inspiring him to consider himself a national, rather than a regional, celebrity. He now has given up the game, however, and is in a private school where competitive sports are limited to swimming, sailing, and soccer. "I just got tired of football," he said recently. "Hell, I played seven years." Bradley King is fifteen.

# A COUNTRY LAWYER
# AND HOW HE GREW

**T**hough there are some two hundred thousand practicing attorneys in the United States, the average layman might be forced to include Perry Mason if asked to name a dozen. The sweethearts of the national press come immediately to mind: Edward Bennett Williams, Louis Nizer, Melvin Belli, Percy Foreman, Jake Ehrlich, F. Lee Bailey. To round out their lists, however, several friends I asked fell back on such ancient memories as Tom Dewey, included Supreme Court justices, or searched their newspapers to confirm that Sirhan Sirhan was represented by Grant Cooper.

Nobody submitted a single name from among the thousands of country lawyers who battle in obscure courthouses where personal freedoms, economic futures, and traditions of the American system of jurisprudence are daily at stake. Such men are rarely known outside their home precincts; many fully deserve their anonymity as they prosper from bail-bond brokerage and divorce mills, or chase ambulances from their musty offices directly above the lairs of loan sharks or next door to some Salvation Army mission. Others enjoy respectable practices in genteel surroundings, where they may either specialize in civil litigation or more sedate "office" practices catering to probate or tax work. Though these remain faceless, their incomes may run to six figures.

110

A third category of country lawyer numbers only a handful. These are restless, vibrant men who have attained a certain regional fame or notoriety: lawyers so diversified in their talents as to have successfully defended a long line of alleged rapists or murderers, and also to have consistently won satisfying (and occasionally astronomical) sums in civil litigations. There is much of the actor in them, and their tastes often run to exotic clothes, super-cars and private airplanes, and luxurious homes. They become grass-roots legends, and everything they do is either maliciously magnified or lovingly aggrandized: let them take two drinks in public and it quickly becomes a quart; let them win a fifty-thousand-dollar verdict and within the year it's worth a quarter million.

Perhaps the thin line between these regional lions and their more famous national counterparts amounts to little more than that the former never had the luck to represent a Candy Mossler, a Richard Speck, a Jack Ruby, a Jimmy Hoffa. The country "super-lawyer" himself willingly accepts this assumption, for these are competitive men, sometimes brash or cocky, always full of pride.

There is both a great exhilaration and a certain secret sense of unspecified doom in such men: they are a little feverish, tending to great emotional peaks and valleys, and quite often they threaten to run for Congress or to write books. Usually, however, for all their threats or flirtations, they remain true to their bitchy mistress, the law, who requires of them nomadic travels, midnight attentions, and almost constant trial by jury. One of the best of this curious breed is Warren Edsel Burnett, forty-three, a trial lawyer working out of Odessa, Texas.

I had been trailing Warren Burnett for perhaps two weeks when we began the 284-mile drive from Odessa to Del Rio, a drowsy little town on the Mexican border, one afternoon last January near dusk and in uncharacteristic rain and fog. We drove south through miles of oil fields and strong persistent winds, each true to my recollections of that same table-flat country where I had sweated as a grimy oil-field roustabout in youthful summers between school terms. I was much happier here in Burnett's maroon Mercedes-Benz—attended by smoky Scotch

111

only mildly polluted by the waxy matter in the paper cups, a giant pickle jar brimming with chasing waters, a bag of cracked ice soon to puddle the floorboard, and enough cigars to reach Mexico City. In the back seat were three briefcases filled with legal papers, lawbooks, and one of the several prepacked suitcases Burnett keeps within handy reach for emergencies. When we talked, Burnett spoke in his typical deep cadences: a kind of half-profane courtliness probably having its origins in many close readings of the Old Testament, yet influenced by the gleeful exaggerations of backcountry Virginia and the slightly self-mocking observations of West Texas barrooms. Norman Podhoretz, originally exposed to the Burnett rhetoric, staggered away labeling him a "master of the high sardonic."

The emergency of the moment centered on another attorney, Mike Gonzalez, whom Burnett had volunteered to represent without fee because he saw in Gonzalez a victim of community vengeance. Lawyer Gonzalez, as Burnett explained, originally came from "typically wretched Tex-Mex circumstances" and had "grunted his way through law school on guts and tortillas." Affronted by what he considered shameful treatment of his poor working-class (and largely Mexican-American) clients, Gonzalez had filed a series of suits charging several gun-toting old sheriffs, prosecuting attorneys, and others with having violated their civil rights. He had also become involved in the only recently semi-militant activities of Texas's long-docile Latins, representing among others a chapter of the Mexican-American Youth Organization (MAYO) which, if not yet as bold as the Black Panthers, is motivated by kindred inequities. In towns like Del Rio, Eagle Pass, Uvalde, or Crystal City, Mike Gonzalez quickly became less than appreciated in certain powerful quarters. Soon he could hardly visit the streets without being stopped for speeding or checked out for drunkenness.

"There was nothing especially artful about Mike's harassment," Burnett was saying, "until suddenly they charged him with smuggling liquor and cigarettes from Mexico. On evidence, incidentally, that looks pretty suspect. When Mike is charged with smuggling, his bond is made in the amount of several thousand dollars; a condition of the bond was that he could not leave the

jurisdiction of the court where he was charged—a common condition, though one not infrequently if informally ignored, especially when the defendant retains home roots within the court of
jurisdiction as Mike surely does.

"Immediately on posting bond, Mike tells his lawyer—I wasn't
yet in the case—that he's been framed. That, indeed, he had been
warned in advance by a friend across the border that he *would be*
framed. So Mike and his lawyer scoot across the Rio Grande
to talk with the friend—who verifies Mike's story.

"They are across the border less than one hour. Though there
patently is no attempt to flee prosecution, they hardly get home
before Mike is arrested for having departed his bonded jurisdiction. Well, now, goddammit! The only thing he's really guilty of
is carelessness in failing to appreciate the vitriol of his enemies!
So the hearing tomorrow is to prevent the forfeiture of Mike's
bond. Should it be forfeited he'd have hell's own time making another, in which case he would go directly to jail. And on a chickenshit deal like this, he doesn't have jail coming to him."

Burnett began the Del Rio drive in damp spirits, fretting not
only over Gonzalez's problems but over an El Paso case returning only a disappointing $3000 when he had been convinced that
his client, a twenty-nine-year-old Mexican maiden, had suffered
far more expensive damages in the auto crash of record. Indeed,
though his law firm had in the final quarter of 1968 collected
$350,000 in verdicts or settlements (of which he retained one-
third in fee) Burnett's practice of late had proved strangely dis-
satisfying. No case had truly excited his soul, as when a year earlier he had represented an antiwar college professor in a libel suit
against an El Paso newspaper,* or as when he'd won a six-figure
verdict against a railroad for its careless contribution to a grade-
crossing accident. He had recently come to toy with accepting
the offer of a New York publishing house to write a book on his
courtroom experiences, or vaguely spoke of moving the main
body of his law practice from Odessa to Houston or some other
large city where unspecified diversions might be found more re-
warding. For the truth is, Warren Burnett generally finds himself

* Won by the defendant, though since reversed in a higher court and thus
portending a new trial.

almost comically out of step with Odessa's prevailing mores. And though he affects not to mind, one who has known him for near to twenty years instinctively understands that one's old friend (by nature gregarious and fun loving) far from enjoys this isolation.

To be sure, among Odessa's eighty-three thousand residents are numerous men and women at home with good books, stimulating conversation, and the proper salad fork. Money, oil-based money, permits much travel, shopping sprees to Neiman-Marcus or New York, some few sons packed off for refurbishing by the Ivy League. Even so, Odessa has more working men and small merchants of limited vision than czars of commerce or industry, more chasers after chamber of commerce values than patrons of the arts. It is more a Harold Robbins town than a Harold Pinter, more beer than martini, more with the preachments of Peale than with those of Spock, more comfortable with the traditional moral homilies of "Bonanza" than with the irreverences of "Laugh-In," more Baptist than Episcopalian, less *New Republic* than *Reader's Digest*. Neither beards nor labor unions are highly visible, and the Kerner Report did not exclude this desert city when it spoke of two separate societies, one white and one black, one fat and one hungry.

General Edwin A. Walker, who retired under fire after recommending Birch Society values to his troops in Europe, may have run a poor sixth in Texas when seeking the Democratic gubernatorial nomination—but in Odessa he led the ticket. Though Richard Nixon carried the day in 1968, George Wallace crowded him and HHH limped in third. The safely monopolistic *Odessa American* goes beyond even the town's normally conservative biases in attacking tax-supported parks, schools, playgrounds, or even roads. Though editor Olin Ashley explains that his newspaper does not review books because "we aren't in business to sell merchandise through our news columns," you might see your insurance agency, service station, or jewelry store glorified in columns on the paper's business page, provided you are a loyal advertiser.

In such consensus communities the pressures to conform are not always subtle. That Warren Burnett organized a memorial parade to honor Martin Luther King, that he has offered free legal aid to indigents charged with capital crimes, that he represents causes favored by the American Civil Liberties Union (or black militants who may find it difficult in Texas to attain competent legal counsel), that he not only defends the Warren court in his speeches but had the gall to have his friend Justice William O. Douglas as a houseguest in Country Club Estates (apologizing, en route, for an Impeach Earl Warren sign established near a busy intersection)—well, that he actually and openly does such things inspires (let us charitably put it) certain community misconceptions. Recently a University of Texas law student, whose father is pastor of one of Odessa's stricter churches, wrote me: "Warren Burnett has long been my idol—though most people I knew thought he was at least 'pink,' probably Communist, certainly crooked."

A jaundiced view of the lawyer is not, of course, unique to Odessa. Carl Sandburg was a kindly man and not infrequently a gentle poet, but one day the sweet old man with the saint's face and the halo of white hair wrote, "Why is there a secret singing when a lawyer cashes in?/ Why does a hearse horse snicker, hauling a lawyer away?"

The layman, speaking from the mires of legal ignorance (and, it's true, sometimes from the sour marshes of his personal experience) knows the answer to mysteries Sandburg could only raise in poetry: lawyers are shysters, cynics, drunks. They are forever ganging up on clients to take it all for themselves. Lawyers gag on the truth by nature and by nature they belch lies. (Did not Ambrose Bierce define "liar" as "a lawyer with a roving commission"?)

Perhaps one reason why lawyers often fail to come off as dashing knights-errant is that 15 per cent or so of our practicing attorneys probably *are* outstandingly inept or in some way rotten apples; while this percentage of spoilage may be no higher than decay rates normally associated with other occupational groupings, lawyers—like football coaches—remain highly visible when they err. The corporate, or "office," lawyer is not nearly so visible (nor so often maligned) as the trial lawyer, who routinely goes forth to defend or prosecute suspected criminals or proximate-causers-of-accidents. By his very role in the advocate system a

115

trial lawyer gathers enemies in a highly efficient manner. The lawyer who wins for the other side is a damnable rascal in whom the truth never reposes because he had done us dirt; the lawyer who loses in our hire is a drunken buffoon, if not criminally on the take, else he would have more efficiently championed so righteous a cause.

Another reason for the layman's disenchantment may be that he knows injustice when he sees it—and, face it, he sees it in American courts often enough. His deficiency is in not realizing that justice was never meant to be always served. Indeed, our laws have largely been made in legislative bodies where corporate, industrial, or governmental interests are more to be feared than flaunted; thus the scales of justice have not infrequently known the weighted thumb. Happily, our higher courts have increasingly come to realize that certain repressive old laws or customs will no longer serve. While the law today is more nearly concerned with individual rights than ever before, only the unwary will presume it to guarantee some pedigreed strain of abstract justice.

And it never can. For by the very nature of the advocate system, no lawyer is more interested in attaining "justice" than in vigorously presenting his client's point of view. No, the lawyer properly concerned with his client's cause has a special (i.e., narrow and judiciously prejudicial) view that, to the uninitiated, may make it appear he chooses the lie even when the truth rests within handier reach. "My clients want freedom," the storied defense attorney Percy Foreman is fond of saying, "not justice." Any honest lawyer will tell you that Foreman's clients are not, in that respect, unique. Candid lawyers make an additional concession: that though the best lawyer does not invariably win, he wins much more often than he loses. If there is implied in this admission the corollary one that the rich shall fare better than the poor, or that the unjust may prosper where the just do not, then one is invited to invoke some plan superior to our jury system.

So lawyers squabble over the fine print, shout and split hairs, persuade judges to free evil men on technicalities—or so it may appear to the old boy in the spectator's seat, to the hostile wit-

116

ness, or to many a disgruntled party to a lawsuit gone wrong. "One of the basic troubles," Warren Burnett said as he drove into the rainy night toward Del Rio, "is that most people just don't understand the Constitution of the United States. It's entirely possible the majority don't even approve of it."

We stopped at a restaurant in Ozona, a rich little town where a statue of Davy Crockett in marble buckskin dominates the square and where the founding money is descended from old ranching profits only later invested in oil. Rancher types wearing Hoss Cartright hats frankly stared while Burnett (wearing forgotten sunshades across the top of his head) telephoned back to Odessa for a report on the personal-injury case he had earlier argued; we had departed for Del Rio while the jury deliberated. When he learned of the $18,800 verdict (in a case, he had privately fretted, that might not return a dime) Burnett whooped, "Come on, let's go drink whisky! I got my balls back!" This declaration, plus his impromptu tap dance toward the door, may have been what prompted the coffee-drinking old cowhands to shift uneasily on their stools while exchanging glances: *That damn dude is a little bit crazy.*

Indeed, the maroon vehicle now zipped along as if slightly crazed in its own right, on a road sweeping over and around scrubby hills, mesas, and canyons from which one half-expected Geronimo to burst in full paint and fury. Hundreds of years ago, even before the coming of the first Spanish expeditions, these mean hills had been roamed by a poor Indian tribe whose survival diet included bugs, earthworms, and fecal matter; even through the rain, and these several centuries later, the pickings didn't appear greatly improved. We rolled past the land's poverty while Burnett grew rich on victory.

"Having won one the computers had judged lost," he said, grinning in the eerie dashboard lights, "I now speak with a conviction bordering on the arrogant. A while back you wrote bugging me to schedule a couple of 'big' lawsuits you could sweat. Well, what *is* a 'big' lawsuit? A 'big' lawsuit is one to which you owe some personal allegiance; conversely, a 'little' lawsuit is one in which you have no personal interest. People will relate the most intimate details of 'my' lawsuit fifteen years after they've forgotten the details of 'my' operation."

Tell me about clients, I said.

"Well, every alternate goofus who wanders off the street into a law office fancies himself another Charles Evans Hughes—when, in truth, the only knowledgeable laymen are those ole boys who have laid around sufficient jails to have leisurely acquainted themselves with lawbooks. Cabdrivers, oil-field roughnecks, graying grannies too old for hysterectomies—they come in and plop down and say, 'I coulda made a lawyer.' Whereupon they instruct you in the fine points of law. I've been given to understand that orphans are legally inadmissible to the electric chair and that it's physically impossible to leave fingerprints on paper."

He laughed, and while drawing from his paper cup missed by a good six inches what I think was an onrushing moving van, spraying roadside debris as we rounded an uphill curve. *"Damn!"* he shouted, fighting the wheel as we slid perilously near a void where the roadside dropped away to frightful depths. When the very real moment of danger had passed he said mildly, "Reminds me of the time I broke my back in that wreck with Charlie Winston." He did not slow down.

Burnett's passenger, momentarily in panic for better reasons than inborn cowardice, had a jillion jagged thoughts that told him much of this man who was his old friend: Burnett, sans crash helmet, speeding the three miles to his office each day on his new Harley-Davidson during a manic period two summers ago; Burnett, a decade ago caught in a West Texas dust storm while flying his single-engine plane, swooping down so low in search of his bearings that he discovered he was flying *inside* a Lubbock drive-in theater only in that final instant when it was marginally possible to pull up and avoid the giant screen; Burnett, ranging from this roulette wheel to that crap table in a twenty-hour marathon in Las Vegas under the mistaken impression he was obeying his physician's order to relax.

Yes, such a driven, gambling spirit was capable of convincing a jury that a back-seat passenger in a car struck from behind, and sent flying out a *front* window, had been more propelled by the mysterious will of heaven than through the careless driving of a

118

Burnett client. Yes, he was capable of saving from prison, asylum, the electric chair, or even an embarrassing guilty verdict a well-confessed eighteen-year-old "model boy" athlete and scholar (who had gently kissed in the moonlight a fifteen-year-old schoolmate before blowing her pretty little head off with a shotgun at the water's edge of a remote West Texas pond) by having the daring to prove that his young client had been so "temporarily dethroned of reason" as to honestly believe he was doing a good deed in dispatching the young lady to "live with the angels" as (testimony showed) she had often begged to do. Such men do not wear suspenders, eat health foods, or content themselves with corporate law.

"The working lawyer must first separate the shoppers from folks who are serious about hiring him," Burnett was saying. "People come in and ask how much to draw up a will, then volunteer that lawyer So-and-So will do it ten dollars cheaper. Or when I announce that I take in fee one-third of all monies recovered by settlement or one-half in trials, they say that So-and-So will represent them for only 10 or 15 per cent. I very pleasantly invite them to please God go *hire* the learned So-and-So.

"I say it, I hope, with pardonable pride—but in most cases the client will prosper by paying my higher fee. For the simple reason that I will likely give him a shot at jackpots beyond So-and-So's dream or comprehension."

I named a lawyer of whom we are both fond, a good man of rare intelligence and no little ability, who is handicapped by being perhaps more than moderately lazy and who certainly is a frequent victim of his own wild excesses. Burnett nodded. "Yeah, and when a client hires him the insurance lawyers know immediately that he'll settle his client cheap because of his own pressing needs. They'll offer five hundred dollars in a case they wouldn't dare telephone me on for less than eight or nine thousand.

"Getting a client to stay hitched in the presence of low settlement offers can be pure hell. This seems particularly true when you have a stout case—one you figure capable of causing record grief in Hartford once the verdict reaches there. Sometimes the only way you can prevent a restless client from accepting a dime on the dollar is by periodic advancing of your own money—fifty, a hundred, three hundred. It's not uncommon for me to have a hundred thousand dollars out in expenses or relatively unprotected advances. So you're exposed. Then somebody you've got a big wad in starts insisting on settling for half of what you've got in him.

"Then you take some ole silly slip-and-fall case, or a sprained thumb, worth maybe five dollars by my father's honest standards or five hundred dollars tops as a nuisance claim by my own, and your client won't settle for less than two acres of downtown Dallas. So you take the doggy ole case to trial and take your gas like a man. Your client rewards you by eating on your rump on account of you didn't prove he caught terminal cancer as a direct result of some fender-bumping accident.

"A lot of horseshit lawsuits come in: somebody gets mad at Uncle Clyde, so screw him, sue him. You can try to talk 'em out of litigation, though at a given point it becomes dumb office politics. See, after you reject him the client will walk across to another lawyer who *will* sue somebody for him—maybe even collect a few bucks in cautionary settlement. Then the spurned client goes around bad-mouthing lawyer Burnett: 'Don't hire Burnett because the son of a bitch won't sue. He's bought off.' That it's a scurrilous lie comforts me only minimally, because such a yarn may knock me out of being hired when some person hearing it has a lawsuit potentially as precious as the sweet name of Jesus.

"The more you win, the more challenging the pressures. Nearly every lawyer out here has a sly little jury speech telling how high powered and clever I am, the coded message of which is: You only hire Burnett if you're guilty or trying to pull a fast one. We're looking into a case of jury misconduct now where one of the jurors—some sour old woman—announced the moment that deliberations began, 'Well, this is *one* case that smarty-pants Warren Burnett ain't gonna win.'"

Del Rio was asleep when we arrived in the rain shortly after midnight: weary, a little fuzzy from cigar smoke, Scotch tars, and steadily deteriorating conversation. There was an unscheduled quarrel when the blubbery motel clerk, who wore a Masonic ring and possibly suspected we were spies sent from the Knights of Columbus, refused to rent us quarters unless we paid in advance. Burnett was incredulous: "How many people drive in here in a new Mercedes-Benz and carrying six satchels of gear and *then* stiff you for your damned old rent?" Even after Burnett named the motel's rightful owner and claimed his friendship, the clerk remained adamant.

By the time Mike Gonzalez telephoned the motel to see whether we had arrived, Burnett had playfully changed tactics: now he confided to the bewildered clerk that we were, indeed, forty cents short of the required rental; if the clerk would only trust us until we could sell some Bibles tomorrow we would see that God blessed him in special ways—might even kick in a free King James version. I paid in advance when it became certain that as a matter of midnight honor Burnett would not.

Mike Gonzalez lived in a tiny frame house on a street of no special merit, silent and dark except for his own home where a small cadre greeted Burnett as if he signified the millennium. There was a young lawyer up from San Antonio with his wife and two infants; a local physician perhaps grown weary of being treated as the "Meskin doctor"; a young teacher down from New Jersey tutoring adult illiterates; a bearded young VISTA worker out of El Paso; Jesus B. Ochoa, an El Paso lawyer and a beautiful heart passionately committed to social reform. Gonzalez, a big bearish man who owns a grin the world has not yet disfigured, recited his harassments dispassionately (the angry physician frequently breaking in to volunteer his own outrage at standard gringo humiliations) while Ochoa baited the young teacher by demanding to know why she wasted time teaching old people to read. ("Goddammit, knowledge will just make the old ones unhappy! But the old ones will not work for change! You should be working with the young ones!")

Near to three o'clock in the morning Mrs. Gonzalez, who has a certain acrid wit, spoke of her husband's predicament and of the social seethings underlying it. Cancellation of her lawyer-husband's bond would deprive the family of any livelihood, she said, and where to go from there? There ensued one of those clumsy moments when one dumbly curses whatever it is gone wrong

121

with the goddamn human race, but is unable properly to apply his tongue to his rage. Then Burnett said, "I think they've got a Mickey-Mouse case. I can't imagine a sane prosecutor convincing a sane judge to cancel Mike's bond on the evidence. If that should somehow happen, I'll pay the forfeiture myself and see that another bond is made. Get some sleep and don't worry." We left after firm handshakes, bear hugs, and God blesses all around: it was a warm moment, one to be cherished in colder times.

Del Rio's Mexican-Americans came to court in their best: plump matrons in hats and girdles; wrinkled old men uncomfortable in their off-center neckties; two ancient crones in black shapeless dresses and shawls, looking like all the old-country mothers of the world; a sizable delegation of MAYO sharpies in neat suits or sport coats, long hair, and some few sets of sideburns.

One of the government attorneys looked surprised when he saw Burnett: "Warren, are you in the Gonzalez case?" "I'm in it until it thunders," Burnett said, "and I don't think it's gonna rain." He managed to get a little Humphrey Bogart in it, a hint of some unnamed menace. Another of the government's lawyers joined the two; the trio then disappeared behind a private door. No more than fifteen minutes later Burnett emerged, beckoning to Mike Gonzalez. After a few murmured words to his lawyer, Gonzalez grinned and winked at his wife. "Let's cut," Burnett called. "They've dropped the charge."

As we trooped from the courthouse one noted the varied reactions: the old Mexican men grinning and gesturing a bit feverishly among themselves; the matrons smiling and silently nodding some mysterious benediction; youthful MAYO lads grouped some distance from their elders: cool, prideful, their faces betraying nothing.

Later, when we started the drive back to Odessa, Burnett said, "Don't kid yourself that those young cats think of us as friends. Oh, they'll *use* us—because they've finally wised up. But don't think they look on us as anything more than fringe participants in causes we don't truly understand." °

° Some weeks later, after thirty-two MAYO youngsters had been charged in Del Rio with parading without a permit, Burnett would return to secure

122

A mile up the road he laughed. "The irony of this morning is that it confirms the worst Latin suspicions. Had there been a trial, and had I won it, they might have staged the first annual *Señor* Warren Burnett *Fiesta de las Flores* or named a bullfight arena after me. But it happened through my getting the charge against Mike dropped—well, the word is rapidly making it around town that the powerful gringo lawyer rode in and bribed another powerful gringo behind a closed door."

Well, what *had* he said to the government's prosecutor?

"I simply told the man he had a Mickey-Mouse case," Burnett said, "and cast some doubt on his ability to win it."

Which is the most he would say, and which probably was not so much untruthful as merely short of the whole truth. For I suspect that Burnett's reputation for excellence and tenacity caused the prosecutor to take another look at his hole card and suddenly find it no better than a deuce. The prosecutor may have been willing to gamble his hand against the average Friday-night poker player but he might have been less than eager to bet it, say, into the teeth of Nick the Greek or the Cincinnati Kid.

The trial lawyer enjoys peculiar thrills: proving to know more about the human anatomy on cross-examination than the physician testifying as a medical expert for the other side; resurrecting a precedent from a long-dead case and applying it anew to a live one. He excels in the quick studies making it possible to be expert one day in diamonds, the next day in ballistics or whiplash injuries, next week in the intricacies of libel or of the gasoline engine. ("Law practice," Burnett says, "requires a diversified range of shallow knowledge.") One bones up as if for midterm exams, then once the test has been passed one pulls the plug to drain the mind of used mental waters.

"Office" lawyers may feel maltreated if required to try three jury cases annually. Last year Warren Burnett tried thirty-odd; his top associate, Jerry Childs, tried almost as many; each of the other half dozen lawyers in Burnett's firm tried from six to ten.

their acquittals on grounds that the city's parade permit law had been given insufficient public circulation. The cool MAYO kids would cheer Burnett as he left the courtroom.

Within one typical ten-day period last January the firm went to trial in thirteen cases at nine divergent points; Burnett personally traveled more than four thousand miles by plane and car, during which he won verdicts or in-trial settlements totaling $67,400 in four cases, none of which carried the potential for really exceptional paydays. He also squeezed in a speech on the subtleties of criminal law to San Antonio lawyers, lectured an assembly of Fort Worth newspaper people on the shoddy way the press has trampled on constitutional rights through lurid pretrial publicity, conferred in Austin with a client charged with possession of marijuana, and in Del Rio attended Mike Gonzalez.

There is a loose locker-room informality about the Burnett law offices. The general milling about would surely deliver efficiency experts to apoplexy and cattle to stampedes. Even as one lawyer dictates a criminal-case pleading, and another takes depositions in a personal-injury case, Burnett may be bellowing into the phone above the whine of Hank Williams ballads coming from his inner-office hi-fi and echoing through the halls. Unwary clients who burst on the scene must quickly adjust to the yellowed bones of a teen-age female (hanging from a wall so that her skeletal toes almost touch the Burnett telephone) on which the resident genius rehearses his anatomy lessons. Books and periodicals are piled and scattered everywhere, a high percentage open or with their pages crimped for easy reference: *Dissent*, *Texas Observer*, *New York Review of Books*, *Commentary*, *New York Times*, *The Village Voice*, *The Economist*, Mailer's *Armies of the Night*, Frank Conroy's *Stop-Time*, Elroy Bode's *Texas Sketchbook*, Jerzy Kosinski's *Steps*, Eldridge Cleaver's *Soul on Ice*, Tom Wolfe's *The Electric Kool-Aid Acid Test*.

Down the hall in the law library a visiting lawyer, a deputy sheriff, a newspaperman, and a used-car salesman may be sharing a game of darts, shouting occasionally when a dart so strays off trajectory that it thwacks into a copy of *Texas Law Review* or *Martindale-Hubbell*. Varied flotsam and jetsam of the human seas somehow wash on by the receptionist to drift backstage: small children lost and crying, a midmorning drunk convinced that "Judge" Burnett is eager to advance him ten dollars against some vague future yard work, two matrons soliciting for some good cause, a client on crutches seeking a two-hundred-dollar advance against a verdict far from certain. Secretaries and lawyers expertly dodge hall traffic, popping in and out of their individual rooms. Jerry Childs (who, in scheduling just which lawyers will try what cases for the firm, is as secretive as the CIA) shouts into the phone to three different persons that Burnett will appear at courthouses in Midland, Pecos, and Odessa on the following Monday; he explains to a puzzled observer that if opposition lawyers think Burnett will personally argue a case they may become more generous in their pretrial settlement offers.

Once or twice each year Burnett vows efficient office reforms: no on-premises beer drinking even after five, no dart games, no lying about being in conference when certain pests telephone. On the average each reform lasts about three hours, and Burnett himself is invariably the original sinner. "I could make everybody walk around in rubber soles and wear their corporate death masks or crappy little Dale Carnegie smiles, but it wouldn't improve my practice and I doubt seriously if it would help my personality."

Burnett came to law by accident. As a boy in Austinville, Virginia, a poor hill-country village near the borders of Tennessee and North Carolina, he read Thomas Wolfe and vowed to become a novelist.* At Virginia Polytechnic Institute he was for one year an indifferent mechanical-engineering student before the U.S. Marines claimed him in 1945. During an eighteen-month hitch in Burma and China he resolved to seek an English degree and then teach. For reasons yet unexplained he entered Lamar State College at Beaumont, Texas. One idle day he visited a Beaumont murder trial—and came away knowing precisely what destiny had in mind for him. Of the several law schools he applied to, only Baylor University at Waco could accept him immediately. He whizzed through, passing his bar exam within three years.

* Tommy Fox, who grew up with Burnett in Austinville and who now cuts congressmen's hair in the House of Representatives barbershop in Washington, once commented on his old chum's success: "I never *was* as surprised to see somebody make good. Ole Warren didn't seem special when he was a kid—hardly ever played ball or went huntin' with us. About all he ever done was lay around and read books."

His first job, in 1950, was as one of many faceless assistant district attorneys in San Antonio. Six months later he came to Odessa as a salaried staff lawyer for a highly successful plaintiff's attorney, John Watts. I was at that point a rather carefree, out-at-elbows West Texas newspaper reporter with few more thoughts of the future than a groundhog; Burnett, however, burned with ambition enough for two. Soon he urged me to go East in search of my fortune as insurance against "working all your life for three hundred dollars a month, tops, while echoing some little pissant newspaper publisher."

Within the year Burnett formed a law partnership with an old Baylor classmate and Odessa native, Paul McCollum (who is now a frequent opponent in court). Odessa's newest law firm did not instantly strike gold. Burnett remembers one of its first cases: "Another classmate hired us in a case up in the Texas panhandle. I drove all night in a clanking '46 Dodge, arriving in time to freshen up in a Texaco rest room before court. Breakfast was one cup of coffee, period. We win the big lawsuit. My old buddy pays my fee with a twenty-five-dollar check representing twice the total of Burnett & McCollum's net worth. Returning home, the old Dodge blows out a tire and I surrender much of the check in purchase of a new one. The check bounces." In 1952, at age twenty-five, Burnett was elected district attorney at $5,100 annually plus five hundred dollars for automobile allowances.

Southwesterners love litigation, else why do New Mexico and Texas have more lawsuits per capita than any other states? A contested divorce or a promising murder trial may attract more spectators than a basketball game. Lawyers whom Yale or Harvard never heard of boast their individual cheering sections, and each village is loyally certain that its hometown favorite is as unbeatable as Rocky Marciano was. When Burnett rose, it usually was to standing-room-only crowds; after each triumph he made his way through handshakers and backslappers like some victorious football hero headed for the showers. In such expansive conditions he cheerfully reigned late in his courthouse office, or some Eighth Street beer hall, not impatiently suffering his admirers' comparisons with Darrow or Bryan. He served two two-year terms; within a year after opening his own private practice (a one-secretary walk-up operation above an auto dealership) he was well on the way to the big Spanish-type house in Country Club Estates with its imported fine woods, stones, and accessories.

As a frequent winner and merciless wager of nerve wars, Warren Burnett is not always loved. "He won't interrupt you while you're talking," I once heard another lawyer say, "as long as you're talking about him."

Recently a West Texas lawyer, opposed to Burnett's candidacy for director of the bar association, gratuitously wrote him a scathing letter saying he was "professionally and morally unfit to serve." Burnett's reply, in full, ran: "It is the opposition of crazy old coots such as you that keeps me young at heart."

"Warren knows there's a game-day psychology among lawyers the same as among football teams," says Bill Alexander, who once was in the Burnett firm. "If he finds your sore spot he'll mash it till it rains."

Sometimes it is little things: rolling of eyes in amused disbelief, simulating anger, dropping a lawbook heavily and then profusely apologizing—anything to destroy a magic moment between the opposition counsel and the jury. Or a lawyer known to despise the morning hours may be greeted early on trial day by the Burnett sing-shout-laugh-whistle-stomp-and-dance routine, inspiring headaches or rages not calculated to prove helpful in court. An opponent known to have a sinful pride in his courtroom abilities may be greeted by condolences boomed to the largest possible audience: "Joe, what in the world happened to you in that Pecos case? I couldn't *imagine* a jury giving that sweet little girl thirty years. Did they stone you out of town?" Then the tormentor may turn piously to inform bystanders, "Poor ole Joe, they poured him out over in Big Spring last week."

"You don't win lawsuits by gimmickry or even by applied psychology," Burnett says. "Unless you're prepared to scuffle on points of law, you're a gone goose. There's simply no substitute for ditchdigging work. Know your law. Know your physical evidence. Visit the scene of the accident or crime. Tie your witnesses down to their testimony. Get the other side's witnesses to talk and talk and talk during depositions—thus increasing their

127

margin for error or contradiction. We aren't any strangers to night work."

Years ago, after night and his office decibel level had fallen, I observed Burnett preparing an accused murderer for trial. After they had discussed physical evidence, motives, and certain mitigating circumstances, Burnett said, "That district attorney is mean as hell. He's probably lying awake right now thinking of how to burn your ass in the electric chair. One of his favorite tricks is putting the gun in the defendant's hand—so the jury will *see* you as a potential killer. Understand?" The client nodded. "All right, now he'll try to get you to take that gun a thousand different ways. *Don't you do it!* If you so much as raise your hands from your lap at any time on that witness stand I'll quit you cold and may shout 'guilty' as I leave." Minutes later, assuming the DA's role in a rehearsal of cross-examination techniques, Burnett thrust a pistol at the defendant with the order, "Well, now, just show me exactly where you stood with the gun and where the late Mr. So-and-So stood." When the client reached for the gun, Burnett knocked him from his chair. On trial day the DA never could coax the defendant to accept the tainted weapon, though he tried many ruses. Burnett's man got off with a suspended sentence.

There are lighter moments. District Judge C. V. Milburn recalls when one of Burnett's witnesses wandered far from his expected testimony, inflicting great self-damage. Despite all the permissible leading Burnett could accomplish, the runaway witness remained on suicide course while opposing lawyers beamed and sophisticates among the spectators snickered. "Finally," Judge Milburn remembers, "Warren rose and said right in front of the jury, 'Your Honor, when is this court gonna shut down for necessary repairs?' " Once, after defending to acquittal a client charged with driving while intoxicated, Burnett was asked by a reporter what defense he would offer for the client in pending civil litigation inspired by the same incident (it being alleged the Burnett client had demolished another car with his own). "We'll probably plead," Burnett deadpanned, "that my man was *far* too drunk to assume responsibility."

The single public performance for which citizens of Odessa

best remember Burnett occurred when lawyers and physicians met at a country-club dinner to alleviate tensions aggravated by courtroom disputes between the two proud professions. Perhaps the prebanquet cocktail party ran two hours too long. When Burnett rose to deliver the welcoming address on behalf of the host lawyers, it was not the speech printed in the official program. "I have watched our learned doctor friends arrive here in their Cadillacs and their wives in precious stones and furs," he intoned, "and have observed their expressions as they considered superior secrets known only to themselves and/or God. I would like to remind our guests that when *their* professional antecessors were teaching that the night air was poisonous, and were setting leeches on George Washington's ass the better to bleed him, *my* professional antecessors had written the Constitution of the United States—as noble a document as known to the minds of men or angels."

One evening last January I consented in El Paso to join a demonstration the following afternoon against a supermarket chain selling grapes from growers being struck by organizing farm workers. Since the demonstration had been described as a "lie-in," one envisioned indelible stains resulting from rutting around in fruit and vegetable bins. Consequently, I dressed on the target day in old slacks and a scurvy sweater.

Burnett, free from court while a distant witness was awaited, advised that I might be charting a course directly for the penitentiary. "Under Texas law," he warned, "should you in any way block that store to customer traffic you could be charged with a felony offense." This should have been disturbing news: one well knew the severity of Texas jails, knew also the accepted constabulatory prejudices against bearded agitators. It somehow wasn't: perhaps because a pledge had been given, perhaps because one secretly glimpsed oneself leading Mailer's Night Armies from the Pentagon to the newer hazards of the grape bins.

At any rate, the irony of Burnett's cautionary lecture reposed in his having recently kicked up a fuss as a prime figure at a conference on legal defenses for political dissidents in the little town of Wimberly, near Austin. That seventy-five Texas lawyers were attracted had caused consternation in Lyndonland, no small percentage of the critics convinced that Castro had leapfrogged Florida or other inferior civilizations to establish the first Soviet-America beachhead on preferred Texas soil. Texans were unaccustomed to their native sons making common cause with New Left activists from among Students for a Democratic Society, Friends of the Progressive Labor Party, representatives of the underground press, persons associated with a much-harassed coffeehouse near Fort Hood where soldiers are invited to critically examine traditional military views—to say nothing of outlander attorneys whose clients included H. Rap Brown, Eldridge Cleaver, and Huey Newton. Though a few brave University of Texas professors participated, their officials had shuddered and denied use of the Austin campus to the conference.

The conference quickly bogged down in structural and procedural squabbles, young activists insisting that certain no-strings provisos attend any help the lawyers might give. Several lawyers were alarmed by the free indulgence of four-letter expressions among the militant young or were affronted by cool receptions. Ultimately, the activists withdrew to one private caucus and the lawyers to another. Theoretically, some acceptable compromises would emerge. In reality, each group began its internal deliberations by excoriating the other.

Burnett listened while wrangling lawyers threatened to pack and go, or else to make their legal skills available only under tightly controlled conditions. When it appeared the conference might go over the brink, he rose to recommend that lawyers not presume the role of "organizational architects" nor otherwise inflict their elder judgments. "We have offered the Movement people our full participation and it seems that gesture may be all we are allowed," he said. "I say we offer them once again our services as lawyers when they are in need of us—and if they can't accept that offer then I say, in the jargon of the Movement, fuck 'em!" The lawyers obligingly returned a proposal saying only, "Create your organization. We are available." The dissidents accepted, and the underground press would hail the Wimberly meeting as an exciting new concept that could become "the model for new and creative approaches to Movement services."

130

As we sat in Burnett's El Paso motel room I asked why he—a comfortable resident of a state where radicals are as unwelcomed as pox carriers and usually are as well quarantined—had become involved. He grumbled that I asked an "affirmation of the obvious." Tell me anyway, I pressed. All right, he said, he had accepted the fruits of a bountiful land while others had been unable even to claim their birthrights as free men. He had thought of himself as a liberal, had blindly believed some ill-defined progress was being made; but in recent years as America seemed to become unbolted, to rend itself with hatreds and killings, he had realized that like many Americans he had led a fraudulent life. The Kerner Report was correct: we had two distinct societies, two sets of rules, two cultures each contemptuous of the other. We were at war with our children: witness Chicago last summer. We forgot the Constitution: witness the government's casual way with wiretaps.

My intellectual friends in the East, he charged, were sitting on their padded duffs at four-martini lunches and the most they now hoped for was that if Richard Nixon listened closely enough to Pat Moynihan we might escape future ghetto burnings. Why, godamighty, ghetto burnings would logically become a thing of the past, since all movements are progressive in that when you reach a certain plateau you push on to another. In the absence of solutions, there might next come torchings of downtown stores where Mister Charley shops for his luxuries, guerrilla-like raids on the lily-white suburbs, industrial sabotage. These would be answered by bloody retaliations from police, the military, Congress, white vigilantes. Conceivably, the American black man might go into the dark night of cultural obliteration and tribal extinction long ago forced on the American Indians. The surest way to avoid blowing the national keg was for every man of decent instincts to start doing something—however small—to make our Constitution do what it says it does. Someone had to communicate, to say *I care*, to say *this won't do*.

He told of an old friend who had telephoned on hearing rumors of Burnett's upcoming flirtation with the Wimberly radicals. "He invoked his personal disapproval, cautioned me against embarrassing my family, and ultimately indicated that if I persisted

131

then the community might become a cold place in which to live. If he hadn't been such a dear old friend I would have told him to shove it, but instead I suggested that such considerations were necessarily secondary to larger problems—and suggested that he, of all people, should advance on Wimberly with me. He started screaming about goddamn Reds and filthy kids and crazy niggers worthy of being marched out and shot. *Shot!*"

The memory depressed him; he slipped into a private mood. I asked why he didn't come out to lie in the grape bins with me. Ah, the hell with it: he might take a nap, get drunk, go to a movie.

In my own quarters I mused that my old friend was something of an American rarity: an uncommon mammal who, though aging and prospering, grew more rather than less of a social conscience. One thought of many persons or institutions gone galloping in the other direction: Hubert Humphrey; the fat and happy American labor movement; the Irish and the Italian and the Jew who having attained a certain assimilation now begrudged the black man his own tardy rise; the nameless freshman congressmen who came to Washington seeing young men's visions but who grew old and powerful and came to wish for little more than that tomorrow could be more like yesterday. No, growing was no small talent.

Jesus Ochoa's telephone call interrupted my reverie: he would pick me up in fifteen minutes, and was Burnett going with us to the grape bins? No, Burnett had other plans. "Tell our good friend," Ochoa instructed, "that that goddamn conservative Edmund Burke joins me in saying, 'For evil men to triumph it is necessary only for good men to do nothing.'" I promised to pass it on. This proved unnecessary, for when Ochoa arrived Burnett was waiting in the lobby with a sheepish grin: "*Hay*-sus, old scout, how you go about getting grape stains out of a silk suit?"

I recently wrote my old friend asking that he drop a note commenting on the one case which he felt had done more than any other to advance his career—and to reveal what, in retrospect, he thought of that particular case or what great lesson he had learned from it.

His response began lightly: "I had been out of law school but a few months when circumstances made it possible to attend court in defense of the liberty of a fellow American. I loaded up with law and investigation. My man was charged as one who had operated a motor vehicle upon a public highway under the influence of the grape that pleases. He was a longtime resident of the small town where he was tried. The arresting officer, a popular sheriff, put poetry to my man in describing his drunkness as producing a condition known as 'limberneck'—a condition, by the way, which produced much pleasure for the sheriff each of the several times he demonstrated it to the jury. I couldn't believe that a case could look so bad.

"Then one of those practical decisions that make the difference in so many lawsuits—as I would learn—had to be made. While stealing a juryward glance I came to believe that one juror had some facial twitch making it appear as though he was winking at me. Minutes later, more damning testimony, another juryward glance, and what now might *very well* be a wink. By God, action was required! If he was winking, and I made no appropriate response, I could lose him; if, however, I was dealing with a facial tic and through returning a nonexistent wink showed my impertinence, then both lawyer and client were in the soup. Probably as tough a call as man ever had to make was made.

"I cut that son of a bitch a wink that could not be mistaken; he then abandoned caution and all sense of decorum, cutting me a wink that could be heard as well as seen. Young lawyer, after making the world's hardest call, relaxed—secure in the knowledge that a hung jury was the worst that fate held. Acquittal followed."

Then he got serious: "State of Texas against Harry F. Butcher. Butcher, an ill-named young fellow in his mid-twenties, is running around the country and ends up in Odessa in the hard year 1953. He gets too much booze superimposed on his other problems, invades a couple of residences, and with gun in hand rapes the resident womenfolk and—to aggravate it—the rapes transpire in full view of the husbands who were earlier bound by their frightened wives. One frantic husband ultimately frees himself, wrestles away Butcher's gun, and shoots him in the leg.

"I was district attorney and as such went to the hospital where the wounded prisoner lay, there to participate in the taking of a confession; at least, by none-too-subtle threats from me, the lawyerless Butcher was moved to confess to the detectives, and to sign it. The confession wasn't really needed, but at that time I had little conscience about gaining advantage for the state, whether redundant or not. Butcher was tried and the death penalty (voted by the jury in thirty-one minutes) was ultimately inflicted.

"Butcher was a big step up for me. Most people thought I did a helluva job. The bad thing about Butcher's case is that it can and will happen again and again. About all that is needed is a broke and friendless sick person who commits a spectacular crime, an ambitious prosecutor who cannot ignore—but who can handily departmentalize—his atrophying sense of moral wrongness, and a public not caring about why things happen.

"The old former DA realizes that we can't get all exercised about one dead man when we kill so goddamn many without any particular conscience in the matter. The thing that now grabs the sensitive and middle-aging old former DA is the chickenshit role he played in making everybody so pleased with the killing."

*Harper's*
JULY 1969

## afterword

My old friend did not make my task any easier to accomplish when, on the exact day I reported to gather story material, he and his wife, Emma (also an old friend), called a halt to their marriage. This was painful beyond the professional complications: I was, and remain, fond of both. Not knowing how that venture would end, I made no mention of their union or of the hilarious scenes to follow. Burnett, ordering an employee to rent him an apartment that first afternoon ("With a telephone number a drunk can remember") insisted that I accompany him in the purchase of housekeeping gear. He bought one sheet, one blanket, one pillow, one pillowcase, a coffeepot, two coffee cups, in-

134

stant coffee, a case of beer, a bottle each of Scotch and bourbon, a hi-fi set and thirty-odd country-western records. Emma, on locating this "house of music" a few days later, took a hatchet to everything but the bedclothes. Relocated in San Antonio, where she is politically and socially active, Emma now can laugh about it all.

Increasingly, Burnett has withdrawn from traditional community involvements. Though he has quietly assisted several disadvantaged youngsters through law school and provided or found them employment, he will not be discovered on chamber of commerce panels, or glad-handing at civic luncheons or at other gatherings of community pillars. His country-club membership expired, unlamented, several years ago. He is the subject of head-shaking or outrage among more conventional professionals, several once numbering among his close friends, who increasingly resent his life-style even more than his legal triumphs. Irrationally, they seem to feel that he has betrayed some vague code vital to the world's continuance. I read it as a penalty against Burnett for his own boldness in a society where conformity is too highly valued.

Following his divorce, Burnett sold the big house in Country Club Estates in favor of more modest quarters in a remote and undistinguished part of town. Though visiting lawyers, writers, assorted radicals, and a few brave politicians frequently make their home his stopping place, Burnett's only close companion in Odessa (except for his affectionate new wife, Ann) is Norman Childress, a used-car salesman and free spirit given to such shotgun observations as "Just dancin' with that ole girl made my dingus hard as Chinese arithmetic." Perhaps a clue to their friendship is an explanation Childress once gave to a young lady with whom he shared quarters about why he drank: "I take a drink, when I wake up, to feel like a new man. Then I have a drink *for* the new man. Then me and the new man get drunk together." A lawyer appreciates such reasoning.

Childress has been an interested observer in several rowdy beer joints when the distinguished attorney found it necessary to physically defend his political views or some vague personal honor; in his most recent encounter Burnett clearly lost a deci-

135

sion to another lawyer, a dedicated biter, who left matching teeth marks on his thumb, nose, and ass.

This postscript should take care of those carpers who said my original piece missed my old friend's rough essence. I don't know how to placate those who insist that I missed his "basic humanitarian sensitivities" unless it is to remark that his four teen-age children seldom receive the conventional parental harassments, coupled with the normal hypocrisies and, consequently, may even like or respect him.

# THE LIBERATION OF JESSE HILL FORD

he young man came to the town where he would eventually kill, in 1957, a navy veteran of Korea, an ex-newspaper reporter and former public-relations flack. Though he had been reared in Nashville, less than 150 miles away, there were those in Humboldt, Tennessee, who considered him an interloper possessed of a strange life-style and vague dreamy motives, one who produced nothing the community could taste or wear or drink. It has happened to other writing men in their rural habitats: to Faulkner in Oxford, to Wolfe in Ashville, to Sinclair Lewis in Sauk Centre, to Sherwood Anderson in "Winesburg" (Clyde), Ohio.

Watching Jesse Hill Ford in his daily peregrinations to the post office, or in his apparently aimless meanderings and random jottings, Humboldtians saw him as a vagabond loafer with no visible means of support save for his schoolteacher wife, Sally. The shopkeepers, agrarians, and clerks of West Tennessee, unaccustomed to the rhythms of a writing man's life, the silent introspections indigenous to his craft, saw only that Jesse Hill Ford looked idle.

Idle he was not. Ford wrote out of the rear office of a clinic operated by his father-in-law, Dr. Charles Davis, who for more than thirty years had attended Humboldt's births, deaths, and recoveries.

He was writing from his own dark, private vision of the town itself, exposing in his short stories and novels its warts and prejudices, its greeds and xenophobia, its secret couplings and official deceptions. Not many understood that Ford loved it—as Faulkner said of the South—"not because of but despite" its crazy contortions, secret broodings, and savage eruptions.

*The Liberation of Lord Byron Jones,* published in 1965, outraged and shocked the town as nothing before. Not that many Humboldtians read the book (even though it became a Book-of-the-Month Club selection), for the West Tennessee village is more interested in its strawberry, cotton, and soybean crops, its feed mills and mop factories and fertilizer plants, its parties and civic clubs and duck-hunting opportunities than in the teachings or musings of literature. Word soon got around, however, that Ford's book was based upon an actual old community skeleton. In the book, as in life, a black undertaker suing his wife for divorce had the temerity to name a white policeman as her lover— and was brutally killed for it. It is the sort of sordid story people detest having told about themselves. Its main theme is that the Humboldts of this world are often cesspools of injustice, societies which honor form above substance, which deceive themselves and oppress others at great cost to their souls. Suddenly the story was in a big book for all the world to read. It was made into a movie—shot on location in Humboldt.

The book made Jesse Hill Ford about half wealthy. He established himself on the outskirts of Humboldt in a fine baronial house, Canterfield, plopped down on twenty-seven acres with a stocked pond, blooded horses, exotic dogs. But Ford's profiteering off the town's mute and buried past—as the town saw it—was another reason for rancor. So it was that more than one citizen whooped in glee or permitted a hidden smile on a moonless, frosty evening in mid-November 1970, when word began circulating through the sleepy streets: *Jesse Ford killed him a nigger out at his place tonight. . . .*

Humboldt is a town of ten thousand people (some thirty-five hundred of them black) and an undistinguished Main Street of gabled tin roofs adorned by one four-story "skyscraper." It sprawls fifty miles from the Mississippi River, dividing Tennessee from Arkansas, is in close proximity to a corner of Kentucky, and Memphis is only a ninety-minute drive away. Though freeways run near by and the same television shows reach Humboldt that benumb Los Angeles or Chicago, it remains as determinedly rural as a Clabber Girl Baking Powder sign tacked to an unpainted barn. It is one of the few remaining American places with deep roots, with a sense of continuity and family blood, and a long community memory.

But for all its Good Ole Boys, folksy habits, and country pleasures, Humboldt has problems, old problems, which it has been reluctant to solve or even to mitigate. It is, and has been, backward in its racial solutions, alternating between white paternalism and pure red-neckery. Local officials, asked to make things a bit more tolerable for blacks, have traditionally crayfished or fought in court or called for the paddy wagons. The people say "nigger" or "nigguahs" or—in attempting to pacify visiting Yankees—"nigra" or "colored folks." These terms are not unknown in Ford's own house, though he rarely is the one to use them.

Jesse Hill Ford's books have captured the absurdities of Humboldt's attempts to maintain hard-line segregation: the druggist who removed his soda fountain rather than serve blacks, the white parsons who refuse to meet with their black counterparts in the Lord's work, the arrests of blacks peacefully picketing chain stores for job opportunities, the double standards at play in the courts or even in the bedroom where white men may surreptitiously join with black women—though a special dishonor, and maybe death, awaits the couple going at it the other way around. People walk softly in Humboldt when racial fevers run high.

During the filming of *Liberation*, Lloyd Adams, a Humboldt attorney with generations-old community roots, hosted a house party for members of the integrated cast and local people—both black and white. A lot of people thought that Lloyd and Bettye Rose had lost their cotton-picking minds. Among the many whites who did not attend was Jesse Hill Ford. In deciding to honor local custom he said, "There's a difference between morals and mores." It was a careful party, liquorless by plan, an orgy of pie and coffee, with a patio recitation of Shakespeare by the black leading man, Roscoe Brown, climaxing the debauchery. Even so, Humboldt police received a number of demands that the revelers be jailed.

In the fall of 1970, under federal court orders, Humboldt reluctantly integrated its schools. The transition was troublesome and hectic. Blacks lost their high school and all its traditions. All social functions—proms, plays, school dances—were quickly abandoned. Eventually all black players on the football team were dismissed when they failed to appear for a practice session as a protest against what they thought was discrimination on the part of the white coach.

Black resentments centered on Jesse Ford's seventeen-year-old son, Charles, captain of the football team and an all-state halfback (now a freshman starter at Furman University) who had replaced a black halfback thought spectacular the year before. Charles Ford began receiving threatening phone calls; during the homecoming parade downtown—on the Friday before his father would fatally shoot a black man—some blacks threw stones at the car in which Charles was riding.

For some time, Jesse Ford later would attest, his family had experienced a series of small desultory harassments—obscene telephone calls, "unidentified people who'd drive up and scare us," garbage strewn across his lawn—which accelerated when the movie version of *Liberation* played in the local theater. But with the troubled opening of school last fall, those harassments—which presumably had been the work of whites—assumed a curious inversion: they began coming from blacks. And where *Liberation* had once drawn only white ire, young blacks now charged that it castrated black males, made sluts and parasites of black women, defamed and misrepresented blacks in general.

Jesse Ford long has been preoccupied with violence. His writing is replete with tales of ambush, betrayals, trickery, murder, mutilations. Nor have all his thoughts on those subjects been confined to the page. While building Canterfield, he read Truman Capote's *In Cold Blood*—the story of a Kansas family slaughtered in their beds—and had the home redesigned to provide clear fields of fire in all directions. Trees were felled, leaving the house standing on an open plain, looking a bit scraped and raw. Each family member was assigned a window from which to defend. "Somebody might break in here," Ford said, "but they wouldn't get out. We've got guns and we all know our jobs." Five giant mastiffs, weighing up to 175 pounds, huge beasts with great crunching jaws—of a type trained to hunt *lions* now, in Africa— patrolled the Ford acres. Signs on the approach road warned against trespassing. Heavy iron grillework protected the front door. Fort Ford.

On the night of November 16, 1970—a Monday—at approximately ten o'clock, Sally Ford heard a car circle the front driveway. It then took a sharp turn on the approach road, pulled off on the grass near a small clump of trees, and parked—facing away from the house, facing toward anyone who might try to reach the house. Sally woke her sleeping husband: "Jesse, I don't think that's Charles."

Charles was studying at the home of a girl friend. His father— later insisting that the unidentified car was in perfect ambush position—felt a premonition of fear for his son. Jesse Ford had himself twice dreamed of being pursued through his own house and shot in the head, "exploding into a dark nothingness, and then I would wake up." These thoughts flashed briefly as he pulled on a jump suit and a light jacket and loaded a deer rifle. He moved swiftly across the grass, on a blind and moonless and frosty night, toward the now-darkened car.

"I fired a warning shot in the air. Nothing happened. I mean, just *no* reaction. I went closer and banged on the car trunk with the rifle butt and yelled, 'Get out with your hands up, I've called the police!'

"The car started moving away. Just *lunged* away. I snapped the rifle up and fired—not to kill anybody, I didn't even aim the gun. But goddammit, my family had been harassed and threatened and I was damn sick and tired of it. I was *determined* to stop that car! I had to know what was happening here.

"All of a sudden the car stopped. Just stopped. The lights were still on, you know, and the motor was still running, but there wasn't a *sound* from inside. Nothing. I thought, *Oh, my God— something's wrong. Something's happened.* Then, all of a sudden,

141

the side door flies open—*blam!*—and this girl with a little child is running like hell down the road. I thought, *My God, is this a family? What have I done?*

"I ran back up to the house and told Sally, 'Sally, I think I just shot somebody.' After a while the ambulance got here and the police came up to the house and asked me, 'Did you shoot at 'em?' I said, 'Yes. Didn't anybody get hurt down there, did they?' And they said, 'Looks like that fella is in pretty bad shape.' And I said, 'Oh, my God! Oh, my God!' I never went back down there to the car. Never saw the fella. . . .'"

Ford's random shot had killed George H. Doakes, a twenty-one-year-old black soldier from nearby Trenton who eleven days earlier had come to Humboldt to marry the mother of his infant daughter. His companion—the young woman Jesse Ford had seen bolt from the car and clatter down the road—was his sixteen-year-old second cousin, Allie V. Andrews, in the company of a four-year-old girl she was baby-sitting when Doakes picked her up, ostensibly to get a hamburger. "After the second shot," Allie Andrews remembers, "he just said, 'Ah.' I felt blood . . . his head fell on my shoulder." Doakes's body was found sprawled across the front seat, his trousers gathered loosely around his knees. He was as dead as Lord Byron Jones, the right side of his head blown away.

The next morning Jesse Hill Ford heard on his car radio that he would be charged with first-degree murder—Murder One. He seemed trapped in the most airless holes of his darker literary plumbings: a victim stepping out of his own pages.

Through the months from November to June, awaiting trial, Jesse Ford often seemed to regard the disaster as some capricious and malicious vandalism of fate against the ordered pattern of his life. He insisted that prosecuting attorneys were proceeding against him with unusual vigor just because he was who he was, or out of some vague, ill-defined conspiracy. At such moments it seemed impossible to rhyme him with his work.

As if sensing this, Ford offered explanations to the clots of friends, newsmen, and visiting journalists he almost constantly entertained—and somehow desperately seemed to need. Presid-

142

ing over Canterfield with its groaning feasts and well-stocked liquor cache, he often said, "Look, I didn't want that fella dead. I wish to God he were alive now. I'd shoot off my own leg. But we've gotten tough about this whole thing because we've *had* to. I'm in a bad situation, it's a nightmare, and I've just got to get through it. And until I do, by God, I can't afford to have any human feelings." Yet sometimes the guard came down. He was given in random moments to fits of weeping. It might happen as he read aloud, played the piano, or gazed with sightless Orphan-Annie eyes across the dead winter fields toward the barns and stables. These attacks were like small repeated shatterings of some fragile inner glass.

He seemed indeed a man of many parts: a man of many conflicting truths, each of which he believed deeply in odd moments but none of which he could trust the day through.

One could see in him the two contrasting law partners [in *Liberation*]—hear, at once, the voice of young lawyer Steve Mudine, who argued passionately for an abstract, perfect justice, and likewise hear the voice of the older lawyer, Oman Hedgepath, so bent on preserving the Old South status quo that he lent himself to the protection of a murderer. Contrasting forces and ideas appeared to bang around inside Ford's head, colliding like bumper cars at a carnival, yet he seemed unaware of these repeated collisions. In one moment he might sound as crass and brassy as a bell; in another, he would weep at the sight of one of his mastiffs—bloody and groggy after a Caesarian birth—and deliver a sensitive, agonized discourse on man's fear of the dark and mysterious pits of unconsciousness.

It is not unusual for imaginative writing men—who can create their own private worlds—to sometimes lose touch with the world they and the rest of us live in, nor is it unique for men in private stress to fluctuate wildly in their emotions. Ford had a double dose: he was a writing man in private stress.

In some curious near-tribal way, Ford now appeared to draw closer to the town he had so summarily judged in his books. Even to defend it. "What I've liked about living in Humboldt," he said, "is there just isn't all that convoluted inbred literary discussion going on around you all the time. Somebody will find out

I've had a novel or short story published and they'll say, 'I heard you sold an article. That's good. I sold a tractor today myself.'"

But while he may actually have entertained this whimsy, the difficulty was that he didn't deal in tractors or shingles or even hospital insurance. His was a more private enterprise, and it gave him a manner more remote, the air of someone secretly practicing witchcraft. In a local pool hall–café, the proprietor, leaning on the counter under a Double Cola sign and swatting a flyswatter against his khakis, said, over the click and nicks of cue balls, "Damn, I don't know, the man's just different. Keepin' to hisself all the time, stuff like that. He acts real funny sometimes. Only time he ever come in here, I never could figger out what it was for, but I sat talking with him for it must've been two hours and he used words, you know, I didn't understand half of 'em. And I know I ain't all that ignorant." A lawyer friend recalled that in his infrequent visits to the country club Ford would "just sort of barge around real noisy and clumsy for a little while, or sit off at a table kind of stiff, and be gone again." Someone else remembered Ford's odd transports after being issued a traffic ticket for easing through a stop sign: ". . . and, sonuvabitch, for *three weeks* after that he was going around taking down license numbers of other folks he saw going through stop signs."

A local business mogul, one of those driven men who live in the big white house on the hill and devote their life's breath to the dogged accumulation of wealth and power—and who, a few weeks after the killing, would call in eighteen thousand dollars in notes Ford owed the bank—said, "He just *tries* to be peculiar. He's brought black marks on this town, writing all that trash. He hasn't even *tried* to fit in here."

Yet, in his darkest hour, the white community seemed to rally to Ford and he to it. He entertained more than formerly, plunged into beer joints and coffee shops and wrung hands on the street "almost as if running for office," one observer would say. He moved, now, with an entourage: people who had not read his books, for the most part, and some few who once had damned them. A journalist who had long admired Ford's work, and who grew close to him in adversity, alternately wondered whether Ford might be conducting a clever campaign designed to produce a friendly jury or whether—in his great and private confusion, concern, and need—he simply and quite desperately coveted the touch of humanity's hand.

Humboldt's black community originally had expected Ford to be acquitted: white jurors would see it as just another nigger killing, no cause for alarm. But in the spring a Humboldt policeman —acting on a case of mistaken identity—attempted to arrest a black man at a café near The Crossing, that place where the railroad tracks divide Uptown from Niggertown. The black man fought back, an angry crowd collected, a mini-riot ensued. For the first time, Humboldt's blacks broke windows, looted, and shouted. "It scared ole whitey to death," a young black educator later would say, grinning. "We decided maybe Jesse Ford might be convicted after all. We didn't think whitey dared let him go after that. We thought they might make a little sacrificial offering." Indeed, for the first time Humboldt officialdom began to make small surrenders: the city council was reorganized by precincts to assure the election of one black, a biracial committee magically sprouted forth from the chamber of commerce, a young black group gained the unaccustomed use of public buildings, the school colors of defunct Stegall High, which had been the black school, were resurrected for assimilation by Humboldt High. Little things, yes, but more than had gone before. "What Ford's trial will prove," a local black said, "is whether he is more unpopular than we are. I've got to think they'll at least slap his wrists."

And, in June, Jesse Hill Ford was found not guilty of Murder One. And not guilty of unpremeditated murder. Not guilty, even, of involuntary manslaughter. The jury was composed of eleven whites and a lone black.

Almost everyone has an explanation for why Jesse Ford went free. Down at The Crossing they say, "The dude killed a nigger," shrugging away all mystery. In a beer joint where the jukebox bleats hillbilly laments of unrequited love and truck-driving fools and whisky widows, a white bartender, sucking a toothpick, says, "That nigger boy had no business slippin' around old Jesse's place like that. He flat couldn't-a been up to no good, and he mighta been up to real mischief."

Others say the prosecution was awkward: while disputing whether Ford had his place properly posted against trespass, the prosecution introduced into evidence a photograph of George Doakes's body that revealed quite clearly a large "posted" notice on a nearby telephone pole. Though claiming Ford fired only one shot, not an additional warning shot as the defense alleged, the state somehow admitted to having found *three* spent shells from Ford's deer rifle.

Jerry Cox is a twenty-one-year-old prelaw student at Lambuth College in Jackson, a rising leader among local blacks, and hopes to be Humboldt's first lawyer of his race. "Frankly," he says, "I didn't trust either side. Probably the defense attorney and the prosecuting attorney are cousins; that's the way it works down here. But, you know, I thought they might give Ford a suspended sentence.

"Ford had that book going against him with whites, but when it comes to push or shove the white folks stick together. That book—as a black man, I loved it and I hated it. Because it was true. After I read it, that old murder of Lord Byron Jones came back to me. I remember asking about it as a kid, and all the Uncle Toms said, 'Shhh, boy, don't ask no questions.' After reading it, I wanted to *get* those cats. But that book's not just about this town. It's about the whole stinking society. Not many whites would have written it, I give Ford that. I didn't get this light color in a crackerjack box, you know. Ford told it like it was. I had real mixed feelings about what I wanted to happen to that dude.

"Will his acquittal cause more trouble here? Hard to say. I think among the younger kids—teen-agers—it had a pretty big impact. One more lesson from whitey: niggers don't count, not even their lives."

Late in October, nearly a year after the shooting, a bulb-nosed little man who served on Ford's jury explained the jury's thinking. "We just didn't believe the state's witnesses," he said. "That Andrews gal, she couldn't explain what they were doing there. Said they had got lost and—well, we saw those pictures with that boy's britches down. Naw, we didn't take old Jesse's ambush

146

theory too much to heart. Oh, I think *he* believed it but—excuse me, Jesse—it seemed a little farfetched.

"The law's clear: if Jesse believed that he or any member of his family was in imminent danger, then he had a right to shoot. We thought those threatening calls could account for the fear in him. And then, too, that little Andrews gal, she claimed to have seen Jesse right down to the color of his jacket and his hair. Well, there was just *no way*, dark as the night was and him staying out of the headlights."

"She saw me in the light when she came back with the police," Ford injected. "We proved that in court."

"Well," the juror said, "we didn't intend to let 'em railroad you, Jesse."

The conversation was taking place in Ford's kitchen around a big round table just at dusk. Outside, one could observe the roisterings of giant mastiffs. Down at the entry to Ford's property stood a half-completed stone gatehouse. It will feature iron grillework, electronic controls, and a two-way intercom connected to the main house. Sally sometimes jokes that the gatehouse represents "locking the barn door after the horse got out."

The juror, who had reddish hair and the round, comic face of a clown, leaned over and grinned. "Hell, Jesse, they couldn't have found a jury in all these woods that would have convicted you."

"No, now, I don't know," Ford said, disturbed. "I mean, Bernie, come on, they *tried*. The bastards really *did*. The state wanted to convict me real bad. We won it on merit, now. This thing has cost me thirty thousand dollars in real money and Lord knows how much in lecture fees. I lost nearly a year's work, Bernie. Hell, I went broke . . ."

Later that evening, well liquored, Ford retraced the fatal night as he had so many times before. He seems to discuss it almost compulsively, displaying an amazing patience with prying journalists. "Hell," he said in benediction, "I was protecting *my family, my home*. Why can't people understand that? Hindsight's wonderful; but it doesn't allow for the passions and adrenalines and fears of the moment.

"Let me tell you, when you're indicted by the state, facing the state's millions and its buckles and guns, and the helicopters they fly over your place taking pictures for evidence, and when you face their battery of lawyers and investigators *and know they've got it in for you*—buddy, you'd better find out who's gonna try you, what their case is, and how you can counteract. You're on trial for your *life*, your *freedom*, your *property*. The man who fails to understand that, and to conduct his defense accordingly, he's gonna be hung for a fool.

"I don't see any betrayal of my values, or that I profaned my work, no sir! When you're up against the nitty-gritty, the name of the game is *win*. Why should I be expected to roll over and play dead for the state? The trouble these days is that people think that anything that's black is automatically beautiful. Well, they're just *people* to me—like the rest of us, hell, that's the whole point of my work—and I'm not gonna treat 'em like Brahmins.

"If the rest of this country ever succeeds in the total alienation of the white South, God help it. Who's gonna keep the store? We educate and export our best people. What if *all* of us left? This is the breadbasket of the nation down here."

He lurched to his feet and poured another drink, eyes marble-like, hard gray agates, his round face somehow flat like a pie pan. "I'm sorry as I can *be*, goddammit, but I don't thresh around at night moaning 'God forgive me, I killed a man.' It was a . . . a tragic *accident*, but you can't linger over it forever."

There had been numerous racial incidents in Humboldt recently: a gang fight at a local drive-in, whites writing "Niggers go home," blacks stoning whites. Did Ford think his act had harmed race relations in the community?

"How could it? No race relations to speak of to begin with. It may have even helped. That sounds funny, I guess. But there's a fella here's got a pond, and some blacks had been swimming in it without permission—on his *private property* now—and when he told 'em to move on, they'd just laugh or give him lip. After I shot that fella, by God, he didn't have to tell 'em not to swim there any more. They stayed away.

"If anything has harmed race relations here it's been those snot-nosed kids fresh from law school, those HEW and Justice Department hotshots. We've got a school superintendent trying to make integrated schools work, and all he hears is threats and intimidations from Washington. They should get off his back.

"Anybody can get on a soap box. I work quietly. Maybe once every three years I can say to some ole boy down here, 'Do you *really* believe a Negro is less than human?' and he'll study about it and say, 'Naw, not really.' Well, that helps a little. You stay in there with 'em, you hang on, you chip away, do what you can.

"The race thing is complicated down here. Its roots go deep in history and blood. You won't change it overnight. Right now the races are more hostile to each other than they've ever been. The politicians told everybody to expect instant brotherhood, got their expectations up, told 'em the problem was solved when a few civil rights bills passed. Hell, we haven't even scratched the surface."

The talk switched back to the Doakes case again, became repetitious, and everyone began to talk a little louder, wave their arms more, take on a whisky flush. Ford fell silent, brooding, and suddenly said, "You can know what's happened to you, you know, without really understanding it." Then, quite abruptly, he padded upstairs to bed.

On a Saturday afternoon, Ford drove three visiting journalists and a photographer on a tour of Humboldt. At the railroad tracks—The Crossing—photographer Jim Karales was enchanted by a collection of old black men, dressed in the rags and tatters of the country poor, sunning on long benches. He insisted on stopping, despite a nervous reluctance on the part of the journalists, who did not think it prudent for Ford to flaunt himself in black precincts. "These people won't hurt you," Ford reassured. "They're good folks, most of 'em."

Soon, however, Ford hummed and jangled with his own tensions. He drove around the block slowly, worry in his eyes. He parked on a vacant area near the railroad tracks. "These people don't like this," one journalist blurted. "They consider it 'looking at the monkeys.'" Nobody said anything. There were quick, darting sippings of beer. Ford spoke softly, as if fearing that his voice might carry: "Isn't it terrible when a man has to be afraid in his own country?"

Karales continued to snap away, apparently oblivious to the building tensions and the gathering crowd. Where earlier there had been only the old men sunning their bones and exchanging Saturday marketplace gossip, there now appeared young men with swagger in their steps, Afro-haired and dressed in the colorful garb of street dudes or hustlers. "Hey,    an," one hard-eye ordered, "take my picture." Karales obliged. "What you cats up to, man?" another demanded. Suddenly, a young black man pulled his car alongside Ford's vehicle and silently stared into his eyes. Pure hate was there. Then he spun off, tires slinging gravel. Now blacks were pouring into the streets, eyeballing Ford's vehicle: dry, hot electricity crackled. Abruptly the black man who had departed in a spray of gravel reappeared—with three other young blacks in his car. They got out as if to approach Ford's car.

Ford called to the photographer, "Get in the car, Jim!"

Karales, true to his breed, begged, "Just one more."

Ford began shouting: "Get in the car! Get in the car! Goddammit, *get in the car or I'll leave your ass!*" Startled, Karales jumped in just as a police car, attracted by the commotion, roared up. Ford accelerated rapidly, turning back across the tracks to safely white precincts. One had seen, briefly and terribly, a flash of the panic and fear that had prompted him to snap off that fatal shot almost a year earlier. Had felt, too, something of the tensions he had been living under and realized that no man who has not been through them could judge what he might do in the same circumstance.

Ford monitored the rearview mirror. "I don't like this. There's a car following us, and I don't know who's in it. There have been threats on my life from the blacks since this thing." He quickly pulled in to a service-station lot, permitting the mystery car to go harmlessly past.

"I just don't come to town any more," Ford said. "Right after my trial, I went in a beer joint and a guy who looked like a redneck that had worked his way up to white collar jumped me: 'If it had been me, Mr. Big Shot, I'd be doing time.' I said, 'Goddammit, am I gonna have to fight some sonuvabitch every time I go out in my hometown for the rest of my life?' Well, the owner of the bar threw the guy out, but I decided right then, by God, just not to expose myself any more."

He remains in the big barred house, working until midafternoon. Then, walking in a surge and roll of mastiffs, he fishes his stocked pond, swims, perhaps rides. On weekends, usually, several Humboldt couples come in and there is a great deal of laughter (Ford's exploding without warning, crashing about like fragments of the concussion bomb he carries in his legs). There are jokes and light conversation about inconsequential things. It is pleasant enough, but to the outside observer it seems a bit feverish, sometimes forced, and maybe it is a form of therapy. "I'm happy," Ford often says on such occasions, hugging Sally or one of the children. "I'm working well now, and things are leveling out. I'm real, real happy."

After the company has gone and the family is in bed, Ford may sit staring into a cold marble unlighted fireplace, drinking, alone out there somewhere at the edge of his mind where nobody can follow, where no journalist can probe, where no one can demand that he explain—once again—that which really is unexplainable.

*Today's Health*
DECEMBER 1971

# THE POLITICAL
# ARENA

hese two political stories furnish examples of the opposite poles of reporting technique. "The Road to Power in Congress" represents more than eight weeks of interviews with dozens of congressmen, Capitol Hill employees, lobbyists, newsmen, and political hangers-on indigenous to the halls of power; all 254 House Democrats were polled, after the majority leader election, to determine why they had voted as they did. (About 45 per cent responded.) The object was to show how a national institution conducts itself in its inner tickings; to go behind the dry press résumés that the South went for this candidate or the liberals for that one. Conversely, "Goodnight Chet, Goodnight David, Goodnight Rosemarie" required only a few hours of ogling television —and my wife's fine, stoned commentary. Originally I was to have covered one of the major 1968 political conventions for *Harper's;* David Halberstam was to staff the other. At the last moment, however, Norman Mailer became available for both chores (resulting in his fascinating book, *Miami and the Siege of Chicago*), thus leaving the King-Halberstam duo idle in front of their boob tubes. Watching the GOP convention, I began making notes out of habit and for my own amusement; they turned into the short piece included here.

# The Road to Power in Congress

NOT ALL THE WORLD knows the importance of becoming House majority leader. The odds and traditions virtually assure that one sweet day the majority leader will become speaker—and that is the point where they begin naming massive office buildings after you, marble edifices costing many millions and housing thousands, as they did for Sam Rayburn, Nicholas Longworth, Uncle Joe Cannon. The majority leader—i.e., the future speaker—knows in that green glade where the ego blooms that he shall leave behind a well-marked grave.

In his own right, the House majority leader is a king among dukes and princes. The job is limiting only to the extent that the man holding it invokes limitations—or, perhaps, that a strong speaker may. His is the opportunity to push his party's or his president's programs through Congress, or to ambush those of the opposition. He advises his party's committee-on-committees in its vital selections. He transmits to the president his party's viewpoint or leanings in the House, bringing back direct word of the president's mood. He is assaulted by cameras and questions and has difficulty staying out of the newspapers.

The majority leader influences when specific legislation will be debated, and in what form or under what rules. He has countless favors to bestow, making the calling of debts most pleasant. He is paid $5000 more in salaries than the $42,500 going to common garden-variety congressmen and is provided enough staff hire, operating expenses, and fringe benefits to delight middling emperors. Where lesser congressmen are limited to look-alike suites in one of the three House office buildings, he is assigned commodious Capitol Building quarters with impressive chandeliers,

153

thick carpets, and scenic views. He is hauled around in a sleek limousine, stationed hard by the Capitol steps no matter the parking problems of mortals, over which uniformed policemen stand guard. A little luck, and some years he can help make a president.

Above all, the office is a vital affirmation. If politicians are any one thing they are egotists. Were they not natural competitors they would not be drawn to lives of wars with short knives. And they are visionaries or schemers, complex men, warmed like the rest of us by cheers from the crowd. The possibility of defeat—of public rejection—is at once the fate they fear most and the hag with whom they must live.

Most of the 435 men and women in the House are unhappy in varying degrees. Some few are thrilled by the miracle permitting them to be called congressman, content to sit in the back row and wait; a fair number are able to trim back their ambitions along with their visions and faithfully apply themselves to drudgery. Often, however, the deadening processes begin: plagues of intellectual dry rot, a certain institutional humdrumism, or a general malaise. Many proclaim themselves happy and fulfilled, not minding—so they say—their slow upward inchings on committees while becoming experts in matters of federal contracts or public roads. You may believe some of them. Catch others drunk, however, and they make liars of themselves in singing sad songs of depleting losses: their youth, golden opportunities, hope, and pride.

Little wonder, then, that any internal election may unsheathe the sharpest blades, or that the majority leader's prerogatives are so desperately coveted—or, even, that men who themselves have no hope of receiving the honor may prove reluctant to pass it on.

Morris (Mo) Udall arrived in Congress from Arizona's horse latitudes in 1961, replacing his brother, Stewart, who had become secretary of the interior for John F. Kennedy. The Udalls are an old political family, furnishing Arizona with legislators and judges, and before Mo was out of grammar school in St. Johns village (where he lost an eye in a childhood accident) he was thinking of the law and Congress. He was not, however, the kind of boy who might be delighted with a black briefcase for Christmas. He enjoyed the small-town diversions of the place and period: the rodeos, Halloween pranks, and old jalopy cruisings. Though he was an outstanding athlete and honor student, his Mormon parents worried over a "wild streak" because he drank an occasional beer and harbored a casual appreciation of doctrines. Discharged an air force captain after World War II service in the Pacific (he somehow smuggled the blind eye past military physicians), he entered the University of Arizona in pursuit of a law degree. After graduation he joined brother Stew in practice, and in 1952 was elected prosecuting attorney of Pima County. In 1954 Stew claimed his right as elder son to grab the only available congressional seat. Mo wrote a textbook on Arizona law and campaigned for John F. Kennedy. When Stew joined Kennedy's cabinet, Mo easily won election to succeed him.

He was then a month short of thirty-nine and looked something like a rodeo hand in short burr haircuts, bow ties, and a wide leather belt studded with ersatz stones with a silver buckle; there was about him a disconcerting combination of painful country-boy shyness and a bawdy cow-lot humor. He had played a vital role with brother Stew in pirating Arizona's Democratic delegates away from an astonished Lyndon Johnson in 1960, delivering them to JFK, so he could not have been pure green gourd and hayseed—though on arrival he wrote a letter of impossible length and complexity to Speaker Sam Rayburn, a man congenitally offended by a single word when grunts or smoke signals might do, ending with an open offer to discuss the world's failings and solutions. Udall's assumption—that he mattered more to Washington than the realities—is a common freshman malady.

He campaigned successfully for a seat on the House Interior Committee, not because it excited his soul but because an upcoming water project vital to Arizona would be processed there. He was named to the Post Office Committee, not because he might invent the zip code but because a Democratic vacancy existed and he was an available freshman. In Congress, New York

City freshmen sometimes land on Agriculture, while newcomers from cornfield Nebraska somehow achieve Merchant Marine and Fisheries.

Udall became an activist in the liberal Democratic Study Group, an internal organization much suspected by the old House bulls. He slowly earned laurels as a serious legislator and witty speaker who knew the parliamentary backwaters. If perhaps a shade brighter or a touch more ambitious than the average junior, he was not yet atypical: he paid deference to his elders and kept his institutional nose clean.

Yet a storm was forming. He was being exposed to the more restless personalities of the House, the young liberals of their day, and was beginning to agree that reforms were required against ailing and standpat old committee chieftains—against group inertia, foot-dragging procedures, and built-in slumbers.

By late 1968 Mo Udall was a different breed than he had been eight years earlier. A new wife, Ella, had vastly improved his wardrobe and tonsorial habits, though you had to get inside his head to discover that coyotes now howled in his soul. He had seen Gene McCarthy and Lee Metcalf, despairing of House reforms, go off to the Senate, while others quit to run for governor or mayor. He had seen the coming of the age of protest and had observed Congress fiddling while the nation burned. He knew that when Congressman Richard Bolling of Missouri had become too critical of House procedures, he had plummeted from being a favored Sam Rayburn protégé to becoming an outcast whose name caused the old bulls to snort and choke.

Udall learned something of the mixed political blessings and dangers. When the House appeared determined to expel Harlem's Adam Clayton Powell for his flamboyant excesses, Udall devised a plan to strip Powell's seniority while allowing him to retain his seat. This solution removed many from behind the eight ball, not the least of whom was Congressman Powell, who —after throwing his arms around his benefactor in gratitude— walked to the Capitol steps where, in front of television cameras and busloads of his angry Harlem subjects, he branded Mo Udall a "Mormon racist." In 1967, before it became fashionable, Udall declared the Vietnam war a major miscalculation, admitted his own error in having originally supported it, and urged others to recant. This inspired LBJ to charge his secretary of the interior with an inability to prevent unreason in the immediate family and aroused congressional hawks.

Udall wrote critically in national publications of the seniority system, of loose and deceptive campaign laws, of unsupervised lobbyists, of general congressional anemia and harmful fuddy-duddyisms. He knew he might forfeit the smiles of House elders, but for all the institutional chill there was a counterwarming: young House liberals looked more and more to Udall as their natural spokesman, and perhaps here he saw his first private visions of power.

Democrats in late 1968, following the fratricides of Chicago, appeared hopelessly divided. The White House had been lost to yesteryear's reject; the Democratic National Committee had been reduced to bones by Lyndon Johnson. The congressional wing did not show to advantage on television when represented by the mild, pipe-sucking homilies of Senate Majority Leader Mike Mansfield or the fading bombast of Speaker John McCormack, at seventy-seven gaunt and white-haired and acting on memory. "When I came here," Udall told intimates, "House Republicans were the old guys and Democrats wore the bright young faces. Now it's the other way around." Speaker McCormack had long been criticized for ineffectual leadership, but the House has never been noted for killing its kings. Few dreamed that anyone might challenge the Old Speaker.

On Christmas Eve Day, 1968, Mo Udall telephoned Old John McCormack in South Boston to announce that after only eight years in the back row he would run against him when the Democrats caucused in January. It was difficult, because the old man kept hoo-hawing season's greetings. "I finally took a deep breath," Udall says, "and told him. He did not keep me on the line long."

Udall sent out an eight-page single-spaced letter to House Democrats. For all its diplomatic language, it could not have brightened the Old Speaker's New Year. Should he win—Udall wrote—he would step aside to allow a *second* election permitting congressmen more freely to vote their hearts once the giant had been slain. There was much of personal conviction in it, the demands of the times, and other high-minded soundings. Old John McCormack may not have bothered to read it all, and if he did, it likely registered as superfluous information or as the ravings of an organizational madman: how does an old man of seventy-seven, who has campaigned funeral trains, understand a young one who pledges to surrender the spoils unused?

Old John McCormack had risen through the ranks, where you were loyal to the block captain past his death. As with all instinctive partisans or doctrinaires, he abhorred deviation or fratricide. He had learned as a young and disadvantaged South Boston Irishman that lesson of tribal truth common to all who must fight group oppression or exclusion: solidarity above all. He was a natural product of ward politics, a poor boy who had left school in the eighth grade to sustain a widowed mother by working for four dollars weekly in a law office; at night he "read law" to prepare for the bar exam. As with so many ambitious South Boston products who had no opportunity to become priests or prize fighters, he made the earliest possible connection with the Democratic party. You did not need to be Harvard or rich to thrive in The Organization—merely loyal, persistent, and a little lucky. The old man could no more comprehend Mo Udall's symbolic candidacy than an orangutan would be capable of grasping the concept of infinity.

Mo Udall went to the Democratic caucus in January of 1969 counting on a respectable 81 votes, the number he interpreted as honorably pledged. The secret ballot, however, went against him a thumping 178 to 58. This did not prevent maybe a hundred statesmen from later seeking out Udall to whisper that they had stubbornly stayed hitched.

Visiting Arizona one night, Udall confided to a newsman that amnesty was not one of McCormack's virtues. A few days later, approaching the House chamber, he was confronted by the speaker. "Maurice," the old man said—he always South-Boston-ized Udall's name to "Maurice U—dahl"—"I want to shake your hand." Udall inquired as to the honor's purpose. The old man was sadly reproving. "Well, Maurice, I received a clipping quoting you that I won't shake your hand." No, Udall said, he had referred only to certain of the speaker's supporters. "Why, Maurice, *who* said that?" Udall mumbled, scuffed the marble floor, and wished a quick deliverance. "Maurice," Old John ultimately offered, "let bygones be bygones." Udall himself could not have suggested a better deal. They traded reassurances of mutual high regard, the speaker disavowing any wish to extract reprisals. Mo Udall remembers a giddy euphoria. Outside of official receiving lines that was the last time John McCormack offered to shake his hand.

Rumblings in early 1970 had Udall again contesting the speaker. Udall had maintained contact with his small cadre of true believers, and their hopes kept him viable in cloakroom and newspaper speculations. Publicly he said nothing.

Soon, however, the Old Speaker found himself in embarrassing waters. His friend and top staff assistant, Martin Sweig, was indicted for perjury. Another crony dating to South Boston days, an energetic little hustler named Nathan Voloshen—one of those political-fringe studies so darkly fascinating to Edwin O'Connor —had been convicted of influence peddling, often operating out of the speaker's office, on the speaker's private telephone, and, incredibly, even in the speaker's good name. No one suggested that Speaker McCormack had known of the improprieties. Old John was the next thing to a monk. Book a bet that if Old John ever accepted a questionable dime he promptly surrendered it to the Catholic Church: colleagues called him the "gentleman from Vatican City" behind his powerful back. But even the good and pious get old.

The old man had been in Congress forty-two years, since Morris Udall was six years old. For three decades he had been one of those fortunates who made the big wheel spin, fussed over by presidents and by retainers who wouldn't permit him to open his own doors or light his own cigars. Shortly before Sweig and Voloshen shot him down, the old man had announced (a full year ahead of the necessities) 167 pledges of renomination for speaker, which was many more than enough. We may be certain that Old John McCormack only reluctantly abdicated.

He concealed his bruises behind an old-world courtliness and florid rhetoric, always speaking well of the nation's institutions. These tricks were sufficient to see him through the obligatory testimonials inflicted by civilized people in turning their old bulls out to pasture, as if such charades might somehow green the retirement grass. Privately, however, he loosed his bile. He did not rail excessively against old associates who had betrayed him, or even against the kibitzings and meddlings of The Goddamned Press—which, as everyone on Capitol Hill knows, loves ruin and trouble above all other gifts. No, it was that damned fella "Maurice U-dahl"—*he* had started all the trouble back in '68. And he would whack his desk with the flat of a bony hand, wildly scattering ashes and public documents, growling like some wounded old lion.

Speaker McCormack's endorsement of Carl Albert as his successor was a popular choice. It also served tradition. Albert had shown a remarkable ability to climb the leadership ladder without stepping on fingers—no small skill. He had risen from a reddirt Oklahoma farm and a rural school called Bug Tussle to become a Rhodes scholar. His homefolks affectionately called him "The Little Giant" in tribute to his intellectual qualities and in recognition of his diminutive dimensions—at five feet four inches he was the shortest of congressmen. On Sam Rayburn's recommendation in 1955, Albert had been named majority whip—the third-ranking party slot in the House. Six years later, on Speaker Rayburn's death, Albert became majority leader when John McCormack ascended. The only question about Carl Albert was how tough he might be.

Some Udall red-hots insisted that he oppose Albert. "No," he said, "Carl's in line, he's respected, and I think he'll do a good job." There were protests: Albert was not a strong personality; he might easily be commanded by the old committee czars; an earlier heart attack may have robbed his vitality. Udall could not be persuaded. No, he would seek the number two job—and he would begin with an open endorsement of Carl Albert. "We didn't expect Carl to shout Udall's praises from the Washington Monument," a Udall adviser recalls, "but we did hope he might wink at somebody." Instead, Carl Albert proclaimed a hands-off policy: he would express not the slightest hint of a choice among majority leader aspirants.

Some read this decision as a backhanded swipe at Hale Boggs, the Louisiana congressman who had served nine years as House whip: "If Carl Albert wanted Boggs, all he'd have to do is lift a finger." In a body where what one does not say is often more important than the utterances, people are alert to small signals. Observing Albert and Boggs in their casual encounters became popular, and people vainly read the careful poker faces of Albert's closer Oklahoma colleagues.

Hale Boggs, for many, was open to interpretation. Elected to Congress from New Orleans in 1946 at thirty-two, he was now a ruddy-faced man gone a bit to suet and puddings. He dressed like a dandy by the timid House standards, running to sporty ties, colorful pocket handkerchiefs, and gay shirts. There was something of the old smoothie about him in a 1930-dance-band-leader sort of way—maybe the near-middle parting of the hair did it. At times he might appear wild or foolish: he had a high appreciation for good whisky, and even the best brands sometimes loosen tongues or inhibitions. Yet one sensed a hard core in the man, some sly, tough, intelligent power, an essence hinting that if times got hard and he had no other choice, then Hale Boggs might go on the road and very successfully sell lightning rods.

Hale Boggs, too, had been tapped for the cozy inner circle by Sam Rayburn. Rayburn felt a deep affinity for the House, a proprietary and paternal interest so urgent he seemed compulsively to seek sons worthy of carrying on past the father. The old man never selected a dummy in his life and was better than most in judging men for their organizational potential. When Rayburn died in 1961, Hale Boggs had served a long apprenticeship on the inside and was named majority whip.

He was no Tory or Dixiecrat. Boggs supported most New Frontier and Great Society programs, was generally friendly to labor, and, on the basis of cumulative voting records compiled by liberal organizations, scored a respectable 79 per cent to Udall's 86 per cent. Boggs was influential on the Ways and Means Committee, and he had served on the Warren Commission and as platform chairman of the 1968 Democratic National Convention.

By early 1970, however, Boggs had suffered slippage. His problems had begun a couple of years earlier. "Hale's personality seemed to change overnight," a Texan remembers. Often gregarious, once voted by Capitol Hill secretaries as the "most charming" solon, Boggs became by turns glacial and wildly exuberant; he might stalk by old friends without recognition. "He would rush on the floor just trembling with energy," a colleague recalls, "and there was *no way* you could shut him up. He made long-winded speeches, maybe brilliant in one sentence—great imagery, sophisticated language, all the oratorical thunders—and then the next sentence might be absolutely meaningless." Once, while the embarrassed Speaker McCormack gently tried to gavel him down, Boggs so heckled his own committee chairman, Wilbur Mills, that friends had to half lead him to the cloakroom. He held an improbable press conference of his own for more than two hours, alternately reading from news clippings, the Democratic platform, his personal-appointments book, and the Bible—interrupting himself to seat latecomers. After monopolizing a White House conference with a forty-minute monologue, he startled Richard Nixon by disappearing on the grounds that he had an "important appointment."

Such history caused Morris Udall to doubt whether Hale Boggs would emerge as his strongest opponent. Perhaps others were more dangerous: Thomas (Tip) O'Neill or Eddie Boland of Massachusetts, California's John Moss, Chicago's Dan Rostenkowski, Michigan's Jim O'Hara, maybe Brooklyn's Hugh Carey or other potentials. When Boggs passed around informal word of his candidacy, a number of Democrats snickered.

Early on, Boggs knew that he must show more dedication to duty. He renewed the garden parties for which he had become celebrated, elaborate functions sometimes attracting a thousand guests with Dixieland bands imported from New Orleans. Boggs circulated among his guests (heavily weighted toward House Democrats and their ladies) carefully sober and highly visible.

Old John McCormack officially disavowed taking sides, though he vacated the speaker's chair at the smallest opportunity to place Hale Boggs on display as presiding officer. He greeted Boggs with glad cries at social functions, plucking him from the masses to park him in receiving lines. Soon people began to take Hale Boggs seriously.

Udall began—months before his announcement—by reviewing other leadership fights. He was impressed by two studies, one written by Robert Peabody, a Johns Hopkins University political scientist, and one by Nelson W. Polsby of the University of California. Peabody's works treated Gerald Ford's 1965 upset of Charles Halleck for House minority leader; Polsby's study was of Carl Albert's careful preparation for becoming majority leader in 1961. Albert's campaign was so successful that his only challenger, Richard Bolling of Missouri, withdrew because, as he said, "I have no chance to win." Udall knew he was vulnerable to the charges that killed Bolling: he, too, had raised the hackles of senior members resentful of leapfrogging juniors.

Udall thought he had less a personality problem than Dick Bolling—less a reputation as an aloof loner. Bolling's evident brilliance (of which, perhaps, he sometimes seemed excessively aware) had not gone down well with many old congressional heads. There are valid reasons why one might guard against flaunting brilliance: not all congressmen are themselves blessed with superior mental equipment—they fancy their constituents to suspect intellectualism—and many are so conditioned to avoiding discussions exposing their philosophies to disagreements or disapproval that a vacuous smile is often preferred to the risking of profundity. Congressmen are instinctive social creatures, hand-crushers and hoo-hawers, so that a half dozen meeting for lunch may shout merry greetings and pound backs all around even though they shared morning coffee. Tribal instincts are at work; conduct not conforming is easily suspected.

Knowing these things, and mindful that Peabody's and Polsby's studies credited Gerry Ford and Carl Albert with helpful "good-guy" images, Udall took care to be an old-shoe regular. He knew that many well-placed seniors would not vote for him with guns at their heads, but he attempted to reduce their hostilities through the jokes, greetings, and small talk indigenous to the tribe; he showed he had no horns by playing paddle ball in the

House gym with his ideological opposites and through regular appearances at congressional prayer breakfasts.

Udall drew fifteen conclusions from Albert's success and nine from Ford's, circulating them among his loyalists. He would emulate Carl Albert in keeping his race an internal matter, i.e., he would not encourage outside organizational pressures as Bolling had, nor would he take his case to "Meet the Press," because he knew the House to be jealous of its internal prerogatives. Like Albert he would maintain "extensive personal contact"; if unsure of the senior man in a given delegation, he would begin with friendly juniors and work up. Like Gerry Ford in his winning Republican challenge, Udall would appeal to the frustrated bit players in the House by indicating that he would spread the power and glory around.

"A vital element in Ford's victory," Udall wrote his insiders, "was the fact that he had fifteen or twenty activists meeting almost hourly and into the night, checking, cross-checking. . . . The Ford supporters were able to contact everybody at least once. A number of Republicans never heard from Halleck, including at least two freshmen." This became the bedrock of Udall's effort: he would gather the maximum advocates and persuade them to work aggressively among the 255 House Democrats, keeping running totals of persons Solid for Udall, Leaning Udall, Unknown, Solid for Opponent, Leaning Opponent.

The Udall brothers, New Jersey's Frank Thompson, and Florida's Sam Gibbons began the roundup. Ultimately, thirty-odd active proselytizers were enrolled. Stew canvassed among former colleagues, including some who were sullen over Mo's attempts to leapfrog them. Special attention was given to old Wayne Aspinall of Colorado, chairman of the Interior Committee, in his seventies and occasionally touchy as a rattlesnake. Aspinall was thought to represent the best hope of bringing aboard one of the established senior powers, but he gave no immediate sign of commitment.

Udall also borrowed from Gerald Ford in campaigning among potential freshmen. Such men often are long shots and treated like stepchildren unknown to Washington's powers. Udall sought out these lonely grass-roots hopefuls, helpfully singing their accomplishments. Should they come to the Ninety-second Congress as new Democrats, they would be much in his debt.

Both Udall and Boggs came with built-in weaknesses. If Udall threatened tradition, Boggs might prove an erratic playboy. If Boggs had permitted a fat-cat builder to perform forty thousand dollars worth of improvements on his Bethesda home at a fraction of costs, then Udall was a "jack Mormon" who had married a Capitol Hill secretary the second time around. If Big Labor did not trust Morris Udall because he had voted against repeal of the right-to-work provision of Taft-Hartley, Big Oil newly suspected Hale Boggs because he had voted to reduce by 5 per cent the sacrosanct oil-depletion allowance. Dixiecrats shamed Boggs for his latter-day civil rights votes: "He did it," a Mississippian said, "so let him live with it." And of Udall a Massachusetts statesman shouted, "He ruined old John McCormack."

Udall's immediate worry was a third announced candidate, James G. O'Hara, a serious-minded liberal from Michigan. Few thought O'Hara could put it together, though everyone realized his basic appeal struck at the Udall core: those who were liberal, black, young, or otherwise disaffected. Labor preferred O'Hara over all others: if Chicago's Dan Rostenkowski was tagged "Daley's man," then O'Hara was thought of as "Reuther's man" or "Meany's man."

At forty-five, Jim O'Hara had a dozen quiet congressional years behind him. "I know I'm no personality guy," Jim O'Hara said. He was sitting behind his desk, eating brown cookies, drinking brown coffee, wearing brown shoes and brown hair. "If they decide it on charisma, I'm afraid I won't fare well. If they're looking for someone who's been active on the floor, in debate and so on, maybe I'll make it." O'Hara had had more time than most public men to read and reflect in the night, to wonder at the big purpose. Among his seven children are two small sons, hemophiliacs, who require constant attention and have astronomical medical bills.

The fact that Mo Udall liked and respected Jim O'Hara did not solve his problem: "I've got to blow in strong on the first ballot, and Jim O'Hara will take away votes." Feelers went out: if

O'Hara saw an early doom, would he withdraw in Udall's favor? Though there were multiple discussions among the two camps, this point would eventually provide massive misunderstandings.

Southerners continued to suspect Hale Boggs, leading to a talent search headed by old Bill Colmer, Mississippi's fiery octogenarian, by Florida's Robert Sikes (an oil, military, and National Rifle Association enthusiast), and by Omar Burleson of Texas, an ex-FBI agent who is personable and witty and owns the ideological instincts of the early primates. These veterans, all safely past sixty, sought a man made from bedrock, one more respectful of careful institutions. They selected Congressman B. F. Sisk, fifty-nine, from California's San Joaquin Valley, a land of small towns and rich farms—Rotary Club and Jaycee territory. Originally a moderate liberal, Bernie Sisk had grown increasingly conservative. Liberals complained that in executive sessions of the Rules Committee, where individual votes are not officially made public, Sisk was an outright reactionary.

When Sisk came to Congress in 1955, he had the weathered skin of his native Texas region and he looked like a road drummer stuck with Appalachian territory. By 1970 Bernie Sisk was wearing tasteful suits and manicured fingernails and reminded observers of a banker whose specialty was taking the sting out of loan refusals. "I'm low pressure," he said. "If I can't help a man, I won't hurt him. If I can't say something good about a colleague, I won't say anything. I've done a lot of favors here in fifteen years."

The fifth candidate was Wayne L. Hays, a Middle America conservative with the wispy gray hair and piercing blue eyes of a stern school superintendent. Hays represented a rurally oriented Ohio district, one with no city larger than sixty thousand, and boasted of being a "lifelong resident of Flushing." In Congress since 1949, he was a screaming hawk of the Foreign Affairs Committee and famed for his volatile eruptions both here and abroad. The word most frequently applied to Hays was "abrasive"—a description the Ohioan reviled as "one of those words like 'restructuring' or 'syndrome' that everybody uses without meaning a goddamn thing. They're just words of the moment. I'm a plain-spoken fella, and a lot can't stand the truth."

With no ideological or geographic unit claiming him, Congressman Hays appeared to have no natural base. Why had he declared? "Well, last summer when Hale Boggs was drinking and making a horse's ass of himself, he asked me to talk him up. I drew a blank. People didn't want him. They didn't want Udall and his bunch of clowns. I figured what the hell, it was wide open."

Newspaper stories early labeled him the certain tail-ender, causing him to sometimes sound rather . . . well, abrasive. When the five candidates assembled to establish caucus procedures, Hays said, "Listen, you bastards, I'll bet any one of you a hundred bucks I don't finish last." Everybody laughed, but nobody called the bet.

An early edge was Udall's. He was first in, better organized, more visible. Boggs seemed to have trouble untracking: there remained the nagging question of whether he suited Carl Albert. Had Udall been able to score a major breakthrough in November or early December, Boggs might have collapsed.*

A key factor was the Northeast Democrats. Udall knew New Yorkers to be generally indifferent to him, and Massachusetts remained cool out of loyalty to Old John McCormack. He made special efforts to land Brooklyn's Hugh Carey and Eddie Boland of Massachusetts, a Jack Kennedy favorite. Both were assumed to have special influence within their delegations. Udall soon judged Carey "extremely evasive"; Boland appeared friendlier but cautious.

Meanwhile the Northeast Democrats were searching their own ranks. Hale Boggs, seeking a breakthrough there, ardently courted Tip O'Neill, a tough fifty-seven-year-old liberal from Cambridge. Once speaker of the Massachusetts House, he had eighteen years in Congress and was well placed on the Rules Committee. Though O'Neill had a fine antipathy to Udall dating back to the McCormack challenge, he did not commit to Boggs: he was thinking of making his own race.

* A Georgia Congressman approached Udall during this period, asking whether he would accept the majority whip's role and run on a Boggs ticket. Udall declined.

Eddie Boland, as it turned out, was also bothered by ambition. He had cemented many friendships as a Jack Kennedy man in the glory days, he sang a pleasant baritone, served on Appropriations, and was known as a specialist in urban affairs. Boland went so far as to describe himself as an "unannounced candidate" and a "fallback choice" for liberals. Somehow, though, he would never put more than a toe in the water.

Another possible challenger was Dan Rostenkowski. At forty-two, chairman of the Democratic caucus and on the powerful Ways and Means Committee, he was assumed a certain additional clout as "Daley's man." A big man with a thick ex-athlete's body, Rostenkowski looked like a Marine DI and did not always warm quickly to strangers. Some contend that machine politics dull the personality or the political senses; if the theory holds, it probably numbers Rostenkowski among its victims. "Those southerners have a way of eating their young," he once told a newsman, pissing off every congressman south of Baltimore.

In early December Rostenkowski claimed "a number of people who have said, 'Hey, boy, it's time to get your hat in the ring.'" He was not "working for the job," however, and "no colleagues are soliciting for me." "We've got to have a strong majority leader," he said, "or Carl Albert won't be strong. I could settle for Bernie Sisk, Hale Boggs, Eddie Boland. Maybe even Wayne Hays." Obviously Udall and O'Hara ranked well down. "When they heard I might run, they pushed me over to the conservatives. That's where *they* say I belong. Well, let 'em sweat it." (The same week he said this, Rostenkowski shared a friendly session with Mo Udall in the House steambath, telling him, "This thing is between you and Boggs." Udall received the impression that Rostenkowski would endorse "the one of us that can show him a hundred first-ballot pledges.")

When Congress came back for a bobtailed postelection session, the conventional wisdom ran that neither Boggs nor Udall could go over the top; O'Hara and Hays were seen as horses too dark to show. Bernie Sisk, only recently declared, had almost immediately created excitement. Many of the old bulls were reported friendly. "I think in the case of Bernie Sisk the office sought the man," a Texan, Jim Wright, said. "I'm pledged to Boggs, and I'll

168

stick. But there's growing Sisk sentiment in my delegation." By mid-December, Sisk predicted one hundred first-ballot votes—far more than anyone thought he had, though many accepted the potential.

The swing toward Sisk came just as Hale Boggs thought he had slowly brought himself back. For weeks he had tirelessly confronted his colleagues, going first to the powerful old seniors: *Look, I'm on the leadership ladder, I deserve a chance, this is the way it's always been done. I'll be embarrassed back home if I'm rejected. People will wonder what's the matter, and it could cost me my seat.*

It wouldn't do, however, for The Goddamned Press to continue heralding Sisk gains in Florida, Georgia, North Carolina, Texas. Nor would it do for rumors to flower that Arkansas's influential Wilbur Mills, chairman of Boggs's own committee, was giving Bernie Sisk sympathetic looks. Boggs decided the wavering Dixiecrats simply had to be scared witless. They must be convinced that should they split off to encourage Sisk, then Mo Udall's "death-wish liberals" would take over: *The South is about to be screwed. You may not always agree with Hale Boggs, but he's subject to the same constituent pressures: he's a blood brother.*

The Boggs "southern strategy" then received an incredible break from unexpected sources. It began with a letter from Congressman Glenn M. Anderson of California, announcing that a majority of his delegation would unite behind their home-state colleague, Bernie Sisk. Paul Shrake, western region director of the United Auto Workers, hotly challenged Congressman Anderson: "Your position is most difficult to understand with [Sisk] . . . voting in support of the Republican-Dixiecrat coalition. You cannot sell me on the idea that . . . Mr. Sisk will do much about helping this troubled nation. . . ."

Anderson responded on Christmas Eve with a "Dear Paul" letter. The key paragraph said: "In the case of Bernie Sisk . . . I find with respect to COPE labor ratings [that] he had four at 100 per cent, four in the high 90 percentile and one in the low 90 percentile and only one below 90. In reviewing the record of other majority leader candidates . . . I find Bernie Sisk's ratings above most, relatively equal, or better than others . . ."

Congressman Anderson told a secretary something about distributing copies of the exchange: perhaps he had in mind friendly California Democrats or all pro-labor Democrats. His secretary, however, thought he meant *all* Democrats—and so sent copies to every labor-hating old mossback in the House. A Boggs staffer remembers, "They began to call in here and come in saying, 'Hail, Hale, if ole Sisk is *that* liberal, I'm a-comin' home.'"

Soon after, dogged by a friendly newsman, Wilbur Mills said for the record that yes, he would vote for Hale Boggs all the way. At a small celebration in the whip's office, Dick Rivers, press secretary to Boggs, offered a prophecy: "Gentlemen, I think it may be ultimately said that Sisk's march through Dixie was halted just outside Little Rock."

Udall was not alarmed by reports of the Boggs consolidations. He had expected from scratch that Hale Boggs would obtain a natural southern majority. His own visible southern strength was limited to a few strays. Though the official propaganda didn't admit it, Udall would have been delighted by fifteen first-ballot votes from among the sixty-seven Democrats in eleven southern states. He approached some few "hopeless" Dixiecrats only through routine circulars and sought secondary support among most. If he directly asked anything, it usually was to be remembered as their backup choice.

More worrisome to Udall was labor. Reports reached him of word circulating loosely in the Democratic Club, where labor lobbyists frequently water, that Mo Udall wouldn't do: "What the hell do they know about collective bargaining in Arizona?" George Meany detested Udall's dovishness. The CIO's top lobbyist, a former Wisconsin congressman named Andy Biemiller, was known to prefer Hale Boggs should Jim O'Hara collapse. Labor proved a hard foe to close with; Udall emissaries were treated courteously, smiled at, given vague conversation—and soon would come reports of new hatchetings. The paramount hope was that an endorsement from Jim O'Hara might ultimately rally pro-labor votes.

By January 1, eighteen days to balloting, it shaped up as a

Udall-Boggs showdown. Bernie Sisk bravely whistled while passing the graveyard: "I keep reading that I'm out of it. Udall and
Boggs have done a wonderful propagandizing job on the press.
Personally, I'm optimistic. The people who started with me are
still with me."

"I know I'm supposed to have *some* strength," Jim O'Hara said
privately, "but when it comes to counting hard votes, I just don't
find many." For the record he was "hopeful"—wryly adding that
he would avoid supplying optimistic head counts "out of a sincere wish to create no wider credibility gap between Congress
and the public." O'Hara, beginning with a few friends from his
Michigan delegation, an inside track with most blacks, and a
scattering of pro-labor congressmen, had added little else. Jack
Brooks, a liberal Texan who greatly resented Udall's "leapfrogging," had been counted on to achieve the miracle of bringing
O'Hara a sizable number of the twenty Texans. The bait was that
Brooks—at forty-nine a veteran of nine terms and a man of consuming personal ambitions—might become whip, restoring one of
Texas's own to the leadership circle. The Texas delegation, however, abounds with unsentimental Tories. "Jack," one of them
said, "we'd like to help your career. But Jim O'Hara is just too
damned liberal. We wouldn't take him if you wrapped him in
tinsel and put him under the Christmas tree." One had difficulty
locating the stray admirers of Wayne Hays, and few congressmen
admitted even having been contacted by him. Still, Hays vowed
he wouldn't finish last.

Any hopes of Tip O'Neill, Eddie Boland, or Hugh Carey that
luck might make them compromise choices had been shattered:
the five announced candidates, meeting with Dan Rostenkowski
in his role as caucus chairman, jammed through a rule that nominations would not be permitted from the floor once balloting
began. Their reasoning was as human as it was simple: why
should they have sweated for months, only to see some sit-tighter
walk off with the prize if a deadlock occurred?

Washington's pols may enthusiastically revile The Goddamned
Press, but few ignore it. Columnists are probably more influential
than is good for either themselves or the country. They are read,

particularly if they appear in the *Washington Post* or *New York Times,* and politicians gossip like fishwives of what they say. Udall fretted that Boggs was "winning the battle of the columnists."

On January 6 Joseph Alsop disposed of Bernie Sisk as the "rather colorless Californian," freshly reminded readers of who bossed O'Hara, and awarded poor Wayne Hays not even a dishonorable mention. Hale Boggs would win, perhaps by "considerably more than two to one." Morris Udall represented only those "hard-core liberals . . . too sure of their own exquisite rectitude"—men who, when not permitted their desires, "lie down on the floor, drum their heels on the carpet, and howl. . . ." Joseph Kraft named Boggs the front-runner in crediting him with leadership ability, "charm to burn, and plenty of brains." Feeling badly damaged, Udall went a-courting.

David Broder listened to Udall's explanation of how he would win, then wrote a column leaving out the best propaganda. Thomas Braden and Frank Mankiewicz appeared impressed: Udall searched their column for days, wondering why they hadn't printed anything.\* Jack Anderson, knowing that he must live with the winner (the highly placed being crucial to his "inside Washington" slant) mulled it over and did nothing; a devout Mormon, he may have been put off by Udall's having left the church. Only Evans and Novak responded. Having disposed of B. F. Sisk as a threat to the Boggs southern base, they now credited Udall with "impressive gains in the South" and hinted that Eddie Boland was almost persuaded to nominate him.

Exactly a week before the voting—on January 12—the morning *Post* headlined: "Udall Leads Race for Majority Leader." The afternoon *Daily News* and *Star* confirmed it. The headlines resulted from a confidential poll conducted by the *Congressional Quarterly,* a news periodical specializing in Hill matters. With 129 of 254 House Democrats responding, *CQ* reported Udall the first-ballot choice of forty-six, Boggs of thirty, Sisk of eighteen,

---

\* Later, he would learn that Gary Hymel, Boggs's administrative assistant, had produced Hale Boggs for a breakfast with the columnists, and Boggs had performed with such charm and persuasion that Braden would say, "We were on the verge of writing a pro-Udall column until that session."

O'Hara of eleven, and Hays of six. Udall was the first, second, or third choice of seventy-eight, Boggs of sixty, O'Hara of fifty-one, Sisk of forty-one, and Hays of . . . well, six. Hays got mad as hell and said for the record what other candidates were whispering behind their hands: "Udall stacked it. His organization was keyed for this. The rest of us didn't attempt to fix it for propaganda purposes."

Hays was right. Udall had circulated word among known friendlies to mail their ballots in, with the corollary instruction to say nothing that might arouse sleeping dogs. Reading the papers, he had to think it had worked: "Udall ran strongest of all the candidates in the Northeast, Midwest, and West and second to Boggs in the South" . . . "surprising is Rep. Udall's support from the South and Midwest" . . . "the head counts disclose Rep. Boggs's backing is not solid enough to survive repeated ballotings."

That night Udall happily told a friend, "If we aggregate all my first, second, and third choices with O'Hara's, there are 129 for me. The aggregate for Boggs, Sisk, and Hays totals only 107." Blinded by the headlines, he did not reflect on the possibility that he might be guilty of improving his own propaganda.

In the whip's office, however, they had noticed something. Gary Hymel had studied the poll carefully in search of salvage: he feared that Udall had scored a timely propaganda coup and felt a bit foolish at having been outflanked. Finally he picked up the telephone: "Hale, I think everybody's misreading this poll. I think we can turn it against Udall." Why? "It shows he doesn't have the freshmen locked. You've got seven of sixteen, and it's *his* goddamned poll."

Of thirty-three freshman Democrats, Udall was generally conceded the most. ("Mo will get twenty-five or more," Jim O'Hara confided.) Old bulls looked their new colleagues over and, shuddering, saw flesh-and-blood verification of the Revolution.

New York's Bella Abzug attacked the Pentagon, war, the seniority system, and other revered targets; her uninhibited swearing could be heard in all boroughs, and she threatened to violate House tradition by wearing her big floppy hats in chambers. Cal-

ifornia's Ron Dellums, up from the black ghetto, wore Afro hair
and bellbottoms and had hit back fiercely when Spiro Agnew mis-
quoted him. Les Aspin of Wisconsin, former McNamara Whiz
Kid, wanted to correct insanities he had discovered in the Pentagon, and held degrees from such untrustworthy campuses as
Yale, MIT, and Oxford. James Abourezk—a Lebanese—was a
peacenik who had grown up on a South Dakota Indian reservation, identified with have-nots, and favored abolishing seniority.
Father Robert Drinan of Massachusetts—first to wear a Jesuit
collar in the House—kidded himself as the "Mad Monk," declared we should feed the world's hungry, counseled the antiwar
young. The old bulls just naturally assumed such strangers to be
children of the reformist Udall—and so, for that matter, did
Udall's opponents.

Except for Hale Boggs.

Not for nothing had Boggs sat all those years at power's right
hand. He had watched tough-talking freshmen come and go, had
seen the revolutionaries of three decades turn uncertain and
humble on first encountering the trappings of power. He knew
freshmen to be new kids on the block, a bit fearful of the bully,
and he knew that something universally human in them silently
cried out for acceptance: new breed or no, they were politicians.
Experience assured Boggs that these new revolutionaries, too,
would accommodate the basic realities. In time they might cause
all the trouble they now promised, but initially they would require a period of adjustment, time to rally themselves, and Boggs
knew he would be dealing with them at their most vulnerable.

The morning following their victories in November, all Democratic freshmen received nice telegrams from Hale Boggs. Knowing there were houses to rent, schools to consult, curiosities to
satisfy, Boggs warmly welcomed the new kids to town and offered to open doors. He wrung their hands and put them at ease
with harmless questions about themselves. He buzzed staffers, ordering them to relieve this rookie or that of some nagging Washington worry. The freshmen sat in the deep soft chairs, and every
time Hale Boggs pushed a button, another small miracle happened: this guy knew his way around.

Eventually Boggs might inquire the freshmen's committee

desires. Naturally, everybody had a vital one. Perhaps Boggs here said a word on the difficulty of freshmen attaining their primary selections—regretfully, of course—quickly coupled with observations on the importance of committee assignments to the congressional career. Then he would surely let it slip that as a member of Ways and Means—"the committee-on-committees, you know"—he was fortunately situated to help. And then the cake's icing: introductions to three or four Boggs friends on Ways and Means, including, of course, the all-important chairman, Wilbur Mills. Only later would the friendly pressures be applied: debts called in by way of firming up prior understandings.

Udall could provide some of the same services and occasionally did. He did not, however, have the natural advantages—the prestige of internal office, the trappings, the crucial committee connections. He could not risk introducing people to Old John McCormack, or presume ceremonial claims on Carl Albert's time as easily as the whip might. And these things, too, Hale Boggs knew.

Now, the *Congressional Quarterly* poll had provided evidence that Boggs's freshman campaign was scoring. It provided new ammunition with which to assault undecided Democrats: *"Look, Joe, using Udall's own stacked poll you can see that I'm making inroads into one of his hard-core groups. And if Mo Udall can't even get the freshmen, where in hell will his votes come from?"*

"I get the feeling just dozens of guys are uncommitted," one repeatedly heard on Capitol Hill in that final week. Serious examinations were accorded the wildest rumors: Hugh Carey had told somebody over dinner at Paul Young's, "Hell, no, I'm not for Udall. I've been working for Hale Boggs all along"; Jim Wright of Texas might switch from Boggs to Udall; Hays or O'Hara or Sisk would pull out.

Mo Udall continued to woo Eddie Boland in hopes of a nominating speech. While he couldn't make any deals, Udall told him, "Those people who serve the cause well will be the first I consult and counsel with as leader." Boland read this as meaning that he had excellent prospects for becoming whip, and he read it right. Each of the candidates used nominating or seconding opportunities as bait, for they wanted the best men out front as visible loyalists.

On January 13, six days before balloting and one day after the revelations of the *CQ* poll, Eddie Boland telephoned Udall to say he would be honored to nominate him. Udall was ecstatic. He could envision uncommitted northeasterners rallying around, and believed that liberals leaning to O'Hara might now decide against wasting their first-ballot votes. "I think I turned the corner today," he telephoned Ella. Fired with new energies, he stayed late to telephone colleagues and to supervise preparation of Boland's nominating speech. A press release went out stressing the importance of Boland's endorsement and—for the first time— flatly predicting victory.

By noon on the following day, Udall was back on the down escalator. He had a report that Hale Boggs would "for certain" announce on Sunday, the seventeenth, his endorsement by Dan Rostenkowski. Boggs would claim a resulting profit of twenty-five votes—enough to put him over the top. "Danny denied a deal with Boggs to me again just the other day," Udall morosely said, "but in a slightly different form than usual. It should have made me suspicious." (Sunday would come and go without Rostenkowski's "certain" endorsement being announced.) There was another cause for alarm: Udall's fresh contacts with the northeast, following Eddie Boland's encouraging capitulation, had reaped only the same old evasions or—more ominously—unanswered telephone calls. This congressman was out, or that one in conference; he would call back (he seldom did).

On Friday, January 15, Jim O'Hara circulated to a dozen lieutenants a private memo headed "Where We Stand"—which, within the hour, would leak and go public.

"The battle is not yet won by anybody," the O'Hara document claimed. "Our count shows no one having more than Boggs' seventy to eighty first-ballot votes. Udall still stands at about fifty or sixty. O'Hara has forty-two hard commitments on the first ballot without counting the probables. Sisk and Hays have about thirty-five votes between them. The forty or more who haven't made a decision are mostly in the northern big-city delegations.

"Neither Sisk nor Hays have taken off. Their first-ballot votes will include some pretty potent people, but they are two ballot votes at the most [and] will [later] go elsewhere. . . . Udall can't get most of the uncommitted or most of the Hays-Sisk strength. *We have identified fifty or more of these seventy-five votes who simply will not go for Udall under any circumstance.*

"As for Boggs, even his first-ballot strength includes some people who are 'soft.' Ninety to one hundred votes is his peak. Our contacts among the new members indicate they are pro-O'Hara, though some of them are obligated to honor first-ballot commitments they have made to others. By the time it's fish or cut bait, they will be fishing in O'Hara waters.

"The Udall bandwagon rumors may start most anti-Udall people moving toward Boggs. If enough of the undecided votes turn to Boggs, and if they begin to frighten off even a small number of O'Hara's hard-core support, the game could be over on the fourth ballot. *If it boils down to Boggs vs. Udall, it will be Boggs who will win.* Your job, then, is to let the hard-core O'Hara vote know what the real count shows. . . ."

Late in the day, Udall took another blow. The new rumor (correct, for a change) said that Tip O'Neill would not follow Eddie Boland to Udall but would shortly declare his intent to nominate or second Hale Boggs. Another lick followed: Shirley Chisholm (whom Udall had counted for himself and whom Jim O'Hara also counted among his solids) would support Boggs in exchange for a seat on the Education and Labor Committee. As Mrs. Chisholm was one of the more militant-talking blacks, and there was a general presumption that the dozen House blacks would vote together—they had formed an internal black caucus to promote their unit effectiveness—this story was particularly unsettling.* Bob Tiernan of Rhode Island, long counted safe, was wavering under pro-Boggs pressures from some of his more vital campaign contributors. A New Mexico freshman, Harold Runnels, who had received grass-roots campaign help from Udall, was a Vietnam

* How Mrs. Chisholm voted is a matter of continuing intrigue. Hale Boggs thinks he got her—and she did receive the desired Education and Labor assignment. Jim O'Hara recalls that, only moments before balloting, Mrs. Chisholm turned to him to specifically discredit her rumored agreement with Boggs and to affirm her loyalty to O'Hara. A poll she later answered, however, indicated she had voted for Udall all the way.

hawk who'd had second thoughts about Mo's dovishness. Nick Galifianakis of North Carolina, early counted a Udall man, was receiving a going-over from pro-Boggs lobbyists for textiles, tobacco, and furniture manufacturers.

Then somebody came in waving a clipping from the *Elizabeth* (N.J.) *Daily Journal* quoting Congressman Edward J. Patten: " 'Boggs will be elected pronto,' or on the first ballot. . . . Patten said he had learned that Rostenkowski was promised the whip's post in return for the Illinois delegation's support of Boggs. That delegation almost to a man will vote for Boggs. . . ." Until then, Udall believed he had a chance for Patten's vote.

Udall's worried supporters decided to have another go at manipulating The Goddamned Press. Florida's Sam Gibbons called in reporters to reveal the latest head count: Mo Udall had almost a hundred firm first-ballot votes and would win no later than the third. Gibbons frequently consulted a document in claiming so many from this region or that. An enterprising reporter slipped behind Gibbons, and every time the congressman stopped waving the paper the reporter memorized names. An hour later, Udall's office was chaotic: of four allegedly pro-Udall congressmen telephoned by the reporter, three flatly denied having committed to him and one offered "no comment." One of them, a New Yorker, who had privately told Udall that he must vote for him only in the darkest secrecy because of powerful counterpressures back home, came in angry enough to chase tigers and to subtract himself from the Udall projections. All Mo could do was to apologize and agonize. But he knew his head count was now suspect on a wide front.

By Saturday night the Udall family had suffered what appeared to be their personal Chappaquiddick. Mo received a distraught telphone call from brother Stew: "An *incredible* thing has happened . . . a *horrible* experience . . . stupid blunder . . . never forgive myself if it beats you. . . ."

Stew had entered a drugstore in a Virginia suburb at noon, dressed in old clothes, to obtain wine, house paint, and cigars. Anxious to reach a basketball game—his young son played on the team Stew managed—he grabbed two ninety-cent packs of cigars and then had difficulty locating the other desired items. The store was crowded. Stew was late; he paid for one pack of cigars and rushed out the door. A store policeman grabbed him. "You're under arrest. You didn't pay for those cigars in your pocket." *"My God!"* Stew Udall said. "You're right. I shoved one pack in my jacket because I intended to open the other. I forgot it was there." He produced a dollar. "It's too late," the store cop said. "You'll have to come along to the police station." The manager was off weekending; his assistant claimed no authority to intervene. Stew was hustled to the Fairfax police station, dazed and mumbling at the incredible stupidity of it all, where he was fingerprinted, charged with concealment of merchandise, and released under $250 personal bond. "Stewart Udall Accused of Shoplifting Cigars"—the Sunday *Washington Star* played it as a front-page embarrassment.

Mo assured Stew that the mishap made no difference to his campaign: people would understand that it could happen to anyone, another of those insane mistakes and sorry jests of the human experience, a dash of Kafka. He tried jokes: "Well, Stew, they accused us of stealing Arizona from Lyndon long before they accused us of stealing cigars." And, "I'll tell 'em on the Hill I meant to pass out cigars, but my brother failed to adequately replenish my supply." *

Monday night. Tomorrow they vote. It is a night for gathering the loyal to an ancient political ritual of attempting to bolster tribal morale while taking a final hardheaded look at the realities. Not surprisingly, bursts of outrageous optimism frequently surface among the assembled pols: it is their way of singing before battle.

In Jim O'Hara's office the official cheerleader is his campaign manager, Michigan's Bill Ford. A short, stocky bundle of nerves, Ford plunges about compulsively and predicts forty-four first-ballot certainties, with victory coming on the fourth or fifth ballot. O'Hara seems not so sure. The candidate is quiet and reflective, and about nine o'clock he abruptly goes home. Wayne Hays leaves his office about the same time, after a day of telephoning

---

* The drug chain later agreed with Stewart Udall that his arrest had been a mistake, apologized publicly to him, and withdrew all charges.

and conferences with his campaign manager, Dr. Thomas Morgan of Pennsylvania. Hays still has that obsession about not being last and asks "Doc" Morgan to hit the Pennsylvania and West Virginia delegations again early tomorrow. In the whip's office Hale Boggs has an attack of prebattle jitters. Gary Hymel reassures him: "We've got at least 110 locked in, maybe 117, and *possibly* enough to win on the first ballot." Boggs shuffles through the head counts, occasionally questioning whether this or that congressman is pure of heart. Hymel makes soothing sounds. Mo Udall's young staff members are especially confident. John Gabusi and Terry Bracy talk in terms of ninety to a hundred first-ballot votes. Udall himself has the look of a man working to improve his mood. Little optimism cavorts through the Sisk office. Bernie Sisk has privately known for three weeks that his campaign has floundered and is no longer extending himself.

Mo Udall reaches his home in suburban Virginia after midnight. Ella is asleep. Udall recalls thinking it strange that he should feel so anticlimactic: he would have assumed wild fevers and brittle tensions near the end. He mixes a drink, turns out the lights, and sits in the dark watching logs burn in the fireplace. For more than an hour he stares into the fire, risking the painful dangers of self-exploration.

Udall concludes that he has deluded himself, has ignored warning signs, has been guilty of soft counts and wishful thinking—especially in the final week. Too many colleagues have responded to his hardest pitches only in terms of general admiration; too many have failed to return his telephone calls; too many have waved brief greetings, glancing at their wristwatches before rushing on to some vital appointment rather than lingering to chat. These are ominous signs. He thinks: *Any truly viable candidate at this point should have to beat his colleagues off with a stick.* He knows enough of power to know that power attracts. Boggs has almost all the old House bulls, the deeply rooted powers—Udall admits to the dark—while he has absolutely none. His election, which he has so firmly believed in for so long, appears in these final hours to require a miracle. The miracle will be possible only if he can gather no fewer than eighty-odd votes

180

on the first ballot while holding Hale Boggs to ninety-five or below, thus preventing bandwagon boardings. Mo Udall's last sleepy thought is that he probably cannot do it.

The next morning, well in advance of the gavel hour of ten, a crowd jostles for position in the marble hall dividing the speaker's rooms from the House chamber: reporters, photographers, Hill staffers, congressional wives. Officious policemen hard-ass the troops, flattening spectators against the walls. The overflow spills into the speaker's rooms, peopled by outgoing McCormack-ites: potbellied old men and ladies a shade long in the tooth for the most part. Old John McCormack has not gone home to South Boston but has joined seven hundred other former congressmen in Washington whose Potomac fevers run too high ever to be soothed again in their original precincts.

An old pro-pol is present, a Marylander defeated in November, who just couldn't stay away. He works the crowd, shaking the hands of strangers from habit, whispering inside information or seeking the same. Each time the elevator stops he darts over to greet his former colleagues, making them a bit nervous with the memory of his loss, before fading back into the crowd. He is past seventy now, and for the first time since World War II he is not entitled to enter a Democratic caucus: cannot know what is happening in that polished and padded chamber where he had used up thirty years and would have preferred to die.

In the chamber the majority leader candidates greet colleagues, consult their loyalists, and try to avoid each other. There will be other business—including the cut-and-dried election of Carl Albert as speaker—before their own fates are settled. Jim O'Hara sits apart, permitting his lieutenants the last-minute solicitations. He arrived on Capitol Hill thinking to quit, and said as much to Bill Ford and to Minnesota's Don Fraser; they vociferously objected. Over a final cup of coffee, O'Hara decides what the hell: he has gone this far, why not see it through?

Hale Boggs approaches Sidney Yates of Illinois, whom Danny Rostenkowski has been unable to deliver. Jovially he says, "Sid, what's this nonsense I hear about you being part of the Udall bloc?" "I don't know that I'm part of any bloc," Yates responds, "but what you hear isn't nonsense." "Sid," Boggs says passionately, *"what in the hell?"* Yates smiles no more than a nickel's worth, shrugs, and moves away with eyes on his back.

Boggs is uptight. By varied circumstances, four votes he had considered certain—and two probables—have been lost. South Carolina's Mendel Rivers is dead following heart surgery; Tom Abernethy of Mississippi and John Dowdy of Texas are hospitalized; Brooklyn's Manny Celler has been called away by a death in the family; Oklahoma's John Jarman, vacationing in Jamaica, has ignored his urgent telegrams begging contact. Then, North Carolina's Richard Preyer has paid an early call this morning to say, *Sorry, Hale, I like you but I'm going with Udall.*

Udall is also fretful. He has learned shortly after entering the chamber that two votes he hoped for—Ken Gray of Illinois and Bert Podell of New York—must be scratched because they are giving seconding speeches for Wayne Hays. Ron Dellums, the black freshman from Berkeley, grabs Udall's arm to volunteer admiration for his antiwar efforts. "I hope I can count on you today," Udall says. Dellums gives him a friendly pat and moves off, leaving Mo to wonder. Wayne Hays ranges among West Virginians, Ohioans, and Pennsylvanians; Bernie Sisk is gladhanding Texans.

Shortly, the packed hall outside buzzes in alarm—the political creature's instinct when mystified by events. Shocking word has seeped from inside the chamber. Congressman Olin (Tiger) Teague, a Texas conservative offered as a surprise candiate for caucus chairman, has upset incumbent Danny Rostenkowski, 151 to 92! Boggs partisans pale: *Migod, is this a year for throwing the rascals out?* Pop explanations make the round: it's a rebellion against the long-rumored deal by which Rosty would deliver Illinois to Boggs in exchange for becoming whip. No, there has been a secret deal between Bernie Sisk and the Texans: in exchange for Texas votes, the Sisk crowd has supported Teague. No, Udall will most directly profit because Rostenkowski's rejection clearly was a slap at Boggs. No, it couldn't have been a slap at Boggs because "Tiger" Teague is friendly with the old bulls themselves most loyal to Hale. Texan Jim Wright leaves the chamber to tell newsmen his delegation put Teague forward "simply because we

182

had no representation in the leadership, and we wanted to rectify that." Few are willing to believe less than the most exotic intrigues, however, and people sneer in Wright's face. The normal anxieties return when Carl Albert is elected speaker, 220 to 20, over the tardy candidacy of Michigan's John Conyers, perhaps the most articulate and savvy member of the black caucus.

A veteran House employee, doorkeeper William (Fishbait) Miller, prepares for the vital majority leader balloting. "Fishbait" supervises stacks of multihued cards, a different color for each ballot. When his name is called, each Democrat will receive a first-ballot card, mark it, and drop it unsigned into a dark green wastebasket held by "Fishbait." If there is no winner the process will be repeated until someone has received 128 or more votes. Two hours are consumed in the tedious nominating and seconding speeches, all the conventional things being said about men of great vision and virtue, everyone careful to get on record as loving each of the candidates deep in his heart. Congressmen slip out under the cover of this oratorical flak to refresh themselves in the House restaurant and grab a smoke.

Suddenly a policeman, reading from a scratch pad, bursts into the hall: "Awright, here we go. First ballot: Mr. Boggs ninety-five, Mr. Udall sixty-nine, Mr. Sisk thirty-one, Mr. Hays twenty-eight, Mr. O'Hara twenty-five. Second ballot commencing immediately." Reporters sprint for the telephones; secretaries squeal or moan. In the speaker's rooms one of the old men telephones another old man in his Washington hotel; he glares at a journalist who asks Old John McCormack's reaction. Inside the chamber, a single thought has flashed through Mo Udall's head: *I've had it.*

Word comes that Wayne Hays, having achieved his ambition not to finish last, has withdrawn with—for him—a warm endorsement of Hale Boggs.* Five minutes later comes word that Jim O'Hara has withdrawn—without endorsing Udall as expected.

Quickly, it is over. Too quickly, it seems, after all those months of work and worry, dreams and schemes. Even before the officious policeman can satisfy his need for drama, spectators near

* It would develop that Hays and Boggs had a secret agreement that should either drop out he would endorse the other.

him take a look at his scratch pad and begin crying, "It's Boggs, it's Boggs!" The confirming figures are delivered in a shout above the general hubbub: "Mr. Boggs 140, Mr. Udall 88, Mr. Sisk 17." Note to the sociologists: Early that morning Hale Boggs had rattled and banged into the city from Bethesda in Gary Hymel's old Volkswagen bus, the abandoned toys and debris of eight Hymel children underfoot. Late that night he was chauffeured home in a long black limousine with his feet reposing on pink clouds.

There was a mirthless wake in Udall's office, a joyless gulping of deadening liquors from paper cups. Like a private funeral, it attracted only the family and a few intimate friends. The action that mattered was occurring two blocks away, in the Capitol quarters of Hale Boggs, where photographers fought for footholds among merry shouts and huggings. Boggs entered to cheers, buoyant and beaming, grabbing hands and repeating, "I can't believe it, I can't believe it . . ." Joe Alsop and Carl Albert were among the many paying their respects, and telephone congratulations came from Lyndon Johnson and Richard Nixon. Old John McCormack had phoned in his delight earlier.

Udall entered his own office wearing his campaign button turned upside down, so that it read ow instead of mo. He paused near a huddle of disconsolate aides to repeat an old political joke: "Do you know the difference between a cactus and a caucus? Well, a cactus has all its pricks on the *outside!*" The staffers smiled like men with broken backs. They had the numbed look of survivors viewing one of God's disasters. All they could do was mill around among the debris, wondering how and why it had happened.

The vanquished plopped behind his desk, accepted a drink, and put his feet up. "Well, troops," he said, "now let's slide back into obscurity." "Mo, honey," Ella said, "I'm glad you didn't win. I won't have to play Mrs. Leader all the time. We can take vacations, Mo." Her husband, recognizing a consoling lie, patted her hand. "It was closer than it looks," he said. "Ten more votes on the first ballot— it could have happened. I got seven, eight calls last night and this morning from guys who said, 'Look, I know I promised you—but Wayne Hays is my neighbor, or we've served on a committee together for twenty years, or I owe him a favor, and he's crying that he'll be last unless I go with him.' I told those guys if they didn't stay hitched I could be in trouble. They hurt me. They killed me."

"So did Jim O'Hara," said a young secretary red-eyed from crying. "He's pure chickenshit, and you can quote me!"

College interns and other Udall staffers chose to be bitter. Most were incredibly young, bright kids who had believed they could work for change within the system and now, suddenly, were no longer sure. They sang of corruptionists, liars, and frauds abounding in Congress. "Those goddamned kids," Mo Udall said of his staffers. "They've worked their tails off. I just don't know what to say to them."

Well, Udall went on, he simply hadn't been able to crack the South or the Northeast: the first had feared his liberalism, while the second continued to punish him in memory of Old John McCormack. He hadn't realized rancors ran so deep; had presumed he had made peace, erased fears. "I thought the Revolution had come to the House," he said. "I thought the House was ready for it. I was wrong. The biggest disappointment was the number of '50s and '60s liberals who went for Boggs, or even for Sisk. In the House, yesterday's revolutionaries become today's elitists."

Someone remarked on the amount of duplicity congressmen had accomplished: several had been discovered privately pledging their honor to multiple candidates. "You've got to take into account the human misunderstandings," Udall said. "What one guy offers as a generality, another may accept as a specific. Politicians, you know, are shaped to tell people what they want to hear. Take Father Drinan—a sweet man, a great guy. He says to Jim O'Hara that he has long admired his general liberalism. He tells me how courageous he thinks I've been on the Vietnam war and another matter or two. I don't know what he told Hale Boggs, but he was probably warm and complimentary—it's just in Drinan's nature. So each of us had hopes of getting his vote and may have listed him as a certainty. Very understandable." He took another drink of beer. "And then," he said, laughing, "there are all those no-good goddamned *liars.*"

Someone offered a hint of hope: maybe an unexpected opportunity would present itself. "The big windows open around here about once every ten years," Udall said. "Even if something opened up, I'm not sure I'd want to go for it. One more loss, and I'm Harold Stassen."

The day after his defeat for majority leader, Udall attempted to run for whip.

It began when five liberals—Udall and O'Hara types—sought out Speaker Albert before breakfast. Should the House establish a tradition of elevating the whip to majority leader and thence to speaker, they said, then the whip should no longer be appointed but elected. Otherwise the cronies of past leaders could rise to the ultimate heights without the caucus having more than a negative veto power. Albert agreed: the whip should be elected. The happy delegation spread this word, cranking up a dozen frantic campaigns. Udall consulted with his advisers; go for it, they said. "I don't want to wait ten years for another opportunity," he told them. "I won't be the young reformist of forty-eight then. I'll be fifty-eight. Let's shove the stack to the center of the table." The Udall men sprang for the phones.

Meanwhile, Albert and Boggs were sharing a stormy private session. The particulars are closely held, though Boggs is said to have insisted on appointing Danny Rostenkowski: Rosty had delivered Illinois as promised and had his reward coming. Speaker Albert replied that it could not be a unilateral decision: *he* had a say coming. The caucus had ousted Rostenkowski from a lesser office, Albert reminded, and to ignore that action would fly in the face of a substantial majority. Besides, Danny had been pretty free in his opinion that Carl Albert wouldn't be a strong speaker: well, maybe now he would change his mind.

Forced to yield on Rostenkowski, Boggs quickly mobilized to stop the election of a whip: he might get stuck with Udall or another unfriendly; dangerous precedents threatened. Soon the old bulls bellowed at Carl Albert. Northeast liberals protested: should Udall win, the leadership apparatus would reside solely with the South and Southwest. Within two hours, rumors floated that Speaker Albert was having second thoughts. Yes, he soon admitted, he had reversed himself: the members did not want an election, opposition was widespread, the new leadership should not presume to establish so drastic a precedent.

Udall sought him out: "Carl, I don't understand." Well, the speaker said, the choice was not his alone; he had to obey the majority. Udall questioned whether the speaker had obtained a majority reading: at least permit a resolution on the question of *whether* to ballot for whip. If the majority voted no, so be it. Albert demurred: he personally would be well pleased to have Udall for whip, but there was the geographic imbalance to consider. If the members wanted to offer a resolution to ballot, that was up to them. He couldn't support it, however.

Ken Gray of Illinois threatened to offer such a resolution. Wayne Hays made a tough speech saying if they *did* decide to elect the whip—and personally, he didn't give a damn whether they did or not—but if they *did*, "Then I will run and I will win."

Potentials who hoped to be appointed circulated against Ken Gray's proposed resolution. It was never offered. By late afternoon Mo Udall brought word to his disappointed staff that the antielection forces were in obvious control, and the rebellion had petered out.

Hale Boggs and Speaker Albert met to decide between Brooklyn's Hugh Carey or Cambridge's Tip O'Neill. There was unexpected opposition to Carey, headed by a New York colleague ("a case of the pigshit Irish being jealous of the lace-curtain Irish," a bitter friend of Carey's would later say). By processes largely remaining a mystery, the two made their choice for whip. Hale Boggs picked up the telephone and told Tip O'Neill the glad news.

JIM O'HARA: "You get tunnel vision. I began as a casual candidate, then the juices flowed and I lost my perspective. I forgot some things and had to relearn them. One, the typical congressman doesn't really care *who* is majority leader as much as he wants to be with the winner. . . . Two, to the extent that most congressmen *do* have a preference it's more likely to be based on old friendships or personal favors or dislikes than on ideology, geography, or leadership potential.

"I was shocked and embarrassed by being low man. Everyone

thought Wayne Hays would be low. When I was, it stunned me. I voted for Mo on the second ballot. I wish he had won, but contrary to rumor I had never agreed to endorse him; I wouldn't presume to dictate how any other man should vote. It's regrettable, but good friends fall out in these things. Relationships get as bitter as those 'friendly' divorces you hear about. I'll go see Mo after a cooling period.

"I feel like a nonperson around here—like Khrushchev. Nobody comes by. The phones don't ring." (Laughs.) "I'm starting over, just like a freshman. My slate's clean. I've nothing to lose. And you know what? I rather enjoy the freedom."

BERNIE SISK: "It became evident, in the week before Christmas, that my chances were very slim. Udall was the key: the members had very definite pro or con opinions about him. Had I put it together in early December—and it was initially encouraging—then I would have defeated Udall in the finals. Anyone would have, except maybe O'Hara. A number of the members like Udall personally, but they're afraid of his people.

"I feel terribly relieved to be from under the gun. I see a rocky road. I'm no reactionary, but some of these new birds—well, what I hear them say scares me. It wouldn't be any pleasure to try to hold this bunch together in the House."

WAYNE HAYS: "I guess I didn't work hard enough. I find it difficult to ask favors. I've made a number of people mad.

"Udall didn't have a chance. People didn't like his bedfellows. I said all along I was the most relaxed, the least ambitious of the candidates. That probably means I'd have made the best leader."

GARY HYMEL, assistant to Hale Boggs: "I think Udall's people did some pretty foolish things. If you accept Mo's premise that the House is controlled by the chairmen, then you wonder why he had fifteen or twenty of the most antiestablishmentarian and antagonistic members running full steam ahead. That was certain to turn the power against him. I think Udall personally realized this and tried to divorce himself from some of the more radical reforms and reformers—but he had the taint.

"Many of Udall's people were amateurs when it came to inhouse politics. They didn't count very well. Hale Boggs has spent

188

many years counting votes. He's been on the inside, with the leadership and part of the leadership, and that helps you develop a sensitive feel for internal matters. You don't learn this place overnight.

"We always saw it as between Hale Boggs and Udall, and figured early to win. Hale came up from scratch. He had problems, but he knew how to overcome them.

"We didn't leave any unturned stones. We didn't concede anybody except the other candidates and their known lieutenants. We may have taken fifteen or eighteen freshmen from Udall. We got five blacks for sure on the first ballot, maybe seven; and I think we got nine on the second.°

"Being on the leadership ladder was an advantage, sure, and Mr. McCormack was helpful. Those things didn't mean automatic promotion. Hale Boggs had to project a certain image, and he did. He worked hard and touched all bases. Give him credit.

"The only thing I can't figure out" (laughing) "is how we got less than 110 votes on the first ballot! I've gone over the count two dozen times and I can't find the . . . ah, *disappointments!* There are fifteen or twenty real smooth political operators running loose somewhere around here!"

MORRIS UDALL: "The Dixiecrats didn't beat me. I never counted on their votes. I was defeated by a combination of defecting freshmen, labor, and liberals with ten to fifteen years in the House. Labor hurt me badly, though I've been with them much more than not. I could just never bring myself to jump like labor commands.

"I had this image of myself as being acceptable to both basic ideological camps. I presumed I had been thoughtful, responsible, and personable enough to come off as less than a bomb-thrower to conservatives and liberal enough to deserve the help and trust of liberals. In truth, it seems I was suspect in each camp.†

"The leadership-ladder bit—tradition, promotion, seniority—

---

° O'Hara still believes he had nine or ten of the dozen blacks, and that most then went to Udall.

† Following Edward Kennedy's upset loss to conservative Senator Robert Byrd for a Senate leadership post, Udall phoned Senator Kennedy: "As soon as I get this liberal buckshot out of my rear, I'll come pull those liberal knives out of your back."

was stronger medicine than I originally thought. This House apparently just insists on people getting in line, serving time. Boggs knew this and exploited the sentiment very effectively. He worked his ass off, and he used all his tools. In the South, the Boggs people put the heat on recalcitrants through lobbyists for various industries: oil, tobacco, textiles, and so on. They snatched six or eight votes from me there. He played the freshmen like a virtuoso: he could pass out more goodies than I. The big-city boys came to him through a combination of his contacts with mayors and other politicians I didn't know externally, and through such guys as Rostenkowski and Carey and a few of the old deans. Boggs had people all over Washington—lawyers and lobbyists and bureaucrats—dating back to the New Deal, and almost all of them knew somebody to pressure for him.

"The remaining bitterness over my McCormack race surprised me. I thought I'd conducted myself like a gentleman, and so I guess people just hated the idea. At a critical juncture somebody brought word that Tip O'Neill had said he couldn't buy me under any circumstance. I said, '*Goddammit*, I've got a lot to learn.' I remember trading funny stories with Tip O'Neill, and once we had a marvelous time on a trip. It's easy to translate such personal experiences into potential support—easy to forget that Tip O'Neill's shared friendly moments with others and for longer. I knew that Ken Gray of Illinois had been sore at me over a Post Office bill I had handled —he thought it encroached on his subcommittee's territory—but I assumed that old difference settled long ago. Then, late in the campaign, I heard he was still talking about it.

"I'm too naïve or maybe too egotistical. Always wanting to believe the best. Right after my defeat I wrote myself a memo: 'If I ever get in another one of these things, remember that the man who gives only general expressions of high esteem should be marked on the *other fellow's* ledger.' Looking back, I know that when I talked to twenty guys, say, and found them generally complimentary but unwilling to commit themselves, I'd tell myself, 'Well, I won't get all of those guys, but surely I'll get six to eight.' The fact is, you'll get none of them. Anything short of 'Yes, I'll vote for you,' means they *aren't* going to vote for you. There's a story from pretty good sources that one of my original lieutenants may have been a Boggs plant, a spy from among my thirty-odd loyalists. Maybe I need to face the realities, but that's *one* story I can't bring myself to accept.

"The liberal or progressive newspapers didn't serve the role they might have. After years of complaining about the need for House reforms, they gave pretty shoddy coverage. The *New York Times* didn't have a line in the Sunday edition before the Tuesday election, and then *after* the vote cried editorially of the result. Big help that was. The *Washington Post* seemed terribly pro-Boggs to me. Those are influential newspapers in Congress, and had they editorially remarked on the race or given proper airings to the issues, then they may have made a difference. I don't remember reading anywhere any in-depth story saying what the candidates stood for, or how they expected to operate as majority leader should they win.

"Right now, of course, I feel that I know much more about the House and about the personalities than I did during the campaign. Even being much more enlightened, however, I'm not sure I could do any better. I did the things I meant to do and said the things I had to say. In the final analysis, it just wasn't there for me."

Ten days after the election, goodies had been distributed to the deserving. John McFall of California, a Boggs man, was named to one of the two newly created deputy whip jobs. John Brademas of Indiana, an O'Hara man, was named to the other as a concession to Midwest liberals. Deserving freshmen achieved their best committee hopes more than normally. Some few of the original Boggs men from among the middle ranks improved their positions.

Udall, despondent and tired, thought he knew one slot where "I might accomplish a little something." Swallowing pride, he campaigned for a seat on the Ethics Committee: there he could assist reforms in reporting of campaign expenditures, situations breeding conflicts of interest, lobbying procedures. Two senior members of Ethics—crusty old Wayne Aspinall and an aging Louisiana Tory, F. Edward Hébert—were reportedly quitting because of more important duties. Udall heard nothing for several days. One afternoon he received a call from Ways and Means sources: sorry, but Aspinall and Hébert had reconsidered. There would be no vacancy.

"I got the message," Udall told a friend. "There's nothing here for old Mo. I'm catching on." He laughed. "When I was a viable candidate, the employees from the service offices here—the folding room, cafeteria, the cops, and so on—were extremely cordial. This morning one of my staff people called the electrical-equipment office to have a typewriter repaired, and got his tail chewed."

Udall prowled his office restlessly. "When I came here, I was forced to get on the Interior Committee to assist an Arizona water project. It was massive and complex and took eight years. By that time I was a prisoner of the seniority system—I couldn't very well quit it and go to the bottom of some other committee. My secondary assignment was to Post Office. That's a duty post, not one I took by choice. This decision today shows me my future here: I can become chairman of the Post Office Committee, with luck, when I'm sixty.

"If you take the long view, maybe I've helped improve things. My challenge of McCormack two years ago, and the scare my younger libs put in the powers this time, may have achieved some small reforms. We have regular party caucuses now, and they help. We've limited the number of subcommittees or committees one man may serve on, and that helps spread the action around. We've scared a few of the old bulls, so that individual committee rules are being loosened, and that may provide more of a participating democracy.

"If you believe, as some of us do, that time is running out—that the country's problems are accumulating and our society is in crisis —well, then, you have to think about restructuring your career possibilities and your life. What do you do? Run for the Senate and hope it's a little better over there? Teach? Write? Practice law? Where can you be more useful?"

He sighed. "Oh, hell, I've got to quit feeling sorry for myself. Decisions can't be made when you're down and out. The smart thing is to sit tight until I get my bearings. I need a rest. Ella and I are going off on a short vacation. We'll sit in the sun and play in the sand."

Where are you going? his friend asked. "Home," Udall said. That seemed a good choice, for home is not a bad place to heal.

*Harper's*
JUNE 1971

# afterword

Honesty compels a confession: "The Road to Power in Congress," to whatever extent it penetrated a national institution, would have been far less effective had it not been that Mo Udall is a valued personal friend. No worse than ideological first cousins, we liked each other from the 1961 moment we met. Later, Mo married the best friend of my late wife; it was he who gave Rosemarie's final eulogy. We simply keep few secrets. Udall's lieutenants or sympathizers, knowing this, were unusually cooperative.

One might argue, of course, that our close connection made it more difficult to interview Udall's opponents and their supporters. There is some truth in that. Some few congressmen who wanted to masquerade their personal intentions tended to gild Mo's lily when talking with me; others attempted to mislead so as to create confusion in my friend's camp; Hale Boggs granted only one semichilly perfunctory interview and his man, Gary Hymel, admitted after publication that I had "not been fully trusted." Still, I think the close association with Udall helped the piece much more than not. As he revealed himself and his strategy, it became clear what I should look for in other camps; the best questions to ask. He gave me a valuable point of comparison, became the key cross-reference against what I learned (or, at least, was told) in other interviews; though he might be mistaken he would not lie. Days before the actual vote I knew deep in my heart that Udall would be defeated. This claims no special clairvoyance. Rather, it means that my knowledge of Udall—and my more detached view of the proceedings—allowed me to separate the fantasies from the realities (no small art in politics) more easily than one who had a less ready reference point. One of the most difficult things was to refrain from passing on to Udall gossipy and possibly helpful tidbits during the weeks preceding House voting. I hope that decision hurt the Republic but little and my tattered professional integrity not at all.

There is a sad ending: Hale Boggs, as the world now knows, is presumed dead after being lost in an Alaskan airplane crash while campaigning there in 1972 for a sitting Democrat. Tip O'Neill, a mere footnote in the foregoing article, was automatically elevated to succeed him. Udall hoped to run for the third-ranking spot, House majority whip, but the leadership opted to appoint, rather than elect, that official: Mo was not among the several other assistant and regional whips also appointed.

# Goodnight Chet, Goodnight David, Goodnight Rosemarie

WEEKEND OF
AUGUST 3–4, 1968

CLIMAXING WEEKS of shilling their special merits, the three television networks explain on their preconvention shows how they will each prove superior in making Dick Nixon's coronation appear somehow exciting.

"It's not the hardware," David Brinkley had saucily reminded us on countless NBC house plugs, "it's the people." Whereupon John Chancellor's microphone whistled and sang several tinny symphonies, Sander Vanocur's gear lost its electronic voice, Frank McGee's extension cord got hopelessly tangled on camera, and some mysterious explosion in Chet Huntley's headset caused him to jump like he'd seen a snake. My wife, Rosemarie, kept waiting for Brinkley to break in to say it was not the people, it was the hardware.

ABC offers the campaign's first mudslinging: Lord Buckley accuses Count Vidal of writing perverted Hollywood prose, of assorted intriguing neuroses, and of living in Europe; Vidal counters that Buckley practices the politics of greed, is himself possessed of odd neuroses, and is a personal friend of Ronald Rea-

194

gan. One begins to understand why both the Lord and the Count have offered unsuccessfully for public office.

On CBS, Mike Wallace interviews Richard Nixon at his Long Island hideaway, telling us that "Mr. Nixon has the look of a man who has been sleeping very well."

MONDAY, AUGUST 5

*8:04 a.m.* Rosemarie wakes me to say the Republicans are apparently going through with it.

*10:40 a.m.* John Wayne makes a what's-good-for-my-daughter-is-good-for-the-country speech, confessing it has been suggested by Dean Martin. Wayne is full of sour juices over ill-treatment of his pro-Vietnam movie, *The Green Berets*, by "the left-wing press." I change my private delegate count to reflect one Californian leaning to Mussolini.

*High noon.* While John Wayne faces down the barroom baddies in the Fontainebleau's Poodle Lounge, the telly examines major presidential hopefuls. In New York, Nixon has the smug look of a used-car salesman who's just peddled two Edsels and a Hupmobile to Ralph Nader; Rockefeller, oddly intent on public suicide after months of teetering on the ledge, smiles bravely at the firing squad and assures us they're shooting blanks; Reagan says it looks as if the nomination may be forced on him by all these swell delegate-guys, though golly-geewhillikins fellers he sure hasn't asked for it.

*6:37 p.m.* Nixon arrives at Miami airport. He offers a ghost-of-Checkers speech about how Annie-Rooneyish good-all-over he'd felt that morning while standing with his Cuban refugee domestics as they received their citizenship papers. "Haven't we seen this before?" Rosemarie asks.

*6:49 p.m.* The networks abandon Maryland Governor Agnew's endorsement of Nixon in favor of watching Nixon's drive from the airport. "Poor Spiro," Rosemarie commiserates. "This is probably his last chance for national exposure."

*10:05 p.m.* Rosemarie claims she saw a Negro delegate when cameras panned the hall though it was probably a trick of lighting.

195

*10:32 p.m.* Washington's Governor Dan Evans, the convention keynoter, is billed as "a former aeronautical engineer" and immediately begins to read from *The Electrician's Manual.*

*11:08 p.m.* Rosemarie interrupts my armchair nap: "Don't you think you'd better watch this?" Huntley is interviewing Brinkley. Goodnight, Chet, Goodnight, David.

TUESDAY, AUGUST 6

*Night session.* Thomas E. Dewey, Congressman Gerry Ford, and Senator Everett Dirksen torment the English language; the world will little note nor long remember what they say here. (I spotted one delegate cupping his ear as if actually interested, but from his facial expression decided he was nursing an earache.) Not their words but certain indelible impressions remain of the old pro-pols decorating the hall: Tom Dewey, gone to beef and still rationing that slightly foolish grin, retains the ability to take the excitement out of an earthquake simply by showing up to watch it. Congressman Ford is the human equivalent of bread pudding: bland, colorless, outwardly dry, slightly spongy as one plumbs the depths. Senator Dirksen's face is where God has kept His record of mankind's sins; his voice beckons the innocent to merry romps among the brimstones. Once, eons ago, two meteorites harder than marble (though not quite as bright) collided in outer space at supersonic speeds, and there sprang into being Senator Strom Thurmond of South Carolina, The Old Confederacy, The Earth: fully grown, proclaiming wrath, understanding nothing. Ex-Senator Bill Knowland of California, bull-voiced and pugnacious even in prayer, comes off like a former Big Ten guard now running for president of Rotary International on a promise to stamp out beards.

If Nelson Rockefeller really thinks he's nominatable at this time and in this place, he should watch more television.

WEDNESDAY, AUGUST 7

*4:48 p.m.* "It's going to go down as one of the greatest conventions the American public has witnessed," predicts Senator

196

Charles Percy of Illinois. Goodnight, Chuck.

*5:50 p.m.* Mrs. Ivy Baker Priest Stevens, state comptroller of California and former U.S. treasurer, nominating Governor Reagan, slips in lauding Ronnie's "million-dollar—er, -*vote* victory." Future hell is promised looters, draft-dodgers, campus radicals, loafers, bums, snipers, flag desecraters and big-spending bureaucrats. Bankers are apparently safe, thank God.

*6:36 p.m.* Ex-Senator Knowland, also a Reagan supporter, touts delegates off Nixon by warning that first-ballot nominations would have deprived the nation of such great presidents as Rutherford B. Hayes and James Garfield. This fails to touch off the expected panic.

*7:07 p.m.* The governor of Alaska is nominated for president with delivery of the convention's most precious line: "Wally Hickel isn't afraid to make waves."

*7:49 p.m.* Florida's Governor Claude Kirk, who on opening day had indistinguished himself through a speech fearlessly endorsing orange juice, is asked his preference for vice-president and selflessly thinks of others: "Well, my mother wants me and I'll go along with her."

*8:20 p.m.* Riots across Biscayne Bay. Fires. Stonings. Cars overturned. Two or three dead. Only this morning Tony Martin sang "The Glory of Love" while Senator George Murphy did an impromptu soft-shoe.

*9:06 p.m.* Nelson Rockefeller's last forlorn hope to be nominated depends on an oratorical genius: one capable of striking enough verbal thunder and lightning to melt Old Guard stone. So out comes Pennsylvania's Governor Ray Shafer, a cross between a Groton headmaster and Charlie McCarthy, who sounds as if he's quoting the Pittsburgh phone book.

*10:15 p.m.* Governor Agnew nominates Richard Nixon, though for a moment—when he declared, "The nation needs a man to fit the times"—Rosemarie shouted he was switching back to Rocky. Goodnight, Rosemarie.

*11:18 p.m.* J. Robert Stassen, a Minnesota delegate, nominates his Uncle Harold. Delegates cheer when Stassen announces the family plans no floor demonstration.

*1:09 a.m.* Technically, it's tomorrow. Somewhere along the

197

way Senator Clifford Case was nominated for being "loved and respected across the length and breadth of New Jersey," that great Chinese-American Hiram L. Fong of Hawaii was offered, and we ran out of wine.

*1:10 a.m.* Rosemarie bolts the convention for bed.

*1:50 a.m.* Nixon's The One.

*1:52 a.m.* Rosemarie sleepily requests the latest bulletin. "They stopped Stassen," I say, "but not until he'd outpolled John Lindsay exactly two to one."

THURSDAY, AUGUST 8

*Noonish or so.* Nixon recommends for vice-president one Spiro T. Agnew. Where are you now that we need you, Hiram L. Fong? Wally Hickel, make a wave!

*1:43 p.m.* "Uncle Spiro's The Two," I say. Rosemarie stares, uncomprehending. "You gotta be kidding!" she shouts, becoming in that moment The Voice of America.

*8:22 p.m.* Ronald Reagan is back in the bleacher seats, just another Swell Guy with a 1937 haircut in a white coat and wearing his Nixon button; just another slugger from the Three-Eye League who couldn't hit the big-time curve. Nelson Rockefeller has earlier appeared before the convention, donating another little slice of his soul to Party Unity, handing the scoundrels his sword, going home at least four presidential years older and six million dollars poorer, not counting cuts and bruises. Delegates gave him a two-minute ovation and called it a decent burial.

*9:07 p.m.* The hall has long stirred with rumors that New York's Mayor John Lindsay will contest the Agnew nomination. "This convention is coming apart," John Chancellor proclaims for NBC. Now, John, you've talked to one New Yorker too many; look around at the old midwestern doughfaces in their flat Nixon skimmers, at the calm way Ev Dirksen sits there digesting his supper Scotch, at the brittle little dragon ladies impatiently puffing their filter tips, at the lean Bright Young Men in their corporate collars, and you will see there is not one insurrectionist bone in a carload.

*9:11 p.m.* Lindsay endorses Spiro Agnew in a stilted, dime-store

198

Churchill style tinged with overtones of unctuous Episcopalian and then—only slightly sullied by his small surrender—gratefully escapes into the night.

*9:17 p.m.* The delegates are all shapes and sizes (if not colors), though one most remembers the old doughfaces with their flat straw skimmers and sightless button eyes. Fred there, he owns the hardware store and has scientific proof that the kind of infantile paralysis that afflicted FDR slowly rotted the brain—just like syphilis. Ole Bill tells the funniest stories you ever heard, sings tenor in the Baptist choir, owns a few rent houses, and loans money at extra-special rates to the niggers; he's the finest old boy you ever seen but don't cross 'im or he'll skewer you on his pocket-knife. Sam, the one whose false teeth fit a shade too casually, suffers from gallstones and from the way that gang in Washington has ruined his hired hands by coddling them with a minimum wage and unemployment insurance. Carl owns the weekly news-paper and is best remembered for his hard-hitting grocery ads. J.B. owns the bank and Carl and a piece of Fred and a generous slice of his congressman. When you see a senator or a governor or a congressman dancing to some secret music, these are the un-seen old spooks piping the tunes.

So George Romney—a token candidate against Agnew—suffers one last and sadly glorious humiliation; for unlike ancient ele-phants The Old Boys do not come to the burial grounds to die but to slaughter.

*10-ish p.m.* Rosemarie and I wager on the music King Richard will select for his grand entry theme. She selects "I Believe in Yesterday," then berates me for frivolity when I nominate "Dark Town Strutter's Ball." The music is not "Dixie" (which may have been the only decision Strom Thurmond lost) but when Nixon enters to the strains of "Buckle Down Winsocki" it is funnier than anything we'd thought of.

So there they are on the platform, Dick and Pat, together again, incredibly durable ghosts from another time, the great dazzling spotlight mercifully blinding them to what they have become. It is easy to pity them now, for one knows something of where they have been: the midnight compromises and the man-datory a.k.-ing, the insane grins and the eternal hot pursuit of the impossible dream, the sapping rituals and excesses of their peculiar trade. The Nixon daughters are there of course (for we demand the sacrifice of Abraham on our political altar; we want to see Isaac's blood), Tricia a dwarfed vision in virgin white and Julie—with her David Ike—all so determined a neat, sweet throwback to the bobby-socks era, that one wonders where they rented their costumes. When the time comes I shall pity Hubert and Muriel the same hard journey.

*10:50 p.m.* I believe Dick Nixon dissipates pity quicker than any other of God's children. For in stepping up to accept the crown, Big Daddy invokes Dwight D. Eisenhower's tired old heart ("Let's win this one for Ike!") so as to somehow imply that if Winsocki will only buckle buckle down then ancient cardiac scars shall miraculously heal, Whittaker Chambers shall witness again, respectable Republican cloth coats shall once more be in fashion, and somewhere in dog heaven the faithful Checkers shall wag his tail in glee.

Goodnight America, wherever you are.

*Harper's*
NOVEMBER 1968

# THE LOST FRONTIER

As the nation moved West seeking new frontiers, Texas, a rude young empire won in blood, was inhabited by restless and adventurous men chasing their own special dreams. One of these was Oliver Loving, a legendary cattleman who, passing through the barren reefs adjoining New Mexico in 1867, was shot, scalped, and left for dead. He crawled eighteen miles, chewing an old leather glove for sustenance, and emptied his pockets of valuables to a roving band of Mexican traders against assurance that he would be packed in charcoal and returned East to Weatherford—almost five hundred miles—for burial. It was perhaps typical of the breed, the period, and the place that Oliver Loving stubbornly refused to die until he had arranged his own terms.

Our literature and our legends abound with tales of the frontier spirit, of men who lived out of saddlebags or sod huts, carving and sweating a new civilization in which they attended their own fractures, made their own rules, and raised their sons to independent and taciturn ways. In 1893, twenty-six years after Oliver Loving's death, a county bordering on New Mexico in the westernmost part of Texas was named after him. Loving County today is the most sparsely populated county in the contiguous United States, 647 square miles with 150 people scattered among

451 producing oil wells. This is land no less desolate than in an earlier time, and it is reasonable to suspect that the folks who remain here—the sons and daughters of gritty dry-gulch farmers, wild-horse tamers, and oil-field roustabouts—would naturally retain their forebears' adventuresome pioneer spirit, coupled with their own stubborn dreams of self-fulfillment.

Once the nation drew its strength from these lower regions, masses of individual songs melding into one symphony of hope and pride and individual doing. Now so much in America seems to have homogenized and dulled us that it is not too much to imagine that one day soon we shall all sound like Jack Lescoulie. Perhaps out on those few old frontiers where there is still elbowroom, we can rediscover charms, virtues, and vitalities that speak well of our roots and suggest options for our futures. These are the hopes, at least, that one can bring to an examination of Loving County.

The best place to meet Loving County's last frontiersmen is in the town of Mentone, and more specifically in Keen's Café, popularly known as "Newt's and Tootsie's." Keen's is the only place in all the county where one may purchase a beer—or anything else of value, though they do sell marriage licenses across the street at the squat county courthouse. On this boiling day, Weepin' Willie Nelson is warning on Newt Keen's jukebox of all the gratuitous troubles love provides when another kind of trouble—wearing a big-brimmed hat and a snub-nosed pistol—clatters through the front screen door.

Granville Lacy, ruddy-faced to the bone, is toting the snub-nosed pistol under the aegis of the Texas Liquor Control Board. He has driven from Odessa across seventy-eight miles of burning desert sands—past oil-well pumps, nodding in their rich extractions like gentled rocking horses, and past infrequent hardscrabble ranches—to serve a seven-day suspension notice of the beer permit entrusted to Keen's Café.

Newt Keen, proprietor, is a graying former cowboy with jug ears and a sly country grin that says he knows the joke and the joke is not on him. He seems to harbor some secret mirth, a submerged mysterious bubbling that has survived tornado funnels, droughts, bedroll rattlesnakes, rodeo fractures, and the purchase of a ranch from a salty old pioneer woman who, it developed, did not own a ranch to sell. Equipped by seasoning and history to expertly sense disaster in its many forms, Newt, on spotting the lawman, mumbles, "Oh, hail far! It's liable to get a whole lot drier around here."

Newt greets the liquor agent aloud, however, as if in the hire of Welcome Wagon: "Come in! Come in! Y'all been gettin' any rain over your way?" He crashes about in scuffed cowboy boots, his body a tad stooped as if permanently saddlesore, and offers the lawman a mug of thick coffee.

Granville Lacy sits at one of the two rickety counters between a factory-tooled sign instructing: *America, Love It or Leave It!* and a homemade sign running alternately uphill and down, as if maybe it had been painted in the dark: *Our Beer License Depends on Your Good Conduct.* The six other customers in the café, which seats a maximum of twenty, watch the lawman with obvious distaste and apprehension.

"Mr. Keen," the lawman says, "I've got some papers to serve on you."

Conveniently deaf, Newt gestures toward the coffee he's poured Lacy: "You want me to cripple that with a little dab of cream? Looks like it was dredged up from the Pecos River bottom." A headshake. Newt tries again: "How's them two big old boys of yours? They doing all right?" Above the counter are likenesses of Newt's own two older sons, Vietnam veterans, proudly in uniform.

The liquor agent unfurls and crackles his official documents: "Now, Mr. Keen, this temporary suspension begins next Monday. . . ." But Newt is clomping across the wooden floor to replenish beer supplies and honor orders for cheeseburgers or chicken-fried steaks with cream gravy.

Agent Lacy inspects his papers while Newt relays food orders to his red-haired wife, Tootsie, who retains a high faith in beehive hairdos. The jukebox has fallen dumb, permitting the lawman to better sample a united community hostility among the oil-field workers and ranchers. It is one thing to retard the flow of alcoholic comforts in any one of Manhattan's countless aid stations—or even one of Odessa's—but it is quite a deeper sin to dry up the only watering hole in all of Loving County. Newt and Tootsie dispense approximately fifty cases of beer each week; a shutdown theoretically would meanly deprive every man, woman, and child in the county of eight bottles or cans. Better Granville Lacy had come to town to poison the water, which leads one to believe that Sheriff Elgin (Punk) Jones—who reported the infraction—will have to pay for his nefarious deed.

When Newt Keen next passes within range, the liquor agent reads in a low monotone: . . . *did on the some-oddth day of August 1971, in violation of section this, paragraph so-and-so* . . . Newt shuffles, pulls an ear, shoots concerned glances at Tootsie. She attends her griddle with jerky motions of anger, slapping hamburger patties with unusual vigor. . . . *nor sell, nor give, nor consume, nor allow to be consumed, any alcoholic beverage on said premise until* . . . Wearing the abashed grin of an erring schoolboy, Newt laboriously scratches his signature.

Newt's formal surrender seemingly reassures the lawman, who jovially says, "Now I got another complaint. You've got four beer signs outside, and you're not allowed but two."

"*Four?* I can't count but three."

"Naw, four. Your main sign counts as two. One for each side of the sign."

Newt, uncertain of the bureaucratic bogs, says, "Well, what's the big gripe?"

"Congestion."

Newt is mute and uncomprehending. This is happening to him in downtown Mentone—population forty-four—where from any vantage point one can see for three days in all directions and still have nothing to tell. He gazes across all that empty territory until his eyes lock on a distant windmill. "Well," he finally drawls, "I sure would hate to cause any traffic jams." When the locals snigger over their well-ketchuped home fries, the lawman reddens. "We've got no choice but to enforce the law. It's an old law the church folks got passed back in the '30s." He makes it out the door unaided by any understanding nods.

Before the lawman's dust departs, all the customers compete to damn the prying old government. Warren Burnett, a prominent Texas lawyer who has paused at the café in midpassage to El Paso, offers to represent Newt for free should he wish to fight the suspension order: "We'll claim cruel and unusual punishment! A man could die of thirst out here. Hell, Newt, your place is more than a community center—it's an *outpost*, by God, offering new beginnings and shelter against the elements. . . ."

"Do it, Newt," Tootsie said.

"Naw, I got to live with that old boy. Besides, this ain't his fault."

"Well," the lawyer said, "come next Monday it'll be a long hot path to beer. So whose fault is it?"

Newt drawls it out like *Gunsmoke*'s Festus: "Accordin' to that batch of official papers, it's mine!" After the laughter abates, he says, "Aw, one night a while back we got to dancing and barking at the moon in here and, well, maybe we run a little past closing time. Mister, I been in this country since the sun wasn't no bigger than a orange and there wasn't no moon a-tall and windmills wasn't but waist-high, and I've learnt that when you can *sell* something out here—you better not worry about what time it is."

Tootsie says: "That ain't the whole story."

"Well, OK, mama. Awright, I *was* dranking nearly as much as I was selling and business wasn't too bad. The sheriff—old Punk Jones—he come in and caught me and snitched to the liquor board."

"You oughta run for sheriff yourself, Newt," one of the locals suggests.

"Naw sir," Newt says. "I ain't gonna say a mumblin' word against old Punk—right on up to election day." Appreciating the laughter, he fishes in icy waters and pops himself a beer. "Punk, he don't have nothing to do but enforce the closing laws in this one little old place, and I sure wouldn't wanta interfere with law and order here in Loving County."

The dominant political strain in Loving County runs to an abiding conservatism. The natives—well off and poor alike—

reject anything smacking of charity, and so they regard federal
aid as being no less poisonous than the ever-present rattlesnake.
When a federal court instructed every county in Texas to participate in the Family Food Assistance Program for the poor, Loving
County Judge W. T. (Bill) Winston said: "We don't need it, we
don't want it, and we can't use it if we're forced to take it."
Snorting and jiggling his beer glass in Newt's and Tootsie's now,
Judge Winston gloomily says, "They finally forced it on us.
We've got nine people getting it—seven in one family. And
*they're* Mexicans." When the Department of Health, Education
and Welfare ordered the county to either racially integrate Mentone's sixteen-pupil school or lose its federal money, Judge Winston fired off a terse letter informing Washington that Loving
County: (1) had no black residents, (2) had never received a
dime's worth of federal school aid, and (3) didn't covet any.

Television has brought the problems of New York, Watts, and
Saigon to the attention of the neglected territory. Everybody
worries about blacks or dope or crime or the Vietcong just as if
they had some. Newt Keen no longer goes off and leaves his café
doors unlocked to accommodate stray customers because "you
can't tell when somebody might come over from Monahans or
Pyote and clean you out." But the Mentone jail has not had a
customer in seven years, and Loving County's crime wave last
year consisted of a profitless burglary of the schoolhouse and the
theft of several rolls of steel cable from an oil lease.

Ann Blair, a pretty young blond who works in the courthouse
for her mother, county clerk Edna Clayton, frets that the outside
world may taint her two small children. "Let's face it, it's boring
here for adults, but there's no better place to raise kids," says
Ann, a graduate of Odessa Junior College. "We have a good family life. My fifth-grade boy has learned work and the value of a
dollar. When I went off to college, I saw wild kids and all kinds
of temptation. And it's so much worse now, with drugs and sex
crimes."

Inconvenience is taken for granted. The nearest moviehouse,
beauty shop, physician, lawyer, bank, weekly newspaper, cemetery, or grocery store is from fifty-five to ninety round-trip miles
away. Fifteen of sixteen Mentone School pupils are bused in

from six to sixty miles away. Sixth graders and above are bused almost eighty round-trip miles to Wink.

Despite the riches of oil and gas under the earth, each Loving County family must provide its own bottled-gas system. And there is no public water supply. Water is hauled in a tank from Pecos at fifty cents per barrel. Even cattle balk at drinking the brackish product of the Pecos River, long ago polluted by potash interests in upstream New Mexico, a fact that, surprisingly, no one here rails against even though their forebears always raised hell at anything—fences, sheep herds, squatters—infringing on their freedoms or presuming to prosper at their expense.

The land is stark and flat and treeless, altogether as bleak and spare as mood scenes in Russian literature, a great dry-docked ocean with small swells of hummocky tan sand dunes or hump-backed rocky knolls that change colors with the hour and the shadows: reddish brown, slate gray, bruise colored. But it is the sky—God-high and pale, like a blue chenille bedspread bleached by seasons in the sun—that dominates. There is simply *too much* sky. Men grow small in its presence and—perhaps feeling diminished—they sometimes are compelled to proclaim themselves in wild or berserk ways. Alone in those remote voids, one may suddenly half believe he is the last man on earth and go in frantic search of the tribe. Desert fever, the natives call it.

And while the endless dry doomed land and eternal sky may bring on the fever, so, too, can the weather. The wind, persistent and unengageable for half the year, swooshes unencumbered from the northernmost Great Plains, howling, whining, singing off-key and covering everything with a maddening grainy down. Court records attest that during the windy seasons the natives are quicker to lift their voices, or their fists, or even their guns, in rage.

The summer sun is as merciless as a loan shark: a blinding, angry orange explosion baking the land's sparse grasses and quickly aging the skin. In winter there are nights to ache the bone; cold, stinging lashings of frozen rain. Yet even the weather is not the worst natural enemy. Outside the industrial sprawl of the prairie's mini-cities—on the occasional ranches or oil leases or in the flawed little country towns—the great curse is boredom. Teen-agers in the faded jeans and glistening ducktail hairstyles of another day wander in restless packs to the roller rink or circle root beer stands sounding their mating calls by a mighty revving of engines. Old men shuffle dominoes in the shade of service stations or feedstores. There is the television, of course, and the joys of small-town gossip—and in season a weekly high school football game may secretly be considered more important than even Vacation Bible School. Newt Keen laments the passing of country socials where people reveled all night at one ranch house or another: "Now you got to go over to Pecos to them fightin' and dancin' clubs. But, you know, it ain't near as much fun to fight with strangers."

The young and the imaginative in Loving County are largely disaffected, strangers in Jerusalem. And those who can, move on when they can. Today's desert youths belong to a transitional generation. Born to an exhausted frontier where there are no more Dodge Citys to tame, no more wild rivers to ford, no more cattle trails to ride or oil booms to follow, theirs is a heritage beyond preserving. The last horseman has passed by, leaving only myths and fences. Industrialization has come and gone: having drilled and robbed the earth, the swaggering two-fisted oil boomer, heir apparent to the earlier cowboy or Indian fighter, has clattered off to the next feverish adventure, leaving behind sterile sophisticated pumps and gauges and storage tanks that automatically record their own dull technological accomplishments. Only the land remains, the high sky, the eerie isolation. The wind hums mocking tunes of loss and the jukeboxes echo it: *"Just call Lonesome-seven-seven-two-oh-three . . ." "I'd trade all of my tomorrows for just one yesterday. . . ."*

The songs are of rejection, disappointment, aborted opportunities . . . of finishing second. And the music is everywhere, incessantly jangling, the call of the lonely. Even many graybeards who have trimmed back their dreams—if they ever had any— cannot sit still unless the jukebox or radio is moaning to them of old loves lost, of the tricks of the wicked cities, of life's rough and rocky traveling. Few know that the music says more about them than they say of themselves.

The young sense the loss of a grander and more adventurous past. It is these—the young and those who secretly know they never will be truly young again—who prove most susceptible to fits of desert fever. And so they sometimes go lickety-splitting down the rural highways at speeds dizzy enough to confuse the ambidextrous, running like so many Rabbit Angstroms, leaving behind a trail of sad country songs, beer vapors and the echo of some feverish, senseless shout. Some may find themselves at dawn howling in the precincts of a long-forgotten girl friend, or tempting the dangers of "fightin' and dancin' clubs" with names like Blue Moon Bar or Texas Taddy Jo's. Some keep running: to the army or to a Fort Worth factory or maybe to exotic Kansas City. Others, their fevers cooled and with no place to go, drive back slowly—a bit sheepishly—to rejoin the private chaos and public tediums of their lives.

Newt Keen's son Jack begins to boot stomp across the wooden floor in a jukebox dance with a tall visiting airline hostess. Jack is dipping snuff and wearing an outsized silver belt buckle he has won riding bulls. Over the whines and thumps of the music he regrets that after next weekend he can't rise at four thirty each morning to cowboy on one of the area ranches because school is imminent. Jack does not appear to be real partial to school, where they take a dim view of twelve-year-old eighty-three-pound boys who appreciate snuff more than arithmetic. To somebody who first dipped at age five, who slew his first snake at seven, and who is impatient to ramrod his own ranch, the arbitrary restrictions on scholars can be mighty vexing.

Tootsie worries about her son. "Till school takes up, Jack's the only kid in Mentone. The rest live on ranches or oil leases. All he's ever been around is adults and he don't get along real well with kids." Jack proves his mother right on the second day of school, decking another boy who has earned his disapproval. Jack's reward is three licks from the principal's paddle. "It stung," he admits, taking a pinch of Copenhagen from his personal tin. "I got to sign the paddle, though. You ain't allowed to sign it unless you been whupped with it."

"What'd you hit that boy for?" Tootsie demands.

Busy roping a cane-bottomed chair, Jack says, "Aw, he's about half silly."

"Yes, but what'd he *do*, look at you cross-eyed? Jack, dammit, stop roping them chairs. This ain't no rodeo arena."

Disengaging his lariat, Jack says, "He put his hands on my book."

"Oh," Tootsie says, apparently mollified.

Newt is amused. "Jack despises school much as I do a rattlesnake. He swears he's gonna quit when he gits to sixth grade."

"Or the seventh," Jack says. "Maybe the eighth."

"Why, Jack," Newt says, "you're liable to wind up a full professor. What's got into you?"

The boy, vaguely embarrassed, tilts his western hat over his eyes: "Mr. Knott says sixth grade ain't enough any more."

Charles Knott, forty-three, is the new schoolteacher in Mentone. When asked why in mid-career he has deserted El Paso's modern school system for the lesser ecstasies of Loving County, he says, "I like small towns. I had thirty-odd kids to the class in El Paso, damn few of them Anglos. The kids here are eager. You take little Jack Keen. Now, he may wind up ranching and live here all his life. If he wants that—well, fine. But he ought to have options. He ought to know that another life exists. You know, kids from small towns—well, there just seems to be more *to* them. I grew up in a little old East Texas town—one picture show and a one-gallus night watchman. And a higher percentage of the kids there made it than ever will make it in El Paso. They were more aware of themselves, aware of life. Maybe it's nurturing their isolation, having time to think things through. Whatever, I think small-town kids use more of their potential."

The next day, as school lets out, Tootsie is gazing through the shimmying heat waves when suddenly she says, "*My Lord*, little Jack must be sick. Yonder he comes wagging his school books *home* with him." Apparently she doesn't realize that Jack may have a growing dream.

Day after day, as the suspension lengthens, the mood in Newt and Tootsie's beerless free-enterprise café grows more and more subdued. Since the suspension, Sheriff Punk Jones—who rose to his present eminence after serving as courthouse janitor—has begun to hear rumors that a disgruntled Newt Keen might oppose him on the ballot after all. A good country politician who knows that a handful of votes might return a sheriff to mopping the courthouse, Punk Jones begins to stress the vast stores of bookwork attending his office; it is well known that Newt's painfully concocted customers' checks for chili or cheeseburgers require more translations than the Rosetta Stone.

In the café, customers are infrequent. Those who drop in jangle around aimlessly, some lamenting the lack of liquid comforts with the sorrow of one whose dog has died. Tootsie sits at a table near the soundless jukebox, making do with coffee. Abruptly she says to her husband behind the counter, "Newt, what we doing in this fool café business anyhow?"

"Well, hon, I just got plain tard of being governor, and the gold-mining business was boring me."

Irked, Tootsie helplessly shakes her head. Daring for once to question life's random assignments, her reward is another of Newt's drawling jokes. One has the impression she suddenly requires answers to questions that did not exist for her before. Something in the restless sweeping of her eyes hints that she has come on some new, if myopic, vision.

"We've made a living," Newt defends, walking over and putting a quarter in the jukebox.

"Yeah," Tootsie says. "I don't buy a whole lot of diamonds."

"Naw, mama, but you don't live in some old line shack and cook for the range camp neither." They are silent while Willie Nelson sings of how "it's a Bloody-Mary mornin' since baby left me without warnin' sometime in the night. . . ." "Say," Newt says, "you remember when we was fresh married and lived in that old dirt-floor dugout?" Tootsie nods, smiling, her face softened by some special old memory. "Well, hon, I always wanted to ask you something about that: when you snuggled up so close to me that first winter, was it on account of you loved me so much or because you was scared of the rats?"

In a monotone as flat as sourdough biscuits, she says, "I was scared of the rats." They look at each other and laugh.

"All this will straighten out in a day or two," Newt promises, seeming to have missed the point of her question, her mood.

"Hail, we got more food business than we do beer sales."

He shuffles over and sits at the table beside Tootsie, who is stirring her mug of thick coffee. The two of them gaze out the screen door at the lost frontier. Nothing, absolutely nothing, is moving on the ribbon-straight highway. They sit and stare, their faces in repose as melancholy as a plain old three-chord hurtin' country song, while Eddy Arnold croons to them of big bouquets of roses.

Something old and precious and a close kinsman to steel— some abiding chemistry of hope and grit—seems to have disappeared from the frontier blood. The men who shaped and settled this desolate waste relied on a fierce, near-savage independence coupled with a vision that made them feel captains of their own fate. That vigor, that vision, is gone now, as exhausted as the frontier itself.

It is sad to see people so tamed and hobbled and timid and dreamless in a land born wild. The descendants of the old breed may roar like wounded lions at distant menaces—the pretensions of sociologists, the pious prattlings of politicians, the mod and the unfamiliar—but they grapple ineffectually with their immediate concerns: their boredoms, small, mean jobs, polluted rivers, and officious bureaucrats. In the old days the people simply would not have tolerated the closing down of their only communal outpost: no, they would have told Punk Jones that they would drink when thirsty, by God, no matter the preferences of some chair-bound Austin bureaucrat with nothing better to do than sign suspension orders. This lethargic acceptance of fate's happenstance gifts, with no more than a shrug or a token gripe, gives one the sense of being a visitor at a wake, of witnessing some final burial of the spirit, of watching people without purpose merely getting through another day. Frontiers were made for better uses.

Still, one does encounter qualities to admire and enjoy here. A withered rancher who will identify himself only as Jesse contentedly saws into one of Tootsie's steaks and says, "This country's soothin'. The country's *close* to you out here. You feel a kinship with it. It don't have no boundaries." Newt Keen says of his neighbors: "We come together like a family when there's trouble.

You take over here in Kermit"—he jerks a thumb toward the highway—"this stranded family stopped at a church one Sunday to ask for a little food and gas money. All they got was a promise the congregation would pray for 'em. Well, they limped on over here. We supplied 'em a big box of groceries and took up a collection for gas."

There is little Jack Keen, who probably has spunk and survival instincts superior to most children and surely has more room to discover himself. Some essence of the pioneer woman's endurance survives in Tootsie. Newt is improbably cheerful in a time full of frowning; he at once preserves the old colloquialisms and speaks a native American poetry.

That much has survived and must be clung to. But over the years, generation by generation, the resources and the spirit of Loving County have been dried up, and there is a lesson to be learned here. As in the nation as a whole, each generation spoke much and thought little of the future requirements of its heirs. Hereafter we must plan far better with far less.

*Life*
MARCH 1972

## afterword

Newt Keen ran afoul of personal ambition. In the same week that a certain key issue of *Life* made its appearance, Newt upped and announced for sheriff against his old tormentor, Punk Jones. Since Warren Burnett and I perhaps had a bit to do with that decision, telling Newt how he was sore needed in public office when we took on a shade too much beer, we sent him twenty-five dollars each and our good wishes. Newt Keen was accused of a lavish campaign financed by outside interests and he lost, fifty-three to thirty-eight. In mid-1973, Newt sold his café and took a job in Pecos.

# REQUIEM FOR FAULKNER'S HOMETOWN

*I feel sorry for these millions of people here.
They don't live in Oxford.*

—WILLIAM FAULKNER,
WRITING FROM NEW YORK TO A FRIEND

hey're ruining my riding path," William Faulkner complained only a few days before his death in July of 1962. "They" were cutting a new interstate highway through the wooded cradling little red-dirt hills on the outskirts of Oxford, Mississippi. The town's most famous son (Member, American Academy of Arts and Letters; Nobel Prize for literature, 1950; two Pulitzers; one National Book Award) did not approve of trading greenery for asphalt and calling it progress.

The bulldozers are working still in the Jefferson chronicled by Faulkner in tales of his mythical Yoknapatawpha County. Already they have birthed neoned motels, drive-in banks, all-night truck stops and glass-adorned pizza parlors enough to have robbed Oxford of much of its special character and charm. The Confederate soldier guarding Faulkner's beloved Square, his sightless stone eyes turned forever south, beholds a mixed marriage of the modern and the neglected; even with perfect vision he would rarely chance to look upon the preserved or the restored.

There are ghostly glimpses from the past, certainly, in the old courthouse with its white plaster columns, crowning cupola, and the sign inside promising a five-dollar fine for spitting on the floor. The old nesters with their weather-seasoned necks poking

214

up from khaki or blue-denim work shirts whittle and gum away their solitary afternoons on courthouse benches, sitting as perpetual judges of mankind, playing out roles assigned them by custom, fate, and Faulkner. Here and there Negroes move about on errands of commerce or mystery, passing into The Golden Rule ("1¢ to $1 Bargains") or into Sneed's Hardware or Smallwood's Dollar Store. A huge painted Confederate flag serves as an advertising decal for Rebel Cosmetology College. A few old dented and muddy pickup trucks are parked willy-nilly around the Square; on warm summer days farmers at the curb market hawk their fresh eggs or watermelons.

The Square's concrete watering trough is gone. So are most of the second-story wooden balconies on business houses ringing the courthouse where—in *Requiem for a Nun*—lawyer Gavin Stevens vainly battled for the life of Nancy Mannigoe ("a Negress, quite black, about thirty") charged with the willful murder of an infant white child. The iron fence around the courthouse is no more, and a dozen years ago man began paying tribute to parking meters. Gone, too, is the brooding jail, built in 1870, where Hollywood filmed scenes for *Intruder in the Dust,* and of which Faulkner wrote, "If you would peruse in unbroken—ay, overlapping—continuity the history of a community, look not in the church registers and the courthouse records, but beneath the successive layers of calcimine and creosote and whitewash on the walls of the jail, since only in that forcible carceration does man find the idleness in which to compose, in the gross and simple terms of his gross and simple lusts and yearnings, the gross and simple recapitulations of his gross and simple heart." A new jail has risen unworthy of the old: a modern pastel structure with a masonry-grill front reminiscent of a second-rate beach resort. One knows, instinctively, that it is altogether too antiseptic to purge the sinner of his baser wrongs.

Oxford's community bones have known much pain. The town, chartered in 1837, was burned by General "Whiskey" Smith's Union bluecoats in 1864, suffered Reconstruction, was staggered by the Great Depression extending well into the 1930s for the poor countryfolk of northern Mississippi's knobby hills. Oxford has known flood, drought, and fiery passions: here, in William

215

Faulkner's imagination, the dirt-poor Snopes family by wile and guile conquered a society and a culture of rural aristocrats just as did their real-life counterparts; and here, in 1962, with the aid of bayonets, tear gas, the Kennedy brothers, and after one screaming night-long riot, James Meredith racially integrated proud Ole Miss—previously known for its efficient football teams, shapely Dixie dolls, and generations of fun-loving sons of planters or merchants.

For a time Oxford was split and made sullen by the "second Civil War" with its occupying federal troops. Those most recent wounds are slowly healing. Some one hundred Negroes are now enrolled on the University of Mississippi campus. Apparently they peacefully coexist with the sixty-seven hundred white students. Within two or three years, the dark, human trickle may approximate an incoming tide. Speakers who dare inveigh against the Vietnam war or describe themselves as integrationists are now invited on campus and tolerated in town. Oxford's leading citizens have passed word that no retributions will be permitted. "We don't claim to like all these changes," a businessman admitted, "but we *do* recognize them as inevitable. New riots or incidents would only ruin our community—both spiritually and economically." Local residents are solicitous of visitors. One senses a special effort to put the best community foot forward. "Townies" have even become passably tolerant of youthful folly: few were moved to apoplexy when four hundred jeering Ole Miss students, weary of driving twenty-eight miles to Holly Springs for beer, marched on the mayor's home in protest after a local-option beer election was narrowly won by the "drys." (Though Oxford prohibits beer, liquor is sold at package stores and mixed drinks are available in some few restaurant-connected lounges.) Shudders were held to a discreet minimum last spring when a dozen campus hippies were charged with possession of marijuana.

Excluding its university population—Ole Miss is a separate corporate entity embracing eighteen hundred acres—Oxford has grown from the 3,956 persons counted in the 1950 census and the 5,283 recorded a decade later into a sprawling town now estimated at just short of 10,000. This growth has dismayed some of

216

Oxford's older heads or more reticent sons of the soil. One of these is Jimmy Faulkner, forty-four-year-old nephew of William and son of another novelist, John. "The town's getting too damn big," he says. "I stay out on my farm unless I'm forced to go in."

Jimmy Faulkner's rambling old house, built with slave labor in 1850, is one of several antebellum homes opened to candlelight tours during Oxford's annual Pilgrimage each April when for three days romantic notions of the Old South revive. Gentle ladies lay out their finest crystal, silver, and linens. A Confederate tea, with southern belles in formal white gloves and floor-sweeping gowns, brightens Mary Buie Museum. Jimmy Faulkner holds an Old South plantation barbecue in the same yard where General Grant's troops camped in 1862; at sundown, to a blaring of bugles and Rebel yells, he leads a troop of horsemen thundering across the grounds in one final defiant Confederate charge. It is difficult to imagine William Faulkner participating in the perpetuation of such old romanticisms, except to horselaugh a bit, unless perhaps he had reached fathomless depths in his bourbon jug.

The younger Faulkner, a look-alike to his famous uncle and said to have been Brother Will's favorite relative, is an intensely private man. "I don't know why writers keep coming here to write about the Faulkners," he grumbled. "Everything's been said. Each one pumps me as if he will learn the Big Secret. Well, he won't learn it from me!" Well, what *was* the Big Secret? Faulkner's head jerked around and he reddened. "There ain't any," he snapped.

Oxford has at least one open secret, however: deep community division over how accessible William Faulkner's home, Rowan Oak, should be made to the public. Under terms of a ninety-nine-year lease granted the University of Mississippi by the author's widow—now living in Virginia—Ole Miss has primary custodial care of Rowan Oak's fourteen acres. Its actual control of the home, however, is no more than nominal. The lease may be canceled by the Faulkner family upon sixty-day notice, and until her recent death Mrs. William Faulkner's sister, Dorothy Oldham, was the only person authorized to admit visitors.

To the chagrin of many Ole Miss officials and chamber of commerce boosters, Miss Oldham was diligently selective in ruling who may or may not visit Rowan Oak. "They're not going to turn this into a commercial gimmick," she declared in her final days. "If Faulkner scholars or special student groups properly apply to me, I bend over backwards to receive them at Rowan Oak. Why, if you opened that home to the public then people would strip the place of books, bricks, or boughs—anything they could pack off. The idly curious, people who haven't read so much as a single *word* of Faulkner, would be trampling through the gardens. Common tourists!"

Miss Oldham required the better part of a week to determine that my own credentials were in order. She greeted me at the door of the 121-year-old house (purchased by Faulkner in 1930) in a cheerful mood and conducted a gracious tour of the grounds. Here was the old pear tree, felled by a windstorm, which Faulkner had propped with a log and nursed until it again bore fruit; there was the old carriage house where he cured his meat; he had built the stables and whitewashed fences—now peeling—himself. "Mr. Faulkner died without telling anybody the formula for his whitewash," Miss Oldham said. "One of the colored said *he* knew—but, of course he didn't and it's still flaking."

The exterior of the two-and-one-half-story twelve-room antebellum house is well preserved. The interior (or that portion Miss Oldham consented to show) is comfortable but surprisingly shabby; it is not the home of a pretentious man, one preoccupied with form or show. The library is much as Faulkner left it: books scattered on a large center table and lining shelves on two walls, three paintings by Faulkner's mother (one of her most famous son, age twenty, hangs over the fireplace), a favored wood carving of Don Quixote, a stuffed owl. A soft if aging couch is centered before the fireplace; there is a generous stock of firewood stacked in one corner.

Faulkner's main workroom, adjoining the library, is spartan and small. He wrote sitting in a severe straight-backed chair, on a rickety table of his own craftsmanship, his view taking in the stables and the woods beyond. On the fireplace mantel rests an unframed painting of a mule, a container of Faulkner's favorite blend of pipe tobacco, and the long wicks with which he brought fire from the fireplace to his pipe. A corner desk holds a ledger in which Faulkner kept his farm accounts, a bottle of horse liniment, a tobacco can, a dish containing fishhooks, buttons, and screws; there is a half-bed on which Faulkner napped after hard stretches of writing.

The most interesting item is Faulkner's day-by-day outline of *A Fable*, written in his hand on the north and east walls and now protected by coats of clear varnish. The headings range from "Monday" through "Sunday"; symbolically, "Tomorrow" is hidden behind a door.

These two rooms, and an entrance hall, are the only ones Miss Oldham showed. The rest is private; she was oblivious to hints that one desired to see the large sitting room where Faulkner once spoke the final elegy over the Negro nanny who raised him, and where his own final rites were spoken before burial in St. Peter's Cemetery.

Reluctantly, and only after much civic begging, Miss Oldham permitted Pilgrimage visitors to walk up the driveway from Rowan Oak's padlocked outer gate to the beginning of a brick walk. (As curator of the Mississippi room in the Ole Miss library, Dorothy Oldham presided over a special Faulkner collection containing his works in thirty-eight languages, other books of and about him, and a revered glass display case holding many of the medals, prizes, and scrolls he won.)

Exploratory talks have been held with officials of the United States Department of the Interior in hopes that Rowan Oak will be designated a national historic site and thereafter operated by the government. Businessmen, envisioning floods of monied tourists—and some members of academia—support the plan. Unless Faulkner-family attitudes rapidly change, however, it seems a remote prospect. "We're embarrassed," one city booster said, "when visitors come from great distances to see Faulkner's town only to discover that we haven't preserved much of it—and much of what we have preserved is locked up. Why, do you know that the pitch to tourists on our official state highway maps fails to mention either Faulkner or Oxford?"

More and more, local citizens have come to speak of city ordinances requiring that existing Faulkneria be preserved and that future construction conform with an ill-defined Faulknerian period; radicals would go a step beyond, requiring even modernized buildings to remodel along older lines. Local authorities have been slow to act, because not everyone favors the restoration scheme. An Ole Miss professor explained why: "Many people here are convinced that they—or their ancestors—were somehow maligned in Faulkner's work. Others are just plain jealous of him. And the surviving Faulkners are neither the most outgoing nor the most popular people in the world. Then in a small town such as Oxford one must allow for the 25 per cent who oppose *any* community planning out of sheer cussedness and old blood."

An old Faulkner chum, "Colonel" J. R. Cofield, who for thirty years made the most and best photographs and portraits of his idol, is enraged because Oxford has failed to give "my little friend" proper homage: "Bill Faulkner was the most respected novelist of his century—a genius who walked among us. Some of these old soreheads around here are too stubborn to realize it. Why, Oxford has been so desecrated that they can't film Faulkner's last book, *The Reivers,* here in his hometown! They're looking in other sections of Mississippi and over in Tennessee for a town that's retained more of its old flavor. That's a crying shame, podner!"

Still, the persistent visitor finds numerous Faulknerian scenes. One may, for example, enjoy the same stroll to town that William Faulkner took almost daily. It begins at the padlocked outer gate at Rowan Oak, on the outskirts of town on Old Taylor Road, near Baily's Woods with its blackjack oaks, wisteria, and kudzu tangles, turns left on South Lamar, and continues for approximately one mile—past old homes, narrow streets, brooding old trees—to the Square. Thence to Gathright-Reed Drugs on Van Buren Avenue, where W. M. Reed (known to everyone as "Mister Mack") visited most mornings with William Faulkner on crops, politics, and sometimes on writing. Faulkner always brought his manuscripts to Mack Reed for wrapping and mailing; the old-timer remembers that as he wrapped Faulkner's last book he heard him mumble, "I been aimin' to quit all this."

From Gathright-Reed, Faulkner crossed the street to take a shortcut up the alley to Colonel Cofield's photographic studio. Here he might linger for a few moments, listening in amusement as the loquacious Colonel entertained him with outrageous tales or cajoled him to autograph one of the many Faulkner photographs he still displays there. Colonel Cofield is a lean, bushy-haired man who rolls his own cigarettes, and visitors find him capable, in top form, of back-to-back lectures on William Faulkner, St. Paul, Pericles, H. Rap Brown, the Ole Miss football team, and the majesty of the mule.

Faulkner made his way around the whole of the Square on his "good" days, pausing to chat with old friends or greeting familiar faces. In more vague times (when, Oxfordians came to suspect, he was "mentally writing") Faulkner might fail to acknowledge old friends at five paces or might prop against a building to stare mutely at some private vision. Ultimately, dodging traffic circling the courthouse, he made his way to the old red-brick post office (still standing) where he picked up his mail and returned home.

One may find on a lonely hilltop in Oxford the old Chandler house with its iron fence along which, in *The Sound and the Fury*, the feebleminded Benjy wandered, thinking his furious and solitary and disjointed thoughts. In William Faulkner's youth a handicapped young boy lived there; doubtlessly the budding author observed him inside the fence, his demented gaze open and yet somehow afraid. Several Ole Miss college boys recently shared the old Chandler house, braving the obvious comparisons from fellow students relative to their respective mentalities and the fictional Benjy's.

On a back lot near the intersection of South Eleventh and Buchanan streets is a paint-peeled old house, vacant now, where Faulkner first lived when he came to Oxford from Ripley, Mississippi, as a five-year-old child. Scholars presume this house is the one that sheltered the fictional Miss Rosa Coldfield, that tragic and outraged southern child-woman. Colonel John Sartoris's bank, owned by William Faulkner's great-grandfather until taken over by "a shrewd countryman named Joe Parks," still stands on the Square, much modernized. (Colonel Faulkner, like his fictional counterpart, Colonel Sartoris, was a soldier, statesman, author, railroad builder and duelist; he killed two men and was himself shot to death by a former business partner who had become his political rival.)

Fifteen strides away from the Square is the one-story red-brick building, topped by a rounded corner turret, where Faulkner's lifelong friend, mentor, and onetime literary agent, Phil Stone, practiced law. Here, too, in Faulkner's youth, Oxford's younger set—self-described as "The Bunch"—gathered to debate, flirt, and plot mild mischief. Stone, now dead, is generally said to have been a loose model for Gavin Stevens, who appeared in at least a half dozen Faulkner novels.

St. Peter's Cemetery of Oxford suggests—in the words of Ole Miss professor Evans Harrington, among the best of the Faulkner scholars—"that hill-rimmed, cedar-shaded destination of so many Faulkner characters. Its tombs and epitaphs, indeed, bear a strangely mingled testimony of the author's real life and his legends. Here in the Faulkner plot a medallion of William Faulkner's grandmother, Sally Murry Faulkner, is strikingly similar to that which Gavin Stevens placed on the tomb of Eula Varner Snopes. . . . Beneath the medallion [is] the identical biblical quotation, with the omission of a few words, which Flem Snopes selected for Eula's epitaph." Because there was no remaining room for the most-heralded Faulkner in the family plot, he is buried some distance away on a slope separating the old section of the burial grounds from the new; his tomb is shaded by three giant oak trees whose roots reach toward his grave.

One rainy night in Oxford, a night full of thunder and fearful electrical crashes, I was made depressed by post-cocktail-party blues and by the characterless assembly-line motel-room furnishings among which I sat, blankly ogling color television. I crossed to the window to gaze on a block with a sign boasting of Oxford's historic importance and contributions to the past. Neon blinked over my motel, and occasional lightning flashes illuminated neighboring structures: a neo-Colonial savings and loan building, two service stations displaying the gaudy shields of oil companies, the new funeral home. From my vantage point Oxford might have been any of the mindless, modernized towns now defacing a nation's soil. Suddenly, I resented it: resented it as much as William Faulkner had resented the despoiling of the bridle paths he rode, the woods he hunted, the old jail where solitary poets spilled out "their gross and simple hearts."

And then, unmindful of the rain, I was out in the streets, seeking something more and better. Lost, uncertain of any certain goal, I became aware of the barks of strange dogs and the imagined hoots of tree owls; of the stormy night and of the vast dark reaches of Mississippi mud. In time, with the aid of a city map and matches to read it by, I wandered to St. Peter's to search out William Faulkner's grave. (Later, when a friend drove me to St. Peter's, I strangely did not tell him of my nocturnal visit.) The tomb is a simple one for so illustrious a man, its white marble headstone marked only "Faulkner"; the darker marble slab running the length of the grave bears his full name, basic dates (born September 25, 1897; died July 6, 1962) and a single quotation ("Beloved, Go With God"). I squatted under one of the dripping oaks, realizing then that I was more than tipsy and was being more than moderately theatrical. Yet I wished, as a favor to Faulkner, that I had brought along a taste of fine old Kentucky bourbon, for which he had a definite appreciation, to flower his grave. And I tried to recall those words Faulkner once wrote to a friend on the subject of man's mortality: "You know, after all, they put you in a pine box and in a few days the worms have you. Someone might cry for a day or two and after that they've forgotten all about you." Well, even Faulkner could be wrong. God love the whisky soldiers.

Later, drenched and sobered and back in town, I toured the lonely Square. The rain had stopped and the night had grown warmer while Oxford slept. In the shadows and dim night-lights the town appeared infinitely more mysterious, more Faulknerian, and yet it seemed somehow as familiar and comforting as an old friend. Perhaps it should have, for like thousands of others I had read William Faulkner's description of the mythical Jefferson where "life lived, too, with all its incomprehensible passion and

223

turmoil and grief and fury and despair, but here at six o'clock you could close the cover on it and even the weightless hand of a child could put it back among its unfeatured kindred on the quiet eternal shelves and turn the key upon it for the whole and dreamless night."

*Holiday*
MARCH 1969

# HOW TO SUCCEED
# IN TEXAS
# WITHOUT REALLY

The state of Texas at this writing has not yet decided whether to try Ernest Medders again or forget it and hope the Medders case —with all its majestic embarrassment to bankers, cattle barons, Neiman-Marcus stores, an order of Catholic nuns, Dallas socialites, and politicians, including the president of the United States —will, like a Texas tumbleweed, just dry up and blow away.

It isn't likely; the Medders case is simply too much of a human comedy to quickly pass from view. It involves three million borrowed dollars, barn dances for the rich, bankruptcy, the most expensive mink coat on record, Guy Lombardo, Keystone-Cop financial blunders, congressmen and senators and Dean Rusk, an unlettered pauper posing as a millionaire, red faces all around, and maybe Cinderella, and universal avarice and greed tossed in. You can see it done up in the movies with the same big-screen treatment Hollywood gave Edna Ferber's *Giant*—a bringdown of all the hoo-hawing, oil-slick, Big Rich Texas known and unloved by all.

Hollywood would have to find a composite cowboy to play Ernest Medders: someone with a touch of Slim Sommerville's slouch, Hoss Cartwright's country-boy earnestness, Maverick's flair for gambling, Wallace Beery's half-roguish bumbling, Fred MacMurray's air of faint bewilderment, and someone with the kind of blind faith Roy Rogers had in Trigger.

It is the wife, however, who would *really* be difficult to cast. Possibly Ava Gardner, Joan Crawford, Marjorie Main, and Ina Ray Hutton's All-Girl Band could never grunt up the élan, executive know-how, spunk, and brass necessary to play Margaret Medders the way Margaret Medders has played Margaret Medders in real life.

While everybody sweated out the jury's return, a shriveled old-timer in wrinkled khaki clothes and a cattleman's coiled hat recited an ancient talmud long favored by defense attorneys: A happy jury won't hurt you.

"You get 'em to smilin'," the old nester proclaimed, "and they're a-fixin' to turn somebody a-loose. It's them jurors come stompin' out lookin' neither to gee nor haw, with their jaws so set you'd swear they was chompin' on rocks, that's a-gonna put folks in jail."

And so, on this steamy late-June day, in the courthouse at Gainesville, Texas, when Ernest and Margaret Medders heard laughter coming from a jury room occupied by twelve of their peers, they smiled. They clutched hands like first-daters at the picture show, looking hopeful beyond any singing of it, and they packed up their possible two-to-five-year-jail-sentence troubles in their old kit bag and smiled, smiled, smiled.

The old nester in the beat hat and violated khakis was one of a breed forever populating courtrooms, vicariously enjoying triumphs or disaster. When the jurors laughed he preened: "See! See?" The prophet shot a glance at the Medderses' attorney, Jack Gray, who was prowling the courtroom corridor with an expression on his face that said he was stepping off fifteen-yard penalties against the world. Gray is a tall, lean Texan who habitually pushes back from the table while he's still a little bit hungry and who is reported to have laughed aloud once in 1948.

So the jurors laughed and deliberated and played dominoes and argued and didn't do the Medderses any real harm, maybe, but they didn't do them any particular good, either. They just couldn't agree on whether Ernest Medders was guilty of selling mortgaged property with intent to defraud (in this case cattle mortgaged to a Tennessee bank) and after two days of fruitless

226

scrabbling they reported themselves hopelessly deadlocked (nine to three for conviction, a juror told newsmen). The mistrial declared by District Judge Hill Boyd was about as satisfying as a bath with boots on.

Having heard all that happy laughter ringing in the jury room, Ernest and Margaret Medders had seemed prepared for acquittal and possibly a night on the town. They had joked and laughed with reporters as much as Jack Gray would allow, but at the deadlocked end they sagged into a moody silence. Lawyer Gray had predicted victory earlier ("Hell, it ain't against the law in Texas to sell cows, is it?"). Now he grimly announced that his clients "still haven't done anything wrong, nor have they been convicted of doing anything wrong." County Attorney Bill Sullivan, speaking for the prosecution, wearily mumbled, "Now it's all to do over again."

Margaret Medders, forty-eight, has a firm jaw, steady eyes, a stout figure, and a chemically induced white streak running through her hair. Vivacious and outgoing, she rarely meets a stranger. She gives an impression of strength. It is amazing how frequently people who know Ernest and Margaret Medders remark that she is stronger than he. Not smarter, not better, not smoother, but *stronger*. "Ask him a question," it has been often said, "and she'll answer it."

Mrs. Medders has long shown a rare ability to survive adversity. When her first husband, Eugene Riggs, died in the mid-1940s he left her virtually penniless with four children to raise. She moved from her native Jellico, Tennessee, to Memphis, placed her children in St. Peter's Orphanage, and then talked her way into a job there so as to remain near them. Later, with the help of friendly nuns at St. Peter's and at nearby St. Joseph's Hospital, she got her two sons admitted to Subiaco Academy in Arkansas. Room, board, tuition, and books for the two boys ran about fifteen hundred dollars annually. Somehow, Margaret scraped the fee together from her meager earnings as a practical nurse.

She married Ernest Medders in 1948, ten years after he divorced his first wife. He had two children by his first marriage;

he and Margaret would have four of their own. Ernest Medders did not turn out to be much of a breadwinner. Plagued by illness, he was periodically unemployed. His wife worked sixteen-hour shifts to take up the slack.

By the testimony of a Memphis bank executive, Margaret was the wheeler-dealer in the family. "Mrs. Medders did all of the loan arranging," he testified. "I don't think I ever talked to Mr. Medders." Between August 9 and October 19, 1966, Margaret's chats with the Memphis banker netted $310,000 in loans. All but $125,000 of this amount was apparently unsecured.

It was Margaret, too, who obtained approval from the Memphis bank official to sell one-third interest in a mortgaged Angus bull, Red Comanche. She also claimed to have received approval from the banker to sell *other* mortgaged cattle; he denied it. The Gainesville trial turned on this dispute. Hours of cross-examination did not shake Margaret Medders on that vital point.

She is a woman with a quick eye for business. Visiting Washington, D.C., in the spring of 1966, the Medderses met James S. Melton, a well-fixed General Motors dealer. When Melton flew to Texas last November to be Ernest and Margaret's houseguest, he'd hardly unpacked before Mrs. Medders sold him a one-third interest in Red Comanche and eleven other head of cattle for $36,873. Indeed, with Margaret handling most of the transactions the Medderses claimed a profit of more than $100,000 in cattle sales last year.

No one doubts that Margaret Medders can hold her own in a horse trade, or that she spends money in loads that might stagger a government mule. An account she is writing of her life tells how when she was a girl in Tennessee her father opened a charge account at a drugstore, and how she immediately bought gifts for all her little friends because "I didn't know you had to pay for all those things."

When news got out that the Medderses had not a farthing of their own, Margaret came under a doctor's care for "acute depression." But there were moments when she appeared to be wholly detached from the calamity about her. While lawsuits piled up, while public-auction sales were forced, while a prominent Dallas man was filing a bad-check charge against her, while the *New York Times* ran seven-column headlines telling all—while all this battle raged somewhere above her head, the lady of the Medders house sat calmly in her fifteen-room Colonial-style mansion on the outskirts of tiny Muenster, Texas, and began to speak gaily of future plans.

One of her listeners, an old friend, made an impatient gesture. "Margaret," he snapped, "the party's over." Then he pointed outside toward a gold Cadillac sporting personalized license plates emblazoned "Mrs. M.M." that told the world the importance of being Margaret. "That golden chariot out yonder has turned back into a pumpkin," he said. A few weeks later when the *New York Times* again trotted out its big headlines ("3,500 Attend Bankruptcy Auction of Texas Couple's Estate: $450,000 Is Realized in a Day") the golden chariot was knocked down for $4,150 and was the first item to go. Every dime went to satisfy creditors.

Cinderella isn't yet afoot, however. On a hot afternoon in the June week before the Medders no-decision trial, three late-model cars and six bicycles lined the rear driveway of the family home. The Medders children frolicked in their private swimming pool and under the spray of sprinklers recessed in the green landscaped lawn, with its collection of stone cherubs and cupids. Red roses and exotic blossoms of bright yellow entwined on the Cyclone fence running around the family compound; nearby, an orchard of peach, pecan, and apple trees sweetly bloomed. From the black-topped highway running in front of the house, two hundred yards distant, a visitor could hear the syncopated wails of some rock 'n' roll group blaring through a speaker.

Even without the odious teenybopper concert, the scene was not as idyllic as it appeared. A quarter mile distant, the rambling structure where a thousand tuxedoed and smartly gowned guests had several times danced all night (to the live music of Guy Lombardo or Wayne King or Jan Garber) sat padlocked and silent, its once-gay Japanese lanterns sagging from the ceiling and weeds growing all around. No cattle lowed in the fancy feeder pens; the locked horse barn housed only a handful of blue ribbons won by champions long sold.

Another padlock, bringing together a great chain, shut visitors

229

out from the arched gate that proudly proclaimed "Colonial Acres Farm" in raised stone and that also guarded a driveway leading to the main house with its four white columns out front. Somewhere behind the locks moved Ernest and Margaret Medders, honoring their attorney's order not to speak with any known newsmen and no strangers at all.

Perhaps even then Ernest Medders sat there in the big house under his prized autographed photo from the president of the United States ("As ever, Lyndon B. Johnson"), wearing one of his four-hundred-dollar silk ranch suits, and coolly puffed his oriental water pipe while Margaret watched color television or shined up her personal jewelry. For one of the great ironies of our little tale is that Ernest and Margaret Medders, though (1) officially bankrupt, (2) charged with felony crimes, and (3) alleged to have spent three million dollars in the last five years, may come out of their rags-to-riches comic opera smelling sweeter than the famed yellow rose of Texas.

Under the lenient terms of the Texas Homestead Act (enacted at a time when many Texas settlers were themselves fleeing creditors or other old shames) the Medderses stand an excellent chance to hold on to the 185-acre farm with its big house, swimming pool, guest cottage, party barn, and show barns. Additionally, they have filed papers to retain one Cadillac, one late-model pickup truck, two monogrammed saddles, personal jewelry worth five thousand dollars, and household goods valued at ten thousand dollars. Lawyers familiar with the Homestead Act predict they will be permitted to keep it all. And, though the Medderses may not sell Colonial Acres Farm while under the shadow of bankruptcy, they *can* lease it. The showplace cattle farm might bring up to twelve thousand dollars per month in rental fees.

Now, twelve thousand dollars per month sounds like chicken-feed to J. Paul Getty. But then, less than a decade ago J. Paul Getty wasn't raising a houseful of children on a total monthly income of less than four hundred dollars like Ernest Medders was. As recently as 1961 Medders was a fifty-dollar-per-week mechanic and sometimes fruit peddler in Memphis, Tennessee.

A family photo taken in 1955 shows the couple with six of their ten children on the steps of their low-cost housing unit. Bits of

230

paper sully unkempt grass at their feet. Two of the six children seem to be crying, another seems on the verge, and to the very last in number they appear to be wiggling or otherwise in motion. Margaret Medders looks dowdy in a shapeless dress. Her hair is parted on the left and then pulled across her head as if for purposes of storage and nothing more. Ernest, his skinny arms poking from a short-sleeved pair of mechanic's overalls, wears workman's brogans and peeps through horn-rimmed spectacles as if faintly puzzled by nature's order. In short, the Medderses looked like your average time-payment-strapped, insolvent, lower working-class family badly in need of both a miracle and a baby-sitter.

But that was before the Inheritance.

Talk of the Inheritance began in the Medderses' humble home in 1961 when Ernest learned that he was one of 3000 hopefuls who might be the rightful heirs of the famed Spindletop oilfield in Texas. A Mississippi lawyer filed a five-hundred-million-dollar lawsuit in behalf of the alleged heirs. All laid claim to some descending connection with one Pelham Humphreys, a long-dead bachelor who once owned much of the original Spindletop land. (The Mississippi lawyer lost the suit all the way up to the Supreme Court of the United States, which in 1965 tossed the suit out. Lawyer Jack Gray, however, still insists that Ernest Medders is the grandnephew of Pelham Humphreys.) The other 2999 potential heirs presumably continued to live their lives of quiet desperation. Ernest Medders was soon to know rapid change. For Ernest Medders soon came to believe that he would inherit great gobs of money as surely as the sun must rise. "The Inheritance gave Ernest hope," his wife said.

No doubt he needed it. Life had not been exceedingly kind. In 1959 his six-foot frame carried no more than 150 pounds. He had a blood-clotted leg and had just been retired for medical reasons by a major oil company. He couldn't always sleep at night and complained of heartburn. Though Margaret's sixteen-hour shifts kept the family in bread, there was precious little cake. You can see why Ernest might be motivated to believe in the Inheritance.

No one knows exactly when anyone first got the notion that

231

Ernest stood as *sole* heir to the Spindletop millions. Indeed, there is conflicting testimony on whether the Medderses even made this particular claim. It is clear, however, that this impression got around. Possibly the idea first came to flower at St. Joseph's Hospital when Margaret worked there. However it happened, the rumor that the Medderses would very shortly be ahead of the hounds by a distance approximating five hundred million dollars soon came to be accepted.

Think on how much money that *is*. Dwell on it. You'd have to spend a mere million a year for five hundred years—or five million a year for only one hundred years—to get rid of it. And what could you buy for your five million green dollars per year? Well, it's hard to translate into hamburgers, four-dollar shoes, or anything that makes any hand-to-mouth sense. Just say that one year you might buy the Washington Redskins, and the next year Jackie Gleason, and the year after that either Albania or Mexico.

Now, money is a funny commodity. It makes people rush to help you and wring your hand. It attracts and dazzles and beguiles. One of the nuns at St. Joseph's Hospital proposed to her order's headquarters in Mishawaka, Indiana, that the Medderses be made a small loan to help in their legal battle attendant to the Inheritance. The loan was duly made by the Poor Sisters of Perpetual Adoration.

That opening loan of five hundred dollars was just for openers. For a few months the checks dribbled in and then, suddenly, the Poor Sisters began to wish money on the Medderses in lots up to sixty thousand dollars per month. Two thousand dollars per day will see nearly anybody through the winter.

Nobody has satisfactorily explained just how the escalation process began or why it continued for so long. Though the Poor Sisters are to date $1,940,000 poorer and at least a nickel's worth less perpetually adoring, they choose silence. Perhaps they were casting bread upon the waters.

Ernest Medders's testimony did not throw any blinding light on the subject. In court he was asked, "How did you tell the sisters how much money you wanted?"

"I don't know how they made up their minds how much to

send," he said. "The checks just came in about the tenth and fifteenth of each month."

"What did you tell the sisters you were doing with the
money?"

"I didn't tell them. My wife talked to the sisters."

"Did the sisters ask how you were going to pay it back?"

"No."

"Did you ever tell them?"

"No."

"When did they stop giving you this money?"

"About six or seven months ago."

"Did you call them up and ask why?"

"My wife did," the fifty-seven-year-old Medders answered.
"They told her they thought we had enough to go on our own."

Six years ago, with the money flowing in from the poor Poor
Sisters at a promising pace, the Medderses pulled their Memphis
stakes in favor of Muenster, Texas. Muenster is a vest-pocket
town of 1190 some seventy miles northwest of Dallas and just a
day's pony ride from Oklahoma. There Ernest Medders bought a
modest house in town and began to make friends with his neighbors who lived on wide, paved streets lined with mimosa trees.

The people of Muenster are largely of Teutonic origin: Gehrigs
and Fischers and Biffles and Shamburgers and Schultzes abound.
They are thrifty and hard working. For recreation they cheer the
Muenster High School Hornets down the football field, catch
John Wayne's latest heroics at the Relax Theater, or eat German
sausages, drink beer, and dance the polka down at the Central
Café & Lounge. The Medderses originally made no splashy
show. They attended the local Catholic church, dressed well,
drove a new car, and were generally well thought of. Perhaps a
few of the more industrious citizens wondered why Ernest Medders didn't work and nobody knew much about his background.
In Texas, however, you don't mention a man's past unless he
does. The story soon got around that Ernest Medders was an
investor, retired by reasons of health, who was in search of a
good farm property.

A year after arriving in Muenster, in October of 1962, Ernest Medders bought a 185-acre farm. The $57,000 he paid was only a fraction of Colonial Acres' present worth. "It was just a rock farm when I bought it," Medders has said. It didn't stay a rock farm long. With help from Texas A. & M. University's extension service, the Cooke County farm agent, a private research foundation in Dallas—and, of course, with the United States mail running on time—Ernest terraced and irrigated. Meanwhile, he was building and furnishing the big house at a cost of $250,000. He stocked his place with registered Angus cattle and Appaloosa horseflesh. (Medders prospered physically, too. Soon he weighed close to two hundred pounds and never had felt better in his life. "Colonial Acres was just like heaven to Ernest," Mrs. Medders has said.)

Before long, the gaudy Medders spread was the topic of conversation most often remarked in Muenster. "That ole boy out there is building a bird's nest on the ground," they might say, and there was civic pride in the telling.

But if Muenster was satisfied with the Medderses, Margaret wasn't wholly satisfied with Muenster. The little town did not represent the limits of her social reach. She first ventured fifteen miles away to Gainesville where she generously footed the bill for a community fund-raising dance at Gainesville Country Club. Then she carted Guy Lombardo and a hundred select guests home for a sunrise breakfast. She entertained politicians and community leaders from Denton, Wichita Falls, and Forth Worth.

At Neiman-Marcus in Dallas she bought Paris originals by the dozen, a $75,000 full-length mink coat, a $65,000 diamond ring and an $80,000 necklace, an electric organ, tape recorders, and other baubles; one time the Medderses owed the store $336,000 and some-odd cents. (Later, Ernest would deny knowledge of debts to Neiman-Marcus other than for "three suits I bought there one time." "What about your wife's furs and diamonds?" he was asked in court. "I didn't know she had any diamonds," he said. "I don't know a diamond when I see one. She showed me some rings. She would ask me if I think they are pretty and I said yes.")

To spare her two teen-age daughters the horrors of dormitory life at posh Hockaday School in Dallas, Mrs. Medders bought them a townhouse for forty thousand dollars. She built a beauty shop in her ranch home, equipped it professionally with three dryers, and hired a full-time licensed beauty operator. Some of Muenster's more frugal citizens grumbled about Margaret's habits. "Don't worry about money," the blithe spirit was fond of saying. "*I* don't."

Maybe Ernest Medders didn't know a diamond when he saw one, but he knew oil. Drilling a water well, he discovered that the drilling bit had bored into rich oil sand. He knew, too, that an adjoining farm of 330 acres and another 440-acre place in the vicinity had once been oil-producing properties. Ernest thought that oil still might lurk underground: perhaps he saw a good omen, felt the touch of fate. Could there be any doubt, now, that oil-blood flowed in his veins, that the Inheritance was sure? He bought the two farms, had the abandoned well sites cleaned out and explored, and—sure enough—he soon had thirty-three producing oil wells all his own. Shallow, low-yield wells, maybe. But oil wells, anyway. By now his land holdings totaled fourteen hundred acres and Colonial Acres Farm proudly flew its own orange-and-white flag.

A quarter mile from the big house Ernest Medders built a huge structure (120 by 240 feet) the family doggedly referred to as the "Coliseum." Rome has an older and even bigger one, but then Rome's is not orange. And unlike the Houston Astrodome the Medderses' giant outbuilding was not roomy enough for baseball. It cost $175,000, however, and it was large enough to host horse shows, calf-ropings, parties of a thousand or more and —as it would turn out—a massive auction sale.

They'd hardly turned the last bolt before Margaret Medders gave the Coliseum a christening. Guy Lombardo and The Royal Canadians returned to play the dance. A public-relations man hired by Mrs. Medders persuaded a Dallas television station to film the party. Big-city newspapers gave news space. A special effort was made to attract publishers, columnists, and what Margaret Medders thought of as Dallas society. Soon everyone heard or read of how guests arrived in charter planes, helicopters, limousines, and air-conditioned buses with built-in bars and Muzak. Even the wranglers who paraded the show horses and blooded cattle wore tuxedoes. (Ernest Medders topped his tux off with hand-tooled cowboy boots.) Steaks, oysters, and chicken were served by candlelight. There was a champagne fountain, wee-hours dancing, and at the end of a perfect day Margaret Medders handed out a fifty-dollar tip to each of fifty caterer's helpers. Texas sat up and took notice.

One fine day Governor John Connally dropped by Colonial Acres and squeezed Appaloosa horseflesh to the sweet music of photographer's clicking shutters. Texas congressmen, who understand power politics the way Einstein understood arithmetic, poured over the Medders homestead. Texas Attorney General Waggoner Carr called hat in hand to solicit the support of Medders and eight hundred well-heeled guests in his race for the United States Senate. Congressman Graham Purcell invited the couple to Washington and broke them into the big leagues. The twenty-five-man Texas congressional delegation broke bread with the Medderses as their guests in the Speaker's dining room in the United States Capitol building.

Enter Lyndon B. Johnson. What else was left?

The Ultimate Invitation came to the Medderses of Muenster after Ernest thoughtfully donated several thousand dollars to the President's Club—a fraternal order historically tracing back all the way to 1964 and founded for the cause of keeping the Democratic party solvent. In return for one thousand dollars annual minimum dues, President's Club members are assured of a "personal relationship" with LBJ and other Great Society bosses. So on May 4, 1966, a black limousine pulled under a White House portico to discharge Secretary of State and Mrs. Dean Rusk and their guests. Thus did Margaret Medders enter the White House on the arm of the secretary of state, while Ernest gallantly if a bit stiffly ushered Mrs. Rusk inside.

After a formal reception (at which, Margaret Medders later re-

236

ported, she met "ambassadors, poets, and movie stars") President Johnson invited the Medderses and seven other couples to his private quarters for a late-night snack, a movie, and neighborly chitchat. This "personal relationship" went on until 2:00 a.m. Margaret Medders thought the goodnight kiss LBJ planted on her cheek was life's most thrilling moment—until the next day when even *that* sweet ecstasy was topped by an invitation to return to Texas with the president aboard Air Force One.

Well sir, you just can't fly any higher than that. And sure enough, that was zenith for the Medderses. Nadir rode not far behind.

The Poor Sisters suddenly had tardy second thoughts about lending the Texas couple money. Without fanfare—but with absolute finality—the flow of bountiful blessings ceased. By this time, however, other money sources stood near at hand. Bankers are impressed by money or else they would not be bankers, and they were by this time competing for the prominent couple's favor. "Mr. Medders"—more than one banker said to his eventual sorrow—"we sure would like to have your account with us." Ernest Medders had a stock response: "Well, I been thinkin' about spreadin' my money around a little bit. You folks *do* make loans, don't you?" Yes, they made loans. Sizable ones after talking with Margaret. Soon banks in Wichita Falls, Muenster, and Memphis had loaned her $730,000 and thanked her for taking it.

With the borrowed bank money the Medderses went on a final spree. There was a huge wedding for son John, twenty, and then a party for twelve hundred young 4-H clubbers. There was yet another grand horse show, a swinging charity ball, and a five-hundred-dollar-prize contest advertised in several cattlemen's publications to name the new foal of the Medderses' grand champion mare, Queen Ann. There was a wingding for Jeane Dixon, the Washington woman who claims a "gift of prophecy," though she apparently saw no cloud on the crystal ball where her hosts were concerned.

At Christmastime the Medderses bought spots on area radio stations to extend season's greetings to the less fortunate. On New Year's Day a special train brought their daughters' Hocka-

HOW TO SUCCEED IN TEXAS WITHOUT REALLY

day School classmates out to the ranch; a band provided music so the kids could rock in the aisles while the train rolled along. There followed a big feed on the grounds and a barn dance. Maybe nobody knew it then, but that was to be the last hurrah.

In February, the alleged relatives of Pelham Humphreys—who had been among the three thousand persons hopeful of inheriting Spindletop's millions—brought a lawsuit to force Ernest and Margaret to reveal the source of their obvious wealth. Apparently they thought the couple had somehow managed to gain the entire inheritance. Though this not-illogical premise blew up in court, it also exploded some other notions.

When the Medderses publicly admitted their lack of solvency, their creditors lost little time in mourning. A feedstore demanding more than three thousand dollars won the race to file the first suit. Neiman-Marcus closed Margaret's account and attached one of Ernest's farm properties. Creditors cried payment for food, flowers, and liquor. The telephone company removed mobile phones from the family cars. Utilities were cut off, making it impossible to water the cattle until twelve hundred dollars in back bills were settled. Lawyers swooped down to serve writs and to subpoena. Bankruptcy proceedings followed and then the giant auction sale with its jostling crowds, humiliating headlines, and bad jokes.

A grand jury in Sherman indicted Mrs. Medders for allegedly giving a fifty-six-hundred-dollar bad check to Angus Wynne III, a prominent Dallas man who directs an entertainment agency. Another grand jury returned the indictment against Ernest for allegedly selling mortgaged property.

Truly, midnight came to Cinderella.

The way Ernest Medders told it at his bankruptcy hearing, he hardly knew what was going on around him.

"I never went but to the third grade in school back in Earle, Arkansas," he testified. He also said he couldn't read or write (except to scrawl his name) because of a condition called dyslexia, which causes one to see certain letters backward. On a courtroom blackboard he demonstrated that he could scrawl his name in a slow, wavering hand. He could not read "the bank notes they stuck under my nose," he said, nor could he read figures above a hundred. He was asked if he knew a one-dollar bill from a one-hundred-dollar or one-thousand-dollar bill. "I know," he said slowly, "that a one-dollar bill has a one on it, and the others have more naughts on them."

(Not everyone sees Ernest Medders the way he came off in the courtroom. "He's no dummy," lawyer Jack Gray has said. "He is as nice a feller as you ever saw," Congressman Graham Purcell remarked. Kent Biffle of the *Dallas Morning News* once heard Teutonic wits gathered in one of Muenster's twenty-six beer halls jocularly refer to Ernest Medders as "Ole Dutch Cleanser." And Wayne Cook, the brash millionaire auctioneer who handled the bankruptcy sale, says: "He comes on countrylike, stronger than Ole Nellie's breath. But he's not. That man's brilliant.")

In her seven hours on the witness stand, Margaret Medders wept and claimed virtue. "We never meant to defraud anybody," she protested. "We've *never* cheated anybody." Mrs. Medders was exceedingly vague about some fairly large details. "I never paid much attention to things like that," she sobbed when asked how much money she had borrowed from the Poor Sisters. "If they say they let us have $1,940,000 then that is correct."

How did the Sisters know how much money to send each month? "Well, we would send them plans and when they approved them, they would mail us the money." About all you can gather from Margaret Medders's testimony is that mail call meant almost as much to the folks at Colonial Acres as it did to our fighting men overseas.

Margaret shunned the big auction sale that began at 9:00 a.m. on May 25, 1967, and continued long past midnight. Ernest appeared in the rear of the Coliseum, unannounced, after the bizarre huckstering of his wares had gone on for twelve hours. "I think we're gonna be all right," he said. Then he ducked by newsmen through darkness back to the big house.

More than three thousand persons crowded into the show barn and possibly another four thousand milled about the grounds. It was not a place for a sensitive soul. "I'm just like a sewer, folks," cried auctioneer Wayne Cook. "I'll take anything you give me." And: "All you Muenster folks sell your tuxedoes and spend the money here. You'll never need your tuxes again." Mrs. Peggy Levine of Fort Worth wanted a big trophy case containing more than two hundred trophies for her husband's jewelry store. "Some of these trophies and ribbons will sell high," she said. "If a person wants a souvenir, he'll pay ten dollars for something worth twenty-five cents." One of the gawkers who came "just to look around" was Judge A. W. Moursound, attorney for President Johnson. A Fort Worth caterer sold five thousand pounds of barbecue to cowboys, fretting children, investors bearing letters of credit up to two hundred thousand dollars, and housewives in shorts, all standing heel to toe in the dust and heat.

When Cook's gavel fell, he had auctioned more than seven hundred items for about five hundred thousand dollars. There were bargains in more than three hundred head of cattle, eleven horses, farm implements, cans of vodka mix, horsewhips, forty thousand dollars worth of indoor and outdoor Christmas tree decorations, card tables, cans of hair spray for horses, a 1912 Weber wagon, tools, cattle prods, business machines, electric fans, televisions, two farms (one with eighteen oil wells; one with fifteen), the Dallas townhouse, a 1964 jeep, a 1966 Cadillac, a 1966 Oldsmobile, a 1964 Ford, thousands of feet of four-inch aluminum pipe, horse trailers, chairs, a miniature kitchen range, ashtrays, candelabras, and possibly left-handed monkey wrenches.

The citizens of Muenster strain few muscles rushing to discuss the Medders case with strangers. A veiled resentment is shown toward prying outsiders: four of six persons asked for directions to the Medders homestead claimed not to know (though the place is almost visible from downtown), and two others gave information reluctantly. Those who do talk take pains not to let their names escape. Given enough time and their due cracks at the tap beer in the Central Lounge, however, some local gentry may come on opinionated.

There was this big Levi-clad cowboy on the third stool from the end, near the television blaring a colorcast of baseball's Game of the Day, who sported what may have been the widest belt buckle in the United States of America. His hand wrapped around the thick, frosted beer mug until it almost hid it from view. "You never did see *Mister* Medders pushin' hisself on people around here," he said. "But that ole lady—now *she* come here to play Miss Queen Bee. Not just in Muenster, either. Over in Gainesville . . . Denton . . . even Big D and Washington!" He dipped into the beer mug. "I reckon she's singin' a altogether different tune now," he observed with satisfaction.

One of two young men playing shuffleboard paused. He said to the cowboy, "J.D., what you reckon they're living on? Them being bankrupt and all."

The cowboy made an inelegant sound with his lips, causing an old man with a pinched face to look up from his barbecue plate in astonishment. The shuffleboard ace took careful aim down the board with a round metal disk. Then he straightened up without taking the shot. He said, "I would of lit out of here for Hawaii."

"Not if you had several tons of brick house settin' out here on the edge of town," the cowboy disputed. "Anyway, you can't run from somethin' that big. Law would hound you plumb to the grave."

Someone remarked that Ernest Medders had testified that his only current income is a small monthly disability check from the federal government. A fat, fringe-bald man in coveralls recalled when Ernest Medders brought golfer Byron Nelson out to his farm to discuss building a private golf course. Grinning, he asked whether the cowboy thought Medders would ever build it now.

"Well if he ever *does*"—the cowboy paused for effect and waved his beer mug—"I bet and guaran-damn-tee you it'll have electric lights, velvet fairways, and dancing girls for caddies. And ole Ernest'll give a golf tournament to put that big tournament over in Fort Worth in the shade." Vastly pleased by the appreciative laughter, J.D. bought the house a drink.

A visitor asked the cowboy if he'd ever been out to Colonial Acres Farm. "Not until they sold everything off at auction," he said, "and I cain't claim no particular honor in *that*. All of Texas and half of Tennessee was out there."

Slyly the fat man said, "Didja see Lyndon Johnson out there?"

"Shoot! I expect Lyndon Johnson's had all of the Medders business he *wants!* Yessir! Why, he'd a heap rather get tangled

241

up with ole Castro than with Margaret Medders again."

Had the Medderses hurt Muenster?

"Well," J.D. said, "if they think they been *helpin'* us I just as soon not have any more of their help. Our bank got took for a pretty good roll—had to eat about seventy thousand dollars worth of paper—and there's a whole lotta business people still got what looks like bad credit on their books."

"I think there's more hurt feelings here than anything else," the balding fat man said. "Folks feel kind of silly getting took in by a man that can't read or write."

The visitor remarked that Medders reportedly suffered from dyslexia, and explained its symptoms.

The fat man was incredulous: "Say he sees letters *backwards?*"

"Sure," the cowboy said. "It'd be the same if you and me was tryin' to read a foreign language." He looked around the room to make certain he had everyone's attention. "Course," he said, "Medders never seemed to have much trouble with his l's . . . o's . . . a's . . . . n's . . . or s's . . ."

It took the boys a moment to get it, but when they did they broke the joint up.

Not everyone in Muenster sees as much fun in the Medders case as did the boys in the taproom. "Most of their friends have stayed loyal," Jack Gray reports. "They see Ernest and Margaret as the victims of circumstances."

Indeed, some of the family's friends hold the Poor Sisters and the easy-loan bankers to blame. "Ernest Medders thought he would inherit all that money and there's no doubt about it," one old chum says sorrowfully. "In fact, he *still* believes it. And maybe that's the long-range tragedy in this whole mess."

Some of the pain may have been avoided had the Medderses used the slightest caution. Even after the Poor Sisters cut them off, they might have salvaged themselves by judicious application toward their overdue bills of the $730,000 borrowed from banks. With that bankroll, and a cattle business with a potential profit of $100,000 per year, there would have seemed to be hope for the future. Perhaps, however, it was too late even without the final spending sprees. "We just always seemed to be out of money,"

Mrs. Medders sobbed near the end. Evidence backs her up: a $37,000 check—from the sale of unmortgaged personal items—deposited to the Medderses' bank account in Muenster was wiped out at the end of the day because of outstanding checks drawn to yesterday's fun.

The remark of a Muenster matron perhaps serves to give the couple's high living some shade of motivation, and at the same time writes a perfect epitaph to the saga of the bogus country squire and his lady. "Margaret Medders wanted everybody to know who she was," the woman said sadly. "Well . . . now they do."

*West*
SEPTEMBER 1967

## afterword

The Medderses, after several court tests, were permitted—under the Texas Homestead Act—to retain Colonial Acres Farm and vital equipment. "Except for one little charge to which they plead guilty in exchange for a short sentence of probation," Jack Gray reports, "they were never convicted of a damn thing." Several charges were dropped in trade for partial restitution; others were dismissed. To satisfy remaining debts and to pay legal fees, the Medderses in 1969 sold Colonial Acres. They returned to Tennessee where, once more, Margaret works as a nurse.

# THE GRAND OLE OPRY

ountry music has always expressed those simple truths that sharecroppers, village storekeepers, and truck-stop waitresses could understand and cling to. It was born in the early 1920s of a mixture of gospel airs, folk songs, English ballads, and soul (or "race") music, but this native American art form soon came to be associated with the Great Depression. We rootless or ruined Depression Children identified with the drifting hobo, a silver-haired daddy waiting somewhere, Old Shep's death, the spurned lover, a promise of the gold streets of heaven. Our songs commemorated the people and places we knew: whisky widows, sisters menaced by the wicked cities of the American hinterland, deep mines, and company stores; they recounted our pitifully few conquests and reflected our impoverished and isolated lives.

If country music was our liturgy, then the Grand Ole Opry was our mother church. The Grand Ole Opry brought music and backwater wisdom across the miles from Nashville, Tennessee. Its music boiled in our blood the week around: through the hot work of the grain harvest, in the fearful soul searching of midweek prayer meetings, up and down endless rows as we picked six-cent cotton. On Saturday nights in our unpainted rural Texas farmhouse, where one generation had died, one grew to adulthood, and still another was born, that music from our old Zenith

244

battery radio reaffirmed our troubles and refurbished our dreams.

Our poets were Roy Acuff, Ernest Tubb, Lula Bell and Scotty. We depended on Cousin Minnie Pearl for the latest in fashions and gossip out of Grinder's Switch: tales of drinking Uncle Nabob and of Brother, who, it was clear, did not always deal from a full deck; Uncle Dave Macon's honey-stringed banjo caused even our preachers to dance. One of my earliest morality lectures came not from Deuteronomy, but from a song in which a selfless felon advised his sweetheart against waiting for him because "I'll always be an ex-convict and branded wherever I go." My father, whisker-stubbed and solemn as Job, spoke in the circle of pale yellow light from a kerosene lamp at his elbow: "Son, there's a heap of truth in that song."

Grand Ole Opry is the oldest continuous show in the history of radio; it still claims to attract the largest single listening audience in the world. Programmed live for five hours on Saturday nights (and on Friday nights for four) over Nashville's fifty-thousand-watt clear-channel outlet WSM, it is broadcast on a delayed basis each week by hundreds of local radio stations; since 1965 some sixty television stations have programmed one or more Opry hours weekly on videotape. Most of its national sponsors (Coca-Cola, B.C. Headache Powder, Golden Flake Cheese Curls, Martha White Mills, Trail Blazer Dog Food as examples) have advertised on the Opry for more than twenty years. National Life and Accident Insurance Company, which owns WSM, sponsored the first Opry broadcast back on November 28, 1925, and remains the primary sponsor.

The fifty-odd entertainers making up Grand Ole Opry's permanent troupe are all stars in their own right. A bid to join the Opry company is the surest sign that one has arrived in the country-western field. An Opry beginner is paid as little as ten dollars per broadcast; even a big-name old-timer will generally top out at seventy-five. There are exceptions. Roy Acuff, "The King of Country Music," is known to command five hundred dollars per broadcast. Other old heads are suspected of having reached similar under-the-table deals with WSM. Still, country artists clamor to appear. There is that vast radio audience out in the brush (and

245

in the cities also, for Grand Ole Opry is now heard in Los Angeles, Chicago, and is beamed across the Hudson to New York from a Newark station) to buy record albums and songbooks. Opry exposure multiplies personal-appearance fees: Roy Acuff, Ernest Tubb, Porter Wagoner, Marty Robbins, Flatt and Scruggs, and others annually earn $250,000 or more on the road. "Opry billing is at least a $100,000 gift in terms of individual personal-appearance fees," Opry manager Ott Devine says. To remain in good standing, Opry regulars must make no less than twenty broadcasts annually.

Grand Ole Opry fans are no less hardy or far ranging than the stars they canonize. The typical Opry visitor travels 960 miles round trip by car; normally he brings along at least one other member of his family, stays in Nashville for three days, and includes in his itinerary a two-dollar bus tour of Opry stars' homes, a visit to the Country Music Hall of Fame, and trips to such Opry Row institutions as Ernest Tubb's Record Shop or Tootsie's Orchid Lounge, where the performers attend to their burning thirsts after, or during, Opry broadcasts. This typical fan will likely be a blue-collar worker, about twenty-nine years old, and come either from the Midwest or a southern state. Though he will have written for Opry tickets months in advance, he may wait in line for more than one hour. Inside he will sit on cruel, hard-backed benches that once served Satan's purpose in a gospel tabernacle; several generations of dedicated gum-chewers have deposited their rejects on the undersides.

On an average Opry night, fans from twenty states subject themselves to more than one hundred musical laments and hoedowns. In the summer season a capacity sixty-two hundred persons will witness the two shows, paying two dollars for general admission and three dollars reserved; at least a thousand others will be left disappointed on the sidewalks. Opry fans burst into applause at the pioneer notes of a familiar hit; some few may sing along. When their favorites step to the microphone, dozens of shutterbugs surge down to blind them with flashbulbs; they beg autographs on popcorn boxes or souvenir programs. Recent patrons included the conductor of the London Symphony Orchestra, a half dozen U.S. congressmen, and a twenty-year-old

Canadian who, after robbing a branch of the Bank of Montreal of more than nine thousand dollars, purchased a gaudy western wardrobe and headed straight for Nashville.

I arrived at Nashville airport at dusk on a chill January day; from the air the countryside had appeared grayish and smoky, and the Cumberland River, snaking around the city's edge, was flat and muddy. In the baggage area two young men claimed guitar cases; a third young man with a guitar prepared to catch a flight out.

The Opry House—Ryman Auditorium—is an old red-brick eyesore with balconies and churchlike windows, and without air conditioning. (Opry officials deny the frequent charge that they spurn air conditioning in order to sell hand fans and cold drinks.) It is located in a section of Nashville with much to be modest about: curio shops dealing in sweetheart pillows and crockery painted with kitchen prayers; lunch counters, garages, a barber college; and a series of beer parlors specializing in rollicking jukeboxes, dried-beef sticks, and thirty-cent suds.

Nine Cadillacs were lined fin to bumper in the stage-door alley; most showed road dust or signs of general neglect. Backstage, only five minutes before air time, there was a fleeting impression of firemen, policemen, stagehands, loose children, and of all the pickers-and-singers on earth milling aimlessly as strings were plucked and fiddle bows tested. Some performers wore suits of psychedelic hues tricked up with rhinestone patterns in the shape of horsehoes, alligators, or ruby-red lips; most, however, wore outfits only mildly western or plain business suits. "Honey," a cowboy in a yellow shirt and lavender tie called to a red-nosed woman passing by, "how's your music box tonight?" "I got the goddamnedest head cold you ever seen," the lady said without breaking stride.

As a boy I had this private vision of Roy Acuff on stage as he sang "Wabash Cannonball" or "The Great Speckled Bird." He wore threads of gold, no doubt, and on his head was a jeweled crown. When the curtain rose now, however, Roy Acuff was bounding around stage trying to balance a fiddle bow on his chin; as his musicians sawed and pounded, Acuff toyed with a yo-yo. He wore a red jacket, shapeless gray slacks, and white tennis shoes. He spoke in audible asides during the music; at commercial breaks he clowned for the crowd. Later, when I met him backstage, Acuff mumbled thanks to my introductory compliments and then adroitly disappeared. (At some point within the next few hours a midnight discovery was recorded in my notebook: *Roy Acuff is potbellied: he is too much of this world and the flesh.*)

When one performer introduced his small daughter on stage, a WSM official assured me there was no end to the sons, grandmothers, and old army pals who are shoved forward for five seconds of glory. "Opry people are like one big family," he said. "They intermarry . . . name their kids after each other . . . go fishing together. It's great." Well, yes, there is some of that. One would learn, however, that Opry people have their professional jealousies, messy divorces, and sins of the flesh like everyone else. Cousin Jody, a toothless old baggy-pants comedian who claims to have been in show business "since water," dropped the first hint. "Some of these young'uns," he said, "try to play it pretty cooliefied. I don't dance much to their music." An Opry youngster or two would complain of too much bluegrass and hoedown music at the expense of more modern sounds.

"It isn't like it was in the old days," Minnie Pearl said. "We used to stay down there all night, acting silly and carrying on. It *was* one big happy family then. I remember during the war we were on the road and had our thirteenth flat of the tour—using those old war retreads—and Pee Wee King threw a jackstand through the windshield and started cussing in Polish. Pee Wee's real name was Julius Franklin Arthur Chakenski, you know. Oh, we were all so close in those days! That's all changed, though. A while back a fan asked me to say hello to Ernest Tubb for him; he was shocked when I said sometimes I don't see E.T. for three to five months. Everybody thinks we have one perpetual Opry party. Shoot, my husband drives in the alley to wait while I do my ten-minute bit. Then I head straight back to the rocking chair." A few days later one big Opry star would vilify another big Opry star to me in barracks language. Over a three-hour wet lunch I would also learn of the Opry wheel who habitually com-

248

plains if his name isn't in large enough lights. This old and special hero of mine drinks too much and requires band members to mow his lawn. And there is a tainted romance or two around town.

When one Jean Peloquin made a much-heralded guest appearance on the Opry stage, Madison Avenue robbed me of my remaining youthful myths. The story ran that this simple barefoot boy, cleaning stables for a West Coast television studio specializing in westerns, found himself too broke on Father's Day to buy his old dad a gift. So he dropped a quarter in this recording machine, see, and plunking his trusty guitar recorded an original composition, "My Dad." Somehow a recording-studio executive stopped by the stable, or something, and Peloquin happened to sing his song. The executive, possibly weeping, signed him on the spot. Soon the stableboy was written into a TV western series; now, he would sing for the public.

You believe it if you wish. Myself, I have seen Jean Peloquin. Handsomer than Rock Hudson, he does funny Elvis-things with his hips; offstage he jive talks and winks at the chicks. A lady from Peloquin's recording house was made nervous by our conversation. Well, no, Peloquin admitted, this wouldn't *exactly* be his first public appearance: he had performed at a few small parties—and on television. Peloquin grinned when asked how were things over at Actors Studio; the moment he admitted to twenty-seven years rather than the twenty-four listed in the official biography, the lady snatched him away. As he finished his number she coached the crowd: "Come *on*. Get off your damned *hands*. Help him! Encore!" Peloquin got one encore and came off to bear hugs from his chaperon. "Crazy, baby!" he said. "Groovy!" The last I saw of the simple stableboy he was drinking something exotic in a night spot called Mister Ed's while avidly discussing Zen.

Near the end of the show, I crossed the alley to Tootsie's Orchid Lounge for beer. The main room has rickety booths and tables, a counter with stools, a jukebox with an overactive thyroid, beer cases stacked head-high, iron curtains of smoke, cowboys in trick pants, and waitresses who consider a food order in the nature of a personal affront. On the walls are yellowed photographs of everyone who has ever played a guitar. Near a homemade sign that reads No Beer Tabs for No Body—Police Orders were three cigar boxes overflowing with beer tabs.

Tootsie Bess, the proprietress, is a girthy aproned woman of indefinite years and a plain-as-mud hairstyle. "Tootsie," Vic Willis of the Willis Brothers said, winking at a bystander, "one of these nights I'm gonna take you to the wagonyard." Tootsie, popping beer tops, answered without looking up, "Well, hon, you better have plenty axle grease with you when you do." The boss lady of Tootsie's is as good-natured as her clients permit. One night one of the wilder sidemen in a big-name band presumed to win an outrageous bet by displaying his manhood on the bar. Tootsie grabbed a nightstick she retains for just such emergencies and restored order in a particularly effective manner.

The self-professed Athens of the South, Nashville is a state capital city with a metropolitan-area population of some three hundred thousand. It is the site of Vanderbilt University, Andrew Jackson's "Hermitage" homestead, a replica of the Parthenon, the Tennessee State Museum, and Belle Meade Mansion; here the Confederacy launched its last great offensive. More germane to our story, however, Nashville has become a great music and recording center second only to New York.

Music City, U.S.A., has more than one hundred publishing houses, some twenty recording studios, four record-pressing plants, a dozen major booking agencies, more than seven hundred professional songwriters and countless amateur ones, about one thousand union-affiliated musicians, and an estimated eighteen hundred "professional artists" ranging from *Playboy* All-Star Band guitarist Chet Atkins (credited with inventing the famous "Nashville sound") down to obscure mountaineer fiddlers or weird jug-band combos.

Though Chet Atkins calls himself "just another hunched-over guitar player," this forty-four-year-old native of rural Tennessee is probably the most influential music man in Music City. As top artist and repertory executive for RCA Victor in Nashville, Atkins matches some fifty artists with appropriate material and produces their recording sessions. He is a noted songwriter and arranger, his own record albums have sold in the millions, and he designed the world's biggest-selling guitar.

Atkins was discovered by Steve Sholes, Victor vice-president, in the late 1940s. Having heard him play guitar on a commercial transcription, Sholes ordered him tracked down. Scouts found him broke and unemployed in Denver. Atkins's first records went virtually unnoticed. As recently as 1955 he was no more than a seventy-five-dollar-per-week assistant to Sholes. Two years later Sholes placed him in charge of Victor's Nashville office, a decision that now seems star kissed. Working with the kinds of musicians he had grown up with—country boys who read little or no music—Atkins began to create the loose, happy, natural sound for which Nashville is now famed. "You can get the same sound anywhere," Atkins says, "if you've got musicians from this part of the country. They've got soul. It's been suggested that the Nashville sound is no more than an attitude." *

Like everything else in America, country music is being urbanized. Drums, once barred from the Opry stage, are now permitted. Amplified guitars have become commonplace. Echo chambers, even a few winds and reeds, and country sounds with psychedelic connotations may be increasingly found in Nashville studios. There are beards in town, and miniskirts; not all the home-rolled cigarettes come from Prince Albert cans.

On Saturdays forty-five passenger tourist buses depart the Opry House every half hour. The men have those thick, big-boned wrists common to plowboys or interior football linemen; they are partial to western hats or duck hunters' caps. Their women seem all of a piece—faceless, neither young nor old, easily forgettable.

Our young blond guide instructed us that our driver would periodically stop to accommodate photographers. The customers

* In Nashville recording studios, musicians and backup voices may hear a song for the first time at 7:00 p.m. and have it on tape by 8:30. While the artist sings the melody the first time, voices behind him hum and musicians write chord changes on three-by-five cards. They take it from there. "I can read a little music," the local joke goes, "but not enough to foul up my playing."

251

paid only perfunctory attention to spiels noting the church attended by Andrew Jackson ("He was a president of the United States"), Union Street ("One of the greatest concentrations of brokerage commodities outside Wall Street"), or Franklin Road ("The avenue of retreat for Confederate soldiers during the battle of Nashville"). They perked up when we passed Hume Fogg High School ("Alma mater of Dinah Shore and Phil Harris"), Acuff-Rose Publications, Minnie Pearl's Chicken Hut, and the Biltmore Courts Motel ("Where Don Gibson wrote the classic country hit, 'Oh, Lonesome Me'").

There was a stir when we reached the wooded clump where Gentleman Jim Reeves died in a plane crash. Webb Pierce's guitar-shaped mailbox was photographed from impossible angles; his guitar-shaped swimming pool has "the strings painted on the bottom"; his Cadillac has "over three hundred silver dollars embedded in it, zebra upholstery, gun racks, and a set of Longhorn steer horns mounted in front." Photographers climbed down to record Tex Ritter's house; nobody accepted the invitation to pay that honor to Governor Buford Ellington's mansion. We saw the small frame house off Granny Pike Road where Pat Boone grew up, the homes of Skeeter Davis, Faron Young, Jim Ed Brown, and Eddy Arnold—"one of the richest men in the world, though he doesn't act like it." An old nester in a baseball cap laughed. "He don't need to act like it if he's got it."

Our longest pause was at the home of Audrey Williams, widow of the legendary Hank. "That 1952 Cadillac in the driveway is the one Hank Williams died in on January 1, 1953," our guide said, prompting the greatest camera action since Iwo Jima. "Audrey and her son, Hank, Jr., have established a Hank Williams museum in the home. Out back is a forty-thousand-dollar cabana decorated in true Hawaiian style. That is an authentic Civil War cannon and Confederate flag you see in the foreground. Hank, Jr., who is eighteen, has recently married and signed a three-hundred-thousand-dollar recording contract. He sang his father's songs in the movie *The Hank Williams Story*."

Hank Williams's big-time career hardly spanned six years; he was dead at twenty-nine. No country singer since Jimmie Rodgers, "The Singing Brakeman" (and also "The Father of Country

Music") caused such emotional impact or so quickly became legend. Much of Williams's story is dark: he couldn't drink, he became addicted to narcotics (because, friends say, of constant pain from an old spinal injury), his domestic life was stormy; he slept badly and ate hardly at all. Williams died in the back seat of his Cadillac while being driven to a one-nighter in Charleston, West Virginia.

Hank was one of the first elected to the Country Music Hall of Fame, housed in a handsome glass-walled barn along Record Row. There tourists study Jimmie Rodgers's brakeman uniform and railroad lantern, Hank's guitar and boots, Pee Wee King's accordion, the Carter Family's audioharp, the executive chair occupied by Jimmie Davis, "The Singing Governor" of Louisiana; Burl Ives's banjo, Bob Wills's first fiddle, the "first guitars" of Eddy Arnold, Chet Atkins, Gene Autry, and Tex Ritter. One display of relics was salvaged from the plane crash in 1963 that took the life of Patsy Cline, whose biggest record was darkly titled "I Fall to Pieces": her favorite wig, mascara wand, hairbrush, and a Confederate-flagged cigarette lighter which, though battered, still renders "Dixie."

The crash that killed Patsy Cline also took Cowboy Copas, Hawkshaw Hawkins, and Randy Hughes; Gentleman Jim Reeves and his manager were killed in another crash; Minnie Pearl was injured when her pilot husband was forced to crashland in a Tennessee field. "You could buy airplanes around here real cheap for a while," one Opry man said. Opry performers travel so extensively that accidents are inevitable: many play 250 or more road dates annually. Johnny Horton, Jack Anglin, Betty Jack Davis, and Ira Louvin died in auto accidents; dozens of others have been injured. Roy Acuff curtailed his travel schedule following critical injuries three years ago. (One of his old classics is "Wreck on the Highway.") George Jones has seen one of his buses demolished and another plunged into an Oregon lake.

Bus travel is, however, the most popular mode of Opry transportation. Porter Wagoner's own sixty-seven-thousand-dollar marvel includes color television, carpets, and a well-appointed bar; Dottie West whips up her favorite dishes in a mobile kitchenette; George Jones—possibly to guard against a third accident

253

—has carpeted the floors, walls, and ceiling of his latest. By employing two drivers a troupe may roll almost constantly, keep down motel bills, and move in relative safety. Disadvantages include crowded conditions, numbing fatigue, and a terrible disorientation occasioned by odd sleeping hours, marathon poker games, and countless state borders. Many bus tours last twenty or more days.

"Naw," Okie Jones answered my question, "I ain't bitter. Marty's got a world of talent. He rides them high notes out of sight. And nobody writes stronger lines than Marty Robbins when he's doing a certain kind of song like 'El Paso' or 'Fellina.' Any songs I wrote had to be kept simple; I never had enough vocabulary. And my own voice never amounted to much. Too thin." He bent the bus expertly around a curve, discovering new miles of night and the winking lights of several heavy trucks dimly seen through a snow screen. The great rubber wheels made popping sounds on the cold pavement, spinning out dirty little rivers of icy slush on the Ohio landscape.

Okie Jones was driving for the third consecutive night; there would be yet another night of diesels and truck-stop coffee before he reached the house trailer he occupies on Marty Robbins's ranch twenty miles outside Nashville. "Marty's been real good to me. I showed up in Nashville flat broke seven years ago and he give me a job digging postholes." Now he works Robbins's ranch, takes care of his racing cars, and when the boss is singing to adoring crowds about golden sunsets, love, or devil women, Okie is somewhere out front hawking Marty Robbins albums and songbooks.

"My big record come out in 1951," Okie Jones said. " 'Send Me a Penny Postcard.' I bought me a white Cadillac." Okie lit a menthol cigarette and flicked the bus lights. "Marty and me recorded for the same label. But where Marty had that pure, clear voice I was just what they call a personality: I'd jump around and act silly—I guess I was doing what Elvis Presley done later. Only Elvis done it a little better." He laughed, and for a moment his thirty-seven-year-old outdoorsman's face was younger. "A *lot* better. Elvis, he's not driving this bus tonight.

254

"It might seem like a comedown to some people," Okie said, "but I've seen it lots snakier than this. My stepdaddy was a farm worker. Moved from place to place. One summer in Texas we lived under a tree. We lived under bridges or culverts several times. When winter come on, a farmer said we could stay in an old sod hut next to his pigpens—as long as we didn't disturb the pigs! Yeah, I've been up and I've been down, just like the old song says. When I was in the army they sent me to perform on the 'Arlene Francis Show' seventeen times. I wrote a few songs and recitations and got recorded. Then I hit with 'Penny Postcard.' After that I booked out at $550 a night. But if you don't get another hot record or two you cool off, and I never got it." Someone persuaded Okie Jones to invest in the wrong insurance firm; he lost even the aging white Cadillac. "Then I sorta withdrew. Wouldn't play any show dates. Didn't cut any records or write songs. Half the time I didn't answer my phone. It wasn't long before I found myself out of show business.

"Ups and downs go with this business. If a guy's got talent it'll usually work out for him. If he's just another entertainer—well, he goes as far as he can. Then he's got to rethink things." Okie Jones pushed the bus toward Indianapolis and the two Sunday shows awaiting Marty Robbins. After a while he began to sing his old hit, "Penny Postcard." Halfway through he forgot the words.

Behind the driver, in a stateroom with a silver star on the door (symbolic of the fame brought by nineteen records in *Billboard*'s Top Ten Tunes, eight in the number one spot), Marty Robbins slept in red-silk pajamas and a plush bunk bed. In the cramped rear, six members of Robbins's band lay atop thin mattresses on less than exotic double-decked bunks.

Nashville has a star system no less rigid and deadly than Hollywood's. There are the same nervous agents, press flacks, and hangers-on waiting around to sneeze should the star catch a head cold. Our star, Marty Robbins, was not aboard his bus when I began this grinding journey with it; he had flown ahead and would join us in Trenton, New Jersey.* Taking a twenty-seven-

* Robbins played a Trenton club on Friday night; the WWVA Jamboree in Wheeling, West Virginia, on Saturday night, and joined an Opry package

dollar poker lesson from Robbins's band boys, I was instructed on how to get along with The Chief: "The Chief don't like a lot of big betting. When he checks a bet then *we* check." Again: "We don't ask The Chief many questions. He'll tell us when to tune our boxes." It was suggested that The Chief preferred not to talk about his family, his money, or politics; should he get a "far-away look in his eyes" one would do well to cease talking altogether. I would later note that none of Robbins's men sat at his restaurant table without specific invitation; they were careful not to get the better of The Chief in roughhouse banter and seemed instinctively to know when he had tired of the game.

Marty Robbins has instructed his drivers that if even one can of beer is discovered to "put it off along with the man who brought it aboard." (A wise rule. More than one country star has missed show dates, wrecked vehicles, or engaged in boxing matches for lack of such a rule.) Every member of the Robbins group has some extra duty to perform: singer-guitarist Don Winters handles travel arrangements; bass man Henry Durrough cuts The Chief's hair and massages him each night with an electric vibrator; this one is responsible for Robbins's guitar, that one for his costumes. Robbins's hirelings average about $150 weekly. Before they got into music they were farmers, barbers, students, soldiers, and factory hands.

Robbins himself held dozens of jobs before stumbling into a music career. "I'm in this business," he says, "because I despise honest labor." He was ditchdigging in Arizona when a local country-western bandleader offered him ten dollars to play substitute guitar, and he kept the job. One night in a roadhouse tavern he sang, and the house roared. Robbins claims that he didn't know he could sing: "I'd seen every Gene Autry movie as a kid and tried to imitate him, but not seriously." He formed his own group and began to work rodeos, political gatherings, radio stations, and high school gyms. Grand Old Opry signed him in 1953. His first big hit, "Singing the Blues," was at the top of every country chart; a few years later his own "El Paso" was so

show in Indianapolis for Sunday afternoon and evening performances. The two-thousand-mile bus trip consumed four nights and three days. Robbins was paid a gross of four thousand dollars.

large that he virtually quit personal appearances for a year because of tax considerations. At forty-four Robbins now owns four
music-publishing companies, a six-hundred-acre ranch, a house
his band boys privately call "Marty's Ramada Inn," racing cars,
beef cattle, and assorted real estate.

For all this success, Robbins is insecure. He does little television because "it scares me"; because his latest records have not
been smashes he is changing recording sessions from Nashville to
New York; he talks of needing new songs, new writers, new arrangements, new approaches. "When did I know I had it *made?*"
he said in an all-night diner somewhere in West Virginia. "Hell, I
haven't got it made yet! I dropped a bundle building a racetrack
in Nashville; then some oil deals turned sour. And the damned
federal government can ruin a man in thirty minutes!"

Robbins campaigned for Goldwater in 1964; this year he is
red-hot for George Wallace and manages to plug him at every
show. (He introduces guitar man Jack Pruett as "my good friend
from Ala-*bam*, George Wallace"; his band strikes up "Dixie"; in
New Jersey, West Virginia, and Indiana this got big hands.) A
farm boy of older and simpler times, Robbins believes that every
man can achieve success if he persists: doles, foreign-aid, or anti-
poverty programs are deterrents to ambition. He looks to George
Wallace to stop riots and looting. Surprisingly, perhaps, Robbins
opposes the Vietnam war: "It's senseless. I love my country and
all that, but if you win the damned war what have you got? Another nation to feed."

"What Marty would really like to be," one of his band boys
confided, "is a frontier sheriff. He'd enjoy a 'High Noon' shoot-
out every day." Robbins's favorite songs are about cowboys,
hangings, posses, dance-hall queens; on moody nights, strum-
ming his guitar, he may sit alone in the darkened bus singing of
these subjects in a sweet, haunting voice, and one senses not to
go near. Last year he wrote and published a pulp western, *Small
Man*, in the hope he will play its gunslinging hero in the movies.
He flavors his speech with Red Dog Saloon terms: "Playing the
road is just like robbing Wells Fargo. You ride in, take the
money, and ride out."

There are certain road hazards, however: crowds seeking autographs, heckling drunks, reckless young women in tight slacks and with hot promises in their eyes. Most persistent of all are The Regulars—those odd characters who single out a given star to haunt at impossible points, seeking him out backstage, knocking on his motel door, asking him to shake hands with an old uncle. "Marty," a middle-aged woman in Indianapolis said, "here's a picture I made of you in Oklahoma last year. And this one I made in Maine." A New Jersey couple regularly adapts their two-week vacation to Robbins's road schedule. An Ohio woman delivered a container of fresh strawberries and carefully seeded grapes, then displayed the latest photos of her grandchildren; Robbins politely murmured how much they had grown. "Those good friends and neighbors *mean* well," Robbins sighed one night after a particularly dogged regular had invaded his dressing room. "They buy your albums, they love you, they're loyal. They'll do damn near anything for you except leave you alone."

Sunday afternoon, Indianapolis: Robbins prowled his dressing room in skintight electric-blue western garb, restless, drumming on tables, flicking imaginary dust from his shiny black patent-leather cowboy boots. The crowd rumbled into the Indiana State Fairgrounds Auditorium. "God loves a promoter," Robbins said. "Ole Dick Blake will rake that loot in today. He'll fill this thing twice—twenty-two thousand people. All right, say Dick pays between six and seven thousand for his talent, maybe about that much more for advertising, hires all his help—hell, he could bank twenty-five thousand dollars easy. *I'm* the cat working for peanuts."

Dick Blake, the promoter, would later admit to eighteen thousand paying customers and a thirty-nine-thousand-dollar gate; a huckster he pays ten thousand dollars annually to shill a dozen big promotions added another four thousand dollars from the sale of assorted merchandise. Counting the house while he stood with Marty Robbins in the wings, the promoter said of his pitchman, "Listen to that guy. He's the best in the world." Within minutes I came to think of the pitchman as "The Golden Fleece": he confided to the good folks that he could make this special offer "by authority of the Continental Optical Company of the

258

Orient." This meant he was willing to part with made-in-Japan binoculars at a nice profit. Then he shilled playing cards "with pictures of your favorite country-western stars in resplendent colors. Roy Acuff is the king of diamonds, Dottie West is the queen of hearts."

Dick Blake, who works out of Nashville, has packaged country-western shows for seventeen years. His promotion had played to eight thousand in Louisville the previous night; there had been a fifty-thousand-dollar gate in Detroit and a forty-thousand-dollar one in Pittsburgh. "Country radio operated right has been the key to our success," he says. "The hip stations program with the same top-forty format that only pop-music stations once used. The good country disc jockeys don't talk down to people. None of this 'Cousin Jake' stuff, or barnyard humor. Your country-western audience is much more sophisticated now." Perhaps so. One must remark, however, that Blake's pitchman sold everything he brought with him.

They come to Nashville with songs in their hearts and young men's visions. The odds favor their leaving within one year. Police and Travelers Aid Association workers know the telltale signs: an old car, out-of-state tags, a stingy wardrobe hanging in back, a stringed instrument. Warm nights they sleep in their cars; colder nights they seek out twenty-four-hour Laundromats. Unless they are especially cursed, there will come one burning morning when they breakfast on a single glazed doughnut that tastes like crow, and wire home for money. Suddenly the hometown gas pump or the family farm looks good. Nashville struggles along with one less genius.

One night I talked late in a Nashville motel room with Mickey Newbury, a young songwriter with Acuff-Rose. Two years ago Newbury literally was on the street; today he owns a gold Cadillac convertible, a sharp wardrobe, and apartments in Houston and Nashville. As we talked, sipping good Scotch, there came from the street a thunderous wail. We stepped to the balcony. Below, under a streetlight, slouched a young man in western blue denims and an outsized hat, a small canvas bag in one hand and a guitar in the other, repeating again that mournful howl to

259

the empty streets. "Listen to him," Newbury said. "He's trying to communicate! With just *anybody*. That was *me* a couple of years ago. Man, you're looking at *me!*"

The lonesome cowhand moved toward the dim lights of a gloomy YMCA building, hesitated, walked six steps one way and perhaps eight steps another, then chose a dark side street to lead him toward some uncertain rendezvous with his personal destiny. "He doesn't even know where he's going," Newbury said.

The unknown young man could not know. Not yet. For the carousel was spinning before him, playing merry tunes with their promise of golden Cadillacs and a certain feathery fame. The young man would eventually lunge at it, but until that moment he could not know whether he would be pulled aboard for the fast sweet ride or whether the carousel would spin on by, leaving him sprawled in the Tennessee dust.

*Harper's*
JULY 1968

# TWO
# PASS IN REVIEW,
# FAILING

**W**e who write for a living without the benefit of oil incomes or rich wives do a great deal of judgment-passing on our peers. Our excuse is that we need the money. Big deal. The approximately twenty books I review each year probably bring in under twenty-five hundred dollars. The fact is, after witnessing the brutal surgery performed upon our own books, we enjoy our turns with the scalpel.

It is far better to review bad books than good ones. They lend themselves to one's humor perversions, to spleen venting, and to brighter writing. Good books must be taken "seriously"; when writers decide to be "serious" they almost invariably become pompous or ponderous. Never is it a good policy to review a friend's book. You cannot please him even if you vote him the clear nod over Shakespeare or G. B. Shaw at their finest. I offer in evidence a fine collection of former friends. An opportunity to review a book by a special old enemy, on the other hand, can make the week.

Of the two books here reviewed, neither is likely to be confused with Art. The review of Sam Houston Johnson's book is offered as typical of the light essay-review, in which the critic mines his own past or external knowledge while the book itself becomes secondary. Also I included it here because (1) it's interesting to see how the former president's secret brother saw "one man's family" from the inside and (2) ole Sam is a pretty fascinating character in his own right. The review of Jacqueline Susann's silly exercise is included to prove that even us hacks got our literary standards. The day I learned that *Publishers Weekly* credited my review in the *Chicago Sun-Times* with keeping Miss Susann's book out of the number one spot on the best-seller list there—a distinction earned by no other city—I wept in gratitude at my best contribution to American letters.

# LBJ's Secret Brother Meditates on History

FEW OUTSIDE TEXAS or select Washington circles knew in his old days of power that Lyndon Johnson had a brother. Given patience, good legs, and woodsman's knowledge of many endless dim corridors, however, you could find Sam Houston Johnson somewhere in the catacombs of the old Senate office building. I first made the trip one morning in the mid-1950s, coming over from my new job on the House side of Capitol Hill as assistant to a Texas congressman, intrigued by the news that our Senate majority leader kept a secret brother in the basement.

The event provided unique high adventure to one so newly arrived from the provinces. Most young men who abandon their native villages for the sources of power are not strangers to ambition; second-banana politicians certainly are no exceptions. I was anxious to take an accurate reading on the Great Man's brother (who might, even from subterrestrial stations, somehow prove useful in a future political battle), and so I approached his undistinguished little alcove more than moderately alert.

Sam Johnson looked up from a long government-issue table heaped with yellowing old Texas newspapers from which he had been clipping mysterious items. He had a vexed look, as if irritated at having to direct yet another damnfool lost tourist to more celebrated Washington landmarks. I was momentarily in confusion: Sam Johnson in that instant so strongly resembled his famous brother that for one flashing moment I feared I had intruded on a private retreat while LBJ was personally bringing his scrapbook up to date. When Sam understood that the visitor had actually sought him out, however, friendly lights blinked in his face. He seemed almost pathetically grateful for someone to talk with and within five minutes had challenged me to luncheon drinks. We would share the cup a fair number of times over the next decade, and I would learn that Sam had inherited the Johnsonian love of good political talk and a midnight fascination with the telephone.

One night Sam telephoned to ask that I get in touch with Lyndon for him. Well, hell—I said—if the Senate majority leader's blood brother couldn't get through, how was a rinky-dink to make connections? "Lyndon won't come to the phone if he knows it's me," Sam complained. "Walter Hornaday of the *Dallas News* has been wantin' to write a feature story on me for two years. I kept on discouragin' him because Lyndon expects me to hide my light under a damn bushel. Well, Walter wrote the story anyway. As soon as Lyndon got ahold of the damn thing, he called up to cuss me for hoggin' the headlines—then he hung up on me. He won't return my calls, and all I want is a chance to explain."

Sam was misused more than once. Occasionally, when a visiting Texas grass-roots politician appeared distressed because he wasn't permitted three hours in idle chatter with the majority leader, they brought Sam upstairs, put a necktie on him, and soothed the offended by offering up, if not LBJ, then a brother who looked like him.

At the start of LBJ's career in the 1930s, and for some years afterward, Sam was at the core of the action: campaign assistant, adviser, speechwriter, pal. As LBJ's star ascended, however,

263

Sam's did not always keep pace. Although he was a paid member
of LBJ's Senate staff, he was seen and heard less and less as Walter Jenkins, John Connally, Horace Busby, Booth Mooney, George
Reedy, Jack Valenti, and Bill Moyers proved unusually skilled at
office politics. While LBJ wheeler-dealered in his ornate Capitol
suite of crystal chandeliers and gold-embossed doorknobs (where
a bigger-than-God oil portrait of himself caught the indirect light
in a flattering way) Sam, a solitary and rather shadowy figure, accomplished grub work in a series of gray rooms without even a
snapshot of himself on display.

One wondered, back then, what natural juices of frustration or
even brotherly rage may have coursed through Sam Johnson. He
was often a brooder, and one night when I introduced him at a
party as "LBJ's first victim—he was only six when persuaded that
'Lyndon' was a more politically potent name in Texas than 'Sam
Houston' was," he became very angry. Sam liked to hint that it
had several times been necessary to save his brother from some
strategic or tactical mistake. If, however, Sam might subtly suggest his own superiority, or turn his rough Texas humor against
LBJ in a private moment, his hackles quickly rose should anyone
else do the same.

By the time LBJ became vice-president, Sam Houston Johnson
lived back in Texas and was rarely seen in Washington. Sam's
absence from official circles was variously explained: he had
grown tired of taking big brother's authoritarianism, or Lyndon
was convinced Sam tippled too much and wasn't serious enough
in his purposes. It depended on who told the tale. Perhaps small
grasses of truth grew on both sides of the fence: being the junior
partner by six years in a sibling relationship is seldom easy even
when one's big brother has no long-range plans to rule the free
world.

Sam Johnson and I spent the Kennedy-Johnson inauguration
eve together, in January of 1961, at the home of mutual friends,
Glen and Marie Wilson. Late in the evening, with a record snowstorm blowing outside, LBJ telephoned hot complaints that Sam
had not chosen to join other family members for the night. ("Dammit, Sam, all the *Kennedys* are together," LBJ invoked as an ap-

peal to blood.) Though Sam rarely defied Lyndon in those days, on this night he remained unimpressed. At ease in cowboy boots and an old dressing gown, he sipped clam chowder with satisfying sound effects while LBJ raved. Sam finally replied that the inaugural ceremonies had attracted him "only because you insisted it was a damned must," going on to lament his required presence on the official platform "in a silly top hat and ass-deep in snow, but without a damn thing to drink." When LBJ hung up dissatisfied (thinking, perhaps, that goddammit here he wasn't even *sworn in* to the powerless vacuum that was the vice-presidency, and mutiny already had extended even into family ranks), Sam proposed an enthusiastic toast to an overnight blizzard grand enough to cancel ceremonies required by the Constitution. Distressingly near dawn, however, an LBJ staffer materialized to get Sam into his formal attire and to deliver him to his appointed place, deep in snow and New Frontiersmen.

Washington whispered that on Sam's high-spirited visits from Texas he was shadowed by LBJ's staff members. I was in Sam's company one afternoon at the bar in the Carroll Arms Hotel when he spotted two of Lyndon's gumshoes at a distant table, looking as if they might give a month's pay for a potted palm to hide behind. Sam asked a waitress to take his guardians complimentary drinks, along with the warning that he planned a big evening. Later Sam would have his own bedroom at the White House, and a dogged secret-service agent, Mike Howard, whom he enjoyed accusing of stool-pigeoning to the president on Sam's carousing. After his well-supervised outings, Sam frequently crossed his wrists to simulate a prisoner in handcuffs as the limousine bearing him entered the White House gates; sometimes he playfully shouted his desire for rescue to the White House guards. By Sam's own testimony, his big brother not infrequently awaited within to deliver stern little lectures on the dangers of strong drink and stray women, or to grill Sam on his associates: "There were times when I was tempted to tell him I'd been kidnapped by a whore and confined in a cathouse for forty-eight hours, but I resisted the temptation." Once, in the Senate days, when LBJ came in potted from the golf course, he woke Sam and said, "Yes, by God, I want you to take a damned good look at

265

me, Sam Houston. Open your eyes and look at me. Cause I'm drunk, and I want you to see how you look to me, Sam Houston, when *you* come home drunk."

Still, if Sam sometimes suffered semibanishment and bedroom lectures, or if he sat alone among stacks of old newspapers while LBJ pressed the flesh of visiting pharaohs or depended on Bobby Baker for his partisan nose counts, he frequently saw his brother on intimate terms. Maybe Sam didn't grin at you from the Huntley-Brinkley show, or you didn't find him quoted by Evans and Novak, but he had opportunity in the privacy of family quarters to serve as a sounding board, to lend an ear, to witness the presidential mind or heart bared because, after all, ole Sam was blood kin and burdened presidents must sometimes sit in the dark and unload themselves.

Now Frankenstein has come out of the basement: Sam Johnson has written a book, *My Brother Lyndon*, about those private moments or emotions which eventually his brother's own memoirs may choose to refurbish, fumigate, or ignore. When LBJ first heard rumors of his brother's book, his old friends combed their connections in the publishing world to beg a copy of the manuscript, and Sam (who had thoughtfully removed himself from Lyndon's board before secretly turning author) was sought in distant places. This time, however, it was Sam who chose not to receive his brother's calls.*

It is just possible Sam Johnson felt some urgent need to proclaim his own identity after all those silent years in LBJ's giant shadow, even if his identity could be nothing grander than Lyndon Johnson's backstairs Boswell. Sam may have been freed from his White House imprisonment, but his book makes clear he is not yet exorcised of his little-brother complex. On the one hand LBJ is the classic hero figure, a white knight leading a reluctant America to greatness although beset by smart-aleck Ivy Leaguers, Ho Chi Minh, bearded peaceniks, ambitious "sycophants" of the White House palace guard, and a forest of goddamned

* Ultimately, with no help from Sam, LBJ's agents obtained a manuscript. A request for some two hundred deletions or amendments was denied by the publisher.

troublesome Kennedys: a protector who rescued Sam from play-ground bullies and cried real tears on seeing his little brother en-cased in plaster following an accident. On the other hand, Lyn-don appears as a scheming boy who skinned Sam in a bicycle transaction and as a president who not only had mean moods but who habitually cheated at dominoes, as a born meddler and bully forever attempting to dictate to everyone around him, as a mark Sam Johnson not infrequently found easy to outwit in gaining inside political information, and as bumpkin content in "baggy, ready-made suits from Sears and Roebuck." Since much of the book is a defense of LBJ as well as a war cry against all his detractors, one assumes that in Sam's mind The Good Lyndon eventually triumphs over The Bad Lyndon. That proposition might not carry on the LBJ Ranch by very much, however. The Ranch may note the rather pointed dedication of Sam's book to a sister described as "my favorite of the family," which pretty well informs the reader who was not.

There are times when Sam tarnishes the LBJ image even in at-tempting to gloss it. In reciting how he contritely told Lyndon of having double-crossed an old school chum on some minor matter years earlier, Sam writes: "He looked at me as if I were pulling the scab off an old sore. 'Why in hell do you want to brood about a little old thing like that?' he said. 'The past has passed, and there's no sense harping on it.' " Nor are the sensitive to be com-forted by LBJ's notion that the business of man is business, while "culture is the business of womenfolk." Here is the young LBJ flying off the handle to a prospective wife who erred in quoting her father's prediction that the Johnsons collectively would never amount to a damn: " 'To hell with your daddy,' he said. 'I wouldn't marry you or anyone in the whole damned family. . . . We sure don't need to mix with your family to get along. . . . And you can tell your daddy that someday I'll be president of this country. You watch and see.' " Observe Lyndon Johnson in an early congressional race, telephoning his brother Sam in Washington to practice the politics of deception: " 'Are you sure Sam Rayburn said that? . . . You actually heard him tell Wright Patman that Avery would be a weak sister?' Since I had said nothing of the sort, I realized he was just pretending for the benefit of someone listening to his end of the conversation, perhaps some local politician who was wavering between Lyndon and Avery. The next time he might come up with: 'When did Jim Farley tell [Congressman] Kleberg that Avery was begging for outside help?' " Such tales may not inspire schoolboys any more than the story of Abe Lincoln jumping out of the window to avoid a tough vote in the Illinois legislature.

Do not consult *My Brother Lyndon* for the specifics of policy decisions. Sam was not often around to hear what Bundy said to McNamara or what Lyndon said to Rusk. Sam Johnson's recollections may prove important to the truth's long-range purposes, however, because, for one thing, he practices no more diplomacy than the Weathermen, and, for another, LBJ in retirement has lately given signs that his own memoirs may prove little more reliable than the *Old Farmer's Almanac*.

We received (I am afraid for history's purposes) LBJ's signal on the first of several one-hour CBS-TV appearances with Walter Cronkite: No, he had spent no time or energies fighting with Bobby Kennedy; why, the last thing the late senator had said to LBJ was, "You're a very courageous and dedicated man"; as a matter of fact, Jack and Bobby's ole daddy had called up to beg Lyndon Johnson to be *his* candidate back in 19-and-55. ("Lyndon hated Bobby," Sam writes. "Bobby hated Lyndon. Lyndon didn't trust Bobby. Bobby didn't trust Lyndon. And each of them knew damned well he was hated and mistrusted by the other.") No, LBJ told Cronkite, being run over by the McCarthy kiddie-corps in New Hampshire's 1968 primary contributed not one iota to his retirement: he had abdicated (like a certain British king) for the love of a good woman and out of patriotic reflexes. Furthermore, he had never wanted to be president and had never sought out power; his every thought had been how to get the national monkey off his back and go home to Texas. What had fueled the prairie Machiavelli through thirty-five years of political head-breaking, cloakroom plots, and partisan schemes had been neither ambitious gases nor the hot coals of power. One wishes for the generosity to believe him, for technically Lyndon B. Johnson is an elder statesman, and perhaps he has been doubted enough for one lifetime. Sam Houston Johnson records enough to the contrary to relieve us of the obligation of blind belief in our former presidents, however. We should be grateful for a number of scenes unlikely to issue from the LBJ typewriter.

*Scene one:* the White House. *Time:* shortly after the convening of the 1964 Democratic National Convention; Sam is attempting to learn, along with the rest of the nation, LBJ's vice-presidential choice; his method is to suggest a series of candidates and then evaluate the president's reaction:

"I kinda like Senator Pastore myself," I said. "He made a damned good speech this evening."

He actually snorted when I said that. "Goddammit, Sam Houston, what in hell's gone wrong with you? How could an Italian from a dinky state like Rhode Island possibly help me?"

"There's Adlai," I said. "He's got the egghead vote good and solid."

"Don't need him," said Lyndon. "With Barry Goldwater running, I look like a Harvard professor to the eggheads."

"Maybe you ought to get a Catholic like Gene McCarthy. He's awful strong in the Midwest."

"He's not exactly what I'm looking for. There's something sort of stuck-up about Gene," he said. "You get the impression that he's got a special pipeline to God and that they talk only Latin to each other."

*Scene two:* the White House. *Time:* shortly before LBJ's announcement of retirement. Vice-President and Mrs. Humphrey are guests. The president baits "poor ole Hubert" for his alleged failure to "influence the midwestern polls for LBJ" to the point where "there were tears in Hubert's eyes, and his lips were trembling a little." When LBJ leaves the room to enjoy a midnight massage, Sam follows him to complain that Lyndon has been too hard on HHH and possibly should not have so effectively humiliated him in Muriel Humphrey's presence. "Hubert can take it," LBJ remarks, stretching out on the rubbing table. When Sam voices a wish to give Hubert a little gratuitous political advice, LBJ orders the nation's vice-president into the rubbing room. LBJ pretends to doze under the hands of his masseur while Sam carries on:

269

"Senator * . . . you've let some of these damned fuzzy-brained liberals put you on the defensive. . . . You're going to have to convince them you're still as liberal as they are: *without* pussyfooting on Vietnam. You can't abandon Lyndon Johnson on that issue. You've got to back him and prove you're a liberal," blah-blah-blah. LBJ listens, eyes closed, with a "flickering smile on his lips."

"I went on in that vein for about a half hour," Sam says, "putting it as strongly as I could, without a single interruption from Lyndon. If I had said anything he didn't like, I'm sure he would have broken in with a gruff order for us to leave the room. 'You two are ruining my rest,' he'd say. 'Go talk somewhere else.' His silence was approval of what I was saying, and Humphrey undoubtedly knew it. He was doubly certain when Lyndon mumbled, 'Goodnight, Hubert. See you, Sam,' as we left the room."

After being a party to the humiliations of the rubbing room, one wonders where Sam Johnson got the audacity to write in anger of the humiliations LBJ himself suffered as vice-president among the despised Kennedys. Sam's dislike of the Kennedys is very well displayed. When promoting his book on the David Frost television show, he spoke so warmly of the passing of old Joe Kennedy and of Senator Ted Kennedy's troubles at Chappaquiddick Bridge that Frost, in some disbelief, remarked that Sam seemed to be speaking from some inner glee. "I am not going to say that I was overwhelmed with grief," Sam writes of the assassination of RFK, "because that isn't true." Robert McNamara, McGeorge Bundy, and Bill Moyers are given several types of hell for their deficiencies, it being carefully noted that among their more horrid crimes was free association with the Kennedys. Sam's book repeatedly makes the point that he was not the only Johnson who found the Kennedys unlovable. LBJ is amused and gloating in mimicking how Bobby Kennedy "gulped like a fat fish pulling in a mouthful of air" on being told by LBJ that a vice-presidency was not in his future. (" 'Look here,' he said one night

---

* Sam repeatedly and unaccountably refers to the vice-president as "senator" in this scene.

at the supper table, waving a news clipping over his coffee. 'I don't need that little runt to win. I can take anybody I damn well please.' ")

In the old days Sam Johnson practiced a certain populist liberalism. His current prejudices are right out of the mouth of the most unyielding mass of Middle America, almost a parody of the militant know-nothing. Quite often the inference is that LBJ shares many of these views right along with Sam Houston Johnson and Richard Nixon. Only Spiro T. Agnew's "effete corps of impudent snobs" dissents from the holy killing in Vietnam, to hear Sam tell it, and hot wax is poured in the ears of senators who "read a lot of fancy literature," or who "quote a lot of poetry"; Sam's views on people who prefer "snails in garlic sauce" or who have associations with Harvard may make Martha Mitchell's day. Senator Fulbright, "known around the White House as 'Halfbright' "—a witticism, I believe, originating with the late Senator Joe McCarthy—is flailed for his alleged "intellectual Rhodes scholar snobbery."

"Bright scholarly men like McNamara, Bundy, and Fortas had a lot of influence on his thinking because he regarded them as part of an intellectual elite," Sam writes of LBJ. "There was a hint of awe in his attitude toward them. He knew he was basically as smart as they were—smarter in some respects—but their way of talking and their whole educational background— Harvard, Yale, and all that—somehow got to him more than it should. He had known plenty of book-loving ignoramuses with Phi Beta Kappa keys from fancy colleges, had seen them pull damnfool boners on the simplest matters, yet he could suddenly be self-conscious about his own limited schooling at a small Texas college." LBJ erred when he failed to take major military reprisals against North Korea for its seizure of the *Pueblo*, in Sam's opinion, and had Sam been consulted LBJ would have removed every last Kennedy appointee no later than the morning of November 23, 1963. For all of Lyndon Johnson's giant flaws, one concludes that Sam Johnson has probably performed a service to our peace of mind that he probably did not intend: he leaves us with the consoling thought that if America just had to elect a Johnson to the presidency, it elected the right one.

*Harper's*
APRIL 1970

# The Love (Clunk!) Machine

AMANDA (the beautiful model whose biggest worry was her puny bust measurements) did it with Christie Lane (the famous foul-mouthed TV comic) and Robin Stone. Maggie (the actress whose original husband drove her into the arms of others on account of he had no proper respect for what the marriage manuals call "love play") did it with sundry passersby who really didn't mean all that much to her and with Robin Stone, who did. Ethel (the friendly neighborhood nymphomaniac who kept a careful diary recording the Beauty Rest gymnastics of Famous People she met as a TV-network Gal Friday) did it with everybody who came down the pike and, of course, Robin Stone eventually came down it. Judith Austin (the young-at-heart-or-thereabouts, if mummifying, old dowager wife of the president of IBC-TV) presumably did it with her husband on her honeymoon, though as time passed she did it more with Robin Stone should the mood be on him. Which it usually was.

For Robin Stone did it to all the foregoing, plus assorted airline hostesses, go-go girls, actresses, a classy countess whose acquaintance he made at one of your better-class orgies, a transvestite and, for all I know, Dancer and Prancer and Donder and Blitzen.

And if you are one of the mindless millions who will queue up to pay $6.95 for this sorry mess (or some fraction thereof for the inevitable paperback) then Miss Jacqueline Susann and her publisher will have cleverly done it to you. In which case I hope you are beyond the aid of penicillin.

Miss Susann, queen of the nonwriting writers (whose *Valley of the Dolls* a few years ago was the number one best-seller) is, curse it, back again. This is a sad time for all people who love the English language. I cannot say whether *The Love Machine* is improved over Miss Susann's last outing, nobody having paid me to read her earlier work. And it will be a cold day, etc., etc.

From what I learned of *Valley of the Dolls* through osmosis and a sheer inability to turn off the publicity machines, I judge that Miss Susann's profitable formula remains unchanged.

Take a cardboard cutout cast of fast-living, hard-loving, dopey-sounding folk who speak pure soap opera while jumping in and out of improbable situations as casually as they leap from pillow to bedpost. Stir in repetitious mention of real-life celebrities, New York night spots and international playgrounds one favors.

Add generous amounts of Dick-and-Jane prose: "Maggie saw Robin stride into the restaurant. He looked clean and fresh. Then she saw the little blond girl. Maggie knew instantly she had been to bed with Robin. Her hair had lost its shape. Her makeup looked patched." Fold in three parts sex to one part French chef: "[Alfie] came to the beach house and made love to her while Adam lay beside them on the bed. . . . And when it was over, she watched while Alfie made love to Adam. . . . Afterward, they all went into the kitchen and made scrambled eggs."

The story line of *The Love Machine* loosely chronicles the rise and fall of Robin Stone, who in his vertical moments kingpins a television network.

What really counts, above the plot, is stripping everybody down in jigtime so as to offer a Heinz variety of dime-store pornography. I must warn you that even porny paragraphs can be disappointingly done, for even when Miss Susann's characters are unencumbered by garments they move with all the grace of pigs in armor. One comes away from "love" passages feeling as if he had witnessed a wrestling match between Gorgeous George and Jack Paar, so many are the grips and tears.

Say for Robin Stone that boys and girls alike dig him. Chicks who have known him in intimate circumstances carry his bath towels around in their tote bags the better to retain his heady musk. (I don't think I can go on with this.) They scratch his name in the sands, in the spillage of their martinis and possibly on the backs of their substitute lovers. They throw themselves on empty beds to sob in loss of his remembered satisfactions. One lady, in the streetwalking business, fullfills for Robin Stone that ultimate fantasy of every acned All-American boy. In appreciation and in loving tribute she gives him his money back!

I am not making this up.

Would to God Miss Susann hadn't.

"The day is over"—Miss Susann once said in an interview—"when the point of writing is just to turn a phrase that critics will quote, like Henry James. I'm not interested in turning a phrase."

You don't have to worry, kid.

*Book Week*
MAY 1969

# SMALL ADVERTISEMENTS FOR MYSELF

The following twin exercises attempted to exploit bad things that happened to me and Mr. Clifford Irving last year. My misfortune was to be nominated for a National Book Award, an experience proving more humbling than applying for welfare. Mr. Irving's bad luck was to get caught bilking a publishing house out of many gold dollars on the improbable proposition that he was secretly writing the authorized biography of billionaire recluse Howard Hughes. A few years in jail aside, Mr. Irving may have had the better season.

Mr. Irving's adventure caused me one stoned night to write a private letter to my publisher, Viking's Tom Guinzburg, who thought it funny enough to pass around publishing circles. John Leonard of the *New York Times Book Review* heard about it and bought it. Following publication, numerous folk wrote in claiming to be offended; some doubted whether I had actually met with Jesus Christ. It was these I wrote insisting that I had. The second advertisement, all about how I foully lost the NBA contest, was more premeditated in that I wrote it with a sale in mind and to call public attention to myself.

# The Most Greatest
# Story Ever Told

Mr. Tom Guinzburg, President
The Viking Press, Inc.
New York, N.Y.

Dear Tom:

By this letter I offer you a unique opportunity to obtain the publication rights to a manuscript nearing completion. I am asking five hundred thousand dollars advance royalties for myself as the author, and an additional one million dollars for my source.

Over the past fifteen months, in various places throughout the free world, I have met with—and transcribed the life story of—Jesus Christ. Once we walked alone in a garden. Another time I joined my source and a dozen of his friends for supper. Still another time we went to this big picnic where all they served was bread and fish, though there was plenty to go around. We have met at various times in shepherds' fields, in chariots, on mountaintops, and so forth. Because my source insists on complete and total secrecy, I cannot at this point provide additional details. When the time comes, however, I will see to it that you get yours.

My source insists that we accept his story on blind faith. Of course, he is accustomed to dealing under those terms and points out that millions of others have so accepted his story. You, as a publisher, know how difficult writers can be, and I sincerely doubt whether my source will compromise his rule in this respect. He appears adamant and even agitated when one suggests alternatives.

276

The manuscript itself must be closely held. I cannot provide you the stone tablets on which the story was set down by my source and his father: it was necessary to copy from the stone tablets which were then—as I understand it—put in the care of a certain Mr. Moses. I am confident that my source is no impostor. He has turned water into wine for me, parted seas, healed the lame and the halt, etc., to the extent that I am convinced we have the McCoy. Also, he wears a beard, a robe, and has scarred hands.

True, other books have been written on this subject. None, however, were officially authorized. This will be the original first-person treatment. My source informs me, incidentally, that numerous errors of fact exist in the most popular work treating his life. Stories involving his immediate family he finds particularly embarrassing: the fact is, he was adopted. He has on reflection come to believe that a single author may have done a better and more cohesive job than did the numerous authors contributing to the other work—though he does volunteer that, as anthologies go, it sold very well. As to exactly why I was chosen for this work, I suspect it is because of my Texas origins: we have long known that Texas is God's country. Or perhaps my source is intrigued that my agent is a Mr. Lord.

No more than these bare facts may be shared with those bidding for magazine, movie, foreign, book club, and paperback rights. I cannot too strongly warn against *any* leak or premature publicity. This is so as to preserve through publication date the time and place of the Second Coming. My source originally planned that event for his two thousandth birthday, but I believe with persuasion might push the date forward to coincide with promotional activities. Probably it would be better to bring this book out on the spring list. The fall list would conflict with the football season, making it difficult to obtain a stadium large enough to accommodate maximum Second Coming crowds.

These details are, of course, subject to review and/or accommodation as we move forward. (My source naturally wants to stage the Second Coming in Texas, but is dubious about the Astrodome because he fears the impropriety of returning to artificial turf.) By the way, when the Second Coming date and site

277

firm up, please be certain that adequate hotel accommodations are available. As the manuscript will reveal, my source was severely marked by a childhood experience in this regard.

It is futile to request my source to show himself to you or others. No other person on earth has been privy to our meetings or possesses knowledge of them: not Billy Graham, not the Pope, not Oral Roberts. When we can make the official announcement, these and others of the cloth's trade may be depended upon to denounce the authenticity of our claim on the theory that my source rarely moves without consulting them, and on the further grounds that they speak with him or to him with great frequency. (Incidentally, I once heard Reverend Graham say on the radio, "I talked with the Lord the other night in Cincinnati," and my source tells me he has never been there.) Atheists will scoff for their own obvious reasons. We simply must be prepared to ride the storm out, to have—as my source put it—"the faith of a mustard seed."

I only wish that circumstances did not preclude my submitting a recent photograph to convince skeptics, but I am simply locked in. I remain confident, however, that once you discover the rich details in the manuscript—things like the real inside dope on Lot's wife, what really happened with Eve and the apple, what a terrible temper my source's father has, etc.—you will have no doubts of its authenticity. The information simply could come from no other source.

Oh, yes, for the title, I have decided on *Naked Came the Saviour*.

Yours in secrecy,
Larry

*New York Times Book Review*
MAY 1972

SMALL  ADVERTISEMENTS  FOR  MYSELF

# Confessions of a Blackhearted Loser

NOMINATED FOR A National Book Award this year, The Writer swore blood oaths to all that winning didn't matter: being nominated was thrill and glory enough. Not much spectacular had happened to *Confessions of a White Racist.* America's most influential critics or publications had largely ignored the book or found it semiwanting. A high percentage of rave reviews turned up in Oshkosh or Wheeling or had been crafted by old friends (Dan Wakefield, Frank Rich, Marshall Frady, Bill McPherson) who may have permitted their personal loyalties to overwhelm their critical instincts. The Viking Press excited only its accountants in springing for a month-long nationwide promotion tour.

The Writer possessed a royalty statement attesting that *Confessions* had sold 6068 hardback copies before dying a vagrant, leaving a red-ink legacy of $13,913.97 in Unearned Advance Royalties. The Writer had come to think of his book in juxtaposition with 3-D movies, the Edsel, and Ed Muskie. Little wonder, then, that The Writer's mind boggled and his heart accomplished mighty pitty-pats at being nominated in the new contemporary affairs category. Yes, good neighbors, such was fame and glory enough.

For about three days.

The Writer's personal sea change occurred when he began to think of himself as The Nominee. He only had to see it in print once: "The nominees include . . ." Thereafter, it was difficult not to sign his checks The Nominee. He liked the ring of it. It sang to him.

Quickly he disposed of what he soon came to think of as The Minor Candidates:

Except for the Nixon administration, everyone was sick to death of the Vietnam war. Therefore, one might logically dismiss Richard Hammer's *The Court Martial of Lt. Calley*, Don Oberdorfer's *Tet!*, and Ronald J. Glasser's *365 Days*. Sorry, boys, no light at the end of the tunnel for you.

William Irwin Thompson's *At The Edge of History* had not attracted The Nominee's notice until it turned up in competition. It therefore could not amount to much.

*The Last Whole Earth Catalog* by Stewart Brand was . . . well, whatever, it was no *book*. Better to nominate Mr. Sears and Mr. Roebuck, who had been longer in the mail-order business.

Tom Wolfe's *Radical Chic and Mau-Mauing the Flak Catchers* was sometimes funny and perceptive. But wasn't he shooting fish in a barrel? Besides, Wolfe dressed like a dandy and parted his hair on the wrong side: clear disqualifications.

What was Mike Royko's *Boss: Richard J. Daley of Chicago*, other than warmed-over newspaper columns slap-dashed between hard covers? Never mind that The Nominee originally had furnished a rave blurb to its publisher: he now realized he had done so merely to be a good fella.

As the night wore on it became increasingly evident to The Nominee that the war of short knives would be conducted between himself, Victor (*Kennedy Justice*) Navasky, and Norman (*The Prisoner of Sex*) Mailer. The Nominee telephoned to leave a personal encouragement with Mailer's secretary: "Hunny, yew tell ole Nawmin he's my solid second choice." After that display of good sportsmanship The Nominee was required to spell his last name.

The Nominee confided to a friendly book critic unspecified rumors insisting that the grand prize might be between himself, Mailer, and Navasky. When, twenty-four hours later, he read his planted little ego trip in print, The Nominee accepted its veracity and found himself repeating, "I don't expect to win even though the newspapers label me one of the tri-favorites."

Old friends of the trade did their best to preserve The Nominee's humility. David Halberstam required prompting before offering anemic congratulations, then complained of The Nominee's book being singled out where Gay Talese's had not. Larry

McMurtry laughed. Bud Shrake required oxygen.

More and more The Nominee fretted about the judges in his category. One, Garry Wills, had resigned in protest when *The Whole Earth Catalog* had been included. Though he agreed with Wills, The Nominee vaguely felt his loss threatened The Nominee's prospects. With only two judges left, would they flip a coin in deadlock?

Deep in his secret heart The Nominee was near certain of the vote of Digby Diehl, book editor of the *Los Angeles Times*. Had he not many times shared wet goods with Good Ole Digby, and common lusts, and experiences here unmentionable until the statutes of limitations run out? Of Harrison Salisbury, the *New York Times*man, The Nominee was less confident. He did not know him well enough to presume friendly corruptions. Probably such a flinty fellow had no price. If Good Ole Digby proved unable to sway him through logic, might he be intimidated by barroom bracings or bluster? Well, trust Good Ole Digby to find a way, even if it meant cheating in the tie-breaking coin flip.

In a night of unusual perceptions, The Nominee asked his black heart why winning had become so vital: What brought out the Lombardi in him, the Bobby Riggs, the Sammy Glick? Not to identify too closely with Richard Nixon, but The Nominee, too, had heard his childhood trains in the night; had dreamed of Fame and Riches and Power and Applause down many an endless Texas cotton row. Those old fantasies now made him squirm: hadn't he outgrown them, as he had Big Little Books and candy jawbreakers?

The Nominee decided he wanted to win in order to make proud his dear old Texas mother. Except that he knew—in the grip of his ambitious fevers and deep down where the lights don't shine—that between losing and having his dear old Texas mother's arm broken, he would go seeking the Mafia's best bone man. Yes, he would sacrifice two of his three children; turn tail at the Alamo; trade Cambodia, South Vietnam, and North Georgia to the Godless Communists. All for a thousand dollars and a brass plaque.

The assassination of John F. Kennedy had inspired him to new self-examinations: he had changed his life-style and goals for, he believed, more noble ones. He had quit politics with its dirty dogfights, sharp knives, and naked power lustings, vowing never again to wear any man's or party's or corporation's or ex-wife's yoke; he would write that which pleased him, cavort with those he loved as Cupid struck, be a friend to man. What had happened to those resolves to seek the simple life? Was The Nominee no better than formerly?

Not a damn bit. On to Victory.

Now The Nominee achieved new lows of scheming. Perhaps, should Good Ole Digby drop it in Harrison Salisbury's ear that The Nominee's good wife lay hospitalized with serious malfunctions, the sympathy vote might be assured. Or the same purpose might be served should The Nominee—like Dita Beard—suffer a timely and public seizure of angina pectoris. Would it help to shoot himself in the leg? (Probably not. Three of ten NBA winners proved totally dead.) Perhaps he would arrange his own kidnapping.

*Dear Mr. Salisbury: We, the undersigned kidnappers, demand $1,000 and a brass plaque for the safe return of Larry L. King to his loved ones, some of whom are hospitalized.*

Flying from Washington to New York, The Nominee mentally formed his acceptance speech. He vacillated over whether to caustically lash the public, critics, and owners of paperback houses or book clubs for their sad misjudgings of his Art, or whether to come off all sweetness and humility and thank more obscure people than do those who claim Oscars for Best Left-Handed Stage Grip in an Independent Black-and-White Musical Production Made in Japan. Or maybe he would simply read them Faulkner's Nobel address and, after a dramatic pause, issue a husky "Thank you, and God bless." He envisioned a standing ovation going on far into the night.

Good Ole Digby . . .

In five well-spaced phone calls to the Viking publicity department, The Nominee casually implanted the name of the bistro where he just might possibly be reached immediately upon the 2:00 p.m. naming of winners. Tick-tock-tick-tock. Longest day since June 6, 1944. When the phone rang and a waiter beckoned in the direction of The Nominee's table, he was proud of his cool in slouching casually toward his fate. This voice—which, on later reflection, did not sound greatly like Viking's fabled PR genius, Richard Barber—said, "See, I *told* you you should come to New York!" "Well," The Nominee drawled—lazily and with his heart stopped—"so you did, Good Buddy." A short silence. Then: "Am I speaking to Mr. Marvin J. Whitson of Chicago?" "Perhaps," I said, "it is he wrestling me for the phone."

At 4:10 p.m., by which time the average patron had been called to the phone five times, The Nominee placed a pride-killing call to Viking. He spoke with a young lady who seemed unaware of much of the world around her. Ultimately, she was wheedled into asking around to see what she might learn of NBA selections. Two minutes of dead air, and then the unexpected growl of a dial tone. The Nominee wept. Another pride-stabbing call was placed. *The Whole Earth Catalog* was announced as the winner. The whole earth wept.

At the Biltmore reception for all NBA nominees (The Distinguished Losers' Ball, according to disaffected cynics), The Nominee immediately encountered Good Ole Digby. G.O.D. attempted to hide behind two fat ladies. Trapped, he blurted, "Look, Good Buddy, except for me you wouldn't have been nominated. One of the judges wanted to throw your book out and nominate *Yazoo*, by Willie Morris."

On Wednesday the *New York Times* did not find The Nominee's name fit to print: he, alone, went unmentioned among Distinguished Losers in his category. According to the same story, Good Ole Digby had not exactly lost a coin toss. He was quoted: "In a hundred years *The Whole Earth Catalog* probably will be the only book of the year 1971 to be remembered."

I'm not bitter. Contrary to rumors, I did not hit Good Ole Digby in either side of his mouth: accidentally shoved him three or four times, maybe, and reaching for my coat accidentally elbowed him behind the ear and, turning to apologize, spilled his very expensive bottle of wine on his new mod clothes.

No, neighbors, not for a moment did I expect to win. Just being nominated was honor and glory enough.

*New York*
MAY 1972

# LOOKING BACK ON THE CRIME or REMEMBERIN' WILLIE AND THEM

he glory days were those at *Harper's*. Our editor-in-chief, Willie Morris, was in many ways a writer's dream. He encouraged his staff writers (called "contributing editors" out of some primitive institutional urge to indulge grand-sounding euphemisms, though not one of us edited so much as an expense account) to largely choose their own subjects. I think he was right in his conviction we would bring our best strivings to work we personally judged important; often a personal yarn or casual observation made to Willie caused him to say, simply, "Write about that," and usually his judgment proved good. He was generous with space, generally holding with writers in their raging deadline disputes about the final language to be employed. His editing hand was so intuitive that often the writer would be abashed he hadn't written it exactly that way in the first place. Willie bought the first two pieces I sold to a national publication when he was a young editor at *Harper's* in 1964; he taught me, by editing example, to prune, trim, and otherwise improve my prose. It's no exaggeration to say he improved me by 30 per cent in only four or five lessons.

Elevated to editor-in-chief of America's oldest magazine in 1967, at a precocious thirty-two, Willie Morris did not hesitate to scale upward the parsimonious rates *Harper's* had been paying. The magazine incredibly had not, before Willie's elevation, paid writers' expenses in most cases; fees, in the range of three to six hundred dollars, attracted only those able to afford charitable gestures. This made for much pedestrian copy by retired State Department officials, experimental diet faddists, wordy academicians, and holders or seekers of public office. Unfortunately, the magazine had begun to read like America's oldest.

Morris soon landed Bill Styron's moving "This Quiet Dust," all about how he came to be writing *The Confessions of Nat Turner;* for ten thousand dollars he got a chunk of the book. (Morris actually had the book excerpt for seventy-five hundred until new owner John Cowles, Jr., said, "Pay him ten thousand. It will sound better when word gets around in the trade.") For a few dollars more he got Norman Mailer's *The Armies of the Night* and *Miami and the Siege of Chicago,* journalistic masterworks that in hardback won critical acclaim; the former won a Pulitzer. One is awed to pick up back issues of the magazine and take a random sampling of the talents Morris brought to *Harper's,* many for the first time: James Dickey, Jules Feiffer, Robert Penn Warren, Justin Kaplan, Sara Davidson, Jack Richardson, Elizabeth Hardwick, Norman Podhoretz, Arthur Miller, Tony Lucas, George Plimpton, Bud Shrake, Michael Arlen, Joe McGinnis, Alfred Kazin, John Updike, Ralph Ellison, Jeremy Larner, Ward Just, Truman Capote, Herbert Gold, Tom Wicker, Gay Talese, Larry McMurtry, Joan Didion, Philip Roth, John Fowles, Irving Howe—on and on.

More remarkably, perhaps, he brought to fuller flower those he scouted and signed as contributing editors. David Halberstam, the Pulitzer Prize winner, came from the *New York Times* after tours in Vietnam and Poland. He wrote incisive political profiles of McGeorge Bundy, Robert McNamara, Ken Galbraith, Chicago's Richard Daley, Tennessee's populist Albert Gore, Robert Kennedy; his book on Kennedy, *The Unfinished Odyssey,* and his tremendous success, *The Best and the Brightest,* began as magazine profiles. Marshall Frady, not yet thirty, joined from *Newsweek* and free-lancing. He wrote on LBJ in retirement, the Gary steel mills, George Wallace; as an American innocent in the Middle East he found a "collision of the two ages, a blind grappling of two dialectics, two realities, each barely comprehensible to the other." His visit resulted in a fine book, *Across a Darkling Plain;* his *Wallace* is possibly the best and most literate plumbing of an American demagogue since Red Warren resorted to fiction in *All the King's Men.* John Corry, crossing over from the *New York Times,* produced high-quality work on sex in social Washington, Cardinal Spellman, Castro's Cuba, George Meany, an average congressman, New York bartenders, and used-car tycoons. Morris coaxed perceptive personal pieces from his managing editor, Robert Kotlowitz, and his executive editor, Midge Decter. His own books, *North Toward Home* and *Yazoo,* got their starts as articles in the magazine. In my own case, *Confessions of a White Racist* began as a *Harper's* article; fifteen of twenty-six pieces I wrote for Willie Morris have been included in two nonfiction collections, and nine or ten have been several times anthologized.

Morris didn't simply sign up promising writers and then, as some editors do, slice or sanitize their copy until it read like a computer printout or committee report. He believed in giving the writer a free reign in search of his own voice; he was not afraid of innovation, bold language, or outrageously divergent points of view published cheek to jowl. There were no sacred cows, no in-house prejudices or fears to buck. When I first published in the magazine, and Morris was a junior editor, he had to fight his staff elders to salvage this innocent sentence from my maiden effort: "As one who attended several of Billie Sol Estes's Washington dinner parties, I am sure they had more fun at the Last Supper." Under Willie, you could with full confidence write "fuck" when "intercourse" or even "copulation" simply wouldn't do. Such a freedom was not all that common in mass-circulation magazines even so short a time ago; Morris pioneered in American magazines in permitting his writers to write the language as it is spoken, warts and all. For three or four years there we were the hottest and most remarked of popular American magazines. My God, it was heady, exciting, satisfying. Writers woke up wanting to work.

Willie Morris was, and remains, a complex man full of many human contradictions; it is possible to love him and to deplore him over the same beer. While Willie doesn't give a flip if the world disapproves of him in the abstract, he lusts to be loved in the flesh and in the moment. It is a very southern thing, a most political thing, something one is born to and raised with in such places as Mississippi and Texas, where Willie Morris spent his formative years. Being a Good Ole Boy is culturally, economically, and politically valuable in such climes; most families expect it of their sons, and some few demand it. Consequently, like the girl who went bad, Willie seldom could bring himself to say no; his instincts and training caused him, sometimes, to try too hard to please. Often this led to impossible over-promising.

It was disconcerting to discover, on the day a given issue was being locked up, that one to three other contributing editors *also* had been promised the lead story or top cover billing. This sometimes led to interesting shouting tantrums or silent cold angers among the vain brothers. Willie's genius was that nobody stayed mad very long. Over drinks at a Chinese restaurant around the corner from our Park Avenue offices, Willie would put on the hurt look of a mistreated hound dog and say, "Goddammit, now, Larry, that's a *marvelous* piece you did, people will be reading it fifty years from now, and I *know* it deserves to be the leader, but ole Halberstam (or ole Corry or ole Frady) has got the red-ass at me for some strange reason, and I just *had* to indulge him. *You* know how temperamental writers are!" Later he would give the same spiel to other malcontents, merely changing the vital names. We would all commiserate with Willie's impossible chore and apologize and buy him drinks. He could have served to a ripe age in Congress, excluding the possibility of occasional assassination.

After some of the shine wore off, and managerial passions against Willie and his "wrecking crew" had curdled, his detractors would say that he got drunk in Elaine's where he bought impossible pieces never to be used or that he lost manuscripts in taxicabs or that he kept casual office hours or that he didn't get enough haircuts or that he brought the magazine to ruin by overpaying and otherwise indulging his writers. Pap and horseshit. Sure, he got drunk some; I say it as a friendly participating witness. Yeah, he bought a turkey or two. Some days he came to the office in midafternoon looking like third place in a wino contest.

288

He hated to take or return telephone calls, and he was capable of some pretty artful lies. Nobody's perfect.

Before you rack the balls, however, I personally saw Willie Morris suggest, contract for, and bring to publication dozens of truly superior articles in times when he was innocent neither of late hours nor whisky. If he wanted a given writer to accomplish a given subject, he was relentless in pursuit. He perhaps knew more writers, editors, and agents than anyone in New York, and he utilized his sources. The proof being in the pudding, I'd risk the sum total of his triumphs against any other editor you'd care to name for a comparable period. And let us end, right now, the fiction that Our Leader spent *Harper's* into semibankruptcy: our annual editorial budget didn't approach $250,000, which is about what your Brinkleys or Cronkites or Chancellors individually draw down as TV news anchormen. Willie's contributing editors worked for less money at *Harper's* than we got for comparable work free-lancing in other magazines; my top salary was $14,000 in a year in which I wrote five long pieces, one lengthy *Washington Report* column, and several book reviews. Morris himself was being paid only $37,500 when he quit in 1971, some $17,500 less than was being drawn by Bill Blair, the publisher's resident "moneyman," who directed the business side and with whom we on the editorial side soon enjoyed a decided lack of rapport. It was Blair, not Morris, who comforted himself with posh new executive offices. It also was Blair, when the financial squeeze came, who suggested firing Bob Kotlowitz and Midge Decter, trimming the contributing-editor staff, and otherwise retrenching. He did not accept Willie's suggestion to join him in a voluntary salary cut so that others might be retained. Blair was the one who suggested, brightly, that perhaps *Harper's* should seek a special audience such as, well, say, the readership of *Ski*. Vengeance is mine, sayeth the Lord. . . . And ain't it *good?*

Willie Morris was responsible for much of the fun and the sense of camaraderie to be found around the place. A compulsive practical joker who could drop all traces of his Mississippi accent, easily adopting others ranging from British cockney to Hungarian freedom fighter to chairman of the board, he more than once enlisted the telephone.

Shortly after my second book appeared—though not long enough after publication that despair had yet descended—a female voice told me that the book editor of *Time* was calling. After an exchange of pleasantries, I was told to my astonishment and joy that *Time* intended to write a long feature about me in connection with my new work: could I receive a staffer on the upcoming Thursday? Making much of clearing my availability with the calendar and a nonexistent secretary, I agreed. "Of course," the *Time* pooh-bah said, "our man will do an in-depth interview. While you're on the line, however, may we chat a bit about your approach to writing?" Wellsir, I needed no further invitation. For twenty minutes I prattled about my literary influences, writing techniques, deeper secretions and motives. Only after making a pluperfect ass of myself did I realize, from the familiar chortle coming across the wire, that Willie Morris had struck again.

Soon I was told that a powerful national politician was on the phone. "Sure," I said. Damned if Willie Morris would trick me this time. When the politician offered a job writing speeches, hinting that the pay might be worth my time, I was cold, curt, and perhaps a shade vulgar. That's how I came to ask Governor Nelson Rockefeller why he didn't go butt a goddamned stump.

After America's newspapers informed the world that I had been selected a Nieman Fellow at Harvard, and old friends and relatives had been posted, I was packing for the trip when the telephone rang.

"Mr. King? This is Dwight Sargent with the Nieman Foundation in Cambridge."

"Yes, Mr. Sargent. How are you? I'm packing my bags right now. Really looking forward to the Harvard adventure."

"Well, yes. I find it my duty to, ah, ask you what I fear is a rather personal question."

"All right. Go ahead."

"Mr. King, have you ever been convicted of a felony offense?"

"Beg your pardon, sir?"

"A crime, Mr. King. Have you ever been convicted of a crime?"

"Well, ah, no. Good God! I mean, what's going on?"

"It's certainly distressing, Mr. King, but a member of the Harvard Corporation has received information that you're a convicted felon. If so, I'm afraid we'll be forced to reconsider your Nieman Fellowship. Not that we'd preclude you without official inquiry and judicious study—"

"*What?* Preclude me? This is the damndest thing I've heard, Mr. Sargent!"

"You categorically deny it, then?"

"Goddamned right. Categorically!"

"There's no need for profanity, Mr. King. Please understand I'm duty-bound to inquire. Have you, perhaps, been convicted of a misdemeanor offense? One short of a felony, though involving incarceration?"

"No. *Hell* no!"

"Then you unequivocally state, Mr. King, that you have never been in jail? . . . Mr. King? . . . Hello?"

"Ah, well, now, Mr. Sargent, a couple of times in my youth, you know, it hah-hah was just silly little laughable things kids will do. You know."

"Oh, dear. I find this *so* distressing. Would you care to elucidate? I'm afraid I must insist. . . ."

"Well, it was for, you know, fighting and drinking and little things like that, back when I was a kid in Texas. That was a pretty common occurrence of the time and place."

"Perhaps we view such matters with a touch more concern at Harvard, Mr. King. Have you any additional information?"

"Well . . . OK. When I was a kid, see, carrying the mail one summer in my hometown, there was this big ole mean dog that chased me all the time. One day I sort of killed it, I guess, and the owner brought me to court. The case was dismissed, however. Actually, in retrospect, it was pretty funny. Goes over well when I tell it at parties."

"Mr. King, if there's anything else—anything at *all*—I simply must know it now."

"Well, there was the time I hit that gas pump in Texarkana. See, one of my children dropped an ice cube down my back as I pulled up to the pump. It caused some excitement and the police

came and I didn't like the way they deported themselves so—
well, anyhow, I had to pay damages. But I wasn't really jailed,
just booked and temporarily handcuffed. And I got arrested in a
couple of peace marches down here in Washington. That's *all*,
Mr. Sargent. I swear to God!"

"Hey, Larry, you ole outlaw! This is Willie!"

"Willie, you sorry son of a bitch!"

I would be afraid to approach the telephone for days.

Managing editor Bob Kotlowitz often wrote for the magazine
on the fine arts. Somehow Morris discovered a dentist in Manhattan named Leonard Bernstein. When Kotlowitz returned from
lunch, he found a note on his desk to call Leonard Bernstein at a
given number. Naturally he assumed it to be from the famous
composer-conductor. The conversation went something like this:

"Hello, this is Robert Kotlowitz at *Harper's*."

"Yes?"

"I believe Mr. Bernstein called me."

"*He* called *you?*"

"Yes."

"Well, do you want to see him?"

"Sure. Yes, that would be fine."

"Well, he's tied up through tomorrow unless you're in great
pain."

"I beg your pardon?"

"Are you in any pain?"

"Well, no more than usual."

"Then I'm afraid he can't see you immediately. He only takes
emergency patients on short notice. Tell me, is it a bicuspid
problem?"

"No," Kotlowitz said as the light dawned. "I think the pain's in
a much lower region."

Willie Morris, monitoring an extension in an adjoining office,
bounded gleefully in from the hall. "Bob, why didn't you ask him
to play 'Turkey in the Straw'?"

Another Morris ploy was, upon greeting out-of-town writers, to exclaim, "Sure glad you dropped by! I read in Leonard Lyons's column that you would be in town." Invariably, the visiting writer would mask his surprise as if to infer that making the New York gossip columns was old hat to him. Willie spent hours chortling over the prospect of vain writers who forthwith marched to public libraries to kill a half day searching recent Leonard Lyons columns.

At a party given by the William Vanden Heuvels, Willie was standing at the end of a hall bar when Senator Ted Kennedy approached. Preparing to warmly greet the senator, with whom he had shared a two-hour discussion only a couple of weekends earlier, Morris was startled when the senator, mistaking him for a bartender, indicated his liquor preference. Willie mixed the drink. A few minutes later he approached the senator bearing another on a silver tray. For the remainder of the evening he pressed drinks, hors d'oeuvres, and other favors on Senator Kennedy. "Don't I know you?" the senator ultimately asked. "Probably, sir. I serves lots of these fancy parties." Then Willie secured autographs for an imaginary menagerie of loved ones at home.

Morris was invited to a breakfast meeting at Averell Harriman's Manhattan apartment, in connection with eastern liberal establishment efforts to unite behind a 1968 Democratic presidential candidate. He shed the old turtleneck sweater and baggy trousers, usually replete with flecks of dried egg or deposits of ashes, constituting his normal costume. He even shined his shoes, washed his feet, and got a haircut. As he stepped from a cab in front of the Harriman digs, Willie alighted in one of New York's freshest and most impressive mounds of dog shit. Long minutes of cursing and scraping followed before Willie judged himself sanitary. Shortly after he joined the Harriman group, he noted his host inspecting guests while wearing a distasteful expression. Arthur Schlesinger, Jr., sniffed the air suspiciously. Surreptitious looks swept the room. Ken Galbraith, or maybe Cass Canfield, moved to a station more remote from Willie. "By that time," Morris remembers, "that room smelled like a dog pound after a three-day rain." He repaired to a kitchen telephone, where he loudly faked an office emergency requiring his presence. His attempt to bid his host farewell from a safe distance met with full cooperation.

Morris has written of how, when he came to New York a provincial from the *Texas Observer*, he half expected someone to accost him at celebrity-filled cocktail parties and shout, *"Willie Morris, get out of this room!"* Willie's country-boy innocence, both real and affected, peeled off rather quickly under exposure to Manhattan's literary stars and odd neuroses. Soon the old Mississippi boy hosted some of the liveliest dinner parties in the city. I remember one particularly interesting mix of Norman Mailer, Bill Moyers, and basketball star Bill Bradley; each of them admired the others, though none had previously met. It was good fun to hear Bradley quiz Moyers about politics (a field the basketball star plans to enter), to witness Moyers in turn asking Mailer about the creative processes, and to hear Mailer complete the circle by interrogating Bradley on basketball's finer points. Later, as the wine flowed, Mailer amused with outrageous imitations of Moyers's old boss LBJ. On another occasion, after we'd dined with politicians including Senators William Fulbright and Fred Harris and Congressman Mo Udall, Willie asked Marshall Frady —then doing a story on Congressman Wilbur Mills—whether he personally liked Mills. Frady thought for a moment and then said in his South Carolina accent, "Willie, ah lak all the bastards when ah'm with 'em. It's when ah sit down to the typewriter that ah make mah judgments."

For several years, at his country place near Brewster, New York, Willie hosted in the early spring an "Ole Country Boys Party"; it attracted southern writers largely turned into northern-locked expatriates. One lucky enough to be invited could monitor, in front of the old stone fireplace and over an astonishing variety of drinks, the yarn-spinning qualities of Robert Penn Warren, Ralph Ellison, William Styron, Tom Wicker, C. Van Woodward, Marshall Frady, Morris, and a half dozen others. There were black-eyed peas, ham, grits, biscuits, watermelon, and other Dixie delicacies; the longer the night and the more prominent the fumes, the deeper became boondock accents. Late in the evening bogus literary prizes were distributed, the presenters

making exaggerated oratorical declamations full of southern ro-
coco and rhythms quoting, likely as not, from Huey Long's
"Evangeline Tree" speech, Faulkner, the Old Testament, and the
combined works of those assembled. Styron, winning the Bull
Connor Award for the best dog story or some other imaginary
honor, once was presented with a pair of Boss Walloper work
gloves, a tin of Honest snuff, a Mexican fuck book, and a certificate promising three weeks on a desert isle with his choice of
Susan Sontag, Alfred Kazin, or the staff of the *New York Review
of Books.*

On Sunday mornings, as the weekend seeking new fun and old
roots came to a close, survivors gulped bloody marys and sang
their favorite Fundamentalist hymns. The closing number invariably was "Jesus on the Five-Yard Line." Then Morris would lead
the expatriates in prayer, asking heaven to lead us without harm
for one more year through cold dark subways and the racist
preachments of Bronx taxi drivers; begging blessings of Moon
Pies, decent governors for Mississippi, an edge for moonshiners
in their bouts with revenue agents, and for a second chance at
arms against the Damnyankees.

David Halberstam, a good heart and a bright talent, was perhaps the most intense of our *Harper's* wrecking crew. Some
weeks could be ruined by a single letter or postcard indicating
less than ecstasy for his work. Consequently, as we traveled the
country on our varied assignments, Halberstam received messages from "fans" all across America. A typical offering, ostensibly from an eight-year-old Ohio farm boy and replete with original spellings, ran: "Dere Mr. Halbinsterm: I like your riting. I
like it because it is so simple. In fact my mommy and daddy says
you are the simplest riter they know. Love, Bruce." Or an agitated mystic in Washington might inform Halberstam, "If you
have written seven good lines I have missed at least six of them,"
before urging that Halberstam imitate his betters on the mast-
head or, that failing, try plumbing or the civil service. One summer a young lady in North Carolina, Alma Faye Frumpkin,
wrote Halberstam a series of letters divided between obscene
propositions and urging him to use his literary influences to pub-

lish her exotic poetry. My favorite offering from "Miss Frump-kin" was one called "Kites and Wind"; if memory serves, it ran as follows:

*Look! In the sky.*
*Kites.*
*Red. Orange. Blue. Green. And then,*
*I run, freely,*
*The string in my hand.*
*Breaking wind.*

On impulse I once introduced the proud Halberstam to Governor Nelson Rockefeller as "Frank" rather than the appropriate "David." It could not have worked out better had I rehearsed Rockefeller. "Good to see you, Frank!" the governor boomed. "Frank, this is my wife Happy. And this is my brother Laurance, Frank. Now, Frank, say hello to my brother David. Would you like a drink, Frank?"

For all the horseplay and jawboning, we had our serious moments and we made, I think, our contributions not only to an exciting magazine but to each other. Let one of us know adversity, ranging from family illness to romantic troubles or looming bankruptcy, and the others offered support. Though we chided our colleagues about their respective lack of talents, we offered our own experiences or suggestions to any colleague writing on a subject in which we claimed knowledge. Often, in Willie's office on a rainy day or in one of several bars, we'd sit and talk books, politics, philosophy, the magazine business, or just pure trash. Marshall Frady, his southern eyes bright with whisky and travel, might offer in his Old Testament roll, "I'm not too sure it's benign for a writer to spend any great length of time in the company of New York's estate of assessors, appraisers, traffickers in reactions and responses, because maybe, now, you start—after a while—writing from those secondary vibrations instead of the primary pulses and voltages that you can't afford to lose." And Brooklyn native John Corry, cynical and amused by the slightest pretension, might grin and say, "Aw, Frady, horseshit!" and we would be off on a debate about where writers worked best, and why. Or another time Halberstam might speak of young bloods fresh from Harvard or Yale who make mistakes in attempting to work for the *New York Times* rather than seeking out the provinces to learn their trades: "I learned as a cub reporter in West Point, Mississippi, that the same lies they tell you in city hall are the same lies you'll be told later on by senators or generals or diplomats." Sometimes we would be joined by writers from *Sports Illustrated*, Bud Shrake or Dan Jenkins, perhaps, or by any number of writers visiting from Texas (Larry McMurtry, Ronnie Dugger) or George Axelrod fresh in from London or William Styron down from Connecticut just for the afternoon. There are worse ways to spend afternoons, and worse company.

The night seven of us handed our resignations to owner John Cowles, Jr., in support of Willie's dispute with management, there were throat lumps and wet eyes behind the grog cups. "I've just realized," Halberstam said, "that in my career I've never worked with this many talents who also were people I admired and respected and loved. And I never will again. We've been a band of brothers."

A fair amount of nonsense has been written about what really happened at *Harper's* to bring about that mass resignation of spring 1971. Norman Mailer's celebrated piece, "The Prisoner of Sex," was unfairly cited as a prime cause. If it was any factor it was a minor one, and then only because its publication coincided with larger problems then coming to a boil. It *is* basically true that the confrontation pitted the Literary Men against the Money Men, though, again, that's a simplification. Caught in the same squeeze bedeviling many magazines—advertising revenues lost to television and sharply rising postal rates—management wanted to cut back expenses, vaguely change the magazine to some more specialized format and, as we saw it, do damage to not only the oldest but one of the best, liveliest, and most prestigious of American publications. Willie Morris, never very patient with office politics and not excelling in the field, may have abdicated owner Cowles's ear to his in-house enemies at great expense; the rest of us, occupied with our own books and other out-of-house assignments, perhaps took too much for granted in failing to learn what transpired at all those tense Minneapolis meetings between Willie Morris, his detractors, and the harassed owners. Faced with what he read as excessive interference and petty carpings, Willie one day boiled over. His tough letter of resignation may have been intemperate; certainly it was accepted quicker than Willie expected. I don't think he realized how efficiently his in-house enemies had poisoned the pond against him. It could be, too, that so much success and praise had come his way in so short a time that he forgot that if you don't own the mill you remain merely a millhand even though you've been designated foreman.

The rest of us asked for a meeting with owner Cowles. In a confrontation at a Manhattan hotel, Cowles opened by reading a twelve-hundred-word statement that General MacArthur would not dared have addressed to the Japanese on the deck of the U.S.S. *Missouri*. We were a conquered people—he said in effect —with no rights or privileges, and Our Leader was deposed for good and all. There followed three hours of whisky rationalizations, a goodly amount of shouting and blame-placing and, ultimately, the mass walkout.

Nobody has starved. Halberstam, at this writing, tops the best-seller list with *The Best and the Brightest;* Willie Morris is out with a novel, *The Last of the Southern Girls*, that fetched rich paperback rewards. The rest of us have performed modest books and eat regularly through other magazine employment, teaching, lecturing, and an occasional dice game. We continue to see each other with some regularity. Willie Morris and I perhaps saw each other once too often, a foolish drunken fight once erupting in Georgetown. We have lately smoked peace pipes, and I suspect that one day we'll laugh at ourselves in front of the fire.

As this old writing man ages and maybe even matures a smidgen, he has less desire to accomplish much of the type of writing that has been his bread-and-butter staple—and that magazines continue to assign. Let others with more supple bones and fewer years in apprenticeship tear around the country in the company of jazz musicians, ambitious politicians, athletes or movie stars; their pronouncements, or even their life-styles, don't seem that necessary to record any more. There is a vexing impermanence to magazine journalism; it bloweth away on the wind and do fly.

Books appear to take on more importance—and the urge to do them. One wants, more and more, to work from his own experiences: to record in fiction the bruises, deaths, disappointments, lessons, and small triumphs that come to him as part of the human condition. If there are real answers to be found, I think, they will be found there or not at all. I suppose that's why two of the three books I now find at various stages of incompletion are novels.

I closed my last journalistic collection by noting that in so personal a recitation one is expected to name the old friends and associates who made one what one is today; in that case, I said, it might come off as blame-placing, so we'd save the ceremony for the next collection. Then we'd print their names, and the devil take them. It is time, then, for the accounting.

Blame my early infatuation with the language on exposure to Mark Twain, H. L. Mencken, a nineteenth-century Texas journalist named W. C. Brann, and the Old Testament; I also owe the humor and rascality of H. Allen Smith. My late father established the example of personal storytelling, bringing his own native countryman's poetry to his tales; when I was an impressionable young man, Warren Burnett spoke the language as well as I have heard it used since. In that same period I was tutored and helped by a good man and fine city editor named Brad Carlisle, for whom I named my son. David Halberstam and Bill Brammer (author of *The Gay Place*, a novel published in 1961 and still considered the best study of Lyndon Johnson) were influences in Washington in the late 1950s and early 1960s. Brammer, then a perceptive observer of the Washington scene as an LBJ staffer, and Halberstam, newly arrived in Washington for the *New York Times* after qualifying stints on newspapers in Mississippi and Tennessee, accomplished their own first novels in the same year. To one who remained unpublished they were certified heroes, inspirations, proof that others might accomplish the magic of their own books. Another writer, the late Warren Miller, who had read two and one-half confused and mutated novels I wrote in the attic at the end of my twelve-hour days on Capitol Hill (none of which could be salvaged or sold) mysteriously saw enough to recommend me to a New York editor, Bob Gutwillig; my first published novel, *The One-Eyed Man*, resulted. While I was working on that first book, along came Willie Morris with his suggestion that I write a couple of articles for *Harper's*. He was there to guide a neophyte through the earliest shoals and shallows. My late wife, Rosemarie, encouraged me in the uncertain madness that once represented a dim dream and now has become a way of life. They are the culprits; I love them and thank them for their shares of the blame.